IF I'M DYING

Other books by Linda Chehey

Changing Hearts

Eden Experiment

Up In Flames

The Face in the Mirror

My Alien Stalker

IF I'M DYING

Enjoy the adventure

Linda Chehey

Linda Chehey

Rev. date: 02/04/2019

To order additional copies of this book, contact:
Xlibris
1-888-795-4274
www.Xlibris.com
Orders@Xlibris.com
791777

I have loved you since your inception and raised you with all the love in my heart. I am here for you whenever you need me. Please remember me when it counts.

When I am old, don't put me on the shelf like some collectible antique and assume I will always be there.

Keep me in your prayers and in your thoughts.

Don't linger at my grave. I am not there anymore. I am watching from above and loving you unto infinity.

Linda Chehey for all mothers

1

Lillian sat at the breakfast table, eyes downcast, as if the smudges in the bottom of her coffee cup had a message for her. "I don't know what to do, Cora. She never calls me. What did I do to make her stop caring?"

Cora's eyebrows scrunched together as she watched her friend and roommate mope. "Who never calls you?"

"I'm talking about Charla. It's like I no longer exist in her world," answered Lillian, as her mouth drooped into a frown and tears brimmed in her downcast eyes.

"Oh, poop," scoffed Cora. "Our kids just don't realize that we aren't dead until they actually see us in our coffins. Somewhere in between the empty nest and the funeral home, there is a big void where we temporarily disappear, only remembered when they need a babysitter or financial help. Why do you let her get under your skin?"

"Because I moved here for her and now she just ignores me."

"When was the last time you called her?" Cora tried not to sound too serious, for fear of another crying session. She had seen Lillian's depressions before and caught her crying and skulking around the house. It always meant Charla had been neglecting her mother for weeks. Last Christmas had been the worst. Nothing the girls could say or do could bring her out of the fit of depression when Charla ran off to California for the holidays instead of spending them with her own mother.

"I don't know; maybe two or three weeks ago. I left a message but she never called back."

Cora buttered a piece of toast and scooped jelly onto it while she eyed her best friend over the top of her horn-rimmed reading glasses. "Call her right now. Ask her out to lunch. Make the first move. She's your daughter."

Lillian pursed her lips, emphasizing the creases around her mouth. "The last time I talked to her, it didn't go well. She gets so snippy with me. It's like she can't stand to be around me." She bit off a piece of toast, dropping a glob of strawberry jelly onto the front of the pink robe that barely covered her ample boobs.

Cora handed her a napkin and pointed to the red spot.

Lillian frowned as she smeared the mess around and finally gave up, lifting the robe to her mouth to suck the jelly off.

"She's a very busy girl, Lil. Think back to when you were her age. Did you have time for your mother?"

Lillian looked up and straightened her shoulders indignantly. "I always had time for my mother. My conscience is clear on that. When she passed on, I had no guilt and no regrets."

"Okay, okay; I didn't mean to upset you." Cora reached for Lillian's cell phone and handed it to her. "Call her."

Lillian bit her lower lip and hesitated. "She's probably with a client or at a closing and she'll just get cranky with me if I interrupt."

"Who cares? She'll get over it. Call her."

Lillian's round shoulders sagged forward in resignation. "Why do I always have to be the one to initiate contact?"

"Because that's the way it is when we get old," Cora answered firmly. "We have to keep reminding them we're still here."

"Someday that brat is going to regret treating me as if I'm dead."

Cora motioned to the phone.

"Okay, okay, but I'll put it on speaker so you can hear how she talks to me."

Cora scratched an imaginary itch on the top of her head and pulled her fingers through her short brown bob, trying to straighten out the severe case of bed head she wore to the breakfast table. She waited for her friend to make the call.

After the third ring, she heard, "Hello, Mom. What's up? I'm real busy right now."

Lillian smirked as if to say, *"Told you so."*

"I just wanted to talk. We should get together. Could we have lunch today?"

Charla replied impatiently, sounding like she was out of breath, "I'm packing. I have to get on the road."

"Oh, are you going on vacation? Where are you headed?"

"I'm driving to San Diego to visit Ella."

"You mean my Aunt Ella?" Lillian was shocked. "What's wrong? Is there something wrong?" Ella was the youngest of six girls, thirteen years younger than Lillian's mother and the last living member of her mother's generation. She was twelve when Margaret Bailey, Lillian's mother, married and started a family. During Ella's teen years, she had been a babysitter to little Lillian and her baby sister, Martha, whenever Dad took Mom out for date night. Ella's only qualifications for that job being that she was an oxygen breather and she could yell loud enough for people in the next county to hear her. Now Ella was a spry eighty-nine years young and widowed.

"I called her yesterday. She said she isn't feeling well and didn't think she could hold out much longer. I have to go see her."

Lillian paused to absorb that piece of information about her octogenarian aunt. "She never said anything to me. I should be going too."

"She implied I should come and I don't have time to wait for you." Charla's voice was snotty as usual and it brought another smirk to Lillian's face. *Twenty-four hours wasn't enough lead-time to extend an invitation.*

Lillian felt a pang of jealousy creep up on her and she couldn't suppress it. She felt her heart rate increase as her blood pressure rose. What makes her daughter go in constant search of substitute mothers when Lillian had devoted so much time and effort to raising her? Charla filled Facebook with pictures and postings of her women friends, some of whom surpassed Lillian age wise. She was always cooing on FB about how much she loved those friends and how she enjoyed their luncheons, and blah, blah, blah. Lillian's blood boiled every time she logged on.

"You will drive all the way to San Diego to visit Ella, but you won't come across town to visit your own mother?" said Lillian with an obvious tone of animosity in her voice.

Charla replied impatiently, "Well, you're not dying. Now I have to go."

A collective sucking of breath on the part of Lillian and Cora followed that statement as they made eye contact in disbelief.

The line went dead and Lillian sat there in stunned silence. The tears that had been holding back at the edge of her lower lids, spilled over, running down her cheeks and dampening the front of her robe. She could hardly speak. "If she cared anything about me, she would have offered to take me along." She wiped the tears away with her sleeve.

Cora rose and fetched the coffee pot, refilling their cups. "I can't believe she said that!"

Lillian swigged on her coffee and wiped a tear with her napkin. "Sometimes I hate her."

"Who do you hate, Charla?"

"No! Ella!"

Cora snickered and grinned, plopping her tall skinny frame back down at the table. "You can pick your nose and you can pick your teeth, but you can't pick your relatives. Like her or not, she's the only living aunt you have left."

"I prefer *not*," Lillian picked up her phone and scrolled through the numbers then hit the call button. "I'm calling Ella. I just talked to her on Sunday, and she never said anything to me about being sick or dying."

She waited for a dozen rings.

"Hello," Ella sounded out of breath.

"It's Lillian. Are you okay? You sound like you can barely speak."

"No, no, I'm fine. I was working out in front of the television to that funny little Richard person's video. You should try it sometime. It's good for you."

Lillian could just imagine Ella's twinkly little blue eyes and mischievous grin as her wrinkled skin flopped around over bony limbs while she bumped and ground clumsily to the beats of a Richard Simmons workout. She wondered if that sort of thing was beneficial or just a slippery banana peel hurtling the elderly closer to the edge of an open grave.

She tried an aerobics class once at the "Y" but her forty-eight DD knockers bounced around so much during a very vigorous part of the routine that her bra straps snapped. The sudden unleashing of her enormous bazookas threw her off balance, causing her to careen into the next girl, setting off a domino effect, creating total chaos. When she picked herself up off the floor and recovered her balance, the instructor gently suggested she should try riding a recumbent bike instead. The walk of shame to the locker room was humiliating.

"Lillian, are you there?"

"Yeah, I'm here. I just lost my train of thought for a second. I called Charla and she said you were sick and she was rushing right down there to see you. She's on her way out the door now. She didn't even have the courtesy to ask me to ride along with her. She hardly ever makes time to visit me."

Ella let out a wicked cackle. "Lillian, you just don't know how to get her attention. You should have said you wanted to come along."

"I did. She hung up on me. What do you mean get her attention?" Lillian's memory flashed back to some of the stories her mother used to tell of her growing up years with Ella. She was the proverbial bratty baby sister who always had a knack for manipulation and deception. She had outlived all of her siblings and her own children. She now resided in a swanky senior living facility after her physician husband left her well off financially. They raised two gay boys and were disappointed that God had not blessed them with a girl, or any grandchildren, so Ella took every opportunity to woo and molly-coddle Charla as a substitute daughter. She had found innumerable ways to get attention from her, faking illness being one of them.

"She comes to visit every time she thinks I'm about to croak. It's the only time I get to see her."

"So, you pretend to have something wrong with you in order to get my daughter's attention. Isn't that kind of dishonest? Perhaps I need to speak to Charla about your deceptions."

"Oh, no, Lillian, I don't pretend anything. She just jumps to conclusions and runs right down here. She's always thrilled to see me. We have such a wonderfully close relationship. It's as if she's the daughter I never had."

Lillian frowned disgustedly at the telephone. "That's the thing, Ella. You stopped producing too early. Maybe you could have had your own daughter and then you wouldn't have stolen mine."

"You don't have to be so nasty. That's the trouble with you Lillian. You have a jealous streak. You always did, even when you were a kid. You should be happy your daughter has a big enough heart to include your old auntie in her life. She's all I have now, since my boys are gone."

"I'm sorry your boys turned out the way they did. I'm sorry they didn't outlive you, but in all fairness to me, why don't you just find yourself another man and leave my kid alone."

"I'm sorry you feel that way, Lillian. I wish you and I could have had a better relationship."

"We would have if you stopped getting in between me and my daughter. Have a nice visit." She ended the call abruptly and stared pensively into space with her jaw clenched and lips clamped firmly together.

Cora put two more slices of bread in the toaster and waited a few beats. "You have an evil expression on your chops. What are you thinking about?"

Lillian's clenched lips spread into a mischievous grin as the angry stare transformed into an evil squint, emphasizing the crow's feet at the outer corners of her eyes.

"Celia will be up soon. We should have a meeting and put on our thinking caps. Things are going to change and I need the help of both of my roommates."

2

"Okay, she's here." Cora was peeping out the front window watching Charla pull up to the curb and brake to a stop. The hour was early yet, before eight and the Las Vegas sun had not turned the pavement into a hot grill yet. The palm trees in the front yard were swaying to a strong breeze the weatherman had predicted would continue most of the day. The three roommates had been plotting this day for more than a week since Charla returned from her trip to visit Ella.

Lillian climbed back into bed. At this hour, her white hair was a tangled mess after a restless night. Without makeup or blush, her morning appearance seemed pale and ashen. She pulled the sheet up over her threadbare granny nightgown and closed her eyes. On her forehead was a large bandage that Celia had applied with her nursing skills. Lillian's right eye appeared to be turning black and blue.

She had drawn thick drapes closed, leaving only a slit of early morning light coming through to cast dim shadows in the bedroom, making the room navigable but too dim for anyone to see well. The bulb in the bedside lamp had conveniently burned out.

When several minutes passed and the doorbell hadn't rung, Lillian called out, "I thought you said Charla was here."

"She is," Cora yelled back. "She's sitting in the car talking on her cell phone. It must be important. She doesn't appear to be in much of a hurry to come inside."

Cora had phoned Charla around seven that morning and reported that Lillian had fallen during the night and was having dizzy spells. She suggested Charla should come over and see her.

She agreed to visit, but explained that she would be in a rush as this was one of her busiest days. *Rush as in drive slowly and don't be in any hurry to get out of the car,* Cora thought.

When she did emerge from her spotless white Cadillac, the expression on her face was more of impatience rather than a furrowed brow of concern. She kept patting down her long bleached blond hair as the gusting breeze kept trying to whip it into an afro.

Cora chuckled at Charla's efforts to hang onto her purse, her car keys, her cell phone and her hair all at the same time. She could read her lips as the primper clomped up to the door in her stiletto heels and designer suit, frowned and spat the word, "Shit," just before reaching for the doorbell.

Charla had been born with all the good features from her father, Charlie Crocker's, Finnish gene pool. She was tall, slender, and gifted with showgirl features and just the right amount of cleavage to make her popular in Las Vegas. As a talented dancer and statuesque prop in sequins and feathers to advertise the glitz of Las Vegas, she had no difficulty finding gigs during her glamorous years. When age started to drag her assets south, getting in the way of show jobs, she took up selling real estate and worked her way up to opening her own prestigious agency, catering to the rich and famous. Her photo-shopped face and long bleached blond hair were visible all over town on billboards and the sides of city buses, advertising her agency as one of the most successful in the valley.

Cora waited for *showgirl* to ring the bell. She gave it a count to ten while the breeze did further damage to Queen Charla's hair, and then she opened up with a smile. "It's nice of you to come. I'm sure your mother will appreciate it." She spoke the word *mother* a slight decibel louder just to emphasize the word.

Without acknowledging the greeting, Charla stepped inside, looked into the entry mirror and frowned at what looked back at her. She pulled three fingers through her hair in an attempt to undo the damage the wind had caused. "I'm supposed to be at the monthly Realtor's breakfast right now. Where is she?"

Cora straightened her shoulders in indignation. "Well if this is too inconvenient for you, go on to your meeting. She's doing fine with me and Celia looking after her."

"No. I'm already here. I have a second. I'll just pop into her room. She's in bed, isn't she?"

"Yes. I called the doctor and they are prescribing something for the dizzy spells. Celia will go pick it up."

Charla sauntered down the tiled hallway, while Cora followed along behind making an obscene gesture with her traffic finger and smirking.

Showgirl took a left into Lillian's room and paused. "Mom, are you awake?"

Cora watched from the hallway as Lillian answered in a weak voice, "I'm just resting. Come on in. I'm sorry you had to come all the way over here on short notice. They shouldn't have called you. I'll be fine."

Charla pulled up a small ladder back chair and sat down by the bed. She dropped her handbag on the floor, spilling some of the contents, which she hurriedly scooped up and tossed back into the bulging bag. She leaned forward as she reached over and touched the bandage.

Lillian flinched.

"Is it bad?"

"It's a bump on the forehead and a slight abrasion. I got up to go to the pot in the night and got dizzy, hitting the dresser as I fell."

Charla glanced over at the three-drawer bureau near the door. "So it's not serious?"

"I don't know yet. I have an appointment with the doctor this afternoon and some pills to take in the meantime for the dizziness."

"Well, you look okay to me but you should have it x-rayed. These things happen. By the way, Ella sends her regards."

Lillian closed her eyes and gritted her teeth. *Even during a private moment with her daughter, Ella couldn't stay out of the conversation.*

When her eyes failed to open immediately, Charla jumped up and announced; "Well, I have to go. I'm late for a breakfast meeting. Call me if anything changes." She grabbed her bag and without further word or a backwards glance, strode out of the room. Her heels clicked loudly on the tile floor, followed by the sound of the front door opening and closing.

Lillian lay there a while, more angry than sad over the cold woman her daughter had become. There had been no handholding, no pats, and no kiss on the cheek. She felt completely disconnected from the child she bore four and a half decades ago. When Charla became a mother nineteen years earlier, she was gushing all over her parents on the phone begging them to pull up stakes, sell their house in Wisconsin and move to Las Vegas.

"I miss you so much," Charla had begged tearfully.

Lillian wanted to be near her first grandchild and Charlie couldn't wait to be a grandfather. He was a schoolteacher and the schools in this city were literally begging experienced educators to relocate.

That's how they had met Cora and her late husband, James English. They were both teachers and taught at the same middle school as Charlie. The two couples became fast friends and now the widows resided together.

Lillian had always worked in the retail industry so she could get a job anywhere in the country. They made that big sacrifice for their daughter and became one of the many people migrating to Las Vegas from other parts of cold and snowy Northern states.

Lillian thought about the change in her daughter since then. When they arrived here all those years ago, Charla had been a dancer with a new baby, trying to juggle career, motherhood and being a wife to a busy musician, Herbie Romaine. She was exhausted and sometimes bitchy. It soon became apparent that she needed her parents to be babysitters and not much else.

Today, even with her hair blown wild by the wind, she still looked glamorous in her impeccable suit and diamond earrings that sparkled in the dim light of the bedroom.

Charla's marriage had dissolved when Courtney, the only child she had found the time to produce, had gone off to college. Even that girl had abandoned Lillian, seldom calling or writing. Children learn from their parents and Courtney was no exception.

Cora had ushered Charla out the front door and watched her pull out her cell phone. Lingering at the open door, she overhear her say, "It was a false alarm; just some old lady crap. Her roommates handled it. They really didn't need to call me."

As Charla drove away, Cora shook her head. "Now there's a narcissist if I ever saw one."

Lillian shuffled from the bedroom. "That was cold. I'm starting to wonder if she's the one who banged her head recently. Do all real estate tycoons act like that or is it just her?"

Cora patted her friend on the shoulder. "I'm sorry, Lil. We tried."

Celia yelled from the kitchen. "Get in here and eat. Breakfast is ready and we've got some bowling pins to crush in an hour and a half."

Lillian ripped the bandage off her forehead and threw it in the kitchen trashcan. She went to the sink, dampened a paper towel and began rubbing off the makeup Cora had applied around her eye.

"I need some coffee to wash away the bad taste in my mouth. Does anyone know a good estate attorney? I think I need to make a new will."

Celia poured the mugs of coffee and set out an assortment of cereals. "Don't be hasty. We've just begun to teach that little snit a lesson." She had a wry sense of humor and when not in the confines of the somber halls of a hospital, she filtered nothing that came out of her mouth.

"Well if pretending to be injured doesn't get her attention, what will?" moaned Lillian. "Do I have to jaywalk and get hit by a car to bring some feelings out in her?"

Celia snickered, "I have some ideas, but we're not going to spoil our day and be late for bowling. Table it for now and buck up, Lil. We'll find a way into Charla's heart."

Celia Rose dug into her bowl of cereal. She was the short fluffy member of the group, a few pounds overweight and two inches shorter than Lillian's five foot six. Up next to Cora's six-foot skinny frame, she almost looked like a munchkin. Still working in her sixty's, she maintained a head full of short dyed red hair. She contended it helped her maintain a younger appearance. The fluffy part kept her skin from wrinkling and sagging, thus aging her.

"So are we still having lunch at the Senior Center today or are you gals up for some gambling after bowling?" Celia asked between bites.

As an emergency room nurse, Celia made good money and she liked to waste some of it supporting the local economy. She could afford a place of her own, but she shared a house with Cora and Lillian for the companionship it afforded.

She had become fast friends with the two of them after Charlie passed away. Celia was on duty in the emergency room the night he came in. She had tried exhaustively to revive him, but his heart refused to respond. Out of appreciation for her efforts, a few weeks later, Lillian and Cora took Celia to lunch, and from there, the friendship between the three grew.

On this morning, Lillian's mood was slow to improve over coffee. "I'm not sure I'll be in the gambling spirit."

Celia fixed her with a frustrated stare. "I think you are taking this situation too seriously. As for me, I worked my ass off to support my three brats as they were growing up while my ex took all the credit for how *well* they turned out. I'm the one that put them through college—not him. He never did pay up on all the child support he owed me. In the end, I was glad when they all decided to move to other states. I don't have to babysit their kids and I can hang up on them when they call and expect me to be their ATM. Do I look like a bank?" She gestured to her body. "When they call, I remind them that their father has a telephone." She paused to finish off her coffee. "Furthermore, I'm not leaving them anything. I'm going to spend all of my money before I die. I worked for it. I'm going to enjoy it."

Cora grinned. "Don't you miss your boys even a little bit?"

"If I did, I would go visit them more often. I'm too busy to dwell on it."

Lillian sighed. "I admire your ability to cope with abandonment."

Celia put down her spoon and spoke emphatically. "I had a crash course in coping with abandonment when that ass I was married to for eighteen years left me for the church organist. He took the television and the new car. I got the kids, an old jalopy and a mountain of bills to pay off."

"At least he didn't try to take the kids away from you," said Cora.

"He didn't take them away physically, but he took them away emotionally and bad-mouthed me at every opportunity. Then he would send them back home and I had to put up with their sassiness, assiness, and resentment blaming me for the breakup. I'm not the one who left; he was, but somehow, he made it out to be my fault. That's why I don't give a damn if those obnoxious snickers come to visit. I don't want to hear them talk about what a great dad that skinny dick is.

Lillian and Cora burst out laughing. "Celia, you never fail to come up with a new name for your ex every time the subject comes up. Was he really a *skinny dick*?" Lillian asked wide-eyed.

Celia answered by making a fist and extending her pinky finger upwards.

Lillian burst out laughing. "I think I'm cured of the blues now." She rose from the table, loaded her dishes in the washer and exited the room still chuckling. "I've got to take a shower. The vision of skinny dicks made my titties itch!"

As she left the room, Cora commented, "I'm suddenly hungry for a Gherkins pickle."

Lillian was still laughing when she reached her bedroom and commenced picking out some clean clothes before showering. As she pulled the covers up to make her bed, her foot encountered something on the floor. She reached down to pick the object up and examine it. "Uh oh," she sighed. It was Charla's wallet.

She scurried back to the kitchen with the item. "We've got problems. Charla's wallet fell out of her bag when she dropped it on the floor next to my bed. She was in too much of a hurry to notice when she left. She'll be coming back and we won't be here. What are we going to do now?" She held the item up and looked from Cora to Celia.

Just then, the doorbell chimed. Lillian's eyes went wide. "It's her!" She dropped the wallet on the table, ran to the trash and retrieved the bandage she had discarded earlier, slapped it on her forehead, and took her place at the table, trying to look as miserable as possible.

The bell chimed again. "Let her in," she whispered.

Panic stricken, Celia grabbed the snakeskin wallet and made a hasty sprint to the door. She opened it and shoved the object at Queen Charla as if it were a scalding hot potato. "Did you forget something?"

Charla heaved a big sigh and took the wallet, dropping it back into her thousand-dollar designer handbag. "God, I thought I had lost it. I had to leave my meeting early and get back over here. Do you know how scary it is to drive when you don't have your license on you? Thanks." She swiftly turned on her heel and beat it for her Cadillac.

Celia watched her drive away and shook her head in disgust. "She has all that money and she couldn't buy her mother a Christmas present last year, the thoughtless bitch." She closed the door a tad too loudly.

Lillian came shuffling from the kitchen. "I gave that girl everything she wanted when she was growing up. I worked forty hours a week and spent all my off time running her around to her dance lessons and school functions while she played campus queen. I made sacrifices and denied myself things so I could pay for her activities."

"We all did that," Celia interjected with a shrug. "That's what good mothers do. We sacrifice."

"So you agree I was a good mother?"

"I didn't know you then, dear." Celia smiled sweetly and patted Lillian on the arm. "However, I know you now and I would say you were probably everything a mother should be."

"Then why doesn't she like me?"

15

"I don't know the answer to that," Celia said. "But I think we should try to find out."

"Do I need a shrink?" Lillian furrowed her brow. "Am I the one in the wrong?"

"No!" Cora and Celia said in unison.

Cora patted Lillian's shoulder. "You are a good person. Sometimes our children get so involved in their own world that they forget we old farts are still around. We sometimes have to do things to attract their attention. That's all."

"Well not today girls," Celia reminded them as she headed for her bedroom. "The pins are waiting for us. And then we are having lunch at the Senior Center and it's not come-as-you-are Wednesday."

Lillian stopped at her bedroom door and looked back at Celia. "Do you suppose someone there will have some ideas on how to attract the attention of an offspring? Mine seems to have become confused about who her real mother is, because it sure as hell isn't Ella?"

"Lil, I surmise that a good many of those old poops are hanging out every day at the Center because their offspring can't be bothered with them either. I hear about it all the time when I volunteer for health clinic once a month. They get very talkative when I'm trying to listen to see if their heart is still beating. Take it from me; you are not the only parent who feels abandoned by her children. You are just more sensitive about it. We'll figure something out."

"Maybe we need to take a road trip and go pay Ella a visit. We can gang up on her and tell her to back off," Cora suggested.

"What and miss bowling? She's not worth it," Lillian grouched as she headed for her room to shower and dress. "I feel a big game coming on today. I'll pretend the head pin is Ella wearing an expensive red choker I want to knock off her skinny turkey waddle neck."

3

Try as she might, Lillian's intention to kill the head pins she had named *Ella*, turned into another frustrating effort that failed. Preoccupied with the morning's activities and puzzlement over the way Charla had distanced herself from immediate family, took her mind off the game. She finished the third game with little enthusiasm.

Afterwards the three friends headed for the Senior Center. On Wednesdays, meals were half price and the tables were crowded with old men, either looking for companionship or a little activity in the sack. Either way, the girls were there for the food, not the *sack* lunches.

Lillian walked into the cafeteria, surveyed the crowd and groaned, "Oh, God, he's here again."

Cora looked in the direction Lillian was surreptitiously pointing to and Celia strained to see. "Who's here?"

"Jim Boy!" Lillian answered indignantly. "He's always ogling my assets and sidling up to me."

"So he appreciates big knockers. Maybe he wants a date." Celia whispered.

"More like a feel. Quick, grab those three seats on the other side of the room as far away from him as we can get." Lillian sprinted for the seats to claim ownership. Celia sat down to hold them while the other two fell into line at the buffet tables. Lillian kept her head down and tried to be as invisible as possible.

Cora looked over her shoulder. "He's headed this way as if he's on a mission."

"Oh, no," Lillian quickly loaded her plate and tried to ignore the approaching sloth.

Jim Boy, as she tagged him was Jim Boyd, a skinny old man in his seventies with teeth yellowed from chewing tobacco, a balding head with brown growths clinging to his temples and high forehead. The Nevada sun had severely damaged his skin and he badly needed a stylist to bring his wardrobe into the twenty-first century.

He had been homebound for years taking care of a sick wife until she passed away recently. Now he acted as if he were a horny Viagra-fed ram freed from quarantine and turned out into the middle of a field of ewes he hoped were in heat. It was obvious he was lonely by the way he spent so much time hanging out at the Center. Jim was too short for Cora, and Celia had flatly informed him that she had taken the cure where men were concerned. Therefore, he zeroed in on Lillian.

She quickly zipped through the line, paid her money and fled to her seat at the table before Jim Boy could catch up. When Celia got up to go through the line, she plopped her purse down to save the seat so *he* wouldn't get any ideas.

The dining room was noisy with the big Wednesday turnout, so conversation was limited among this crowd of aging ears. The girls concentrated on the meal while Lillian kept a wary eye out, ready to flee if Jim Boy headed in her direction.

When the place began to empty out, Lillian urged the girls, "Can we get out of here. I can't give you-know-who the opportunity to cop a feel. Let's go back to the casino and play for a while."

"But don't you want to discuss your abandonment issues with any of these people?" asked Celia.

"Not today, Celia. Not when he's here." Lillian nodded her head in Jim Boyd's direction. He was engrossed in conversation with Farley, another of the eligible men driven by little blue pills who hung out hoping to get lucky. Cora referred to him as *Fartley* because of his apparent intestinal problems that he wanted everyone to enjoy in his presence.

"Let's do something different," suggested Cora. "Let's go down to the strip and play tourist. We haven't done that in a long time."

Lil jumped up and headed for the door. "I have to go now. He's looking at me. I think he's drooling. Oh, God, he's standing up. Let's leave." She was gone out the door in a flash, leaving her friends to follow behind her.

Celia piped up as they left the building, "We need to find someplace else to eat lunch. She acts like a flea on a hot skillet when we come here."

Lillian was already waiting at the car, anxiously grabbing at the door handle. She nervously glanced over her shoulder to see Jim Boy in hot pursuit.

Cora was behind the wheel as they pulled out of the parking lot. "Let's go see the atrium at Bellagio first. I think they have it decorated for Easter. Then we can walk the middle part of the strip."

Lil sunk as low as she could into the back seat, swiveling her head around, for fear Jim Boy might be following them.

He had emerged from the door and was striding rapidly to his car as they exited the lot.

"That guy is relentless," Celia said with a chuckle. "Maybe you should tell him you're gay. That would discourage him."

"Maybe a hit man in a dark alley would discourage him," humphed Lillian. "He smells like stale cigarette smoke."

"He just needs a nice lady in his life to clean him up and satisfy his…his…" Cora searched for a word that wasn't offensive.

Lil piped up from the back seat, "Well, I am not going to nuke his sausage for him."

Celia laughed. "Lillian, you can be so gross sometimes."

Cora came to a stop at the traffic light. "Changing the subject, I notice Marge Stewart doesn't come to the Center anymore. I wonder where she's been lately. Did she die?"

19

"She's avoiding *Jim Boy*," said Lil, emphasized his name. "She told me once that she accepted a date with him, and it consisted of dinner at Carl's with a buy one get one free coupon and a fast ride to his house where he expected a night of sex."

Celia snickered, "How did that go?"

"She said his house was filthy and stunk like kitchen garbage. She excused herself and went to the bathroom. It was equally filthy. While she was in there, she called a cab from her cell phone."

"So how did she get out of the house?"

"This is the cleaver part, Cora. She told him to go in the bedroom and get undressed and she would join him in a minute just as soon as she put on the little sexy something she had in her purse."

"And did he?" Celia was already stifling a laugh.

"As soon as he closed the bedroom door, she slipped out the front and ran like hell to the corner where the cab was supposed to pick her up. She said she was laughing all the way."

Celia glanced over the seat. "When did all of this happen?"

"Just before she sold her house and moved to Arizona closer to her kids."

"You mean she moved away to avoid that old fart? Isn't that going to extremes?"

"Cora, if he keeps chasing me around, I may have to leave too. But for now, I think I'll find another Senior Center to visit."

Celia's face lightened up with a mischievous grin.

Cora noticed the slight change and asked, "What are you thinking about, Celia? You look like you've just come up with an evil plan."

"I think I have."

"Okay, what are you thinking?" Cora prodded.

As they turned into the driveway to the parking garage at Bellagio, Celia grinned. "Let me work on it for a while. I will let you know."

The three friends were admiring the decorations in the atrium, while dodging people snapping pictures. The place was always a big attraction and it never disappointed.

After admiring the giant Easter baskets, the cute bunnies made of daisies and the colorful eggs, Lillian was just about to walk back into the lobby, when she spotted her daughter entering the front doors of the hotel. Charla strode alongside a good-looking gent. She watched from behind a potted palm tree as the two strode step for step through the lobby, not speaking or touching, but emitting unmistakable sexual vibes. It struck Lillian as two people who were together, but trying to act as if they didn't know each other. *Charla has a boyfriend.* They were coming close enough to see her spying.

"Oh, my God," Lillian gasped as she did a quick U-turn to flee in the opposite direction. That's when she bumped head long into *him.*

"Shit." She sidestepped as if she didn't recognize him and fled out of the atrium away from the lobby.

She could hear him padding after her. "Wait, Lillian."

Acting as if she didn't hear him and keeping a wary eye out, she made her way through the hallway, up an escalator and found she was on the platform where the monorail coach was boarding, preparing to leave. The only way off the platform was to go back down the escalator and risk running into horny Jim, or taking the monorail and abandoning her friends. She opted for the latter. She darted through the closing doors, risking injury and ducked down low in a nearby seat while glancing back toward the escalator. It took a few calming breaths to regain her composure.

Having lost sight of the other girls, she took out her phone and dialed Cora.

It went to voice message as she slid lower and peeked out towards the escalator.

Thankfully, the cars started moving just as her pursuer's shiny forehead appeared at the top of the moving stairs. Dialing again, she breathed a sigh of relief that she eluded her stalker.

"Where are you?" Cora asked without saying hello. "Did you see Jim Boy? He was here a minute ago."

"That's why I'm on the monorail headed for Aria. He was chasing me. I gave him the slip."

"He must have followed us from the Senior Center."

"He's a stalker. Did you see Charla?"

"No. Is she here too?"

"She walked in the front door with a man. I'm supposed to be at home with an injury. I couldn't let her see me, so I was running away when Jim stepped in my path. He apparently didn't see where I went, so can you meet me over there? Make sure he doesn't follow you and don't let Charla spot you, but try to see where they go. You're supposed to be with me at home making sure I don't die. Boy, this day is sure getting screwed up."

"Oh, what tangled webs we weave when first we practice to deceive," Cora laughingly quoted Walter Scott.

"Save it, Cora. I'll wait for you two to catch up. She broke the connection and looked back at the platform. She could make out Jim Boy's rumpled plaid shirt as he stood there watching his prey get away.

She dialed Cora again. "He's still in hot pursuit. Go get the car and pick me up at valet parking in front of Aria. He'll be high tailing it over here looking for me."

"Okay, but I wish someone would introduce me to a guy who thinks I'm worth chasing all over town. I could use a little roll in the sack if you get my drift."

"Nothing wrong with that, Cora, but at least find a roll that's not gone past its 'Best if used by' date." She could hear Cora giggling.

"But Lil, you forget, stale rolls get harder the older they get." More laughter came from the phone.

"Cora, you are a dirty old woman. You're terrible."

Cora agreed readily, "Yeah, I know."

"Now come and rescue me, please!" Lillian pleaded in desperation.

4

Hurrying off the monorail, Lillian took an elevator down to the main floor where she zigzagged around the carousels of noisy slots as she kept a wary eye out for Jim. She resolved to pursue some action to stop his harassment. It's ridiculous that he has the freedom to ruin her day.

She waited anxiously inside the doors of the valet entrance for Cora to arrive.

The time ticked off and it seemed like they would never come. She was pulling out her phone when she spotted the car. Not waiting for Cora to come to a complete stop, she yanked open the rear door and got in. By then her heart was pounding and she felt a headache coming on. She sat back, heaved a sigh of relief and ordered, "Hit it, Cora, I can smell him coming."

Celia peeked over the seat. "You look exhausted. Do you still want to play somewhere? We could go someplace else."

"Go back to the Senior Center. I have a piece of my mind to share with the Director. Maybe he can do something about that old fart. This is an infringement on my freedom!"

"Are you sure, Lil? Maybe we should ignore this whole thing. It could be he's just lonely. It could be a coincidence that he showed up there," Celia suggested.

"I don't think lonely is the right word to describe him, Celia. By the way, did you see Charla? She walked in with a good-looking hunk of burning love. I wonder if she has a boyfriend."

"We saw her," Celia said over her shoulder. "They walked straight to the elevator bank and took the car to the top floor. We followed to see where they were going, just so we could report to you. He looked like he might have some major bucks to his name. They didn't touch each other, but there was enough heat radiating from them to melt polar ice. I've seen that act in movies when someone is having an affair. They didn't fool me. They were going to his room."

"Maybe he's a client," Cora snickered, "and she just sold him a house."

Lillian smirked. "I didn't see any brief cases full of papers. She's having an affair with a married man and I'd bet on it."

Celia sucked in a shocked breath. "Lillian, you don't mean that. How can you say that about your own daughter? We don't know that he's married."

"There must be a reason other than her day job for her to have no time for me."

A few minutes later the trio arrived back where the chase had begun.

The lunch dishes were gone and seniors occupied the tables working puzzles and playing cards.

The three of them marched directly to the Directors office. Lillian knocked loudly on the door.

"Come in."

All three swooped in and took seats at the desk. Darren Washington looked up with a practiced smile. He had been Director for a little over a year and was amicable and efficient at providing hospitality to the elderly class of Las Vegans. The facility provided an affordable social setting that didn't empty their wallets every time they walked through the door. He was good at recruiting volunteers to provide entertainment. He scheduled classes geared to retirees, like computer instruction, crafts, exercise and dietary plans. "How can I help you ladies today?"

Lillian blurted, "We've come to lodge a complaint."

"What kind of complaint?" he asked as his smile faded and his brow furrowed. He settled back in his desk chair and folded his arms over his chest with a *hit me with your best-shot* look. "Is it about the food on Wednesday's menu? We've had budget cuts."

"No," Lillian assured him, "we're not here about the food. We get what we pay for. If we didn't like the menu, we'd go somewhere else to eat. We come here to visit with our friends."

"Then what is it?" He checked his watch and glanced at his desk calendar as if searching for a reason to cut the meeting short.

"It's about the man who seems to have me on his menu," Lillian said in a huff.

Darren's smile faced rapidly. "Whatever do you mean?"

Cora blurted, "You have a stalker in your midst and he's making my roommate very uncomfortable. He hovers around Lillian and brushes against her inappropriately. He ogles her and today he followed us all the way down to Bellagio. He chased her from the atrium to the monorail platform when she was trying to get away from him."

Darren cleared his throat and seemed to hesitate before responding. "And who are you talking about?"

"Jim Boyd," Lillian said indignantly. "You need to get him in here and give him a good talking to about manners and boundaries. I don't like his advances and it has to stop. I suspect we are not the only ones he has bothered. I've noticed lately that there is an obvious drop in the number of females that used to come here compared to what you have now. This place is starting to look like a men's club. I think he's running the ladies off."

Darren took a long pause and heaved an audible sigh, before responding. "Those are harsh accusations. Jim is harmless. He lost his wife and he's lonely. He's a decent fellow. Have any of you made an effort to befriend him?"

"There's a difference between being lonely and becoming a stalker. He's a stalker. Do something about it, or I will." Lillian fixed him with a firm stare to emphasize her point.

"Sexual harassment at a place like this is something the news media would love to sink their teeth into," Cora threatened in an intimidating tone. "It wouldn't speak too well for your job if you let this continue."

Sweat broke out on Darren's broad forehead and he swallowed hard. "This isn't an issue I'm generally asked to address, but I'll see what I can do." He checked his watch again and rose from his chair. "Now if you will excuse me, I have a meeting to attend." He strode to the door and opened it; a clear signal he didn't want to deal with an unexpected complaint of this nature at this moment.

The women filed out as Lillian whispered under her breath, "This wouldn't be happening if we had a lady director."

Celia chuckled. "A lady director would have kicked Jim's bag of nuts out the door by now and barred him from the Center."

"Okay, girls," said Cora, "we've lodged our complaint. We'll give Darren a couple of weeks to deal with it and then we'll come back and have lunch. If Jim is still misbehaving, we'll try something else. Now where do you want to go?"

As they left the building, Lillian took her cell phone out of her purse. "I'm curious to know if Charla has a boyfriend. I'm going to call her."

"You're supposed to be in bed," Celia reminded her. "How will you explain that you saw her on the strip?"

"Just listen." She dialed Charla's number.

The voicemail answered and instructed the caller to leave a message.

Lillian complied and said, "I just wanted to let you know I'm feeling okay this afternoon." Lillian snickered softly. After she ended the connection she gloated, "Yup, I knew it. She's screwing that guy," said Lillian, indignantly. "Meeting my ass—so this is why she has no time for me."

Celia raised her eyebrows and grinned. "Maybe this is just the modern method of closing a sale. He probably bought a two million dollar mansion and she's showing her gratitude."

Cora laughed. "Maybe I should try real estate sales. I'd be willing to take my commission out in trade if the client looked like that man Charla was obviously seeing. Did anyone recognize him? Didn't he look like a movie star?"

"Well if you're that desperate for a date, Cora," Lillian snorted, "maybe you should go out with Jim Boy."

"He's too short for me."

"When you're horizontal, height doesn't matter."

"Yuck!" was Cora's only response as she pulled into the parking garage back where their day began.

"It's time to stop talking about dates and poke some machines instead. I'm feeling lucky today," Celia said as she exited the car, putting an end to any further discussion about Jim Boy.

5

Since Lillian's first attempt at garnering attention from Charla was a monumental failure and she was supposed to have a bump and abrasion on her forehead, she had to wait a couple of weeks, the amount of time a real injury would take to heal without a trace.

Over breakfast Wednesday morning, the three women discussed their next move.

"Are we going to the Center for lunch today?" Cora inquired. Since we skipped last week, does anyone want to see if Darren spoke to Jim Boyd?"

"I'm up for it," Lillian replied as she poured coffee.

Celia popped two slices of bread in the toaster and put out the butter and jam. She had a sly grin on her face that went unnoticed by her companions.

Cora set the table with plates and flatware and then commenced scrambling eggs and pouring them in the skillet. "What if there's no change? What if he's there and his behavior is still repulsive?"

"Then I'll just tell him off in front of everyone. Maybe embarrassing him will help," Lillian replied indignantly.

"If you want to have words with him," Celia cautioned, "wouldn't it be nicer to just take him aside and speak to him privately? There's no need to make everyone uncomfortable. It's easier to be nice than it is to be mean."

"This is coming from an admitted man-hater. However, I suppose you're right. I'll try to be on my best behavior. Maybe there won't be a problem and Darren took care of it."

"From the sweat pouring off his forehead," Celia chuckled, "I'd say we made him a little nervous."

"Unless he wants his Center to be known as an old man's exclusive club, he had better start throttling the offenders."

"Not to change the subject, girls," Cora said as she dumped eggs on each plate, "but what's our next move on the Charla front? The accident scenario didn't work."

"I could stand out in the driveway and let you run over my foot!" Lillian suggested. "If I was rushed to an emergency room, maybe she would feel a little concern."

"Are you nuts? You would miss the rest of bowling season," Celia gasped. "Think of something a little less harmful. Now eat up. We have to go do our exercise in futility and then have lunch at the Center. I checked on line and the menu today includes Cherry Cheese Cake for dessert."

"Cherries, huh," Lillian snickered. "That's something we haven't had since forever."

"Now, who's the dirty old woman," Cora chortled.

Later, when the girls left the bowling alley, Celia seemed to be strangely quiet in the back seat.

"So, what's on your mind, Celia?" Lillian cast a glance over her shoulder as Cora drove. "You are so quiet today. Is everything okay with you? Is there trouble at work? Did you lose a patient?"

"Everything is just peachy keen," Celia replied enthusiastically. "I'm just thinking about that Cherry Cheese cake and working up an appetite."

"Sure you are."

Cora parked and Celia jumped out and headed for the door as if she needed to run for the restroom.

Cora watched Celia disappear into the building. "What's with her? Has she developed a weak bladder? Is she mad at us?"

"I don't know. She's not herself today."

"Whatever it is, she'll get over it. Come on. I'm hungry." Lillian headed for the door. "I hope Jim is behaving himself today."

"We'll see if his little slap down session with the Director helped."

The two friends looked around the dining hall, spotting Celia in the corner talking to someone.

Lillian peered intently at the man with his back to her. "Who is that? I think we have someone new here."

The dapper stranger was dressed in meticulously pressed black slacks, shiny dress shoes, and a turquoise long sleeved shirt. He sported a jaunty black leather tam on his freshly barbered head.

Celia seemed to be in deep conversation until she noticed the girls enter the room. Then she broke off and headed in their direction.

"Who is the new man?" Lillian asked.

"Not new," Celia said casually.

"What do you mean?" Lillian asked as they picked out their seats and placed their sweaters on the chairs to reserve them while they went through the line.

As they waited in line, Lillian felt a tap on her shoulder. She turned around to find herself face-to-face with Jim Boy—but not the Jim of two weeks ago. Her mouth dropped open.

He was holding up her sunglasses and smiling. "You dropped these at the Bellagio."

Lillian found herself staring at the *new man* Celia had been talking with. He looked very handsome in turquoise and black. He was clean-shaven and smelled of cologne. Behind his smile was a row of newly whitened teeth. Her mouth dropped open and she couldn't find words.

"Why did you run away from me? I was only trying to return these. I'm really not a stalker," he said politely, making eye contact.

"I'm sorry," Lillian dropped her eyes to the floor and took the glasses. I don't know what to say. I'm sorry."

"I'm sorry if I bothered you. I will try to respect your wishes and be more reserved. I know I've given the wrong impression in the past, but I will try to be more careful in the future. Now if you will excuse me, I have a lady friend over there waiting for me." He turned on his heel and retreated to the end of the room.

Lillian stared at his back. She could not find her voice as she watched Jim Boyd join an attractive elderly woman at his table.

Cora had watched the exchange in awe. She finally gathered her thoughts and spoke. "What came over him? He's a changed man."

Lillian turned to her other roommate whom now she realized had been absent from home frequently over the last two weeks. "Celia did you have anything to do with this? You did, didn't you? You've been gone a lot with no explanation. I know you weren't gambling all that time. Confess now because we'll get it out of you."

Celia grinned. "I'll tell you about it later. But not here." Her gaze darted across the room at Jim Boyd and a smug grin formed on her face.

Back at home that afternoon, Cora made coffee and the three girls settled around the table for their traditional afternoon coffee klatch.

Lillian spoke first as she took a cookie from the package on the table. "Jim Boyd actually looked handsome today and he has a new lady friend."

"Okay," Cora said, taking a stern look over the top of her glasses and glaring at Celia. "Tell us how you made that happen."

Celia took a deep breath and smiled. "I just felt a little bit of remorse that we were so hasty to report him for sexual harassment. I went back the next day to speak to Darren and we cooked up a plan. Together we took Jim to the store and helped him pick out all new outfits. Turns out, money is no object with him. He's loaded. Then we went to his house. I could see how he really needed some help to clean and organize his home so it would be attractive to any women he wanted to invite over. Darren and I offered to pay for a one-day housekeeping crew to come in and clean it for him. However, he insisted on paying the bill."

"You're kidding." Lillian gasped. "You would have paid someone to clean his house?"

"Relax, it wouldn't have cost any more than a trip to the casino would have, and it was for a good cause."

The roommates stared at Celia for a long silent moment.

Celia continued, "Darren and I felt sorry for him. He's been lonely and kind of at sea since his wife passed. We helped him out this time and left him with a printed schedule of chores he needs to perform religiously to maintain his house. We made a long list of housekeepers he can call on if he gets behind. He can afford it. He just didn't know where to start."

Lillian sipped her coffee and munched on a cookie for a few beats then asked, "Why didn't you tell us?"

"I wanted to surprise you. I felt guilty at how we were talking about him. He's just a lonely old man. Look at him now. He has his confidence back and he met that nice lady at the mall."

"Now I feel like a witch." Lillian felt like crying, she was so ashamed. "All he wanted to do is return the sunglasses I apparently dropped when I bumped into him. What can I do to make it up to him?" She could feel her face turning red.

"Send him a thank you note for returning your glasses."

"It doesn't seem like that's enough after the way I treated him."

"I don't think you can do more. Darren and I had a talk with him about boundaries and manners. He simply didn't realize how he was coming across. He's a changed man. He's happy and we're happy." She searched the faces of her two housemates. "We are happy aren't we?"

Lillian and Cora let Celia sweat for a few beats as they looked at each other across the table.

Lillian finally spoke with a smile. "That was a very noble thing you did. I don't know why I didn't think of it."

Celia waved the air as if to sweep the notion away. "You would have come up with the idea I'm sure, but you're so preoccupied with your problem with Charla, that you were overly annoyed at the distraction Jim Boyd created. You need to find a hobby, dear girl."

"So your new hobby, Celia, is making over the old men at the Center to make them more eligible? Who are you…Oprah—Doctor Phil?"

Cora laughed softly. "Well I found the makeover to be rather titillating."

"But now he's taken," Celia grinned. "Who should we do next?"

"What?" Cora and Lillian chimed.

"That didn't come out right!" Celia gasped. "I mean make over."

"I could make a suggestion, but I think it would be a waste of time," Lillian blurted. "You can make over the exterior, but a heart transplant is the only thing that will improve Charla."

Celia threw up her hands. "Sorry, we're fresh out of available hearts in my ER."

6

Several days passed with no word from Charla, so Lillian decided to try again. She dialed Charla's number. It went to voice mail. She left a brief message to say she would like to hear from her.

She was sitting mindlessly in front of the television in a funk when Celia shuffled into the room in her robe and slippers. She had worked swing shift and awakened late in the morning. "Any coffee left?"

Lillian rose and headed for the kitchen. "I'll make a fresh pot."

"Where's Cora?"

"The school called real early this morning. They needed a substitute for one day. She jumped at the chance."

"I'll never understand why she keeps going back into the classroom," Celia mused. "Kids nowadays are such mouthy brats."

"Well, she has always enjoyed children of any age. Even when they are acting out, she has a way of handling them and it brings in extra money for her. Occasional sub jobs help her cope with the absence of her own grandchildren since Donny packed up his bunch and moved to Oregon."

Celia pulled two mugs from the cupboard and set them on the counter. "I've been to Oregon. It rained every single day. I cannot fathom why anyone would want to leave this state and move up there. It's depressing when the sun doesn't shine for days at a time."

"I hear you," agreed Lillian. "I like the sunshine too."

"Have you heard from Charla?" Celia poured the coffee and set their mugs on the table. She popped toast in and retrieved some knives from the drawer. "Want some toast with your coffee?"

"Sure, and no, Charla has not called me back."

"I wish I understood that girl."

Lillian smeared butter and jelly on her toast and took a bite, washing it down with a swig of coffee. "Are you busy today?"

"I don't know. I just got up."

"I need to drop my car off at the shop. There's a leak in the radiator. Can you come and get me? I can go ahead and take it in and I'll call you if they are keeping it more than an hour."

"Sure. Go ahead. Just call me and let me know where and when."

To Lillian's shock, the mechanic would be holding her aging black sedan hostage for more than a day. It was living up to the name she had dubbed it when it began needing frequent trips to the shop. "*Bat Crap* strikes again," she complained. "Well this is inconvenient!"

"I'm sorry Senora, but we have to replace the radiator and hoses." Jose cautioned, "You shouldn't drive it like that and there's a problem with the water pump and thermostat. When was the last time anyone looked under the hood?"

"I don't know. My son-in-law used to take care of scheduling maintenance. Herbie's been gone a whole year already. I sure miss him."

Jose, the mechanic furrowed his brow and said sympathetically with sadness in his eyes, "Oh, I'm sorry Ms. Crocker. It's always difficult when someone close to you passes away."

"Oh, he's not dead! Charla divorced him and he was so hurt, he moved to New York City to get over it."

Jose emitted a whistle. "That's a drastic move."

"Not for a musician. He can blow his horn anywhere."

"Si," Jose sighed. He handed Lillian the work order to sign. "Do you have a ride home? Should I call a cab?"

"No, I've got it handled. Call me when the work is done." She took out her phone and dialed Celia.

Celia answered breathlessly. "Lillian, I'm so sorry, but I have to rush back to work. There has been a tour bus accident on the freeway and we have multiple patients coming into emergency. I have to go. Please call Charla for a ride." The line went dead.

Charla was probably showing a house or closing a deal; perfect time to interrupt her life! She dialed.

"What, Mom. I'm in a meeting."

"Well get out of your meeting. I need a ride."

"Can't you call your roommates? I'm very busy." The noise from multiple voices in the background sounded like she caught Charla at a party or in a restaurant.

"Cora is teaching school today and Celia had to go into work because of some kind of emergency. My car is broke down and I need a ride home. Is that too much to ask?" She could not help it when her snotty voice took over involuntarily.

"Isn't there anyone else you can call?"

"No! What in hell is the matter with you, Charla? I never see you and when I need your help, you are always too busy. Your crappy attitude is wearing my patience thin! We need to talk."

"Not here and not now, Mother. You'll have to call a cab."

"Thanks for nothing!" Lillian ended the call. "You will pay for this someday," she said to the phone as if Charla were still listening.

So angry she could hardly think, Lillian burst blindly out of the business and began walking mindlessly down the street. She knew she was several miles from home, but was so upset she could barely think rationally. Having walked aimlessly for several blocks, thirst reminded her that she had left home without any water. She stopped at a corner convenience store to purchase a bottle. As she waited in line at the counter, she became aware of the fact that she was the only one who spoke English. She immediately regretted the decision to bring her car to Jose for repairs.

He had been one of Charlie's students. In spite of his impoverished circumstances with immigrant parents, he had managed to finish twelfth grade and attend trade school. With Charlie's mentoring, Jose had opened his own auto repair business. He had always been honest with Charlie and kept the costs of car repairs down. Charlie trusted him and in turn, Lillian did too.

She nervously paid for the water and left the store, keeping a wary eye out and securing her purse close to her body. After walking further west for several blocks, she took a break, sitting down on a bus bench. She uncapped the drink and sipped on it. The sun was rapidly heating up the city and Lillian's armpits became saturated with sweat.

Buses came and went. Riders gathered to board and others disembarked. Lillian stayed put. She had not ridden a bus in years and had no idea where they were going from this stop.

When the same driver came around for the third time and noticed her still sitting there, he hollered at her. "Lady, are you going to camp out all day or are you going to ride?"

That brought Lillian out of her daze. "I don't know. Where are you going?

"This is my last run. Where do you need to go?"

"I need to go to Lone Mountain and Clayton."

"You won't get there on this run. You need to go across the street and up a few blocks. This bus is going east. You should go north."

"What time is it?" Lillian could not even think now. She felt dehydrated.

"It's five o'clock. Are you okay?"

"Yeah, I can call someone now. It's late enough."

"Okay then. Stay safe." The bus pulled away and Lillian was so warm, she began to remove her sweater, but it became tangled up in her sturdy over the body purse strap. Just then, she heard heavy foot falls approaching and her mind jerked to high alert.

A scruffy young man rushed at her and grabbed at her bag. However, he was too slow and clumsy. Lillian knew all about the level of purse snatching in this city, so she kept hers secured across her body by a long heavy strap.

As the would-be thief reached for her bag, she brought her foot up and nailed him squarely in his nuts. He buckled to his knees in front of her, clutching his groin in agony. Lillian wasted no time bringing her knee up and whacking him in the chin, knocking him backwards. Those self-defense classes at the Senior Center had not been a waste after all.

Before the perp could recover and scramble away, Lillian stood over him and kicked him in the face, breaking his nose. Blood spurted from his nostrils as his hands flew up to clutch his newly rearranged face. She dealt a final blow with a foot to his ribs as he lay in a fetal position.

An "Out of Service" bus pulled up just then and the driver, seeing what was going on, put on the brakes and jumped out to help Lillian subdue the thief. He produced zip ties from his pocket and slapped some on the dirt bag's wrists and ankles.

Lillian stood in awe. "What are you, an undercover cop?"

"No ma'am, but we get a lot of purse snatchers and trouble makers on this line. I carry restraints just in case. Wait here please."

He got back on the bus and radioed his dispatcher to give him a location, report the incident, and then he called 911.

"Are you hurt, Ma'am?" he asked as he returned to her side.

"I don't think so. My foot hurts a little, but I showed that snot nosed little piss ant that it's not a good idea to mess with me." She squared her shoulders and gloated. "I took self-defense lessons." She leaned down and grabbed the perp's shaggy hair, turning his face to hers. "Remember this face, Sonny, I'll be testifying against you in court."

Sirens were approaching and a police unit skidded to a stop. Lillian suddenly felt weak as the adrenaline subsided and her body started to relax. She plopped back down on the bench.

The officer directed his attention to Lillian. "What happened here?"

The handcuffed perp whined, "She kicked me."

"He was stealing my purse! I showed him. It's not wise to mess with an angry woman. He won't be boinking his girlfriend anytime soon." She sneered at him and looked at the officer. "Are you going to arrest him?"

"How did he get handcuffed? Did you do that too?" The officer was having trouble keeping a straight face.

"The bus driver carries them. He says he has a lot of occasions to use them on this route."

"That brings up the question as to what a nice lady like you would be doing in this neighborhood. Do you live around here?" The officer frowned.

"No. I brought my car to the mechanic my late husband and I have been using for years. I couldn't get a ride home."

The officer took out his own cuffs, waited for the bus driver to remove the plastic ties and then he cuffed the man. He removed a wallet from the moaning man's pocket, patted him down for weapons, and removed a switchblade knife from his pocket.

"You broke my nose! I could sue you, bitch!" yelled the thief.

"Shut your mouth," the officer responded.

Lillian spit in her attacker's direction and yelled back, "I'll see you in court. Bring your rap sheet with you!"

She waited patiently, feeling nervous. Struck by a sudden panic attack, Lillian feared they would arrest her for assault. Without being able to control them, tears began to flow. She looked away and only then noticed she was looking at an advertisement for Charla's office posted on the kiosk. *This must be the low rent zone for ad space. Logically, she is wasting her money. Nobody around here is going to shop for a million dollar mansion across town.*

She grinned when strangers began gathering around with iPhones, recording the scene. She moved over beside the poster and pointed. "That's my daughter! This happened because she refused to come and pick me up at the repair shop! She was too busy. Wait until she sees this. You are going to post this on the net aren't you?" She grinned.

As the officer took notes regarding the details of the incident, Lillian became aware that a van from a local television station had just arrived to record all of the activity for the news. She gladly responded to the reporter's questions, making sure she included her previous statement, "This never would have happened if Charla had come to pick me up."

The news crew left with their story and the officer escorted Lillian to a unit that would drive her home.

"Can I ride in the front?" she asked. "I don't want anyone to think I've been arrested." She gave her most engaging little-old-lady smile.

"Madam, you just took down a career purse snatcher we've been trying to nab for a long time. If it were in our budget, I would hire you a limo ride. But the squad car will have to do."

When the black and white pulled up in front of their house, Cora came bursting out of the front door. "Where have you been, and why are you under arrest? Celia and I have been frantic. You didn't answer your phone."

"I was busy being interviewed. I needed a ride and this nice officer brought me home. These are my roommates, Cora and Celia."

The officer nodded as he helped Lillian out of the car and turned her over to her roommates. "Check her over and make sure she's not hurt." He handed Lillian a card. "Call if you need anything or remember something about the incident."

It was only when Lillian started up the steps that she felt a severe pain in her nut-kicking foot. "Ow!"

"What's the matter?" Celia took her arm and helped her into the house.

"I think my foot is broken."

"Now how could you have done that? You were taking your car in for repairs."

"That's not all I did today."

Lillian flopped down heavily on the sofa and sighed. Celia knelt down and removed Lillian's athletic shoe. "This looks bruised." She felt around. "Does this hurt?"

Lillian flinched. "Yes. Is it broken?" She pulled her pant leg up and examined the rapidly darkening bruise on her kneecap. "Battle scars!"

Celia felt around further. "I'll get an ice pack and an ace bandage and wrap those. I have a walking boot in the closet. You look like you are dehydrated. Cora, I think she needs some water and something to eat."

When Lillian's foot and knee were iced and wrapped, the three sat in the living room eating an impromptu meal when Cora spoke up. "Okay, now are you going to tell us what happened and why you had a police escort to get home?"

"If you turn on the news in a little while, you'll probably see me. There must have been a half dozen people standing around with their iPhones. I bet I'm on YouTube already."

"So what did you do? Were you mugged?" Cora demanded.

"I nailed a little twit that's been stealing purses."

"You got mugged at the auto shop?" Celia gasped wide-eyed.

"No! I didn't have a ride home, so I started walking and I was taking a break at a bus stop, sitting on the bench, minding my own damn business when this little jerk ran up to me. You'll see it all on the news tonight."

Cora was about to comment when Lillian's phone rang.

Lillian grinned. "It's Charla. She refused to leave what she was doing and come to get me when I needed a ride. Now let's see what she has to say for herself."

"Mother, how could you embarrass me like that?" She was just a decibel short of screaming.

Putting the phone on speaker, Lillian grinned wickedly, "Whatever are you talking about dear?"

"You stood right in front of my ad poster and told that officer that you got mugged because I wouldn't give you a ride home! How could you do that? It will be all over the internet, on Facebook, on Twitter. My email is going to blow up! You made me look like a terrible person!"

Lillian clamped her lips smugly and then grinned and spoke in a malicious voice. "So, me getting mugged is all about you, dear? I'm bruised and my crotch kicking foot might have a broken bone, but thank you for asking about my welfare."

41

"It doesn't sound serious. Celia can fix it for you. This is so embarrassing. If you had called a cab like I told you to, this could all have been avoided."

Lillian's expression swiftly changed to indignation. "If my name was Ella, would you have dropped everything and come to my rescue this afternoon when I asked for your help? Think about that Charla. Be sure you watch the eleven o'clock news. There was a television crew there to catch my interview. You wouldn't want to miss that." She hit the button to end the call.

Cora stood up and gathered the dishes to take them back to the kitchen. She shook her head in disbelief. "What is it with that woman?"

"I don't know. The older she gets the worse she gets." She touched her kneecap and groaned. "I don't blame Herbie for leaving her and moving to New York. He probably got tired of her treating him like a doormat. I sided with him. I think she's still mad at me for that."

Lillian tried to stand, but flinched when her foot hit the floor. She sank back down. "Maybe I should have it x-rayed. I have to pee very badly. Get me the office chair so I can get to the pot, quick!"

Celia fetched the chair and the girls helped her into it, then they pushed it to the bathroom. "I guess we should take you to emergency and get that foot looked at."

"And miss the late news? It can wait. Just help me get to bed. You can examine it in the morning. Bring me some aspirin. I'll be fine."

From her bed that night, Lillian smugly watched the clip on the news of her standing in front of the poster, while iPhone junkies and the television camera operator were recording all the details about the attack. She frowned when she realized the newsroom editors had blurred the company name on the poster. "Charla can relax now. At least the media was discrete."

A mugshot of the accused purse-snatcher flashed on the screen. He owned a long arrest record.

She turned off the set and drifted off. Her foot was elevated on a couple of pillows, but she managed to sleep in spite of the inconvenience.

7

When Lillian awoke in the morning, Celia was still sleeping after her graveyard shift. The foot was aching but she was able to stand on it. She hobbled into the kitchen in the walking boot to find Cora had already started coffee.

"How's the foot?" she asked as she put out mugs and cereal bowls. "I saw the news after you went to bed. That guy looked kind of familiar."

"What! Have you taken to socializing on the dark side?" Lillian heaved herself into a chair and took the wrappings off her knee to examine it in the light. A dark bruise had appeared where the kneecap encountered the perp's chin. She was able to flex it and walk so it apparently had not suffered any permanent damage.

"No, I think he may have been a student of mine at some time. I think I remember little Tyrone Johnson. If he wasn't skipping school, he was stealing lunch money from other kids and sexually harassing the girls. He had a reserved seat in the principal's office. I can't believe you got the upper hand on that career criminal."

"I'll have to thank Darren for bringing in self-defense instructors to the Senior Center."

"You took an awful chance fighting him off. He could have had a gun!"

"Fortunately he didn't and I didn't give him time to pull his knife out of his pocket. The next time he wants to mug a little old lady like me, he better wear a cup on his stinking balls."

Cora toasted some English muffins and put out butter and jelly. "What were you doing at that bus kiosk? You don't ride buses."

"I was angry at Charla for refusing to come and pick me up so I just took off blindly walking. I wasn't thinking rationally." She dumped cereal and milk in her bowl and took a sip of hot coffee.

"Well, you're not going back to pick up your car until one of us can take you. It's not safe to let you out of the house alone." Cora snickered to indicate she was kidding. "I'm sorry I wasn't there for you."

"At any rate, I managed to get Charla's attention! I stayed awake long enough to see the news clip. She's going to be steamed."

Cora peered sternly over her glasses. "But is it the kind of attention you want?"

"Well, I…"

Lillian's cell phone broke up the conversation. She looked at the caller I.D. "It's the shop calling. I wonder if my car is ready."

"Hello."

Jose's distinct Spanish accent spoke hesitantly. "Ms. Crocker, can you come to the shop this morning? We need to talk about the condition of your car. I don't think I can fix it."

"Why? What's wrong with it?" Lillian had managed to drive *Bat Crap* to the shop without incident.

"I have to explain it here. Can you come?"

Lillian was trying to absorb the news. That car was the last big purchase she and Charlie made together before his passing. It had sentimental value. In spite of its age and poor gas mileage, she loved *Bat Crap.*

When Lillian failed to respond immediately, Jose raised his voice, "Are you there Ms. Crocker?"

"Yes, I'm here. Are you saying it's going to cost me more money to get it fixed?"

"Just come by the shop when you can." The line went dead.

By noon, Lillian was able to remove the boot and wear her slip-on sneakers with just a light ace bandage.

Cora drove Lillian to Jose's shop. As they entered the lot, Lillian craned her neck. "I don't see my car out here. It must still be in the bay."

Lillian hobbled into the office. Jose was at the counter and he avoided eye contact as she greeted him. "Okay, want to tell me what's going on? I didn't see my car out there."

Jose's eyes went wide when he noticed her limp. "What happened to your foot?"

"A purse snatcher injured my foot when he ran into it with his groin! Then his chin bruised my knee when he came crashing down on it."

Rendered speechless by Lillian's explanation, Jose gaped at her as if he had just met Super Woman.

"Pay attention, Jose. Where is my car?"

"Come with me." Jose gave Lillian a wide berth as he opened the door to the garage. He stepped a few paces away.

Lillian followed him to the farthest bay. On the floor was a pile of rumpled black metal lying upside down like a dead cockroach.

Lillian gasped. The only thing recognizable was the color. "Is that my car?"

Jose frowned, took another step backwards and looked away. "Yeah, I'm afraid there was a problem with the lift. I fired the mechanic who left it up in the air overnight. He failed to set the safety locks. I have repeatedly told him not to leave them up all night. He's an idiot. I'm so sorry."

Lillian gasped, "I don't understand," as she walked around the wreckage to inspect it.

"My equipment is old," Jose replied defensively. "The hydraulics on one side failed and you see the result. I am so, so sorry. Do you have full coverage on your insurance?"

Lillian turned around and faced the mechanic her husband had trusted for several years. "You're joking! This is not going on my insurance. This is going on yours. You did this. Now you owe me a car!" She took out her smart phone and snapped a picture of the pile of crushed metal. A lone tear escaped her eye as she thought back to the day she and Charlie drove the Chevy Malibu off the sales lot. They immediately tagged the sleek black auto, *Batmobile*. However, over the years as the car aged and needed frequent repairs, she had renamed it, *Bat Crap*.

"It was an accident. I must check with my insurance company to see if liability will cover it and give you something. It was an old car. I'll see what I can do."

"So what am I to do in the meantime? I need my own transportation. This does not make me happy!" Lillian turned and went back into the reception area. She paced back and forth taking deep breaths to try to calm down.

"I can loan you a car until this is all settled."

Lillian thought about that offer for a minute. "You'd do that?"

"Sure. I feel terrible about this. Your husband was a friend. I can't let him down. I have to take care of your needs. Tell you what; my cousin is in the county…uh…uh…away for sixty days. I have his car parked in my storage lot. He won't mind if I loan it to you."

"Is it an automatic? I can't drive a stick with this foot." She pointed to the bandaged defensive weapon.

"Yes, yes. You should have no problem driving it. I'll go get it." He took some keys from his pocket. "Meet me out front." He disappeared out the back door.

Lillian went to Cora's car and motioned for her to roll her window down.

"What's the hold up?" she complained. "It's hot out here. Where's your car?"

"Bat Crap has met an untimely death and is no longer drivable. Jose is loaning me his cousin's car for a few days."

"That's nice of him, but what about your car? Will he fix it and get it back to you?"

"Not likely. I guess I'm going to have to buy a new one."

The blare of a loud horn interrupted them. Jose pulled alongside Cora's car in a bright orange nineteen eighties vintage low rider, painted with red and purple flames erupting from the front wheel wells. Darkly tinted windows, a hood scoop, and chrome hubcaps that kept spinning even when the tires stopped, completed the package.

Lillian's jaw dropped.

Cora gaped wide-eyed, and when she found her voice, she blurted, "You have got to be kidding. That's the loaner?"

Lillian jumped up and down and laughed in spite of the pain in her foot.

"This is perfect! I hope I can drive it."

Cora got out of her car and the two of them walked around the customized vehicle, inspecting it closely as Jose unwound his skinny frame from the driver's seat and stepped aside.

"Lillian, you can't seriously think you can drive around town in this…this…hot rod!"

"Sure I can." She climbed into the driver's seat. "Get in Jose and show me how everything works. Let me drive it around the block first. I can barely see over the steering wheel. Where's the accelerator?"

Jose showed her how to move the seat forward. "There. Now can you reach the gas pedal?"

"That's good."

Cora backed away. "I'll just wait for you here." She watched as her friend pulled out of the lot very slowly. She shook her head in dismay.

When the car returned, Lillian was still behind the wheel. Jose got out, waved, and headed for the shop. She motioned for Cora to come around to the driver's side where her window slid down silently. "I can handle this. See you back at home. This car is so cool!"

Cora looked it over with a skeptical eye. "Cool maybe, but it really doesn't suit you."

"Oh, but it's just the thing I need. Wait until Charla sees this." The window went back up and Lillian hit the gas, bolting forward towards the exit. She was already thinking ahead to what she was going to do with these wheels in the afternoon.

8

Lillian gleefully parked her loaner in the driveway behind Celia's Purple P.T. Cruiser dubbed *"The Purple People Eater."* Cora's conservative sedan the girls had tagged *Brown Betty* pulled in next to the P.T. As Cora got out, Lillian pushed a button on the steering column and the sound of trumpets blared as if it was the start of the Kentucky Derby.

Whirling around, Cora yelled, "What in God's name was that? I nearly jumped out of my skin!"

Laughing like a fool as she emerged, Lillian beamed with excitement. "It's the horn. It has a whole menu of sounds; I can even make it sound like a semi-truck!"

"Are you going insane? This is a quiet neighborhood. Please try to keep from turning it into a circus. We have to live here."

"Relax. Most everyone has already gone to work. Do you notice anyone coming out of their houses to see what the ruckus is?"

Cora looked furtively around. "Just get in the house before you embarrass us."

Lillian stalked to the front door. "Well, you're in a sour mood. You're starting to sound like Charla."

"How long do you have to drive that...that..." At a loss for respectable words, she nodded in the direction of the hot rod parked in plain sight.

"*Spanish Cadillac*," Lillian finished the sentence with a name she invented while driving home.

"When will your car be fixed?"

"Never," Lillian answered matter-of-factly. "I have to call my insurance company and report this. Maybe they can get some money out of Jose's insurance company."

Cora stared open-mouthed and then shrugged and headed for the kitchen to start a pot of coffee. "I think I need some caffeine before I can hear your explanation. That little caper out there in the driveway probably jolted Celia awake. Do you want some toasted cheese sandwiches for lunch?"

Celia shuffled into the kitchen yawning and rubbing the sleep from her eyes. "What is all the commotion? Somebody just blew through the neighborhood honking an annoying horn. We need a noise ordinance in this city."

Cora turned from the counter where she was making sandwiches. "That was Lillian's loaner car. She's feeling her Spanish oats."

"Huh? What do you mean?"

Lillian had disappeared through the door to the garage. "Now where did she go?" Cora dropped what she was doing and went to see.

Her friend was busy rummaging through boxes stored on the shelves. "I can't remember which one it's in."

"What are you looking for?"

"I'm looking for the hat I brought back from Cabo San Lucas the year Charlie and I went there to celebrate our anniversary. I can't remember which box I put it in." She took down another box and shook it.

"Why would you want that?"

"I have plans for it." Lillian stripped the tape from a box that looked promising.

"Look for it later. Lunch is almost ready and Celia will want to know what the problem is with your car. Come on in here." She retreated to the kitchen.

Looking longingly at the stack of boxes she wanted to search, Lillian shrugged and followed Cora back into the house.

As the three roommates sat at the table drinking coffee and eating, Cora urged, "It's time to tell us what happened at the garage. Why can't your wheels be fixed?"

Lillian recounted the tale of the sad demise of her aging sedan and showed them the photo on her phone. "And that's why I'm driving Jose's cousin's car. When he comes up with a check for me, I'll make a down payment on a newer one."

"I could have just given you a ride home. Why would you need to borrow a jalopy like that? If we are both working, you can call Charla for a ride."

"Cora, if I thought I could rely on Charla for anything, I would have done it that way. This is going to be more fun. I haven't driven a hot car like that since I was a teenager and Jimmy Sickle took me for a ride to lover's lane at the lake. When he wouldn't take *no* for an answer, I enticed him out of the car, then I jumped back in, locked the doors and fled in his ride. He had to hitchhike home. After that, my nickname for him was always Jimmy Sicko."

Celia snickered. "That was very virginal of you."

"I know I'm old, but I can still remember the days when we tried to hang on to that moral status symbol until we said our marriage vows. When I look around at the young people nowadays, I have to wonder who got it right, them or us. They are all so much more relaxed with their life styles. Look at that girl on Bachelorette. She tried a bunch of those hunks on for size before she picked one and she did it on national television! Can you imagine what our parents would have done to us if we did such a thing?"

"Well, there was mention of banishment to a convent," Cora sighed. "How long is that...that..."

"*Spanish Cadillac*," Lillian filled in with a mischievous grin.

"Okay how long are you planning to drive it?"

"Just long enough to get somebody's attention."

"Who's attention?" Celia asked skeptically.

Lillian only smiled as she loaded her dishes into the dishwasher and headed for the door to the garage. "I need to find that hat."

After a short time, she returned, prancing and dancing gingerly around in the kitchen on her injured foot. The bright pink velveteen sombrero generously embossed with silver embroidery was perched on her head. She gyrated to the imaginary tune of a mariachi band while her ample boobs bounced up and down, popping the buttons on her blouse. She repeatedly yelled, "Ole....ole!"

The roommates watched in amusement.

Celia finally spoke. "I'm not sure if I should laugh or call the paramedics. I think she's having some sort of brain fart."

"Don't get too concerned. I think that *Spanish Caddie* parked out there has cast a spell on her." Cora stood up and grabbed the hat off Lillian's head. "You can stop now. Just because you drove that ridiculous car home, it doesn't mean you are Spanish. Remember, you are a gringo. You speak English! Now stop it."

Lillian took the hat back and limped down the hallway to her room. "You guys are taking all the fun out of this."

She changed clothes, picking out some orange leggings and an oversized yellow tie-dyed tee that screamed with neon splashes of purple, orange and pink. "Hum, matches the car." She plopped the hat back on her head and admired her image in the dresser mirror. "Perfect." Her foot wouldn't fit into any of her sandals with that bandage on it. She tested it out by removing the wrapping and slipping into a pair of jeweled slippers. It only hurt a little bit.

She downed two more aspirin and headed to the front door with her handbag slung over her shoulder.

Cora yelled, "Where are you going in that getup?"

"I'm going to see someone." The mischievous look on her face hinted at what she was planning. "Want to come along?"

Cora took a moment to think that one over. She cocked her head. "Lillian, you are going to make things worse."

"No I'm not. All this is going to do is stir up some dust. You should come with me and watch."

Celia followed her to the door, pleading, "Lillian, come back here and have another cup of coffee. We need to discuss this and I need to examine your foot."

"It's fine. Now *I* am going to have some fun. If you guys don't want to join in, then you can stay home." She walked out, and shut the door. "My chariot awaits me."

Thirty minutes later, Lillian drove into the parking lot in front of Charla's spacious offices near an impressive development of mansions on the west side of the city. She put the car in neutral to idle the engine and turned up the music. As she did so, she experienced the thrill of sitting in the middle of a giant stereo, booming, woofing and tweeting. She hit the horn and the sound of trumpets blared as if the Kentucky Derby had come to Charla's real estate office. As she played with the devices on the dash, the car started bouncing up and down. She giggled, "This is so much fun! Ole!"

Employees started pouring out of the office to see what the commotion was. One of them tapped on the window.

Lillian rolled it down. "Hey, how are you?" She said casually, "Cool ride. I just got it."

"Madam," said the astonished employee who obviously did not expect to find a little old woman with white hair sitting in the noisemaker. "Could you turn it down a little bit? Ms. Charla has a very important client in there and this is disruptive. Do you have business here?"

"Yeah," Lillian replied flippantly. "Charla is my daughter. I just wanted to show off my new car. Send her out."

"Miss Charla is writing up a sales agreement. She's busy right now."

Lillian reached over and turned up the volume on the stereo. The increased decibels made the car vibrate. "Then I'll wait," she shouted.

"Please, I'm asking you nicely. Turn it down!" the girl shouted over the din.

"Not until Charla comes out." Lillian rolled the window back up.

The exasperated look on the secretary's face made Lillian laugh aloud, although it was inaudible over the racket in the car.

While she waited, Lillian reached over and flipped a toggle switch on the dash. "Whoa!" she exclaimed as the car rose. "Jose should have warned me about that one." She flipped it off and the car settled back down.

There was another rap on the darkly tinted window. Lillian rolled it down and faced the angry expression on Charla's heavily made up face. Eyes burning with anger, she glared at her mother.

"What in God's name are you doing here? And where in hell did you get this…this…" Charla's eyes roamed down the side of the garishly painted car.

"*Spanish Cadillac*," Lillian completed the sentence with a grin on her face, pushing all the buttons to rile Charla.

"Get out of the car, Mother, and turn off that noise!"

Lillian turned off the ignition and secretly welcomed the silence for an instant. *Being Spanish is ear-splitting business.*

"So you don't like my wheels," said Lillian with an impish grin.

Charla cast another disdainful eye over the strange automobile and shook her head. "Where is your sedan?"

"It's upside-down on the floor of Jose's auto repair shop. There was an accident. He loaned me this one."

"Is this his car?"

"No, it's his cousin's. He said that he was away for sixty days and probably wouldn't mind if I borrowed it. I can drive it until I buy another one."

"Then go get another car. In the meantime, get this piece of crap out of my lot. You're embarrassing me and I'm right in the middle of a major sale negotiation. And take off that stupid hat!"

Lillian raised her chin defiantly and pursed her lips. "This hat has a lot of sentimental value. It was the last thing your daddy bought me when we celebrated our final wedding anniversary in Cabo San Lucas. I can wear it if I want."

"Not here and not now." Charla cast a glance towards her office building. People were gawking out the windows.

"Come with me, Charla. We can go to El Pollo Loco for dinner." Lillian could hardly keep a straight face as sweat began to bead on Charla's forehead. Her makeup job appeared to be breaking down.

"Mother, I'm begging you! Just take that thing…"

"*Spanish Cadillac*," Lillian interjected with a smile.

"Just go already. I'll call you later."

"But I want to have dinner with you. Don't you want a ride?"

"No!" Charla opened the car door and tried to guide Lillian into the offensive vehicle's driver seat.

Lillian stood firm.

Charla took a deep breath and let it out. "I know what you're trying to do, Mother. You want my attention. Okay, I get it. You've succeeded. Now take this piece of junk and leave. I'll pick you up Monday, and take you to lunch and then we will go select a more… appropriate car. Hell, I'll even pay for the damn thing. Just get rid of this hunk of junk before somebody shoots you for disturbing the peace! Take it back to Jose!"

"Is that a bribe?"

"Call it what you want. If I close this sale, I can buy a dozen cars. I'll see you Monday."

"Can I have a Cadillac like yours?" Lillian grinned as she eyed Charla's immaculate vehicle parked in the reserved spot in front of the door.

"No! Don't get greedy!" She turned on her heel and stormed back into the office just as her clients were coming out the door as if to leave.

As Lillian watched, Charla directed the buyers back inside with the insulting words, "Pay no attention to that crazy old woman."

The couple eyed Lillian with amused expressions. "Somebody you know?"

"Unfortunately, yes. However, it's taken care of. Come back in please so we can finish up. I apologize for the interruption." She cast a disgusted smirk over her shoulder as she followed her clients inside.

Satisfied with herself, Lillian climbed back in the hot rod and started the engine. She hit the horn one more time while exiting the lot, as if adding an exclamation point at the end of the statement she wanted to make today. It was time to return the car to Jose.

9

Lillian awoke early Monday morning with a feeling of excitement. She had spent the previous day on the internet surfing for possible new cars she might like to test drive. The one she especially liked was a hybrid estimated to give her fifty miles to the gallon. For no more than she used her car, she figured it would be several months in between stops at a gas station.

She had done price comparisons amongst the dealers in town and even picked out the color she wanted. In her dreams during the night, she was driving it all over town. She might even break it in with a trip to see…Ella's face popped up in her daydream, jerking her mind back to the present. "Yeah, like I'd go see *her.*"

Lillian sat up and gingerly placed her sore foot on the floor. She tested it before standing. It wasn't bad. Her instep had turned black and blue, but by now, she figured nothing was broken.

She put on a robe and headed to the kitchen. Cora was making coffee. Celia would still be asleep after her overnight shift. The house appeared dim and Lillian looked out the kitchen window to find the sky overcast. A dark gray cloud in the south looked as if it might dump some rain on Henderson.

"How's the foot," Cora asked as she put bowls and boxes of cereal on the table.

"I guess I didn't kick him hard enough to break anything but his balls." Lillian chuckled. "I think I'm in better shape than he is."

"I hope so. Are you ready to go car shopping this morning?" Cora asked cheerfully.

"Charla said she would pick me up and take me to lunch and then she's going to buy one for me. My little trip to her office Saturday got her attention." She smiled with satisfaction.

Cora eyed Lillian over the top rim of her glasses as if chiding someone in her class. "A simple phone call might have worked better without pissing her off."

"I doubt it. Most of the time, she doesn't answer my calls— damn caller I.D. Anyway, I found a gorgeous white sedan I'm going to name Angel. She's so pretty and will get such good gas mileage that she'll practically be floating on air."

"What makes you think you'll get that particular car?"

"Charla said I couldn't have a Cadillac like hers but she would get me a nice new something. At least I think she meant new. I can't wait." She poured milk on her cereal and slurped her hot coffee. "She didn't buy me a Christmas present last year so she owes me."

"A car is a lot to expect. Is the debt that big?"

"I think it is. I'm going to ask if she will take me to Oliver's for lunch. I haven't been there in a long time."

"Don't you remember why you don't go there anymore? You got food poisoning the last time. That place is a breeding ground for bacteria. I saw it featured on *Dirty Dining*."

"I don't really want to eat there. I just want to see if Charla will lower herself to slumming with her mother." She snickered. "I think I'm catching on to pushing her buttons. Boy, she really hated that hot rod I showed up in Saturday."

"I can't say I was thrilled with it either," Cora snorted.

"Are you getting snobbish too?"

Cora rolled her eyes and turned back towards the coffee urn on the counter. "I just think you need a more appropriate ride for a lady like you."

Lillian quickly finished breakfast and disappeared into her room. She had to search her closet for something to wear to lunch that Charla wouldn't find offensive. She obviously didn't like the outfit Lillian wore to her office, and the sombrero had been stowed back in the box in the garage.

She killed time picking out her clothes and cleaning her bedroom and bathroom. The morning seemed to drag by too slowly.

After a shower and taking care to apply a little makeup and fix her hair, Lillian was ready. She turned on the television in the living room and watched some morning shows, constantly looking at the clock in anticipation of Charla's arrival. In her bag was a printout from the internet of the car she wanted.

The noon news began, and there was no sign of Charla yet. When a game show started at one and she had still not shown up, Lillian dug her phone out of her purse and dialed.

After several rings, Charla answered. "Yeah, Mom, what is it now?"

"Charla, you are supposed to be taking me to lunch today and then get me a car. You promised."

"Oh, was that supposed to be today? Well I can't make it today. We'll have to do it some other time."

Lillian paused for a long moment as tears formed in her eyes. "You told me you were buying me a car today. Was that just so much smoke you were blowing up my ass to get me to leave your parking lot? Are you so ashamed of me that you don't want me around? Do I have to be on my death bed before I can get your attention?" Now the tears came and Lillian could hardly speak.

"I'm just really busy right now. I can't just drop everything. Your roommates can provide you with transportation for a few days."

"It's not their job. You are my daughter and frankly, you should be ashamed of the way you have been treating me. You should apologize." That statement brought a long dead silence on the other end of the call.

"Look, I'll have someone go rent a car and bring it over to you."

"But I wanted to have lunch with you." Lillian was aware of how pathetic the whole conversation was getting. "I don't want a rental car."

"I'll send you something nice to drive for a few days. Now I have to go. Some clients just walked in the door."

"But...."

"We'll talk about it later." The line went dead.

Celia came into the room right then, noting the tears and her heart ached for her friend. "She's not coming."

"No," Lillian sobbed.

"Please don't cry. I'll take you out to look for a car."

"No, Charla said she was buying me a car and by damn I'm going to hold that little liar to her word. She'll think twice before she lies to me again."

"So do you want to go out to lunch with me anyway? I love you, even if she doesn't seem to know how to show her love." Celia tried to grin and fight back tears of sympathy at the depressing situation.

Lillian dropped the phone back into her purse, turned off the television. "Thanks, but I think I'll go change my clothes and read a book." She retreated to her room and quietly closed the door. After removing her outfit and carefully hanging it back in the closet, she climbed back into bed, pulled the covers up over her head. She couldn't stop the tears. She cried until she exhausted herself and fell into a fitful sleep.

10

Thinking that Lillian was going to enjoy a long awaited day out with her daughter, Cora had left after breakfast with a long list of errands to run and a grocery list. She was glad Lillian had finally garnered some attention from that neglectful offspring, however, she wondered if the manner of getting that attention was necessary.

Lillian had returned the car to Jose the evening after her trip to Charla's office, and he had graciously given her a ride home.

The afternoon was nearly gone when Cora pulled up in the driveway, expecting to see Lil's new wheels. The only car present was Celia's purple P.T.

She hauled the groceries into the house, assuming her roommate must be out putting some mileage on her new ride.

Celia was in the kitchen working the crossword puzzle from the daily paper and sipping coffee.

"Where's Lillian," Cora asked as she stuffed fresh vegetables into the refrigerator. "I was anticipating finding a new car in the driveway."

"Not likely," Celia said with a glum expression on her face. "Charla never had any intention of showing up here for a day with her mother. She lied just to get rid of her. Lillian's back in bed, in another depression. I offered to take her shopping, but she's too upset."

Upon receiving that news, Cora's blood pressure went up a few points and she reached for her phone. She started to search for Charla's number and then thought better of it. She knew from experience, that girl would just get snotty and tell her to "Butt out."

Lillian came shuffling into the kitchen just then in bathrobe and slippers. Her eyes were red and puffy. She yawned.

"I'm sorry about your plans falling apart today." Cora looked at her friend with deep concern. "Don't worry about transportation. We can take care of you for now. Did you have car rental coverage on your insurance?"

"No. Bat Crap was so old I only had the bare minimum of liability on him."

"So what are you going to do now?" Celia asked.

Lillian took her place at the table. "I was lying in bed thinking about that. Tomorrow I'm going to call Charla's cell phone every half hour, and when she stops answering, I will fill up her voice mail until no one else can get through. Then I will call her office and make her secretary take messages until she is sick of me. I will get on the computer and send an email every ten minutes until it blows up her mail box."

"Is it really worth the effort?" Celia cautioned.

"I'm going on Facebook and report this whole thing to all my Facebook friends. Let's see what they all have to say. I'm going to embarrass her until she cries *Uncle*."

"Don't they call that stalking?" Cora snickered. "Won't she just get angry?"

"Well maybe feeling angry will start to wake up the emotions in that girl's stone cold heart."

Cora took a soda out of the fridge and sat down. Isn't that going to extreme? Facebook is supposed to be upbeat and friendly. Some readers will be offended if you start bullying Charla in such a public forum. It could result in some negative comments directed at you. It could backfire."

"Then what should I do? Faking an injury didn't do it. The mugging became all about how embarrassed she was at me standing in front of her ad. What the hell was she doing advertising in that part of town anyway?"

Celia suggested, "You can post on Facebook, just keep it civil. You'll get more sympathy that way."

"I guess I could just report the demise of Bat Crap and post my picture of him in his final pose. Then I could mention that Charla promised to buy me a new car."

"That sounds better." Celia agreed.

"And then, as time goes by, I could update it to say I'm still waiting for that new car, without naming names."

Cora chimed in, "You could post a picture of the car you want and remind people that Charla is going to buy it for you. In the meantime, the two of us will make sure you have transportation, won't we, Celia."

Lillian thought about it for a while and nodded. "Okay, but do I still get to make the harassing phone calls?"

"No!" Her roommates blurted. "Try the Facebook angle first. It's less intrusive and more subtle."

Cora finished her soda. "Now, what shall we have for dinner? I got the stuff to make spaghetti and garlic bread."

Celia jumped up. "I'll make some salads."

Lillian headed back to her room. "I can help after I throw on some clothes."

11

By the time Wednesday rolled around, Lillian had gotten over her initial disappointment with Charla standing her up on Monday. She had posted Bat Crap's picture on Facebook and told everyone about Charla's promise to buy her a car. Now she resolved to put it out of her mind until Thursday. It's a new day and it's time to crush some more pins. She was feeling a little more cheerful, now that she had set in motion a new plan to get Charla's attention.

Cora and Celia were making pancakes for breakfast when Lillian walked in and helped herself to a cup of java. "Good morning."

"Are you feeling better now?" Celia asked tentatively.

"Yes, I'm fine. I guess I over-reacted. Thanks for the moral support. I don't know what I would do without the two of you to rein me in when I start to go over the edge."

"That's what we're here for." Cora said as she plopped two pancakes with a couple strips of bacon on a plate and handed it to Lil. "Have a dose of fat and carbs. They will chase the blues away."

"So what are we doing after bowling today? Want to gamble?"

"Let's go play Bingo," Cora suggested. "I checked on the jackpot. It's up to over $70,000."

"Are you kidding," Lillian scoffed. "Nobody ever hits that. How do you think it gets so high? It's rigged."

"I'm no math genius," Celia chimed in, "but I think that would be pretty hard to manipulate. After all, those little balls just blow around in that box on hot air. The caller can't pick which ones will come up the tube. It's kind of like those dating sites. If you agree to meet somebody, they are usually full of hot air and never quite rise to the top of the list to become a winner."

Cora looked at Celia and laughed loudly. "What would you know about internet dating? You hate men."

"Well I'm just drawing a parallel. I hear things."

"Well, whatever. If you girls want to play Bingo today, we can probably make the one o'clock. We'll have do lunch afterward so take an energy bar along. I'm kind of feeling like Mexican food." Lillian chortled.

Cora eyed her sternly. "Residual effects of driving that…that…"

"Spanish Cadillac," Lillian filled in Cora's effort to find the right word.

Celia rinsed her dishes and put them in the dishwasher. "Come on girls. Time is wasting. Will it be Brown Betty or Purple People Eater today?"

"Brown Betty is low on gas."

"So let's get this show on the…" The doorbell chimed twice.

"Who could that be? You don't suppose Charla had a change of heart do you?" Lillian stood up and headed for the door.

The person standing there wore a green polo shirt with a rental car logo on it and a clipboard held in his hand. "Are you Lillian Crocker?"

Lillian looked past him and saw a car idling at the curb. "Yes. Who are you?"

"Your daughter rented a car for you and I've parked it in your driveway. Here's the key. Just sign here."

Lillian opened the door wider and stepped out to view the delivery. Sitting behind Brown Betty was a plain, non-descript white sedan. She recognized the model. "Is that one of them cars that's been killing people when the gas pedal sticks and the ignition switch breaks?"

"Well, I…uh…." The man seemed to be tongue-tied.

"Well, is it or isn't it?" Lillian demanded.

"We haven't had any reports of trouble with this particular car," the man responded defensively. "Do you want it or not?"

"Do I look like I have a death wish? My daughter may be trying to get rid of me, but I'm not ready to die yet. Take it back and tell that bitch, 'Nice try!'"

She turned around and stomped back in the house, slamming the door in the astonished man's face. She grumbled aloud as she headed back to the kitchen. "She's trying to kill me."

"What are you talking about?" the girls chimed in a duet.

Lillian relayed the exchange of a moment ago with regard to the brand of vehicles notorious for crashes.

"Maybe she was just trying to help you out until she can find the time to take you shopping. You should give her the benefit of the doubt," Celia chided. "She's very busy and she probably didn't even know what kind of car the agency was sending over."

Right then Lillian's phone rang. "It's Charla." She took a deep breath and punched the connect button.

"I sent you a car and you refused it. Why?"

"I didn't like it. You said you were buying me a new car. Come and pick me up tomorrow morning and make good on your promise."

"Mother…."

"Don't 'Mother' me. I'm tired of having to beg for some time with my daughter. I'll see you in the morning and no excuses." She ended the call before Charla could respond.

Celia chuckled. "How many years has it been since you spanked that child like that? Do you think it will do any good?"

"We'll see. And now I'm logging onto Facebook to report that Charla is taking me car shopping tomorrow morning." She turned on her heel and headed for the computer desk in her room.

12

After the bowling balls were stowed away, the trio headed for the Bingo Room, just barely making it through the line before the first game began.

The caller drew the Cash Ball for the day, B6.

"My lucky number," Lillian said gleefully, bouncing up and down in her seat.

"How is that your lucky number?" Celia whispered.

"The sixth day of the sixth month is my birthday. It took twelve years to make Charla, that's two times six, although, now I'm not sure if that was lucky; and Courtney was born on my birthday."

Celia cautioned her, "666 is also the mark of Satan." She pointed to Lillian's forehead and grinned as she made a motion as if drawing the numbers there.

"Say what you want, I still maintain six has been lucky for me."

Cora mused aloud, "My lucky number is any number that gives me a Bingo."

As the caller droned on, Lillian was disappointed to see few of her cards showing any hope of winning. Game after game ended and B6 seemed to be lying dead somewhere in the bottom of the Plexiglas box. She started to get bored with the whole activity. The final game was coming up and B6 had still not made an appearance. "This is just one more thing to top off an already crappy day. First, that man tried to deliver the car from Hell to my door. Then the snotty call from Charla. Then we lost all three games bowling. It was another day of splits…" When Lil's machine beeped, indicating she only needed one more number to win the coverall; she stopped complaining and stared at the screen. She needed B6 to win the big jackpot. Her mouth dropped open.

The caller yelled out, "B6."

Lillian's hand shot into the air and she yelled "Bingo!" Another player a few chairs away also called out and raised her hand. It was the thirty-ninth number worth over seventy-six thousand dollars. Lillian's heart raced and she calculated in her head what her share might be even if she had to split it. She was feeling faint and seeing spots.

Celia broke into her thoughts. "Breath, Lillian, breath."

The floor person went to the other winner first, picked up her paper and yelled out the card number. It came up on the large monitor. However, there was a gaping hole. Lillian could see from where she was sitting that the woman had daubed all of the numbers on the sheet. The attendant called out the numbers to verify.

Long seconds elapsed and then the caller announced, "Not verified. O73 was not called."

A collective moan rolled through the room in sympathy for the chagrinned player who had marked the wrong number.

Cora poked Lillian. "That means you win."

The attendant picked up Lillian's electronic machine and read the card number. There wouldn't be any mistake on it because the computer marked the device.

"Verified," the caller, replied. "Are there any other winners?"

Lillian, Cora and Celia all craned their necks to see if anyone else raised their hands. There were only moans and inaudible comments.

"Congratulations to our one winner. Pay that lucky winner, $76,666. This game is closed.

Cora poked Lillian who seemed to have gone into a trance "Now you can go buy a car."

Dazed, Lillian took a few beats to respond. "Did that really happen? Did I win?"

Celia chuckled. "I guess I have to rethink my contention that there are no such things as lucky numbers."

13

With the money safely in her bank account and her roommates sworn to secrecy, Lillian decided to keep playing on her current status of needy mother whose daughter had promised to buy her a car.

She posted daily on Facebook that she was still waiting for Charla to fulfill her promise. For some reason, Charla was not responding.

She was a no-show again on Thursday. The day dragged on and repeated attempts to reach her on the phone failed.

When a week went by, Lillian decided to take a cab. She could afford it now, since she had become the recipient of a large windfall. She had the driver drop her off at the corner near Charla's office. She walked the last half block and entered, thankful when the air conditioning hit her in the face. Spring was unusually warm this year.

She plunked down on a plush white leather sofa and mopped her brow with a tissue. The secretary looked up, recognizing Lillian immediately. "Charla isn't here," she reported bluntly with a frown.

"I'll wait for her. Do you have any bottled water? I forgot to bring some."

The girl rose and disappeared into the back. She returned a short time later with a cold bottle. "Here. I'm afraid you came at a bad time."

"That doesn't surprise me. When will Charla be back?" She downed a swig of water and mopped her sweaty brow again.

"Sometime next week," the sullen girl replied.

"What?" Lillian exclaimed a little too loudly. "Where is she?"

"Don't you two talk? Doesn't she tell you when she's going out of town?"

"If she did, I wouldn't be here now waiting for her to finish up so she can take me to a dealership to buy a car. She promised weeks ago." Lillian could feel her blood pressure rising and her head began to throb. "Where did she go?"

"She went on a cruise in the Bahamas. Didn't she mention it to you?"

"No! Did she go with anybody? Was it that handsome guy I saw her with at Bellagio?" Lillian immediately regretted that reference. She was supposed to be in bed that day, not down on the strip, playing tourist.

"I'm not sure who you could be referring to, and I don't think I'm at liberty to say who she went with. You will have to call her yourself. I'd like to keep my job."

Lillian took out her phone and punched Charla's number. It went to voicemail. "It figures. I'll bet she took Ella with her."

She punched Ella's number in. She could feel her heartbeat increase and pulsating in her head. Ella's number also went to voice. "Damn, damn, damn," Lillian spat the words loudly.

"Please, could you keep it down," the girl glowered at her. "Can I call you a cab? There's no point in you waiting here."

Lillian stood up as if to comply and then asked, "Can I use the restroom while I wait for that taxi?"

"Sure. Go down the hall. You can't miss it."

Lillian ambled in that direction, closed the restroom door, and used the facilities. Then she unfurled the entire roll of toilet paper and filled the toilet bowl. After washing her hands, she hit the flush lever, and quickly shut the door behind her. She casually headed to the front door. "Is my cab here yet?"

"It's just driving up now. You have a nice day. I'll let Charla know you stopped by."

"Oh, you don't need to bother, my dear. I will tell her when I see her the next time. I hope she's having a great time on that cruise. She works hard for her money. You have a nice day, honey." With that parting comment, and the sweetest smile she could muster on her face, Lillian left and climbed into the waiting cab.

14

After returning home, Lillian paced the floor in anger over Charla's behavior. She never could tolerate liars and had tried to instill in her only daughter the importance of always telling the truth. She could just see that girl acting like Ella's little darling on a cruise in the Caribbean knowing how much Lillian would have enjoyed that trip. A vacation with Charla to give them time to re-connect emotionally would have more than made up for the neglect of the past few years. She might even have released her from that promise to pay for a new car.

However, Charla chose to put distance between them and further exacerbate the rift in their relationship. Why would she do that? If she was regretting blurting out the statement that she would buy her mother a car, then she needed to say so. Nevertheless, leaving town without a word was more than hurtful. It was inexcusable and cowardly.

On the other hand, going on a cruise with a handsome boyfriend could be good for Charla. Maybe she would come back relaxed and not so uptight. A week of passion might smooth out her prickly edges. Maybe she would be more amicable and willing to go shopping with Lillian. It seemed Charla had grown more and more uppity since the divorce and Herbie's departure. It could be her way of handling that kind of change in her life, however, if she chose to take Ella with her....

Lillian's phone rang before she completed that thought. The caller identification puzzled her. "Hello."

"It's Ella. I am just calling to see how you are. I saw your posting on Facebook about your car. What a terrible thing to happen."

"You're just calling to gloat. Are you enjoying your cruise with Charla?" Lillian failed to mask the anger.

"I'm not on a cruise. What made you think I went on a cruise?"

"I went to her office this morning. Her secretary informed me she was on a Caribbean cruise. I naturally assumed she was with you."

"Oh, dear, no, I don't like cruise ships. I get seasick. Why would you think she would take me on a cruise?"

"Because she's always doing things for you, and with you, while I have to beg for a moment with her. The rift between us has grown so wide I don't think anything is going to mend it. For the life of me, I can't figure out what is the matter with her. Since Herbie left, she's just a bitch most of the time."

"I do know that she was not happy with you for making a scene in her parking lot. She thought that maybe you'd gone off the deep end when you showed up in that silly car. She told me all about it. You can get her attention in other ways."

"Oh, yes. She was just full of concern when I was injured defending myself against a serial mugger. She chewed me out for embarrassing her. Can you beat that? She's so wrapped up in herself I'm surprised she has any time for you."

"I know you're hurt. When she gets back into town, I'll have a talk with her. Maybe she needs a little motherly advice."

Oh, that was the wrong thing for Ella to say. Lillian's blood pressure soared and she nearly threw the phone across the room. She had to take deep breaths before speaking again.

"*I* am her mother," she screamed, "*I* am her mother! Not you!" She started down the hall to her room when she experienced the worst headache she had ever known. She reached out and grabbed for a doorjamb, slowly sinking to her knees.

Celia wandered out of her bedroom, rubbing the sleep from her eyes. "What's all the yelling about? Cripes, you woke me out of a sound sleep." It took only a second to react to what she found.

Lillian was sitting on the tile floor. "I have the worst headache. Oh, God; my bladder just let loose. Help me to the toilet."

"I'm calling 911. You may be having a stroke." She grabbed Lillian's cell, ending the call in progress and dialed 911.

She grabbed a pillow from the couch and put it under Lillian's head then ran for a glass of water and aspirin. "Here take these."

The loud wail of an approaching ambulance broke the quiet in the house.

"You did it again."

"What?" Lillian tried to focus her eyes but Celia had become blurred.

"You let Charla get to you. What did she do now?"

Lillian tried to speak, but her words were slurred. "Sheee…"

"Tell me later. Here they come." She opened the front door. "We're getting you to the hospital."

The ambulance sped away toward the Emergency Room where Celia worked. She dressed quickly and followed.

While Lillian was up in radiology having a brain scan, Celia called Charla.

It went to voice mail, so she left a message. "Your mother has been taken to emergency. I think she had a stroke. Please call back as soon as possible."

It was late evening when the results reported that Lillian had experienced a TIA, a stroke-like episode when her blood pressure soared. The medical staff tested for kidney damage and treated her for the elevated blood pressure. She was sedated, and kept overnight for observation. Since Celia was working graveyard that night, she would be able to keep a watchful eye on her.

"Bring me some clean clothes when you come back. I can't go home in those." She pointed to the bag of smelly clothing.

"Sure. I have to take a nap and eat. I'll be back when my shift starts."

Charla had still not called back, so Celia called again that afternoon. This time there was an answer.

The sound of clinking glasses and the din of a crowded room preceded the voice that said, "This is Charla."

"This is Celia. Your mother is in the hospital and you should go see her."

"Don't tell me she got mugged again. What happened now?"

Celia rolled her eyes at the sound of impatience in Charla's response. She forced herself to push down anger and reply in a civil manner. "They thought she might have had a stroke, but it was less serious. They are keeping her overnight for observation. Where are you? Can you come and see her?"

"No I can't. I'm on a cruise in the Caribbean. I won't be home for a week."

"Charla, please, isn't there a port-of-call where you can get off and fly back?"

"Why would I do that? You said it isn't serious. What brought it on?"

"What I know so far, is you left town without telling her and you stood her up for that lunch date when you were supposed to take her car shopping. She's been very upset for days now and it's not good for her blood pressure. You need to be kinder to her. She's your mother! I think you should come back."

"She's in good hands. I'm not going to cut this short because my mother has a headache. She does this all the time. It's a bid for attention. I'll be back when this cruise is over."

"Charla, you need to start spending more time with Lillian. She loves you and when you make a point of avoiding her or lying to her, she becomes so hurt and upset that it's starting to affect her health. Can't you find it in your heart to schedule a lunch once a week? A couple of hours to do things mothers and daughters do together would mean so much to her. She's not getting any younger." Celia could feel her own blood pressure rising as she imagined Queen Charla partying it up on a cruise, seemingly not caring about the status of the woman who bore her and devoted so many years to giving her everything she wanted.

"My mother drives me nuts," Charla blurted.

Celia paced the floor angrily, trying to keep her anger at bay. "How can she drive you nuts when you never spend time with her?"

"She does things like the caper with that stupid car. I almost lost a major sale because of her distraction. She needs to call first before she shows up."

"If she called first, you would tell her you don't have any time for her. Your excuse is always that you're too busy."

"I am busy," Charla replied indignantly. "I have a business to run."

"Charla, you left town without telling her. You could have taken her on the cruise with you. It would have made her feel like you still cared."

The long pause at the other end of the conversation made Celia think the call dropped. She pulled the phone away from her ear and checked the screen.

"Charla are you still there?"

"Yes."

"You're trying to think of a good excuse for not at least talking to your mom before you left. She's still waiting for you to honor your commitment to buy her a car. Was that just a lie?"

"I think she misunderstood."

"No, I think you chose to ignore your commitment. She doesn't understand why you've abandoned her. As I said, it's affecting her health. If you keep this up, she could die of a broken heart."

"People don't die of broken hearts," Charla scoffed.

"Are you going to keep testing that theory until it's too late to reconcile and make up for all the neglect?" Celia could barely keep her voice from rising and sounding nasty.

"I said I can't come home right now. She'll be okay. She has you to look after her. I'll get there when I can." The call ended.

Celia sneered at her phone as if Charla could see her.

Re-making that old man at the Senior Center was so much easier than trying to change Charla's attitude. She checked her watch as her stomach growled. She realized she hadn't eaten yet and she needed to catch a nap before going to work. Charla would have to wait.

The house was very quiet. Cora had answered the call to sub in a classroom of sixth graders, so Celia made a quick sandwich and retired to bed.

Sleep didn't come easily as she went back over her conversation with Charla. She wondered if Lillian would be better off just cutting the snob out of her life. That's not a decision she could make for her friend. Celia had a close relationship with her own mother and no regrets when she passed on. She had cared for her personally through her illness. Charla, on the other hand, if she kept this up, was going to rue the day she treated her mother like a disposable plastic bag.

15

Celia brought Lillian home when her shift ended and insisted she go to bed. "You're drinking decaf for a while until we get your blood pressure back to normal."

"I hate decaf. I'll get headaches."

"So take aspirin. You had a close call."

Cora sat down on the bed and looked at Lillian. "You are one of my best friends. I can't have you dying on me."

"I'm not going to die," insisted Lillian. "I let myself get upset again over Ella and Charla's relationship. I know I shouldn't, but it's so hurtful to me when Ella usurps my role as Charla's mother."

"Is that why you got so upset?"

"She said that when Charla gets back she will have a talk with her and give her some *motherly* advice."

Celia and Cora exchanged a brief glance.

"It sounds like she needs to be reminded of her place. It's not as Charla's mother," Cora said with an authoritative tone. "Give me her number. It's time one of us explains it to her in plain language she can understand. She's interfering in your relationship with your daughter. I do believe that's called alienation of affection and some people have been sued for a lot less. You could sue her."

"I'm not spending my hard earned bingo winnings on lawyers. That old woman has to die sometime. She's older than dirt. Maybe she'll do us all a favor and break a hip while she's gyrating to Richard Simmons."

"Yes," Celia piped up, "when people her age break a hip, it's the beginning of the end. Oftentimes they get pneumonia and croak."

Cora chuckled. "You two are just being catty now. Diplomacy is always better than wishing someone bad luck. I'm going to call her and just have a nice chat. Do you mind?" She picked up Lillian's cell and scrolled through the numbers, then dialed from her own phone.

Ella failed to answer, so Cora left a message. "This is Lillian's roommate. You need to call me back. Lillian just spent the night in the hospital and we can't reach Charla. Please call back." She left her own cell number before ending the call.

Celia smiled. "That makes the situation sound dire."

"How else can I get her to call back?"

Cora's phone jangled about an hour later while she was in the kitchen making a snack.

"Is this Cora?" the little voice asked, barely audible above the noise in the background.

"Thank you for calling back, Ella. Where are you? It sounds like you're in Las Vegas."

"I, uh…I'm uh…"

"Are you on that ship with Charla? Are you in the casino?"

"I…uh…I'm in a casino, but not with Charla. I drove up to Las Vegas to look after Charla's house while she's gone. She needed me."

Cora took a deep breath before speaking. "Why would she need you? Lillian would have been more than happy to stay over there for a few days. I don't understand it."

"Well, I wanted to come and play for a while and Charla offered me her house. Is that so wrong?" Ella's voice projected a note of crankiness.

"It is when you assume the role of Charla's mother and upset Lillian so much that she has a near stroke. She spent the night in the hospital. She's so hurt, she cries and her blood pressure is out of control."

"I didn't mean to upset her. It was a slip. I should come over there and apologize, I guess. Will she be home tonight?"

"She's home, but she's very tired and she's on some medication that will make her sleepy. If you really want to see her, come over Sunday. I'll make dinner. You and Lillian need to come to some kind of truce. Your constant interference in her relationship with Charla is affecting her health in a negative way."

"I don't mean to. I love Charla as if she were my own daughter."

"That's the core of the matter, Ella. You are not Charla's mother, but you have stolen her affections from Lillian. It has to stop."

"Oh, dear, the battery in my phone is running out. I have to go. I'll try to make it over Sunday." The call ended.

"Yeah, right," Cora spoke to the silent phone. "Go stick your finger in a light socket, you old reprobate."

Cora thought it would be better not to mention her conversation with Ella. Lillian was sleeping now. She didn't need anything to set her off again.

16

By Sunday, Lillian was up and around and her energy level had returned. "I feel like a fool," she moaned over breakfast. "You guys are so good to me. I don't know what I would do without you."

Cora buttered some toast and handed it to her friend. "Everyone needs at least one loyal friend in their life. You have two."

"Now what should I do? I don't know where to go from here with respect to Charla. Am I just spinning my wheels and burying myself in a quagmire of self-pity? I frankly don't know how to handle being ignored."

"Today we are going to forget about it," Cora stated firmly. "I'm going to fix a roast chicken with all the trimmings. The three of us are going to eat hearty and make merry." She had decided against telling Lillian about her conversation with Ella and the anticipated visit. If Ella didn't show up, it would be another wedge in their already fractured relationship. There was nothing to gain by telling Lillian that there might be a guest for dinner.

"What's the occasion, Cora?" asked Lillian. "It sounds like you are celebrating something."

"Not really. I just think you need to take your mind off your troubles. I'm putting you to work making a Waldorf salad." She pointed to the ingredients she had gathered and set on the counter.

Lillian eyed the apples. "I can do that."

"Good. Now let's have our breakfast." Cora refilled their coffee cups and buttered some toast. "By the way, I stopped by the Y and picked up a schedule of activities. Bowling will be over soon and we should find something to replace it for the summer."

"Aren't we bowling a summer league?" Lillian furrowed her brow. "It's no-tap."

"It's also summertime. We should do something else. The Y is starting a water aerobics class. They're calling it *Belles and Bums*."

"It's a mixed class? I don't want to exercise with a bunch of old bums that only come in there to shower and clean off the street dirt. You know what happens when I jump up and down." She looked down at her ample bosom and frowned.

"There are no hobos in the class. The bum part is not a reference to men." She motioned to her behind. "This is a bum."

Lillian snickered, "So it's a nice way of saying ladies with fat butts?"

"Maybe they could have come up with a better name. Anyway, its *women only* water aerobics. It's good exercise."

"It might be fun," Lillian agreed hesitantly, "or not."

"What might be fun?" Celia asked as she came into the kitchen yawning and stretching. She poured a cup of coffee and sat down.

"Lil and I were just discussing the possibility of signing up for a water aerobics class this summer. It's at the Y in the afternoon, so you could come with us."

"Ladies only," Lillian added, knowing how Celia would rather not socialize much with the opposite sex.

"If you still wanted to bowl on Wednesday, we could sign up for the Tuesday and Thursday classes. The sooner we decide the better. There's a limit to how many can be in each class."

"I'll think about it," Celia yawned. "What's on the agenda today? I hear there's a good movie out."

"Cora is cooking a chicken today. I'm making a salad and you get to decide what we are having for dessert."

"Are we expecting company?" Celia eyed her roommates suspiciously.

"No," Cora said quickly. "I just thought we needed to do something different. If we cook today, we can eat leftovers tomorrow."

"You're just trying to distract me," said Lillian.

"I am doing what's best for you. I think we should go out and shop for your car tomorrow. You have the funds now, there's no reason to delay. You know what you want. So let's do it."

"But what about my resolve to make Charla live up to her promise?" Lillian pursed her lips in a pout.

"That attitude is just going to make you sick if you keep clinging to it. Forget what she said. She obviously didn't mean it and pursuing that avenue is just going to make you miserable while she's off enjoying her cruise. So face it, it's not going to happen."

Celia added, "She's right. We're going to get your car tomorrow. It will make you feel better knowing you didn't have to rely on Charla. From now on, we need to find activities that will take your mind off her. Next time, you could end up with some permanent brain damage. We don't want to see that happen."

"Listen to the nurse," said Cora authoritatively. "She knows what she's talking about. We are looking out for your best interests."

Tears formed in Lillian's eyes. "I love you guys. I am so grateful to have you in my life."

Celia topped off her coffee cup and sat back down. "By the way, I checked Facebook this morning. There haven't been any postings from Charla. I thought for sure she would be posting pictures of her fabulous Caribbean cruise. She's been awfully silent."

Lillian frowned and finished off her cereal. "That's because she unfriended all of us."

Cora and Celia both gaped open-mouthed. "That was a little drastic, don't you think?" Celia gasped.

"How could she unfriended her own mother?" Cora blurted. "That's harsh."

"Easy. She dispensed with me with just one key stroke."

"Don't worry," Celia patted Lillian's hand. "We'll figure out something. In the meantime, I think we should go see what all the hype is about with that new movie."

"Which new movie are you talking about?" Lillian asked skeptically. "I haven't read about any lately I'd walk across the street to see."

Celia placed the movie schedule on the table for the girls to study. "I'm talking about the one with the bunch of hunks of burning junk."

Lillian eyed the ad and sneered. "I wasn't wild about the first one, and now they've come out with a second one? Isn't that for the younger viewer—perhaps twenty something single girls with raging hormones?" She frowned and wrinkled her nose as if she had just smelled a fart. "I just had a minor stroke. I don't need my blood pressure rising at a spectacle like that. I still remember the first movie with a measure of revulsion."

"Come on, live a little. It'll take your mind off your troubles." Celia assured her.

Cora reminded them, "It will have to wait. I have a chicken ready to go into the oven. We can't do that and go to a movie too. This thing is stuffed and ready. It won't keep. But if we eat early, like three or so, we can make it to an early evening showing."

"I have tonight off," Celia announced. "It works for me. There's a showing at five."

"Okay, but if I don't like what I see, I'll quietly leave and go play the slots while you two corrupt your minds," Lillian agreed. "Maybe we can gamble for a little while afterward. I need a diversion."

By four, dinner was over. The girls piled into Brown Betty and headed for the movie theater.

As Cora stood in line at the box office, the thought suddenly struck her and she drew in an audible breath.

"What's the matter?" Celia asked.

Cora shrugged. "Nothing; I just remembered something I was supposed to do, but it's not important." She smiled and turned away. She had forgotten that Ella was going to drop by.

Outside of the house, Ella was ringing the doorbell and knocking. Celia's car was in the driveway, but nobody was home.

As the girls excited the movie theater, Lillian shivered and blurted, "I think I have to go home and rinse the smut out of my eyes and ears. That was awful. I didn't see anything *magic* about it."

Cora snickered. "I think I have to go to the Senior Center and find some horny old man with a supply of Viagra."

Celia gave them the raspberries. "I took a nap. That was the worst waste of money I've ever seen. If I never hear the F-bomb again, it will be too soon. I'm hungry for a hot fudge sundae."

Lillian sneered. "How can you eat after that? I think I need a beer to take away the bad taste in my mouth."

"Okay, let's pick up some beer, pizza and ice cream and go home and watch the Disney Channel," Celia suggested.

"Just hit the delete button and pretend we never saw that piece of rot," Cora commented.

"It's hard to un-see something like that," Lillian snorted derisively.

That evening, when the roommates returned home, Cora hurried from the car. "I have to go to the bathroom. She found a note tacked to the front door, which she grabbed and stuffed into her purse. In the privacy of her bathroom, she read the message. *"I came to have dinner with you and nobody was home. That was rude. Did you forget? Ella."* Cora smiled and flushed it.

17

The next day, the three women set out to find Lillian a new car. She directed them to the agency listed on her internet printout.

That poor sales associate probably regretted not calling in sick that day. When Lillian was informed that the car on the printout had been sold already, he spent the next three hours being brow beat and harassed by the three roommates, until he finally suggested that maybe Lillian's best option would be a three-year lease. It took no time to pick out and test-drive a different car. It took hours to do the paperwork and listen to the associate explain all of the bells and whistles on the vehicle.

Lillian ran her hand over the gleaming white surface of the hood. "She's an angel. And the best part is I don't owe Charla anything." Lillian climbed into her beautiful piece of engineering and headed for home. The operator's manual would be her bedtime reading for the next several nights.

Celia cupped her hand behind her ear. "What's the matter with this car? I can't hear the engine. Is it running?"

"It is battery operated most of the time. It's going to take some getting used to." Lillian smiled widely as she pulled into the driveway. She was turning over in her mind, the idea of keeping up the charade of needy mother without wheels. How long would she be able to fake it? Charla was due back from her cruise in a few days.

After they swung by the house and dropped off Cora's car, the three of them took a drive to break in the new car.

Cora climbed into the back seat and buckled up. "Are you sure this thing is running? I can't hear an engine."

"The salesman said it would take some getting used to. The gas part only kicks in when the battery needs a boost. I think it's nice. We can hear each other talk without shouting. Where should we go?" Lillian asked as she came to a stop sign. "Give me some suggestions?"

Celia piped up. "Let's go have lunch in Boulder City. We can eat at the hotel and browse the shops."

"Let's drive out to the dam. That bridge has been finished for years now and I still haven't ever seen it." Cora dug into her bag and checked her wallet. I need to stop at an ATM. We can go over to the Arizona side to that convenience store and buy lottery tickets. How long has it been since we've done that?"

Celia opened her bag and dug in for some money, checking her balance. "That sounds like fun to me. Go to the bank first. I need some money too. Lillian, do you need some cash?"

"I just bought a car. I can't be throwing money around."

"Bull pucky! It's a lease and it didn't set you back all that much," blurted Celia. "You won all that money playing bingo. You paid cash down. You have money to burn. Loosen those purse strings and have some fun."

"Yeah," Cora added, "You're not going to live forever. Why leave it for Courtney to squander? Kids don't appreciate the money they didn't have to earn. When was the last time that little brat called you?"

Courtney was Lillian's only grandchild whom she helped raise while Charla and Herbie worked. She was a freshman in college in California. "You're right. My family doesn't appreciate me. Let's go to the bank."

After that necessary stop, Lillian headed towards Boulder City. "Let's see how far this thing will go on one charge of the battery."

"Don't push it too much," Celia cautioned. "I don't like long walks on deserted roads."

18

Tuesday evening, Lillian was surfing through the channels trying to find something to watch, when her phone rang. She checked the screen and heaved a sigh.

"Hello Charla. Have you returned from your glorious cruise?"

"Yes and it wasn't all that glorious. I called to see how you are feeling. Celia said you had some kind of stroke like thing. You sound fine now."

"It could have been worse, but I was lucky. I just have a few memory problems. Like when I can't remember somebody's name. But it will come back."

"I guess I didn't miss anything."

Lillian rolled her eyes. "It would have been nice to have my daughter here in my time of need, but I guess that's too much to ask," she said acidly. A long silence ensued, indicating no reply to that comment.

When Lillian failed to comment further, Charla raised her voice, "Mother, are you there?"

"Yes I'm here. Why didn't you tell me you were going on a cruise? You could have let me know."

"It was a last minute booking. I threw some clothes in a bag, flew to Los Angeles, jerked Courtney out of school and we took off. I had no time to warn anybody."

"So what was the big rush and doesn't Courtney have exams coming up? This is a bad time to be taking her out of school."

"It was that or let her ruin her future. I had to get her away for a few days."

"It sounds serious. Do you want to tell me about it?"

"I'm so wiped out, I can't talk right now and I don't want to discuss it on the phone. I have to unpack and I need to get back to the office tomorrow. I'm going to put it on my calendar to pick you up on Thursday and we'll go to lunch."

"Don't make an appointment you have no intention to keep. Don't you want to spend time with Ella?" Lillian could feel her blood pressure jump at the very mention of her archrival. "The last time, you stood me up. Can I trust you to keep your word this time?"

"Ella's leaving tomorrow to go home. I promise I won't stand you up this time. I'll pick you up and we will spend the afternoon together. I need to discuss some things with you."

"Wait! What do you mean Ella is leaving tomorrow? When did she get here?"

"I thought you knew. She drove up here while I was gone and housesat for me. She said she had a conversation with you."

"Yeah, just before my stroke, but she never mentioned she was here in town." Lillian was feeling another headache coming on.

"I have to go. I have a lot to do today."

Lillian hesitated to take Charla at her word. She had been disappointed before. What else could she do? "Fine, but if you stand me up again, I'm going straight to a lawyer and cut you out of my will."

There was a long silence on the other end of the call.

"Charla, are you still there?"

"Yes. I'll see you Thursday around noon."

Lillian ended that call and dialed Courtney's number. The call failed to go through.

It seemed Charla was going to make Lillian stew for a day and a half wondering what was up with Courtney. Did the girl get herself pregnant? That would certainly gall Charla.

Now that Lillian thought about it, Courtney had not called in months to talk to her grandmother. Something was going on. She brightened; *maybe I'm going to be a great-grandmother. I can see it now. Courtney goes off to an expensive college and comes home with a bun in the oven and no degree.* Then another thought hit her. *Now they will both get cozy with me because they will expect me to be a built-in babysitter. Well I have news for them.*

19

Thursday morning started with a bang. That is, a loud crash in the direction of the kitchen.

Lillian started to get up and sank back, waiting for the vertigo to go away. It was another one of those hateful signs of aging. The urge to jump out of bed as if still a kid is hampered by the inner ear affliction of old age. She eased herself up and gingerly put on her slippers.

Cora was picking up pieces of a shattered plate when Lillian shuffled into the kitchen. "Sorry, I didn't mean to wake you. It slipped out of my hand."

"I'll get the broom," she offered as Cora picked at the larger pieces. "Don't cut yourself."

Over coffee, Cora asked, "So what's on the agenda for today? Shall we go shopping and put some miles on your new car?"

"No, Charla said she's coming by."

"You don't look real enthused about that."

"Considering her history, I'm not going to get too excited. Even though, I suppose I should just hang out here. I'll do some house cleaning. If she shows up, fine. Otherwise, I figure if I don't expect anything, I won't be disappointed."

"I think we need to find some new activities to keep you occupied. We should join some senior groups. Maybe some of those groups that go on bus tours and such. It'll take your mind off Charla and her neglect. We'll make new acquaintances and have some fun. What do you say?" Cora looked eagerly at Lillian for a minute.

"I don't know what kind of activities you have in mind," Lillian replied, "but it might be okay. Maybe we could take golf lessons or go on a cruise, like one of those singles cruises? I'm sure there are a lot of lonely old men with a supply of Viagra on one of those ships that would be happy to accommodate you." Lillian chuckled.

Cora glared at her. "You're kidding aren't you? I kid around about it, but I really don't want a man in my life. I loved my husband, but one old man who had to reach to mid-thigh to scratch his balls was enough for me."

Lillian reacted with a burst of laughter, blowing out a mouthful of hot coffee. She dabbed at the mess with her napkin. "So golf it is. See if you can sign us up somewhere."

While she tried to put the idea of lunch with Charla out of her mind, Lillian commenced doing household chores. With all the times she had been stood up, she figured this would be another one of those days, so when the doorbell rang, she was in the process of winding up the cord to put the vacuum cleaner away. She had not showered or dressed to go out. A glance at the clock reminded her lunch time had rolled around.

Charla frowned for a moment when disheveled Lillian answered the door. "Did you forget we were supposed to go out to lunch? You're not even dressed. Is that your housecoat you're still wearing?"

"Come in. It's so nice to see you too. I'm afraid I forgot." Lillian lied. "Come in and relax. I'll fix something for us to eat here where we can talk. The other girls have gone out."

"Are you sure you don't want to get cleaned up and go someplace nice?"

"This is someplace nice. I just cleaned house. Isn't it good enough for you?"

"Mother, I didn't mean that," Charla said indignantly, putting her nose in the air. "Why are you so touchy?"

"Do you really have to ask?"

"I'm just feeling short tempered. I spent all day yesterday catching up on work. Some idiot plugged up the toilet in the restroom while I was gone. We had to hire a crew of plumbers and cleaners to correct the mess. It cost me a fortune."

"Oh, my," Lillian turned away and grinned as she headed to the kitchen. "Who would do such a thing?"

"I don't know, but if I find out it was an employee, they will be fired." Charla plopped down at the kitchen table. "Is there anything to drink around here?" Her eyes roamed over the kitchen that Lillian had just cleaned.

"There's iced tea in the fridge. Help yourself." She placed an empty glass in front of Charla.

"I'm just going to run to the bedroom and wash up and put on some clean clothes. Make yourself at home."

Charla was sipping her tea when Lillian returned. "I ordered Chinese food take-out. It should be delivered any minute," she announced.

"You didn't have to do that. I could make us sandwiches."

"It's no problem." Just then, the doorbell rang and Charla went to answer it. She came back with the bags.

After dishing up portions, Lillian reminded Charla, "You were going to tell me about Courtney and how she's ruining her life? Is she flunking out of school?"

"That was one of the reasons, but worse, she was getting ready to bolt and run off with some jerk she met and fell in love with on the internet for God's sake! One of her classmates became concerned and ratted on her."

"That's dangerous territory for a girl her age. Has she actually met the guy?"

"No. She's only seen pictures on Facebook and email. I grabbed her out of school, kicking and screaming. I took away her phone and laptop and turned it over to a private investigator."

"That's rather bold. I'll bet she's angry with you."

"Angry is a mild term. It turned out the creep is a predator. He's not the twenty-year-old handsome college student she thought he was."

"Then what is he?"

"This is so embarrassing; I can't give you the details. It's humiliating."

Lillian picked up her cell phone and stared at it for a second. "I've been calling her, but she doesn't answer. I've been so worried. Tell me what's going one."

Charla took a deep breath and blurted, "After I got Courtney away and started grilling her about her activities, she claimed it started innocently enough. It's easy to lure people on the internet and deceive them. She admitted she became, caught up in the process and that it was all by design on her part. She was going to play along with the jerk and see how far he was willing to go, so she could use it for the subject of her term paper. The perp was good. From all indications, he thought she was hooked and he was reeling her in."

"So he *thought* he was reeling her in but she was on to him."

"I stepped in and put a stop to it. She's probably going to get an incomplete on that course, but I don't care. This was a dangerous thing for her to do."

Lillian took another helping of teriyaki chicken. "This is really good. So maybe he is a nice young man. Many people meet on the internet and some even end up getting married. How do you know this wasn't going to end well?"

Charla finished her food and daintily dabbed at her lips with a napkin. She finished off her glass of tea and frowned. "My detective discovered that he's a low-life ex-con in his forties and a sex offender. He was trying to lure her out of school to run off and hook up with him in Chicago. He probably makes a practice of it. If anyone did hook up with him, they would probably disappear for good."

"What did she do when your detective reported back?"

Charla pulled an envelope out of her bag and withdrew a picture. "At first she didn't believe me until he emailed me the mug shot of the actual person and his real name. Now she's mad because she said I robbed her of the opportunity to uncover the deception herself. She insists she was doing a term paper on the subject and when I jerked her out to go on the cruise, she missed the deadline to turn in the paper."

Lillian frowned at the disheveled man in prison stripes. "So is she pleased you helped her to uncover his real identify? She would probably get a really good grade on a paper if she could get an extension."

"Yes, but she's still angry. I interrupted her research and withdrew her from school and she'll have to take the class over. She swears it was all role-playing in order to write her essay and she never would have gone off to meet him."

Lillian fingered the photo. "And you couldn't give her the benefit of the doubt? She's a smart girl. So what will happen next?"

Charla stuffed the papers back in her bag. "The detective followed up and reported him to his parole officer. He's going back to jail when they find him. However, I still fear he may come after her."

"Where is Courtney now?"

"Since she was flunking out anyway, I brought her home. She's at my house, grounded for the time being. I'm transferring her to school here where I can have more supervision over her."

"It sounds like she was only doing research. Why are you being so hard on her? Won't she still have access to the internet?"

"No she won't. I put a password on my computer. She won't be able to get on. I had a tech put blocks on her laptop so she can't access any more sites like that."

"She still has her smart phone."

"I confiscated that and now she has a store-bought flip phone and all she can do is make phone calls and answer it when it rings." Charla fished in her purse and took out a piece of paper. "This is her number if you want to call her. But don't tell her I told you all about this."

Charla checked her wristwatch. "Well, I have to get back to work."

Lillian frowned. "I thought we were spending the afternoon together. That's what you said two days ago."

"That's before this whale called and said he was coming to town. He wants a high rise condo and I have one listed."

Lillian sighed. "What about that car you said you would take me shopping for?"

Charla stood and smoothed out her skirt. "It'll have to wait for another day or you could just go buy one for yourself." She picked up her bag and hiked it over her shoulder. "I have to go."

Lillian put her hands on her hips and took a defiant stance. She looked Charla in the eye. "So that day at your office when you said we'd shop for a car together, you were just giving me lip service to get me to go away."

"Mom, you are taking it all wrong."

Lillian raised her voice slightly. "Don't lie to me, Charla."

"Okay! Go buy a car and I'll reimburse you. Will that settle things?"

Lillian thought about her new ride safely tucked into the garage. She had spent all afternoon the day before shoving storage boxes around and discarding trash in an effort to make room for it. She grinned and replied, "Fine, I'll see what I can do. Can I have a Cadillac like yours?"

Charla started toward the front door. "No!" she blurted, "Don't take advantage of my generosity."

"What generosity? You haven't given me a birthday or Christmas present in years. It's like you don't care anymore."

Charla turned and glared at her mother. "It would appear you think I owe you something."

"I think you owe me an explanation as to why you treat me like an old worn out blanket you no longer need."

Charla sighed. "I don't mean to. I'm just so…"

"So…what?" demanded Lillian. "Am I living too long to suit you? Would you be happier if I just died?" Lillian could feel her head throbbing.

"That is a cruel thing to accuse me of, Mother. How could you think that?"

"Because that's the way you treat me. You treat Ella like she's your mother, your best friend, your...your—you treat me like an inconvenience."

Charla stood in the open doorway, open mouthed as if to say something in her defense, and then shrugged. "I have to go." She turned on her heel and left.

Lillian stepped outside as if to pursue Charla, but stopped. "So that's the way you are going to leave things—no apologies—no explanations?"

Charla ignored her yelling and slammed the car door, speeding away as if she were fleeing a fire.

Lillian watched until the Cadillac rounded the corner out of sight and then she ambled back into the house. "Well that didn't go very well." Then another thought crossed her mind. How was she going to present a backdated invoice for the car she had already leased? Charla would know she was being deceitful if she just gave her the receipt. She shrugged and said to herself aloud, "I guess that ship has sailed."

20

After Charla's hasty departure, Lillian felt disappointed once again that she couldn't corral her long enough to delve deeply into the reasons for their growing estrangement. They were supposed to spend the day together, but in the end, she brushed her off like an annoying gnat. Charla had a *whale* to reel in, as she referred to her customer.

Lillian shuffled back to the kitchen and cleared the table. The food was cold and no longer appetizing, so she dumped the whole lot in the garbage and rinsed the plates off, depositing them in the dishwasher. While she worked, she mentally plotted her next adventure into shaking up Charla's world. By the time she was finished, she had a basic plan in mind.

She sat down at the table, picked up her phone and called Courtney. It rang a number of times before she answered.

"Hello." Her voice was dull and raspy, as if she were still in bed sleeping in the middle of the day.

"It's Grandma. You don't sound like yourself. Are you sick?"

There came a cough from the other end of the exchange and the voice became clearer. "Oh, Grandma, I'm sorry. You woke me up."

Lillian glanced at the kitchen clock. "My dear, it's two o'clock. The sun is shining. You should be out doing whatever a kid your age does when the weather is beautiful."

"Yeah, well thanks to my mother, I don't have any people to do anything with unless you count that security guard she's posted outside to keep me prisoner."

Lillian didn't let on as if she knew anything. "Your mom told me you went on a wonderful cruise and now you're going to enroll in school here. I'm excited about that because now I can see more of you."

"Yeah—sure—I don't plan to stick around long. She jerked me out of school for no good reason. I hate this town. I want to go back to L.A."

"Why dear?"

"I can't talk now, Grandma. I'm sure she has ears and eyes on me. Can we go shopping or something? I need to get out of this house. Can you come and get me?" Her voice sounded desperate and whiney.

"Sure, I'll be there in…" *How am I going to do that without revealing that I already have a new vehicle? Charla will find out.*

"I have a rental car at the moment," Lillian lied, "and I can come and get you. Call your mom and tell her I'm taking you shopping and will have you back after dinner. We can talk then."

"Sounds like a plan to me."

Lillian began rounding up her car keys and purse while Courtney was still on the line. "Where would you like to go?"

"Anywhere but here," she replied sullenly. The call ended.

A half hour later, Lillian pulled through the gate of Charla's upper crust neighborhood.

Courtney was waiting at the curb. She flashed her traffic finger at someone as she got into the car and sank dejectedly in the seat, snapping her seat belt in place.

"Who were you greeting?" Lillian asked with a grin.

"The rent-a-stalker mother hired." She was dressed as if Granny were taking her out to a rock concert instead of the mall. She wore a tee with a picture of some rock group with the words "Trash Talk" splashed across it. Her blond hair had a streak of blue through it. The legs of her jeans were torn and frayed in various places. On her feet, she wore flip-flops revealing a variety of toe rings and purple glitter toenails.

When Lillian stared a little too long at the drastic change in her granddaughter, Courtney snapped, "What? Everyone dresses like this in school now. After all, I'm not some nerd!"

Lillian accelerated away from the curb towards the gate, noting the rent-a-stalker following behind. "I guess I'm over-dressed," she said under her breath. Glancing sideways, she noted a tiny diamond stud in Courtney's nose. Opening her mouth to chide the girl, she stopped in mid thought and merely asked, "Is that a real diamond?"

Courtney fingered the stud and smiled. "Sure!"

Attempting to concentrate on driving, Lillian silently assessed the change in her grandchild. When Courtney left for college, she was classy and stylish in expensive clothes picked out by her mother. The little mini-Charla was gone. Something had transformed her, and not in a good way.

Without taking her eyes off the road, she casually asked, "Why do you hate Las Vegas? You were born and raised here. It's a lovely place to live." She glanced at Courtney noting the girl rolling her eyes.

"Sure it is. It's full of homeless people wandering the streets begging; crop dusters walking the strip; and suckers throwing their wealth away in slot machines. It's full of opportunists and criminals. What's not to love about it?" She picked glumly at the frayed slits on her jeans.

"Crop dusters—what are you talking about?" Lillian laughed. "I've never heard that expression."

"Tourists farting their way down the sidewalks. Haven't you ever been down wind of them? Ugh." Courtney wrinkled her nose.

"No, I can't say I have." She glanced over at Courtney's jeans. "Those are interesting denims you have there." Lillian grinned with amusement. "Have you had them long?"

"I bought them at an over-priced boutique on board the cruise ship. Mother almost pissed her fancy bikini bottoms when she walked in on me putting them on in the cabin. We had a huge fight about my choice in clothes." Courtney laughed loudly. "I rang her bell with that one! Then she took away my credit card. What a bitch! Sometimes I get the feeling she hates me and only puts up with me because she has to. I can't wait to be out on my own."

Lillian chose to ignore the disrespectful reference and played dumb. "I'm sure she loves you in her own way. I still don't get why she thought it necessary to pull you out of school. You're not pregnant, are you?" She cast a sideways glance at the shabby girl.

"What! Oh, for God's sakes no! I'm never having any brats."

Lillian pulled into the mall parking lot and cruised around until she found a parking spot. "We can talk about that issue a few years from now. You'll change your mind as you mature. Now let's go find something to buy that will irk your mother." She grinned impishly at the grandchild she adored. "You laughed when you told me about the pants. What can Grandma buy you?"

"How much money can you spend?" Courtney fixed Lillian with a curious look.

"I got lucky at bingo a few days ago. How much do I need to spend to get your mother's goat?" She grinned back.

"I want a set of drums. Can you fund them?"

Lillian stopped walking and raised her eyebrows in surprise. "Whatever would you do with those? Do you even know how to play them?"

Courtney began leading Lillian towards the music store. "My boyfriend has been teaching me."

Lillian stopped in her tracks. "You have a boyfriend and he plays drums?" Now the grungy clothes, piercing and streaked hair made sense. "Is he in a band?"

Courtney pointed to her tee. "Where do you think I got this? We met at a gig this band played in L.A. We're in love." Her face glowed with first time infatuation.

Lillian couldn't help but stare at the child she helped raise. "That's why you are so angry at your mother, isn't it? When she brought you back here, she thought you were just flunking out. You didn't tell her you were taking up music and you want to join a band. Is your boyfriend also a student?"

"The whole group is. Music is a way of working their way through school. They don't have rich snob parents like I do."

"Now, now, your daddy isn't a snob. He's a wonderful man. I'll admit we spoiled your mother when she was growing up, and she's never gotten over her princess complex. She's rich because she has worked hard and is very good at what she does." Defending Charla left a bitter taste in Lillian's mouth.

"I've already called my boyfriend. He's very angry that I disappeared without a word for a whole week. If I don't do something soon, he's going to dump me." She started walking again, and turned her face away, brushing a finger past the corner of her eye as if wiping away a tear. "He's teaching me to take over the drums so I can replace the pothead that's on them now. He's getting too lazy and sloppy to keep up. I need a set to practice on until he can get over here and pick me up."

"So you're not going back to school?" Lillian had to step up the pace to keep up with Courtney. She was running out of breath and frowned in disappointment. "I was looking forward to—oh never mind. You young people have to do your own thing. After all, your father is an excellent musician. It's natural that you would have that same talent. It's in the genes."

Courtney slowed and put her arm around Lillian's shoulder as they walked. "I need to go back to school in California, not here. If I don't I'll lose Lennie. Please don't say anything to my mother. I want to tell her the news in my own way. You'll keep my secret won't you?"

"I agree that you should handle this your way," Lillian responded with an impish grin, "kind of like I handled her with that Spanish Cadillac when I showed up unannounced at her office. Boy was she mad. I thought it was a blast. Honestly, she has no sense of humor. Now we have some drums to pick out."

21

Courtney had suddenly switched from aggravating rebellious teenager to calm, cool and collected behavior ever since she had dinner with her grandmother. The change puzzled Charla. *Mother must have given her a lecture about her unacceptable attitude of late.* "Your dinner with Grandma must have gone well."

"We had Italian. Love that spaghetti at Antonio's Pasta Palace. It's like spice for the tummy." Courtney turned away and rolled her eyes.

Charla's senses shot to attention at the mention of phony cannabis laced with chemicals and packaged like bath salts. "You're not smoking Spice are you?"

"Come on Mother, give me credit for something. I know that crap is poison. I would never try it. I'm just using a figure of speech. Relax."

"That's reassuring."

It was Saturday evening and the girl had been surprisingly pleasant after almost two weeks of heated battles and recriminations. Charla noted that the last couple of days when she returned from work, Courtney was puttering in her room, spending a lot of time straightening her closet and rearranging the furniture. She had even picked up the piles of discarded laundry from the floor and put them in the utility room for the housekeeper to wash on Monday. A few times, she had been talking on her phone while lounging on the patio out of earshot, but overall, things were getting back to normal.

Charla slid the glass door open and approached her daughter, frowning at the blue hair and nose piercing, but careful to avoid the issue. "I will be going out on a date tonight."

"You're seeing someone?" Courtney said sullenly as she thumbed through a fashion magazine. "Who is he?"

Charla looked away and didn't answer immediately as if choosing her words carefully. "I see someone once in a while when he comes into town on business." She walked around the pool as if checking to make sure the pool service was taking care of it properly. Avoiding eye contact, she said, "I'll probably be very late getting in."

Courtney screwed up her mouth. "So what am I supposed to do while you're gone? There's nothing on television on Saturday nights and you won't let me have any friends over. Is the rent-a-stalker going to be out there watching? Maybe I can make his day by flashing him through the living room windows."

Charla whirled around and faced the insolent girl. "Look, Courtney," Charla retorted, "don't start up again. I'll rent a movie for you on Netflix. What would you like to see? Maybe two movies will keep you occupied. I'll order pizza for you."

"Can I have some beer to go with it?" Courtney jumped up and started towards the door. "Have you got any wine?"

"No! You're nineteen. Don't push it. Come on. Let's find you some movies."

Charla had barely left the driveway to go meet up with her booty call when Courtney ran upstairs to unpack the boxes containing her drums. Delivered while her mother was at work the day before, she commenced dragging them out of the closet in the guest bedroom where she had hidden them. She stripped the tape away, anxious to start practicing. *This was going to be fun!*

The movies went unwatched and when the pimple-faced pizza delivery person dropped off her dinner, she wolfed down a couple of slices along with a bottle of coke, and then ran up to her room, leaving the rest to dry out on the counter. *The housekeeper will clean it up.*

She put a CD in the player, put on her headphones, and commenced practicing to the beat, repeatedly starting over until she got it reasonably right.

Mother had still not returned home by midnight, and Courtney's arms were feeling fatigued, so she dressed for bed, threw a sheet over the drum set, locked her bedroom door and turned in. She lay there in the dark, turning over in her head the practice session, analyzing what she did or should have done, until she heard the front door close a little too loudly. She jumped out of bed and looked out the window just as a taxicab was pulling away. *Mother got a snoot full and couldn't drive herself home. My plan is going perfectly.* The bedside clock read four in the morning. She grinned and set the alarm for six. Two hours of sleep and then….

The sudden crashing of cymbals and beat of drums jolted Charla out of a sound sleep. It vibrated through her head, smashing her brain like a sledgehammer coming down hard on a plate glass window. She ripped off her eyeshades and rolled over, peering at the clock. "Someone's breaking into the house."

Jumping out of bed and throwing on a robe, she grabbed her cell and went to investigate. As she staggered unsteadily down the hall, the noise seemed to be coming from Courtney's room. She pounded on the locked door. "Courtney," she yelled. "Turn it down!" She pounded again. "Damn you, turn that noise off!"

The racket stopped and the door opened a crack. Courtney innocently stood there looking at her mother. "You're not as pretty without your makeup."

Charla glared back. "What in hell do you think you are doing, turning the stereo up at this hour of the morning? You woke me out of a sound sleep. What were you thinking?"

"It's not a stereo."

"Then what was that racket?" Charla elbowed her way into the room and stopped in her tracks. "Where did you get the drum set? Did your father send that to you for the specific purpose of annoying me?"

"No." Courtney pursed her lips to keep from laughing.

"Where did you get them?"

"An anonymous benefactor sent them to me." She sat down, picked up the sticks, and started to beat the cymbals rhythmically.

Charla grabbed a stick out of her hand and demanded, "I will ask you again and don't lie to me. Where did you get these drums?"

"I told you, the donor is anonymous." She smiled smugly, and hit the cymbals with the other stick.

Charla heaved an exasperated sigh, grabbing her pounding skull. "Your grandmother is responsible for this, isn't she? I'm going to kill that woman."

Courtney stuck her chin upward and sneered at her mother. "That woman is your mother and you should be nicer to her."

"Don't tell me what to do," Charla said angrily.

"She's your mother and my grandmother and a nice person. You treat her like crap." She smashed the cymbal hard.

"I don't treat her like *crap* and I will thank you to use more ladylike language. I'm very busy with my business and she…she… lately she's been doing things that make me look like a fool."

"So, her attempts to get your attention are all about making you look bad? She told me all about her Spanish Cadillac. I thought it was hilarious. Really, Mother, get your priorities straight and take that knot out of your thong. It's making your ass too uptight."

"Don't tell me what to do and stop talking to me like that! I am your mother!" Charla took a deep breath, ran her fingers through her messed up hair and stared at the noise makers occupying a corner of Courtney's bedroom.

"Back to the drums—why do you seem to think you need them? You're going back to school soon. You need to concentrate on getting an education. When you're an adult, which it appears is not happening yet, you can decide what to do with your…desire for musical entertainment. For now, please, just go back to bed. I need some sleep." Charla stomped out of the room and slammed the door.

Courtney defiantly hit the cymbals one more time. *She didn't even wait for an answer. I still haven't told her about my boyfriend and she isn't interested enough to ask. Mission accomplished.*

22

Charla returned to her room, inserted some earplugs and replaced her eyeshades. She was exhausted after a night in a hotel room with her date. He flew into Vegas with a generous credit card and bottle of little blue pills. He took her to dinner at the top of the Eiffel Tower where they dined, drained a bottle of Dom Perion, and then retired to the five thousand dollar per night suite on the top floor of Paris.

She could still feel him inside her. The thought of his naked body brought on another wave of pulsating desire. She closed her eyes and rocked her hips. The insatiable yearning she felt when she thought about his...big...*ego,* brought a more intense wave of passion. The rocking of her hips became more urgent. Reaching down, she massaged herself until an explosive orgasm ensued.

The release was only temporary. Her mind and body wouldn't let go. Sleep remained elusive. After two hours of tossing and turning, she staggered out of bed and headed for the master shower.

She was starting to regret forcing Courtney to come back home. If she had her house all to herself, they wouldn't have to meet in a hotel room. They could spend the entire weekend romping naked, making love on every flat surface in her house.

After a brisk interval in cool cascading water, she felt refreshed, although still physically drained. However, it wouldn't be the first

Sunday that she was dragging around after a night of love making with her man. Smugly, she referred to him as her "energizer booty."

She dressed in casual clothes and left her room. All seemed to be quiet now. She listened at Courtney's door. She could hear snoring.

After downing two Excedrin, setting coffee to brew and bringing in the Sunday paper, she sat down on a bar stool, picked up her phone and dialed.

A sleepy voice answered.

"Mother, I'm not happy with you." She rolled her eyes upwards as if to see through the ceiling into Courtney's room.

"It's nice to hear from you too," Lillian replied. "So, what else is new? What did I do now to piss you off?"

Leaning her throbbing head on her hands and elbows, she spoke in an accusatory manner. "Why in God's name did you buy that dastardly drum set for Courtney?"

"What drum set are you talking about? What time is it?"

"It's after eight in the morning. Thanks to you, I only got two hours sleep and I'm in a nasty mood, so don't mess with me."

"Why did you only get two hours sleep? Did you stay out all night? That can't be my fault, although it seems you blame me for everything these days. If you can't sleep, take a pill, don't call me." The line went dead.

Charla set the phone down hard on the counter and spoke aloud. "I'm in no mood for her antics today." She took a long swig of coffee and massaged her throbbing temples with her fingertips.

"You look like crap!" Courtney flounced into the kitchen in her pajamas and poured a glass of orange juice. "Is that a hangover I see?"

Charla gazed angrily at the child she regretted having given birth.

Courtney grinned impishly and wagged her finger in her mother's face. "You really should lay off that sauce, Mother. You don't wear the effects very well."

"Don't...."

"Don't what, Mommy dearest?" interrupted Courtney. "Treat you like a child? I saw you come home last night—I mean this morning in a cab. Where's your car? Did you misplace it?"

"I left it at The Paris. I wasn't feeling well and didn't want to drive." She took another swig of coffee.

Courtney shook her head. "Some people just never learn that booze is nothing but poison. Isn't that what you warned me about when I went off to college? If I remember correctly, you said 'I'm sending you to school to get an education, not to party and get drunk.'"

"I'm glad you remembered those words, but apparently you didn't take the advice. You still flunked out. Are you going to lie to me and tell me you didn't skip classes because you were hung over? Be careful how you answer because I'm in no mood for..." Charla suddenly threw a hand over her mouth and raced for the kitchen sink where she emptied the contents of her stomach. She rinsed her mouth and washed her hands. "I think I'll go back to bed. I must have gotten food poisoning."

"Yeah, sure," Courtney reacted sullenly. "Either that or you're pregnant. Don't tell me you've come home pregnant!" She feigned a shocked expression. "How would I ever explain that embarrassing situation to any of my friends? My God—you're so old!"

"Oh, shut the hell up Courtney. I am not." She turned on her heel to leave the room. "I can't deal with you right now. I need some sleep. And kindly stay off the drums today or you might find them smashed out on the driveway."

After Charla disappeared up the stairs, Courtney poured a bowl of cereal, refilled her juice and sat down at the bar to eat while perusing the pile of Sunday ads. "Round two goes to Courtney."

23

Lillian set her cell down on the bedside table and smiled. She glanced at the clock. "I may as well get up." She mumbled, "I can't wait to hear from Courtney how she sprang the drum set on Charla."

She put on a robe and headed for the kitchen to set up coffee. The snoring emanating from Celia's closed bedroom door indicated she had not roused yet.

Cora was already in the kitchen with coffee made. All those years of teaching high school turned her permanently into a morning person. She poured a cup for Lillian when she saw her coming. "Want some toast?"

"I'll make some later." She sipped at the fresh brew and chuckled. "I just had a call from Charla, waking me up. I guess if she can't sleep, nobody sleeps."

"Okay," Cora said with a grin. "What did you do now to get her attention?"

A twinkle flashed in Lillian's eyes. "I bought Courtney a drum set."

"You mean the whole boom-boom clang bang shebang?"

Lillian giggled. "Yes. She wants to play drums in a rock band."

Cora heaved a sigh and leaned back in her chair. "I once had a neighbor with one of those set up out in his garage. He opened the door so everyone in the neighborhood could hear the racket. I had to listen to his incessant pounding and the clang of cymbals until late into the night. It's like a Chinese water torture."

"That is precisely the plan," Lillian said with a mischievous laugh. "Charla is keeping Courtney a virtual prisoner with the determination to enroll her in college here."

"She should finish school," Cora agreed. "She can have a music career later."

"I couldn't agree more, but there is no talking to her. She has to go where her heart takes her and right now, that's back to Los Angeles and to the boy she loves. He's the front man for a band."

"What band—do they have a name?" Cora buttered some toast and bit into it.

"I don't know. But that is what Courtney wants."

"So if she is leaving, why does she need the drums?"

"Her plan is to become so annoying to her mother that Charla will gladly send her back to school in California, just to be rid of her." Lillian couldn't keep a straight face. "I think it's an excellent idea. Maybe if I keep annoying her, she'll buy me a cruise to the Mediterranean. And if we all annoy her enough, maybe she'll book three tickets for us."

"It sounds like you have at least one backup soldier in Courtney to help you make Charla's life miserable." Cora peered over her reading glasses at her roommate. "You are evil," she said with a grin.

"You might say that." Lillian retrieved a bowl and some cereal, and commenced eating.

With breakfast over, Lillian returned to her room to dress for the day. She sat down on the bed and called Courtney who answered right away in a hushed tone.

"How did it go? Did your mother like the drums?" Lillian whispered back.

"The warden didn't get in until four this morning and she was plastered. I waited two hours and then decided to get in some early practice." The ensuing laugh was loud.

"What happened?"

"She flew out of bed and practically broke my bedroom door down. You should have seen her face. She's not as pretty without five pounds of paint on her face."

"So she was pissed?" Lillian felt smug, remembering the look on Charla's face when they argued over the Spanish Cadillac. It had been years since she had seen Charla without any makeup.

Courtney yawned loudly. "That's a mild way of putting it. A wild night of riding her rich stud didn't mellow her out at all. She came home in a cab. I don't know how she plans to get back to the Paris to pick up her car."

"She better not be calling me, but if she does, I may have to be unavailable like she is when I need her. Anyway, do you think we've accomplished what you set out to do?" Lillian was pulling the bed covers up and making her bed as she spoke. "What is she doing now?"

"She's sleeping. She has a hangover. She said if I don't lay off the drums, she would throw them out into the driveway. She sure can be mean when she wants to be."

"Would you like to go out and do something today? I can come and get you. We could go bowling. Then I'll buy you some lunch."

"Sure. I have to shower. Can you be here by ten?" The sound of breakfast dishes landing roughly in the kitchen sink rang out.

"I'll see you then."

24

Lillian broke the silence while driving back home after bowling and downing burgers at Smash Burger. "What if your plan to beat the drums until your mother cries *Uncle* doesn't work?"

"Then we have to think of something else. I could get a pet."

Lillian glanced sideways. "What would that accomplish? She hates pets. She never wanted one as a kid because she didn't want to clean up after it. However, she's gone so much of the time, she probably wouldn't even notice if you brought home a little animal."

"I didn't say *little*. I was thinking about something bigger."

"Oh, boy," Lillian sighed. "Do you know how destructive big dogs can be? Your mom is very proud of the pristine condition of her house and yard. She would not be happy with you at all."

Courtney grinned mischievously. "I know. It's as if nobody lives in that classy ass prison."

"I figured getting the drum set was an innocent thing to do. I don't know about a dog. I'm not sure I can go along with that. If there was a way of borrowing one for a short time, it might work. What would you do with an animal if she finally relented and let you go back to California?"

"Then I'd have to give it back to the pound. I don't really want to bond with one. I just want to use it as an instrument of annoyance. When she objects, I can tell her we are a package deal."

"I don't know about this. It seems like a cruel thing to do to the dog. I mean subjecting the poor animal to the angry reaction of your mother. She might go ballistic. I hope she doesn't own a gun."

They had arrived home and Lillian pulled up to the curb. "Maybe you could rent a dog, because I don't think that arrangement will be very long lived. Shall we check into that? Do you have any friends in town that could use a dog sitter?"

"I didn't think of that. The problem is, all my friends are away at college and their phone numbers are in that Smart Phone my mother confiscated."

"What about the rules in this neighborhood? What if there are restrictions about having animals in this subdivision? There could be fines by the association. All those things need to be checked out first." Lillian checked her rear view mirror. "Your watch dog in the plain black wrapper is still with us. Your mother needs to get rid of him. This is ridiculous."

"She thinks she's protecting me from some sicko. In the meantime I'm going to do some research." Courtney opened the door and popped a smooch on her grandmother's cheek. "Thanks for taking me out of my prison today. I needed this. I love you."

Lillian's heart swelled at hearing those words. "I love you too with all my heart. Let me know if I can help you in any way. Now I'll bet you have some practicing to do on those drums."

"Yes I do." Courtney laughed as she glanced up at her bedroom window. "I think it's time for my mother to haul ass out of bed. She can't sleep all day."

"You go, girl." Lillian grinned as the door shut. She waved one last time and cruised silently away. "That girl has spunk."

25

Courtney let herself into the house. It was silent as a funeral parlor at midnight. A check in the kitchen revealed no additional dirty dishes, so mother had not risen from her drunken slumber yet. The kitchen clock read three in the afternoon. She grabbed a soda from the fridge and headed up to her room. The door to her mother's suite remained closed.

She locked her bedroom door, opened the front window, and sat in the window seat sipping on the soft drink. Eyeing the drum set, she rehearsed in her mind her opening performance to awaken the sleeping dragon. With a grin on her face, she sat down on the stool, picked up the sticks, and announced her presence with a resounding smash of the cymbals followed by a loud drumroll.

She kept up a rhythmic beat for a time until her arms got tired. There should have been banging on her door by now. "Where is she?" she said under her breath. "She should be breaking my door down and yelling at me."

Courtney went to investigate. She crept down the hall and quietly opened her mother's door. The room was dim with drapes drawn. The bed was rumpled, but empty. "Oh, crap. She's gone," she said under her breath. "That was an exercise in futility." She returned to her room, retrieved her cell and dialed the number.

Charla answered.

"Where are you?" she asked impatiently of her mother.

"My date brought the car back to me and I had to take him back to the hotel. We're having early dinner and then I'm taking him to the airport. Is there something you wanted? I see you went out with your grandmother. Did you have a good time?"

"How did you know that? I didn't leave a note." Courtney sneered at the phone.

"The body guard I hired for you called me."

"Oh." Courtney felt total disappointment that her latest effort to annoy her mother had failed.

"You must be feeling better." Privately she sneered into the bureau mirror. *How did she manage to get over a hangover so fast? Mine always last a whole day.*

"I am. I'll be home later. You'll have to fend for yourself for dinner. I have to go now." The line went dead.

Courtney plopped down on the bed. She eyed the drum set. *It's pointless to practice anymore today. Guess I'll go swimming.*

After a methodical ten laps in the pool, Courtney lounged on the steps and surveyed the backyard that looked like something out of some gardening magazine. The perfectly trimmed palms and shrubs, the rockery, the waterfall reeked of money. She looked at the patio and noted the pricey chaise lounges with their plush white cushions looked as if nobody had dared occupy them. Courtney's bedroom was the only area in the whole place that looked lived in. An evil grin formed on her lips. She jumped out of the pool, toweled off and headed for the kitchen to find a phone book. *Would Mom still have one of those antiques?*

Charla had still not returned home by eleven, and Courtney got bored and sleepy. She had already taken a bubble bath in the massive tub and washed her hair. There was nothing on television. She ate all the potato chips and drank all the soda. "Fend for yourself for dinner" was an understatement. Mother was not much of a grocery shopper. She had settled for a nuked chicken dinner that turned out to be tough and tasteless. The majority of it ended up in the garbage. Prison food really was everything the convicts said it was. Thankfully, Grandma had filled her tummy with the best burgers in town before depositing her back home.

The only good part of the evening had been an hour on the phone with Lennie, the love of her life, before her battery ran down. Somehow, she had to get back to him before he found someone else to play drums in his band.

Sitting at the kitchen counter now, she picked up the scrap of paper on which she had made notes. She had explained her desire to do some volunteer work and they responded with an immediate need she might be able to fulfill. She would have to rely on Grandma to run her over there and meet with the person in charge tomorrow.

The sound of the garage door opening interrupted her thoughts. She stuffed the paper into her pocket and ran up the stairs to her room, closing the door. She plugged in her cell and turned out the lights, anxious to avoid any confrontations with the dragon tonight.

26

Sunlight was just beginning to brighten the room the next morning when Courtney jerked out of a sound sleep. Someone was nudging her arm. "Get up. You're going to the office with me today."

She rolled over and turned her back, mumbling, "No I'm not."

"Get up, I said. You've been complaining about being bored, so come on. You can go to the office and do some filing for me and answer phones." The bed jolted from Charla's knee jamming against it.

"I have plans today. Grandma is coming to pick me up and we're going…shopping." She drew the covers up over her head. "Don't you have a minion you like to boss around?"

Charla grabbed the top covers and pulled them off onto the floor. "Yes, but I thought you might like to experience the joy of working for a living." The bed jolted again.

"Not today. I have plans. Maybe I'll feel like being your slave tomorrow."

"Get up, Courtney!" yelled Charla.

"No—go away!"

"I give up," Charla sighed. "You are going to try my patience to the point where I might have to ship you off to your father. The last I heard, he was in France."

"Send me to Europe with all those refugees and terrorist bombers—over my dead body," Courtney replied indignantly as she reached down and grabbed the sheet in an attempt to cover back up.

Charla turned briskly, and spat the words, "I give up. The door slammed loudly, indicating her departure.

Courtney remained in her room until she heard the garage door open and close. She jumped out of bed and watched as Charla cruised away in her Cadillac a little before nine.

Waving goodbye with her traffic finger, she noted the rent-a-stalker had not shown up yet. She bounded down the stairs to the kitchen for a bowl of cereal and some juice.

After dressing in jeans and a tee, she picked up her cell to dial but it rang just then. "Hi, Grandma, can you pick me up? I have an appointment."

"What kind of appointment? Are you sick? Do you have to see a doctor?"

"No, but it's probably better if I don't tell you with whom. I don't want my mother to blame you for what's going to happen next."

"What do you mean what's going to happen next. What are you up to, Courtney? Is it something that's going to get you in trouble? Is it going to get me in trouble?" Alarm was evident in Lillian's voice.

"Um…I'd really rather not give you all the details on the phone. I just need a ride to meet with someone. Let's just say I'm exploring my options. Will you come?" She held her breath for a few beats.

"You know I will."

Courtney heaved a sigh of relief. "Okay. Here's the deal. I don't want my bodyguard to know I've left the house. Therefore, I'm going over the back fence and through the greenway. Meet me outside the gate on Straus."

"Why do we need all this secrecy?"

Courtney looked out the front window in time to see the black car come to a stop across the street. "Because my tail reports to mother every move I make. I don't want her tipped off to what I'm going to do next. It would spoil the plan and we will end up in another big battle. It's better this way."

"It sounds so mysterious. I can't wait for this scene to play out. I wish I could video tape the big reveal, whatever it is." Lillian's laugh through the phone indicated her consent.

"If I still had my iPhone I could do that for you." She picked up her purse and rummaged through it to make sure she had what she needed.

"Then let's go to the store after your appointment and get you a better one than that flip phone. I can add it to my bill. Your mom doesn't need to know."

"Oh, Grandma, that is a great idea. How can you afford it, though?"

"Don't worry about it. When will I need to be there to pick you up?"

"I'm ready now. When can you get here?"

"Give me forty-five minutes. I'm not even dressed yet."

"See you then." Courtney dropped the phone into her bag and hefted it up on her shoulder. She headed for the garage where she dragged a small set of kitchen steps out the back door and set them up by the rear wall. Climbing to the top of the steps, she looked to see if anyone was around. Finding nobody, she heaved herself up on the wall and dropped down between some shrubs on the other side. She took up a jogging pace down the path towards Straus.

Lillian cruised up to the curb where Courtney was lounging on a low brick landscape wall.

She jumped into the car and handed her grandmother a piece of paper with an address. This is where I need to go. Do you think you can find it?"

"Probably...I think. We'll find it together." She put the car in gear and drove on. "This sounds all very mysterious. Can't you simply convince your mother to send you back to California?"

"She's not about to. She needs to be in control of my life. She took my credit cards. When I run out of cash, I'll be reduced to rummaging through her purse to get spending money." A frown crossed her face and she folded her arms in front of her. "She's just being a witch."

Lillian glanced sideways at the child she so adored. She wore the torn denims that irked her mother to the core, along with a tee splashed with neon colored lettering advertising "I'm the Total Package." She chose not to ask what that means.

"Have you leveled with your mother about having a boyfriend and wanting to join a band? Maybe she will relent."

"Are you kidding? Since dad dumped her, she has a grudge against musicians. She tried to get me to go to the office with her today. I'd have spent eight boring hours answering her dumb phones and fetching her coffee."

"Is that so bad?" Lillian glanced sideways at Courtney, silently questioning her new fashion sense. "Maybe she's just trying to find some common ground between the two of you."

"The only common ground I want is the path that leads back to L.A. Besides, slavery was outlawed." Courtney started calling out the streets. "The street where you turn should be coming up soon. There it is. Turn right."

"Should I come in with you? Who is this person? This is a private residence. Are you sure this is safe?" Lillian was craning her neck looking around the unfamiliar neighborhood.

"Relax. I'll be okay, Grandma. I talked to them on the phone and they're going to help me get something. They only want to meet me before delivering the goods."

Lillian's brow furrowed with concern. "Is this a drug deal? Are you into something you shouldn't be?"

"Grandma, you need to have more trust in me! Just wait here. I shouldn't be very long." She jumped out and bounded up to the door.

When Courtney returned, she was all aglow with excitement. "Can we go have some lunch? I'm starving. My mother seems to think frozen dinners and potato chips constitute a healthy meal."

"Sure, and then we need to get you a phone that can take video."

"Grandma, I had no idea you could be such a good conspirator." She leaned over and pecked Lillian on the cheek before buckling up.

"I have selfish reasons. Your mom has built a shell up around her. I've tried to get close and find out what's eating her, but she brushes me off like an annoying gnat. She won't tell me why she avoids me."

"Me neither. I don't know what's up with her. Maybe if we exasperate her enough, the walls will come down."

After a leisurely lunch and a trip to the phone store, Lillian dropped Courtney off at the gate. "Whatever you are planning, post it on Facebook so I can see it." She grinned. "I swear you are a chip off my old block." She laughed and drove away.

Courtney nonchalantly walked through the neighborhood to her house. When the rent-a-stalker saw her coming up the street, he snapped to attention. He rolled down his window and hailed her.

Courtney approached. "Yeah, what do you want now?" she said sullenly.

"I didn't see you leave. Where have you been?"

"It's none of your business. When my mother finds out you were sleeping on the job, she will probably fire you. Good luck on your next assignment." With that said, she walked up to the door, unlocked, and slammed it after her. She watched out the window to see if he was talking on the phone. He wasn't. It was in his best interest not to report that his prisoner slipped out of her cage.

27

The room was flooded with sunlight from the bedroom window when Courtney's bed began to shimmy and shake. She bolted upright thinking it was an earthquake.

"Get your buns out of bed. You're working for me today." Charla stood akimbo at the foot of the bed with a determined expression on her face.

Courtney defiantly lay back down and pulled the covers over her head. "No I'm not. I have other things planned for today."

Charla responded to that statement with a loud clang of the cymbals and banging on the drums.

Courtney peaked out from under the covers to see her standing there with sticks in hands, poised to whack the drums again. "Get up!"

"Go away."

Charla set the sticks down, reached beneath the covers, grabbed Courtney's foot with a firm grip and pulled her off the bed.

She landed with a thud on the floor in a pile of bedding. "Ouch. Was that really necessary?"

"Get up and get dressed," Charla ordered in an exasperated voice. "Wear something appropriate." She went to the closet and searched through the clothes, picking out the least offensive of the items and flung them on the bed. We have to be at the office by nine, so get a move on." She stomped out of the room, leaving the teenager on the floor rubbing her hip.

Courtney grabbed her new phone and dialed. After a few rings, the call answered.

"Grandma!" she blurted. "Would you please phone my mother and inform her that we have plans to go somewhere today and they can't be changed."

"But we don't," objected Lillian. "What time is it?'"

"Early. I can't go work in her office today. She literally dragged me out of bed." She rubbed her hip with her free hand.

"What is it we are supposed to be doing then? What should I tell her?"

"I don't know. It has to be something believable. Do you do any volunteer work? What about something like serving at a soup kitchen to feed the homeless. Do you volunteer at a hospital? Maybe I can wear something with her real estate office logo on it to make her look good. Think of something." Desperation was apparent in her voice.

"Can't you just tell her you have the flu?"

"If I had thought of that first, I wouldn't be calling you. Please help me out here. I have to be at home at noon today or my plans to royally piss her off will be blown." She picked herself up off the floor and headed for her bathroom. She briefly went over in her mind the meeting yesterday where she had to turn on the charm and drop names to get the man to agree to what she wanted to do. He initially objected saying the vetting process would have to take place. However, when she explained that her mother was the very influential Charla Romaine, and willing to donate generously to his cause, he relented and waived formalities.

"Please Grandma, this is important."

"Okay, dear. I'll think of something."

Charla was finishing application of her makeup and combing her hair when the cell on the bathroom counter rang. She frowned when Lillian's number came up.

"Good morning, Mother. I'm kind of in a hurry right now."

"I just wanted to let you know that I'm picking Courtney up today. On Wednesdays afternoons, we eat at the Senior Center and this week our grandchildren are invited to help serve."

Charla frowned into the mirror. "You should have asked me first before signing her up. She's working at my office today."

"But that will have to wait for some other day. This is a special occasion. All the members are bringing their grandchildren with them today. Everyone is participating. I don't want to be the only grandmother there with nobody to show off. They all know I have Courtney, because I brag about her so much and they know she's back in town."

Charla let out a loud sigh. "I'm trying to teach her a lesson."

"What lesson is that dear?"

"She needs to learn that if she isn't going to take education seriously, she will have to learn to work for a living."

"But this is an important lesson too. Maybe you can loan her a shirt with your company name on it to wear while serving tables. It would be good advertising for you. All those people are old and every time one of them dies, the heirs list their homes for sale. Give her a supply of your cards to pass out. This could be a marketing opportunity for you."

Charla heaved another exasperated sigh. "Okay, just this once, but tomorrow she's going to work with me and that's final."

"Whatever you say, dear, I won't keep you." The line went dead.

Courtney's new cell rang. She jumped on it immediately.

"It's all arranged. I told your mother you are having lunch with me today at the Senior Center and I'm picking you up right after bowling. I should be there by noon. She wants you to wear a shirt with her company advertising on it, so act like you are thrilled when she gives it to you."

"Yeah, like I'd wear anything like that. Thanks, Grandma gotta go."

She exited the bathroom just as Charla entered the bedroom and tossed a shirt on the bed. "Wear that today." She set a stack of cards on the bedside table. "Pass these out wherever you have the opportunity."

Courtney picked up the orange polo shirt and eyed it with disdain. *This is going to look like I'm on a prison crew cleaning up some roadside trash.* She put a smile on her face and tried to look enthusiastic. "Of course, Mother, I'm only too happy to help you promote your business. It's the least I can do." She turned her back, rolled her eyes and sneered.

Charla turned to leave the room. "I'll be home by six tonight. I'll pick up dinner. What would you like?" She paused at the door.

Courtney thought for a minute and considered what was about to happen today and then suggested, "Can we have ribs?"

"Those are kind of messy to eat, but sure. I know a place that does take out ribs Texas style with all the trimmings. See you at six."

As Charla descended the stairs and headed to the door leading to the garage, Courtney looked on with an evil grin on her flawless cheeks and a twinkle in her blue eyes. Thoughts of those delicious ribs and the aroma always made the mouth water. Everything was falling into place. She threw the orange shirt into her closet where it landed on a pile of other discarded clothing.

28

Courtney poured a bowl of cereal and started to dig in when the new smart phone in her hip pocket vibrated.

"Hi Grandma, you didn't really mean it when you said I'm going to the center today did you? Mom threw an ugly orange polo shirt at me and told me to wear it and pass out her business cards."

"No, it was made up. You said you needed to be home at noon."

"She actually believed I would do some volunteer work." She took a swig of juice and listened.

"I've gotten good at lying to your mom. Efforts to be honest don't get her attention."

"Yeah, I know. She still hasn't sat down to have any in-depth conversations with me. She's in and out, barking orders and handing out criticism. I can't wait to get out of here."

"I called to ask what in the world you are up to. I think you need to give me a heads-up so I can make up a good response. I know she's going to think I have a hand in whatever it is you are doing to piss her off again. You should tell me so I can start making up my alibi."

"I don't really want you involved, but if you would like to come over around noon and be here for the delivery, you'll see what I'm about to do. You should be gone by the time she walks in after work though…for your own protection."

"It all sounds very mysterious. I hope you're not breaking the law," Lillian whispered in a conspiratorial manner.

"No. I'm just pushing Mom's buttons. This might drive her right over the edge. If this doesn't make her kick me back to California I don't know what will."

"I think you should tell me what you're up to," Lillian wheedled.

Courtney tossed the dishes into the sink and chuckled. "Just come over and you'll see. Be sure to park at the curb because I have a delivery coming that they need to unload inside the garage."

"Now you really have my curiosity in high gear."

"See you soon." Courtney ended the call. She gazed around the large kitchen and strolled through the house, noting the perfectly placed furniture her mother had purchased from the most exclusive store in the city. It all looked like one of her model homes in one of the upper-crust developments where she peddled real estate. She wandered out to the pool and dipped in a hand to test the water temperature. It looked as if the gardeners had been there yesterday while she was out with Grandma. Not a twig was out of place; the patio appeared swept clean to perfection. She looked over at the pricey outdoor furniture with immaculate cushion covers. A mischievous grin spread across her face.

Through the open patio door, she heard the wall clock in the entry chime once. It was nine-thirty—two and a half hours until the expected delivery.

She went upstairs, brushed her teeth, and threw the ugly shirt in the trash along with those business cards that displayed Charla's photo on them. "I have got to get out of here."

Wandering into Charla's room, she began systematically searching the drawers, looking for cash. Asking Grandma for money would be a last resort. *I wonder what a bus ticket costs.*

The doorbell chimed, interrupting her thoughts. She cast a glance around the bedroom to make sure she hadn't left anything messed up to reveal she had been searching her mother's drawers for valuables. Nothing seemed out of place. Bounding down the stairs, she swung the door open, expecting to see Lillian arriving early.

The rent-a-stalker was standing there, impatiently shifting from one foot to the other. "Sorry to bother you, but I have an immediate need to use your restroom. May I come in?" The expression on his face appeared stricken with panic and beads of sweat were dripping from his forehead.

Courtney considered slamming the door on him, but his desperate expression played on her emotions. She stepped aside and directed him to the tiny guest half-bath off the kitchen under the staircase.

He took several steps while holding his backside with one hand in a tight-ass manner. The door closed followed by a loud explosion of anal gas echoing from the small room. Following that sound was a familiar muffled splat of someone with a serious case of Hershey squirts.

Courtney stifled a laugh. "I'm not cleaning that up," she yelled.

When the man emerged, he looked pale and sweaty, wiping his brow with a kerchief. "I think I have to leave for a little while. Please don't tell your mother I deserted my post."

Courtney's brow furrowed. "Are you sick?" She backed up a few feet as if to avoid breathing the same air.

"I have to go home. I'll call for someone to relieve me. Please keep this between you and me."

"You don't need to call anyone. I have no plans for today. My grandmother is coming over to keep me company and have lunch. I promise to be on my best behavior." She headed to the front door and opened it. "I hope whatever is ailing you will get better."

He made a swift exit and practically ran to his car.

Courtney noted a strong odor following him and detected a slight brown splotch on his rear. "That poor man, it must have been a bad breakfast burrito. I hate when that happens." She shut the door and doubled over with laughter.

She walked past the little guest bath, noting the bad smell coming from it, so she scrounged up a piece of paper and some scotch tape. A minute later, she hung an "Out of Order" sign on the door.

Just before noon, the doorbell chimed again. This time she peaked out the window, noting Grandma's car at the curb.

Lillian headed for the kitchen with a sack in her hand. "I remembered what you said about no groceries in the house, so I stopped at Subway and picked up some sandwiches for our lunch." She wrinkled her nose when passing the guest lavatory. "What's that smell? Did the sewer back up?"

"I don't know. I'm afraid to look. Our stalker made an emergency trip in here to use it and then he had to leave. He looked a little sick. If you need to go, use the one upstairs." She pinched her nose as if to emphasize the situation. "I think the maid is going to earn her pay tomorrow."

Lillian put the sandwich bag in the fridge. "Can I have some coffee? I didn't quite get my quota this morning."

Courtney plopped a capsule into the Keurig and stuck a mug in place. "You should've brought a swim suit."

Lillian glanced longingly at the pool. "I used to keep one here, but finally took it home when it became clear I was never going to get invited over anymore." She took a seat at the breakfast bar and gazed about the mostly immaculate kitchen.

"Trying to get your mother to spend some time with me is like trying to catch a pesky cricket in a butterfly net." She pinched her nose and glanced over her shoulder at the offending restroom. "Boy that is a powerful smell. Do you have any air fresheners?"

"Let's go outside." Courtney handed Lillian the steaming mug and opened the patio door, leaving it ajar so she could hear the doorbell if it rang.

Lillian eyed the teenager. "Even if you get back to school, will they let you in—I mean in view of your grades?"

"I don't think it's a problem. Mom pays cash. It's not as if I depend on government grants or loans. Spread enough money around and they make room for you. As long as she pays the bill, they don't really care if I pass."

Lillian sipped the hot coffee. "Have you discussed it with her?"

"Have you ever tried to discuss anything with dragon lady? It's like talking to a computer. Press one for English, etc. etc."

"Either that or it becomes all about how it affects her. I don't understand it."

"Don't even try." The doorbell chimed and Courtney jumped up. "It's show time." She ran to the front door, spoke to the visitor in a hushed tone and then sped to the door leading to the garage whereupon she pushed the button to open the big door.

Lillian followed Courtney inside, waiting patiently in the kitchen while taking a final swig on the coffee. She heard the door to the back yard open and then all hell broke loose.

She followed the direction of the barking and watched as two black and white dogs the size of small horses burst out onto the patio. They ran back and forth around the yard and pool, sniffing at everything. One raised his leg and shot a stream of urine onto the climbing rose along the back wall. The other massive animal dove into the pool and paddled around. When he climbed out, he shook his body and dampened a six-foot swath around him.

Courtney appeared at the patio door with a stranger. "This is my grandmother, Lillian."

Lillian was so stunned that she was slow to respond.

"Hello. Nice to meet you," the man said, extending his hand to shake. "I'm with the Great Dane Foster Care Society. We find temporary homes for these great animals. It was very lucky that Courtney called when we needed somewhere to house these two temporarily. Their master passed away suddenly and nobody else in his family would take them."

Lillian dumbly shook the man's hand, thunderstruck at what was taking place, and the fact that he was so tall, handsome, and her own age group. His hand remained in hers a little longer than necessary as she gazed at his ice blue eyes and full head of white hair. She darted a glance at his left hand. No wedding ring—only a slight white ring and indentation as if there had been one in place at one time. She came out of her stupor when he disengaged his hand.

"Excuse me; I need to get the supplies out of my car for this young lady. I brought food and dishes for these boys. We'll be working on permanent placement. In the meantime, we are thrilled to find such a wonderful place for them to live." As he turned on his heel and headed towards the presumed door to the garage, his eyes roamed appreciatively around the high ceilings and pricey furnishings. Courtney directed him away from the offending restroom door.

Lillian turned back to the yard where the giant invaders were peeing on every bush and slobbering on the chaise cushions. She watched with disgust as one of them squatted and dumped a pile the size of Mount Everest on the pool deck. "Charla is not going to like this."

"What isn't my mother going to like?" Courtney was back and the sound of the garage door closing was audible.

"That!" Lillian pointed to the mess the dogs were making of the back yard. She frowned at Courtney. "Was this really necessary? You know how much she hates dogs. She didn't even want one when she was a kid. She didn't want to clean up after an animal."

"The whole point is to piss her off so she lets me go back to school and back to Lennie. He won't transfer here to finish school. His parents won't help him do that. I have to go back to L.A. The drum set wasn't enough incentive to get my mother to relent. I think this will do it."

Lillian shook her head in dismay. "I can't watch this. Let's have lunch and then I have to go." She slammed the patio door shut. "Please don't let those things into the house." She gazed around. "She'll never forgive you if you let them destroy any of this." She swept her hand around the room, "This is her castle."

Courtney smiled. "Would I do such a thing to the queen?"

A barrage of barking from the back yard interrupted their conversation. The animals' front paws were up on the high concrete block wall and they were enthusiastically barking.

Lillian shook her head. "Have you read the rules for this gated community? I think they have a size limit on allowable pets. This could mean a lot of trouble for your mother."

"No, I didn't bother to read any rules and ask me if I care. She's keeping me prisoner. This isn't where I want to live."

"I understand that. Let's eat and then I think I need to go home. I like dogs, but I can't get excited around any horses masquerading as such." She shook her head and retrieved the sandwiches and bottles of water. "Let's eat."

29

Waving goodbye to her grandmother, Courtney quietly shut the door, noting that the rent-a-stalker had not returned.

They had eaten the sandwiches and watched a game show on television while leaving the dogs to their own devices in the back yard. A cacophony of barking periodically drowned out the audio as they attempted to watch TV. Dog snot smeared the previously spotless patio doors.

She had promised to call Grandma if she survived the anticipated nuclear explosion when the dragon arrived home.

The house phone began ringing incessantly. She let the answering machine pick up. It was one complaint after another from the neighbors, complaining about the barking. The Association called to remind Charla of the noise ordinances in the CC&Rs. Courtney grinned wickedly. One neighbor threatened to call Animal Control.

Finding nothing of interest to entertain her for the next couple of hours, she slid open the patio doors about a foot, leaving only the screen to bar intruders and then fled up the stairs to her bedroom, closing the door behind her. She opened the bedroom window, took a seat at the drums, and launched into a routine. She could hear the incessant ringing of the house phone downstairs, followed by angry voices recording messages on the answering machine. She couldn't make out the messages, but things were going as planned. After a while, the incessant barking stopped and she assumed the animals were napping.

During a pause in her drumrolls, she heard the garage door. Mom was home a little early. She grabbed the new smart phone, cued up the video app, and quietly slipped out of her room. The noxious smell of urine assaulted her senses and a dark wet pool was visible in front of Charla's closed bedroom door. Under her breath she mouthed, "Well, aren't you a nice doggy, whichever one did it."

She crept down the steps, her eyes roaming over the living room below, which was now in disarray with cushions on the floor and vases of purple artificial flowers toppled and broken. Lavender and purple throw pillows littered the floor. Stuffing bulged out of the corner of one white couch cushion where the dogs had chewed it.

She reached the bottom step as Charla entered the kitchen, laden with bags of food from the Rib Kitchen.

Courtney extended her arm around the corner and aimed the phone in that direction just in time to catch two large objects burst right through the hole they had made in the screen. That explained their sudden quiet time in which they ran amok in the house. They galloped across the room and took flying leaps straight for the bags of ribs.

The wide-eyed shock on Charla's face was priceless and Courtney had to stifle a laugh. The dogs grabbed the food, turned, and ran outdoors where they immediately began wrestling and tugging to get them torn open. Ribs, fries, and coleslaw containers flew everywhere as the two behemoths wolfed down the contents of the dinner, stopping periodically to look up and dare Charla to take the food back.

Eyes wide, and seemingly speechless, Charla appeared rooted to the spot.

After pocketing the phone, Courtney sauntered into the kitchen. "Where's dinner?"

Her mother finally recovered, slamming her handbag to the floor and stalking towards Courtney with fire in her eyes. "Where did those two come from?" Her hands clenched in anger and her face reddened in spite of the covering of makeup.

Courtney casually glanced at the beasts. "Do you mean Brutus and Cezar? I'm fostering them for a while."

"No you're not!" Charla yelled. "Call the owners and get them back here. You have crossed the line." She wagged her finger in Courtney's face. "You...you..." she stopped when her eyes began to roam the adjacent family room where plants lay toppled and newspapers were strewn and chewed to pieces. She walked into the living room and cried out, "No, no, no. Look at what you've done."

"I didn't do that." Courtney surveyed the damages wrinkling her nose at the enormous pile of feces on the white carpet in front of a lavender floral armchair. "I was upstairs in my bedroom practicing the drums."

"Then how did this happen?" Charla screamed, "You let them into the house!"

"They were outside when I went up. They must have managed to bully their way through the screen all by themselves." She stooped down and picked up a white sofa cushion, glancing at the wet teeth marks on it. She placed it back on the couch. "I guess your maid will have a big job to do tomorrow. Now can we eat?"

Charla turned on her heel and headed for the kitchen. As she passed by the guest bath under the circular staircase, she wrinkled her nose and sneered. "What is that smell? Did the toilet overflow?"

Courtney pointed to the "Out of Order" sign. "You can't blame the dogs for that. It was your rent-a-stalker. He left that for you before he sped off for home to change into clean underwear." She had to turn her back and stifle a laugh.

Charla let out an exasperated "Ugh!" and proceeded to the telephone on the kitchen counter.

Courtney followed. "Who are you calling?"

Charla ignored her. "I need Animal Control," she yelled curtly into the phone.

Courtney swiftly reacted, grabbing it from Charla. "You can't do that."

"The hell I can't!" She started to dial again.

Courtney's shoulders sagged. "I volunteered to foster them until the Great Dane Society can find a home for them."

"You what—are you insane?" Charla's mouth gaped as the telephone remained poised in the air. "How do you expect to pay the fine that will be assessed because those monsters violate the rules in this area? Look at the mess they've made in here. How do you expect to fix that?" She stared angrily at Courtney.

Her eyes drifted to the patio and yard where they darted back and forth eyeing the damages outside. After finishing off the food, the dogs lazily sprawled on the chaise lounges, licking the remains off their lips and smearing bar-b-que sauce on the cushions. Food wrappers scattered in the breeze, some of them landing on the surface of the pool. "They are not staying and that is final! I'll deal with you later." She shoved the receiver at Courtney. "Call whomever you have to and tell them to come and get the beasts immediately or I will call the city's Animal Control. You have thirty minutes to get rid of them."

Courtney hesitated and looked away.

"Now, Courtney!" She turned and angrily stomped away, ascending the stairs.

Courtney was looking up the phone number in her phone when she heard a scream. She smiled. "I guess you found the new indoor pool," she whispered under her breath.

The nice man who delivered the dogs wasn't so nice when he showed up to take them back. "I thought you said your mother approved of this."

"She did," Courtney lied. "But you didn't warn me those two beasts were a wrecking crew."

"They are puppies. They have to be monitored in the house." He said defensively. "I told you they needed to be kept outside until it gets too hot for them."

She shrugged. "Well they broke down the screen door and got in, doing a lot of damage." She directed his attention to the destroyed living room. "My mother is furious. You will be lucky if she doesn't sue your ass. Now please take them and go." She watched as he loaded the beasts into his van, feeling sorry that she had to use him as a pawn in her game. She was closing the door when he turned and hurried back.

"Did you forget something?" she asked innocently as he stood there nervously hesitating.

He cleared his throat. "I was wondering…"

"What!" she barked impatiently.

"Could…could I have your grandmother's phone number?" He shuffled his feet and looked down, his face turning red as if embarrassed.

"Why? She doesn't like your animals either. She won't foster them." She started to close the door in his face.

"No, please. I recently lost my wife and I kind of liked your grandma and…"

"Lillian. Her name is Lillian. Have you got a piece of paper?"

He magically produced a little notebook from his pocket and a pen, smiling endearingly. "Do you think she would go out with me?"

Courtney looked him up and down. "I guess you have to ask her yourself." After reading off the numbers, she closed the door.

"My, my, Grandma, what big mojos you have," she mumbled under her breath and headed up the stairs. "I guess I should post the video to the net."

The double doors to Charla's bedroom remained closed and a large bath towel in front of them was absorbing the urine pool. Sounds of water running in the shower came from the other side.

"This might be a good time to throw a few things in a backpack and call Grandma for a ride," she whispered under her breath. "I will be sleeping on her couch tonight while the nuclear fallout blows over."

30

Night had fallen by the time Lillian arrived back home with Courtney in tow. She had answered her granddaughter's desperate plea to spend the night on her couch, thereby avoiding the combat zone for a few hours.

After picking her up outside the gated community, they had stopped for dinner. While waiting for their meal, Courtney pulled up the video and together they watched it, laughing so loudly that other people started to stare at them. "This is going on YouTube."

"Do you think that's wise? It might get back to her on Facebook."

"What can she do—kick me out? Send me back to school?"

"It's more likely she will be all over me for this. Now we are both in hot water."

"Oh, snap. So what else is new?" Courtney shrugged and pocketed the phone. "Let's eat."

Lillian's phone rang numerous times in the course of the evening. She ignored it and finally turned it off, choosing to avoid confrontation until they got home. Charla needed a cooling off period and the two of them needed time to prepare their defense.

"What made you think of orchestrating this caper?" Lillian asked between bites.

"It was your comment that my mother never liked pets of any kind, especially big ones."

"Wouldn't a little poodle have done the trick?" Lillian dipped a French fry in catsup and popped it into her mouth.

"What do you think? I figured it had to be something big enough and destructive enough to force her to banish me back to school." She wiped some mustard from the corner of her mouth and grinned.

"Wow. I never would have thought of Great Danes. I didn't even know there was such a thing as foster care for dogs."

"Oh, by the way, Grandma," Courtney grinned and winked. "Remember the nice man who delivered them?"

"Yes. What about him?" Lillian's mind flashed back to the extended handshake and his piercing blue eyes. Her heart skipped a beat. She took a deep breath to calm herself.

"He wants to call you for a date."

The fry she was about to bite into stopped in front of her lips. "No! Did he say that?"

"He asked for your number and I gave it to him. He said he lost his wife and he's lonely. So do you think you would go out with him?"

"I don't know. I haven't considered dating since your Grandpa passed. I don't think I know how. I went into such a panic when Jim Boyd chased me around that I reported him for stalking. All he wanted to do was return my sunglasses. I could have crawled under the floor tile, I was so embarrassed."

"Well, apparently, *dog boy* liked your mojo," she glanced at Lillian's ample boobs, "when he shook your hand. I saw where his eyes landed and it wasn't on your forehead."

"Maybe he just wanted my number so he could chew me out for being an accomplice to your escapade. You did after all use him and those dogs to make a point. You didn't have any intention of actually fostering them for any period of time did you?"

Courtney dropped her eyes to her empty plate. "No." She rolled up her napkin and set it on the table. "I didn't count on things getting so out of hand in such a hurry. I really thought it might take a few days for mother to erupt in a nuclear explosion. She was going to call the Animal Control to take them to the pound. I had to relent and call the Society to come and get them."

"And the mess they made? Who is going to clean that up?"

"The maid comes in tomorrow. It's probably better that I'm not around. She always rants in Spanish when she sees my room." The image flashed in her mind of her un-made bed, and floor carpeted with discarded clothing, shoes and socks. "I can imagine what she will say when she sees the rest of the house tomorrow."

"For now, you and I are on the lam," Lillian chuckled. "We'll lay low and let your mother get over her anger."

When the two mischief-makers burst through the front door, Cora looked up from her newspaper where she was working a crossword puzzle. She frowned over the top of her reading glasses. "What have you two been up to? I ask that because Charla has been calling repeatedly to see if you have come home yet. She's ranting and raving. She says she is going to kill the both of you."

"Gosh, we're scared." Courtney and Lillian mocked in unison.

"You should be. Now come over here, sit down and tell Mama what you did." She patted the sofa. "Then I will decide what punishment you children need." She frowned, but her eyes twinkled, giving her away.

Courtney cued up the video and handed the phone to Cora who watched in stunned silence. "Oh, my God, where did those horses come from?"

"Not horses," Courtney corrected, "Great Danes. I *borrowed* them for a day…okay, half a day. They have gone back now, but they accomplished my purpose." She replayed the video again and then posted it to YouTube.

"Did you make your point?" Cora fixed her with a severe, stern teacher-to-bad-student stare.

Courtney shrank back and shrugged her shoulders. "I might have overdone it a little? I need to lay low over here until the fire-eating dragon goes to work tomorrow and the housekeeper is finished cleaning up. Right now, there is toxic fall out in that area and I would just as soon not be there when Rosario shows up in the morning."

"So, Celia and I are in a positon of aiding and abetting fugitives in your campaign to topple your mother's pedestal. She's been ruling from it for some time now." Cora put down the puzzle and stood.

"We didn't mean to," Courtney replied, "but I guess so."

Cora headed for the kitchen. "Okay then, let's have some popcorn and pick out a movie to watch."

Courtney's flip phone rang again. She looked at the caller's number. "It's Mom." She let it go to voicemail

31

When Celia cruised up in her PT in the morning and pulled into the driveway, Charla was waiting.

"Hey, Charla, you're out early. I just got off work. What's up?"

"I can't reach my daughter. She took off last night and she isn't answering her phone."

"What would make her do that?" She eyed Charla suspiciously. "Did she run away from home? It's none of my business, but did you have another argument?"

"That's putting it mildly. Just let me in the house. I'll see if she's here and if not, I'll be on my way."

Celia eyed Charla who was dressed in her usual flawless fashion reeking of money. Her Cadillac parked at the curb rarely had a blemish on it. She turned over in her mind all the slights over the past years the bitch had done to Lillian. "It's seven in the morning. Everyone is still in bed asleep."

"I just got here a second ago. Would you prefer I ring the bell and pound on the door?"

Celia barely had any tolerance for the woman, but she shrugged. "Okay, but be quiet, and keep it civil." She unlocked the door and entered as quietly as possible. "Be quiet," she whispered.

Charla barged into the living room expecting to see Courtney asleep on the sofa. The room was vacant, the sofa undisturbed. "I expected the little brat to be couch-surfing."

"See, there you go. No wonder you don't get along with Lillian or Courtney. You always come on negative and nasty." Celia opened the door and motioned for her to go. "Now you need to leave."

"Not until I check the other rooms." She stomped loudly down the tile hall on her stiletto heels. "Courtney, come out. I've had enough of this shit."

Cora's door opened and she stood there rubbing the sleep from her eyes, her hair standing on end, styled by a night of contact with a rumpled bed pillow. She whispered to Charla, "Will you keep the noise down? What the hell do you want at this hour?"

Charla turned, with anger in her eyes. "Where is she?"

"You know where your mother's room is. It's no big mystery." Her eyes darted to Lillian's closed door. "I guess I may as well put on the coffee pot. If Charla can't sleep, nobody sleeps," she mumbled as she walked past the intruder, *accidentally* elbowing her in the process.

Charla burst into Lillian's room and switched on the light. There was no sign of either one of them. She whirled around and stormed into the kitchen. "Where are they? I know my mother helped Courtney last night. She's in on this."

Cora turned from setting up coffee and fixed Charla with a shriveling expression. "You need to calm down, sit down, and chill out. Your daughter is nineteen years old. She's an adult. She doesn't need a bodyguard. You don't need to ground her or keep her locked up as if she's a child. She needs to be free to pursue her dreams. You should let go and allow her to do that."

"But I…"

"Don't interrupt me," Cora said with the authoritative voice she uses in the classroom. "I have watched you be nasty to your mother, hurt her feelings, brush her off like a gnat, and cause her to have health problems…"

"It's none of your business…"

As if disciplining a bad student, Cora took a step forward and pointed to the chair. "Sit down and stop interrupting!"

"You can't talk to me like that." Charla squared her shoulders and backed up a step. "This is really none of your business."

"It becomes my business when you storm into my house making demands. Now sit down and let me talk, or get out." She waved her hands wildly and stalked toward the woman.

"Just tell me where I can find Courtney and my mother."

"She mentioned a trip to Laughlin to see a concert last night," Cora lied.

"I didn't give Courtney permission to go anywhere." Charla fished in her purse and came up with her phone.

"She's an adult. She doesn't need your permission."

"I can have my mother arrested for interfering in my efforts to parent my child."

"As I said," Cora raised her voice a few decibels, "Courtney is an adult. Now you should go. I'm wasting my time trying to turn you into a human being."

Charla seemed to be standing her ground.

"Get out!" Cora stalked toward her. Charla backed up slowly, and then turned on her heel and walked swiftly to the front door, slamming it as she exited.

Celia looked out the front window. "She's gone." She turned around and faced Cora. "So where did they go if they're not here?"

Cora returned to the kitchen, poured a cup of coffee and sat down. Celia followed, but opted for a glass of milk. "They did come home last night, but after a lot of discussion, we assumed the dragon would attack this morning, so we made other plans."

"Okay, so where did they go and why is Charla so furious? I feel as if I fell asleep in a movie and missed the whole plot."

Cora commenced filling Celia in on events. She retrieved her smart phone and pulled up the YouTube video to show her. That drew a laugh from both of them. "No wonder Charla is so angry. I suppose she blames Lillian for cooking it up."

"Courtney did it all on her own, but Lillian is guilty by association."

"It's obvious; Courtney has really done it now. This isn't going to help Lillian's relationship with Charla. It sounds like a situation for the Doctor Phil show." She giggled. "I'm sorry I missed the whole thing." She gulped down her glass of milk and set the empty glass in the sink. "I have to go to bed. I'm bushed."

Celia ambled down the hallway, opened her bedroom door and stepped inside. Two shadows appeared from behind the door, startling her. She jumped back and yelled, "Yikes! You scared the shit out of me."

Lillian and Courtney laughed. They stood there in their pajamas grinning. Lillian spoke first. "I hope you don't mind. We slept in your bed last night. Just give me a minute and I'll change the sheets for you."

Celia looked over at her rumpled bed. "Don't bother. You don't have any cooties. But did you have to scare me like that?"

"We're sorry." They hugged Celia and planted kisses on her forehead.

"We figured she would be over here early looking for us, and we knew she would look in my room, so we borrowed yours. She wouldn't barge in here," Lillian whispered.

"You can stop whispering. She's gone. Did you hear the whole exchange?"

"You'd have to be deaf not to hear it." Lillian frowned.

"What now?" Courtney asked Lillian as she closed the door to Celia's room and headed for the kitchen.

"It's a big city with lots of entertainment. She's only one woman. How fast can she catch up to us?" Lillian grinned. "Aren't the fields in bloom in Death Valley about now? We could take a road trip. Cora, would you like to ride along with us? We can stop for lunch somewhere."

"Sit down and have some coffee." She put bowls on the table and an assortment of cereals. "We can't go without eating first. Do you want some juice?"

As Lillian drove up the highway towards Death Valley, Courtney amused herself in the back seat with her new phone. When a giggle erupted, Cora asked, "What's so funny?"

"Cora, I forgot to mention the man who picked up the dogs wants a date with Grandma."

"Really; is he good looking?" asked Cora.

Lillian shrugged. "He's okay. He's tall. Maybe you would like him."

Cora shook her head. "I was married my whole life to one man and we had a loving relationship. I'm not sure I could date again. It would be like cheating on his memory."

Lillian burst out laughing and nearly drove off the road. "Cora, you're always saying you would like a little sack time once in a while. You bring it up all the time."

"Yes, but I'd prefer something younger."

"So, you want to be a cougar?" Courtney asked.

"I guess you could say that. After all, I'm old, I'm not dead."

Lillian laughed. "You had your chance with Jim Boyd, but now he's taken."

"Sorry, Lil, he didn't fit the bill—oh look at the field of flowers!"

32

The hour was very late when the three women returned home. Courtney was asleep in the back seat. Lillian roused her. "Wake up, we're home."

They entered the house quietly. Celia's PT was in the driveway, indicating she had the night off. She was lounging in the living room in front of the television. "Did you have fun?"

"The flowers were beautiful, but remind me to make the next trip up there an overnighter. That's a long drive for one day."

Celia yawned. "I stayed up to make sure my *children* got home safely, now I'm going to bed. Good night."

Courtney took out the flip phone and turned it on. She had missed thirty-five calls. "Doesn't my mother have anything else to do besides call me?"

Lillian sighed. "Give her a call back and let her know we are okay. She can relax and chill out. Tell her I'll bring you home tomorrow."

"Should I tell her where we've been?"

"I don't think she will care. Just tell her you will see her tomorrow. Now I need to go to bed." She yawned and headed to her room. "You'll have to sleep with me tonight."

After Courtney's call to check in, she lingered for a few minutes with Cora. "My mother doesn't like it when she's being ignored."

Cora picked up the remote and turned the television off. "It seems to run in the family. Your grandmother struggles with the same thing. Your mother never seems to have time for her. It's so sad. Lillian is a good woman and a lot of fun to be around."

"I know. I love her so much," Courtney agreed. "I'm going to miss her when I go back to school."

"So you are going back?" Cora raised an eyebrow.

"If I have to take a bus, I'll get back there."

"Where will you live?"

"I guess I never mentioned it. I have my own place. Mom had the idea that living in a dorm wasn't good enough for me, so she bought a little one-bedroom condominium near campus. I can just imagine the condition of it now. We left in such a hurry. The garbage must smell horrid by now. There was no time to empty it before she kidnapped me. The food in the fridge probably looks like lab specimens by now. I really need to go back before she gets any madder and decides to sell it. All my stuff is still there, including my car."

"I didn't realize that. Of course, Charla doesn't tell us very much. We hardly see her."

Courtney rose to go. "Maybe I can get Grandma to drive me back to L.A. I just need to go home long enough to pack up a few things and arrange for shipping my drums. I'm sure my mother will be happy to get those out of her house."

"Just remember your mother loves you in her own way and she felt she was protecting you from making some wrong decisions. You should never leave on a sour note. Try to make things right." She rose from the sofa where she had been drinking a bedtime glass of milk. "Now I'm turning in. I'll see you in the morning."

33

The next day, Courtney sank low in the front seat, as Lillian cruised up to the curb in front of Charla's house. Parked in the driveway in front of the open garage door was a carpet cleaning truck. Another car parked at the curb sporting signs on the side of a house cleaning service.

"Isn't this over-kill?" Courtney scoffed. "Rosario could have cleaned everything up." She exited the car and walked slowly through the garage.

Lillian followed. "I don't see Charla's car. I hope she's at work."

"I hope so too," Courtney snorted.

The two conspirators walked into the kitchen and cautiously looked around. Rosario, the regular housekeeper, sat on a stool at the kitchen counter, scarfing down a burrito.

She quickly swallowed the mouthful and then launched into a barrage of Spanish, shaking her finger at Courtney and spitting saliva and food particles. She slid from the stool and advanced in Courtney's direction, unleashing angry, unintelligible words in Spanish.

Courtney and Lillian sidled towards the staircase, and then turned and ascended them, while the barrage of Spanish followed them. "What do you think she was saying?" whispered Courtney.

"I don't know, but I don't think she was complimenting us on our fashion sense."

They quickly made it to Courtney's room and locked the door behind them. A little surprise greeted them.

Disassembled and demolished drums lay about the room. Punctured as if stomped on, they were no longer useable. Strewn around the floor, the dented cymbals appeared to have suffered from assault by an angry hammer, which lay nearby.

Courtney picked up a pair of sticks as she slumped down on her bed. Tears formed in her eyes as she surveyed the damages. "Why would she do this? I'm so sorry, Grandma. I'll get a job and pay you back for them."

Lillian sat down beside her and sighed. "I haven't seen her lose her temper like this since she was a child. I think she's angry that she can't control you anymore." She swept the room with her hand. "This, however, was uncalled for. Don't worry about paying me back. I'll get it out of her, one way or the other."

"I can't stand to stay here anymore, Grandma. I need to go back to California. Even if I have to get a job and pay my own way, I'll do it. I can wait tables."

"I can help you until you find a job," Lillian said as she swiped at a tear. "Your mother apparently can't accept rejection. I remember the tantrum she threw after losing a dance competition way back when she was nine. It was ugly and embarrassing in front of all those other parents and kids. I had to ground her for a month. She did this same thing to her room."

"What did you do?" Courtney sniffled.

"I gathered up everything she had broken and everything she threw on the floor. It went into the garbage can out on the curb. The trash collector took it before she had a chance to get anything back. She thought twice before raging like that again."

Courtney went to her closet and pulled out a suitcase. She began throwing clothes into it. Lillian made an effort to fold them and pack them more neatly, but couldn't keep up. When the suitcase was stuffed, they headed for the door. Courtney clutched the drumsticks as tears ran down her cheeks. "I think she needs an anger management course."

"I don't think I would approach that subject anytime soon. She needs to have time to chill out. In the meantime, you'll stay with me."

"I think I'm starting to understand her a little more," Courtney sighed. "I always thought she was in control, but now I think she's a tightly wound clock that suddenly snapped a spring."

Lillian paused at the bottom of the steps and watched as the carpet cleaner worked vigorously on a stubborn spot on the white carpet. "She's definitely come undone. I haven't been able to break through her walls since your father left. She's kept everything inside and I still don't know why they split."

Courtney took one last look around the house and spoke wistfully. "I don't think she's keeping it in any longer."

Before they exited the front door, Courtney removed the flip phone from her pocket and placed it on the table in the entry.

"Do you think we should stop by your mother's office and try to make peace?" Lillian darted a glance sideways. Courtney didn't respond as she tugged and bounced the heavy suitcase down the steps. "Cora may be right about kissing and making up before we take you back to school."

Courtney brightened. "Does that mean another road trip?"

"Honey, I would do anything for you. First, however, we should try to make nice with your mother—after she's had time to cool down. Let's stop by her office. She can't make a scene there without making herself look bad."

"Are you sure about that?" Courtney smirked.

As her car pulled away from the curb, Lillian answered, "When it comes to business, your mother is a very good actress. She can put on an appropriate face and play the scene. She missed her calling. I don't think she would go ballistic in front of any customers, or her employees. It's a safe place to try and smooth things over with her."

Courtney suddenly turned pale. "Stop the car. I have to throw up."

Courtney opened the door before Lillian came to a complete stop, and emptied her breakfast on the curb.

Horns honked and cars changed lanes to get around them. "What was that all about?" she asked as she drove on.

"After what I saw in my room, I'm scared to death. My stomach is quivering."

"Take some deep breaths. If it upsets you too much, we can go back to my house." Lillian turned at the next light and headed back in the direction of her home. "I think the two of you need some space. I'll call your mom and tell her you will be staying with me until the weekend and then I'll drive you back to L.A. Maybe Cora will accompany us so I don't have to return alone."

"I'm going to have to find a job. She took away my credit cards."

"Working never hurt anyone. It's a good character building time of life. You might even like it." She tried to sound upbeat, recalling her own struggle as a young girl, working and going to school. Courtney's efforts to become independent of her rich mother might be an even greater struggle, but a lesson she should learn.

Courtney frowned. "When did you ever have to work?"

Lillian shot a shocked glance at Courtney. "I guess this family really does have a communication problem."

"What do you mean?"

Raising her eyebrow, Lillian replied, "I mean, do you think I was born old and retired?"

"Well, no. I know that Grandpa taught school. I know that you were always there to take care of me and tuck me in bed at night when Mom and Dad had to work. I know that Gramps always read me a story. Other than that, I guess what you did with the rest of your day never crossed my stupid kid brain."

Lillian pulled into the driveway at home and cut the silent engine. "Let's have a bite to eat and I'll tell you about our lives. I don't think grandchildren ever really understand where grandparents come from. We are just here. I regret that I never asked my grandmother any questions about her life and now she's gone and it's too late."

Over lunch of toasted cheese sandwiches and tomato soup, Lillian began. "Your grandpa and I were childhood sweethearts. We married as soon as we graduated high school and turned eighteen. We couldn't afford a wedding, so we were married in my parent's living room by a Justice of the Peace and my ring came from Woolworth's Dime Store.

Charlie replaced it on our fifteenth anniversary with a real diamond. We wanted an education, so we both took whatever jobs we could get and we attended a local college. Back then, tuition was as little as thirty dollars for a semester for one class."

"Thirty dollars," Courtney blurted, "I could afford that."

"It sounds cheap, but it wasn't when you figure we worked for a little over a dollar an hour. Charlie worked in a hardware store days and took classes at night. I cashiered in a grocery store and took night classes. We had to live with his parents because we couldn't afford rent. On weekends, we picked up yard work for a few extra bucks. It was hard, but we were in love and anything was possible."

"I didn't realize. I'm sorry."

"Don't be. I suppose I should have discussed this more with you, but kids never seem to be interested in the past; they only concentrate on the here and now. Anyway, it took us several years, but Charlie got a teaching degree and a position. I continued to work and eventually got a Bachelor's in business and continued working in retail. I eventually got a Supervisor's position. We concentrated on becoming financially stable and then we wanted a family. At twenty-nine years old, doctors considered me too old to start a family, but we had Charla anyway. We wanted more kids, but they just never happened. By then I was able to be a stay-at-home mom. I gave your mother everything she wanted. She got dance lessons, music lessons, and costumes. Perhaps I spoiled her. We thought since she was the only one, we would do it up right. I'm afraid in the process she became spoiled and demanding, throwing temper tantrums when things didn't go her way."

"I know all about that. She's gone completely ballistic now."

"Anyway, when you came along, she said you would be an only child, so we packed up, sold our house and moved here. I'm glad we did and we don't regret it one minute. Your grandfather died a happy man because he loved you so much and he had the opportunity to watch you grow up." A tear slipped from the corner of Lillian's eye and she brushed it away. Even though Charlie had been gone three years, the sorrow still hurt like a fresh paper cut in her heart.

"I miss him a lot, Grandma. My best memories are the books he read to me at bedtime. He had a way of giving each character a different voice. He made me laugh. And he never missed a soccer practice or game."

Lillian wiped away another tear and continued. "Anyway, after we moved here, he taught school and I managed a drug store, working the early shift so we could be at your house to take care of you when your parents went to work at their jobs on the strip. It was hard because we got home late at night and then had to get up early to start all over again."

"Couldn't they pay a sitter? Did they pay you?"

"They didn't offer and we would have refused anyway. We love you with all our hearts. It was a pleasure to be there for you. However, what is so hurtful now is my estranged relationship with your mother. This is a time in my life when I expected payback in kind, like some time with her doing what mothers and daughters do together... shopping, lunching, and movies. I feel she's holding some kind of grudge. She has erected walls and she avoids me."

"I told her she should be nicer to you and she said it was none of my business." Courtney held Lillian's hand. "I'm sorry. But thanks for telling me all this."

"I'm sorry I haven't shared more with you in the past. Anyway, the lesson here is, if I can work my way through college and come out strong and financially stable without my parent's help, so can you."

Courtney paused for a moment as if absorbing all Lillian had said. "I think you're right. I'm going back to L.A. and I'm going to get a job. I can do it." She perked up and smiled. "I can do it."

"Yes you can. Now let's talk about your love life." Lillian plopped a bag of cookies on the table and poured herself a cup of coffee. "What's his name again?"

"His name is Lennie Becket and he's very talented. He plays keyboard and guitar and he has an awesome voice."

"You said you met him at a concert. Is he cute?"

"I think he is." Courtney's eyes took on that dreamy shine of infatuation. "He has curly strawberry blond hair and blue eyes."

155

"What did you say the name of the band is?"

"They don't have a name yet. They just call themselves *The Band.* When we talked about a new name, Lennie suggested *Trash,* but I told him I don't like that name and it doesn't shed a good light on our character. He agreed so we decided to wait for something else to come to mind."

Courtney retrieved a soda from the fridge. "I'm afraid to suggest something else until I can think of something better. It's not my band and he might resent me trying to name it."

"Is it a rap group or punk rock? Because that's what the word, *Trash* suggests. It sounds—well…trashy. I think they could improve on it and maybe reinvent the group. Who else is in the band? What kind of music do they play? How successful have they been so far?"

"So far they're still unknowns. They only get small gigs in coffee shops and shopping malls. There are two guitarists, the drummer and another girl. She sings backup. They play mostly current music like the ones you may have heard on the top ten charts. It's not hard rock. If it was, I wouldn't be interested in joining. The boys write most of the music themselves. They can't afford the complications of using somebody else's tunes."

"They don't sound *trashy.* Why don't we get pencil and paper, and have a think session. Maybe we can come up with something a little more appropriate for these young talented people." Lillian grabbed a grocery list pad and pen from the counter and sat back down.

The cookies were about gone and the coffee cold, when Courtney jumped up and down with excitement. I think we've got it, Grandma. I can't believe you thought of it. I love the name, *Pulsation.* I hope I can convince the band to use it."

Lillian kissed her on the forehead and smiled. "I would love to tell my friends that my granddaughter plays drums in a band. I think we've just hit a much better name. I hope Lennie likes it."

"I have to call him! I'm so excited."

Courtney was about to dial when the doorbell rang, interrupting her.

Lillian went to the door and peeked out the window by the front door. She frowned and whispered, "It's your mother."

"Well there's a mood killer." Courtney frowned, putting away her new phone. "Do we have to let her in?"

"It would be rude not to. If I'm going to take you back to school, I should do it on a good note. Let's work out a truce with her." The bell chimed twice more.

"Don't tell her about Lennie. She'll never let me go if she hears about him and my intention to get into the performing arts. I'm going to change my major."

Lillian whispered, "Then you better put on a good act. Grovel if you have to. Apologize, make promises, anything that will convince her you have made up your mind to be good and study hard."

The bell chimed incessantly. "I know you're home." Charla shouted. "Open up."

Courtney grabbed the doorknob. She whispered over her shoulder, "Show time."

Lillian scurried to the kitchen to clear the table, hiding the long list of band names the two conspirators had been writing down.

Charla sashayed into the house and went straight for the kitchen where Lillian was putting on a pot of coffee. "Do you want a cup?" she cast a glance over her shoulder.

Charla's face was sober but her eyes were angry. "What do you think you're doing, Mother?"

"I'm making coffee, dear."

Charla wasn't satisfied. "I mean, you kidnapped Courtney. She left an absolute mess at my house. I'm probably going to have to replace all the carpeting. Do you know how much that will cost?"

She slammed Courtney's flip phone down on the table, directing her gaze to the errant teen. "You left this behind."

Courtney defiantly stared back. "I didn't need it."

Charla retrieved the phone and dropped it into her bag. "Fine, you can learn to live without one. Now get your things. You're coming back home."

Courtney backed away. "No, Mother, I'm not. I'm going back to school. Grandma and I have been discussing it, and I'm going to get a job and work the rest of my way through. I'm not a child anymore, so stop treating me like one."

Charla threw her head back and laughed. "Do you really think you can get along without my money? I'm not giving you back your credit cards. You don't seem to know the difference between what you need to survive, and what you want or think you need. Those disgusting rags you're wearing are a prime example."

Courtney looked down at the torn pants she had purchased on the cruise. The holes and frays had grown with each wash. "I like these and they are all the rage at school."

Lillian glared at the daughter she no longer understood and raised her voice. "If you just showed up here to insult everybody, you can leave now. What you are doing is wrong. I thought you had finally outgrown the tantrums you threw as a kid when you didn't get what you wanted, but I was wrong. You've merely learned to put on an act pretending to be someone you are not. You're still that spoiled, demanding, selfish child. It's no wonder Herbie dumped you and fled to the other end of the world."

Charla squared her shoulders. "He's in Europe working. I hope he never comes back."

"He's the father of your child. Have some consideration for him," Lillian chided her. "Now either sit down and discuss our situation in a calm and respectable manner, or leave now. I'm not putting up with your crap anymore. Do you understand me?" She made eye contact to emphasize her point.

Charla paused, seeming to be pondering a fight-or-flight decision. She cast her gaze back and forth between Courtney and Lillian. After a long pause, she set her bag on the table and took a seat, frowning sourly.

Lillian poured coffee and set one of the mugs in front of Charla.

"Courtney, do you want anything to drink?"

Courtney shook her head negatively and took a seat meekly. She mumbled under her breath, "I still don't see anything wrong with my jeans."

"Who does that new white car in the driveway belong to?" Charla asked bluntly.

"It's mine," Lillian answered. "I got tired of your empty promises and I leased a new car. Do you want to bitch at me about that too?" She glared at Charla who seemed to sink a little as if deflating.

Lillian took a seat and sipped on her java.

Charla opened her mouth to speak, but Lillian raised her hand to silence her. "I'm going to do the talking," she said firmly.

"I don't know what your beef with me is and frankly, I no longer care. My primary concern is to get Courtney back on track and in school where she wants to go. That is at UCLA, not UNLV. Therefore, this weekend, I'm driving her home to the condo."

"What if the school won't take her back?" Charla asked indignantly. "She's been out for two weeks."

"Part of that time has been spring break." Courtney interjected. "We'll have to lie about the rest of the time."

Charla's coffee sat untouched, as she seemed to contemplate a response. "What would you suggest we tell them?"

Courtney questioned, "Are you going to help?"

Charla heaved a loud sigh of defeat. "It appears we have a two against one situation here, so I guess I must do something since you are determined to go back."

Lillian raised an eyebrow. "You're giving up easier than I would have thought. Why?"

"You saw what she did to my house. It's let her go or risk more damage. What do you want from me?"

"I'll drive her back," answered Lillian. "You can return her lap top and write a letter to the Dean explaining her absence." Lillian waited while Charla mulled that over.

Courtney piped up. "Tell them you jerked me out of school because I needed an emergency appendectomy. That's a good excuse to be absent. Tell them I'll re-enroll in the classes I screwed up, and take them over." She seemed to brighten and even smiled with enthusiasm.

Charla fixed Courtney with a hard glare. "I will only help if you promise to stop playing around on the internet. That was a dangerous thing to do."

Courtney rolled her eyes. "I told you that it was research for a paper I was going to turn in for extra credit, but you didn't give me a chance to explain before you went all ballistic. I'm never going to speak to Suzanne again for calling you and tattling on me. She got it all wrong and you got it all wrong."

"All the same, find another subject to write about. One good thing did come out of it. My detective contacted the authorities, and that predator went back to jail on a parole violation."

"Oh, yippee," Courtney mocked, "there are thousands more out there doing the same thing and now I can't expose them."

"It's not your job to expose them. That's my terms. There's to be no more net surfing such as you were doing. In return, I'll pay your tuition. You get a job, and buy your books and pay for your own car insurance and gas. You don't get a credit card funded by me anymore. Get your own if you need one. You will pay most of your own expenses."

"Do I get to stay in the condo?"

"You get passing grades in your classes, and you can use the condo. Start screwing up again and I'll start charging you rent."

"That sounds reasonable to me," Lillian agreed. "How about you, Courtney, does it sound like an arrangement you can live with?"

Courtney nodded. "What about my drum set?"

"What about it?" Charla asked with a hard expression on her face.

Courtney opened her mouth to speak, but only shrugged, and said, "Forget it." Her eyes met Lillian's as if to apologize again for the wasted expenditure.

Lillian nodded, almost imperceptibly. She rose from the table as if to adjourn the meeting.

Charla rose and picked up her heavy bag. "Are you coming with me," she directed her gaze to Courtney.

"I'll bring her home later. You can go back to work. How about meeting us for dinner somewhere?"

"Okay," Charla agreed. "Let's meet at Chili's; the one near my house?"

Courtney nodded. "Okay."

"See you at five." Charla turned and left without another word.

The two watched her drive away. "I don't know, Grandma. This all seemed too easy. I'm almost scared to step foot in her house again."

"I'm one phone call away and it's only until Friday. Now let's find something for you to wear for dinner that won't piss her off again."

34

Charla had just walked into her office with the intent to finish some paperwork and put a new listing on the internet for an impressive ten thousand square foot mansion at the Ridges. She plugged her phone into the computer to download the photos she had taken. The sale would bring her a nice fat commission.

She finished the upload and disconnected when her smart phone rang. The caller I.D. registered Ella's name and number, which brought on a delighted smile. Lately she had been too busy to call the aunt she adored. She answered.

Ella yelled loudly, "My Lord, Charla, I just saw the YouTube video. What were you thinking when you got two big dogs? What in the world are you going to do with them?"

Charla drew in a breath. "What are you talking about? I didn't get any dogs. Courtney thought she would pull a fast one on me, but the dogs were sent back immediately."

"Well that's a relief. The video is shocking and nearly knocked me off my chair laughing until I realized it was you."

"What video—what YouTube are you talking about?"

"It's posted on the internet—the one with the dogs rushing at you and stealing your dinner. I assumed Courtney recorded it. How is she anyway?"

Charla sat in stunned silence for a beat until she heard laughter coming from outside her office. "I'll have to call you back, Ella."

She ended the call and crept up behind her secretary's desk where several agents gathered around, all eyes on the monitor. Her hand flew to her mouth when she saw the dog attack. "How did that get on the internet?"

All the viewers turned in wide-eyed surprise to see an angry boss confronting them. "We…we…don't know," her secretary stuttered. She turned off the monitor and stood up nervously.

"I took Courtney's smart phone away. It had to be her, but how?"

Everyone shrugged and backed away, heading to their desks. "Maybe she borrowed a phone," the secretary suggested. "You'll have to ask her."

Charla turned on her heel and marched to her office. "My mother had something to do with this. I am sure of that." She closed her office door, sat down at the desk and clasped her hands to stop the shaking.

After taking a deep breath to calm her nerves, Charla poised her fingers over the keyboard and typed up two documents. She hit the print button, retrieved and stuffed them into her bag. A glance at her gold wristwatch indicated it was time to go kick some butt. She breezed past the receptionist. "Lock up for me, I'm going home."

Chili's parking lot was crowded and having to park way out and walk in her stiletto heels did not improve her mood. Charla was so angry that Lillian and Courtney had conspired to embarrass her that it took all her effort to remain composed in a public place. The people at this restaurant knew her well and she couldn't break character while in their presence so she took a deep breath and plastered on a smile as she entered the restaurant.

"Good evening Miss Charla." The girl smiled back. "Will that be a table for one tonight?" She grabbed a menu.

"No, I'm just dropping off something to some clients." She craned her neck and looked over the crowd. "Oh, there they are. I'll only be a minute. Thank you anyway." She marched resolutely to the table where Lillian and Courtney were engaged in pouring over their menus. She took a seat and placed her handbag in her lap.

Lillian smiled. "This is something the three of us haven't done in a long time. Here we are having dinner together. It's nice."

Charla didn't smile. "I saw the YouTube posting." She directed her comment to Courtney. "How did you manage to get a video of the dogs attacking me?"

Courtney shrank back and cast her eyes downward. "I have a new smart phone. You took my other one."

"How did you get that?" Antagonism was evident in her voice.

Courtney looked pleadingly at her grandmother, as if silently seeking help.

Lillian blurted, "I bought it for her. So sue me."

Charla glared at her mother as if she hated her. "You want a relationship with me yet you go behind my back and interfere with my attempt to teach my child a lesson."

"I disagree with your methods. I'm trying to counteract the damage you're doing."

"You embarrassed me in front of everyone I work with and employ. They found the video. Ella called and alerted me to its existence. I'm *never* going to live this down. How could you do this?"

Courtney raised her voice. "Grandma didn't do it. It was all my idea and my entire fault. She had nothing to do with it. Don't be mad at her. Be mad at me."

"Very well," Charla said in a snotty manner. She pulled the papers out of her bag. "This is the excuse you need to get back into school."

Courtney picked it up and read it. "Thanks."

Charla handed her the other paper. "This is an eviction notice. You have thirty days to clear your crap out of the condominium. I'm selling it. From now on, you pay your own way."

Courtney's mouth dropped open.

Lillian started to speak, but stopped.

Courtney replied in a near whisper. "What about tuition. Will you still be paying that?"

"The money I paid at the start of the school year is still on deposit. You can draw on it for tuition until it's exhausted. Then you're on your own." She picked up her purse and left abruptly.

35

Lillian watched Charla sashay away, and smile at the host as if nothing was amiss.

"Sometimes I hate that woman," Courtney said as tears formed. "I'm not hungry anymore. Can we leave?" She peered around at the diners, all of whom were enjoying their social time. She placed her napkin and menu on the table and rose to leave.

"Come on. We'll fix something at my house." Lillian steered a crushed Courtney out the door. "You're staying with me."

"I think I crossed the line with the dogs. She's really gone bat crap crazy now," Courtney said glumly. "Where am I going to live?"

As they put on the seat belts, Lillian heaved a sigh. "I didn't want to do it, but I think it's time to call your father."

Courtney's eyes went wide. "Why would you do that? Are you going to tattle on me about all the pranks I've pulled?"

"No," Lillian grinned. "We're going to tattle on your mother. Herbie loves you and he won't stand for what she's doing."

Courtney swiped away a tear. "He's in Paris right now. How's he going to help us from there?"

"If I know him, he'll find a way."

The aroma of a skillet meal met them when the pair walked in. "Have you eaten yet?" Cora asked as she turned from the range. "Dinner's almost ready."

Lillian answered, "Our dinner was ruined when an angry bitch walked in, made a scene, and spoiled our appetites. We decided to grab something here."

Courtney sniffed the concoction in the skillet. "It smells good enough to eat."

"Then wash up and set the table. I'm just popping the garlic bread in to warm it up."

When the delicious meal was over, Lillian and Courtney cleared the dishes and cleaned up the kitchen.

"What time do you think it is in Paris by now?" asked Lillian.

Courtney checked the kitchen clock and counted on her fingers. "I think it might be around six in the morning. I don't have Dad's number. It was in the phone that Mom repossessed." She turned away and whispered, "The bitch."

Lillian ignored the comment. "Don't worry, I have it. She retrieved her own phone from her purse, selected the number, and motioned for Courtney to sit down next to her at the table. It rang a number of times.

A sleepy voice came on the line. "Hello." Grunting and rustling sounds emitted from the phone and then the voice cleared. "Oh, hello Lillian, do you know what time it is over here?"

"Herbie, I have you on speaker phone. Courtney is here with me." She nudged the girl. "Talk to your dad."

"Hi, Daddy, we're sorry to bother you at this hour. Its evening here, but this is an emergency."

"Is something wrong?" Herbie's voice cleared and grew louder. "Are you sick? Are you hurt? Why are you talking on your grandmother's phone? What's going on?"

"Relax, Dad. Nothing like that is wrong. Mom is on the warpath. She jerked me out of school and brought me back home."

"Why?"

Lillian intervened. "We have a lot to tell you so listen up." She launched into the events of the past two weeks, including the part about the dogs, and concluding with the eviction notice.

There was a long silence on the Paris end.

"Herbie, are you still there?" Lillian spoke a little too loudly.

"Yes, I'm here. I'm glad you told me all this. Where is Charla now?"

"We don't know," Courtney whined, "but you can always reach her on her cell. Are you going to call her?"

"You bet I am. You two sit tight. I guarantee there will be some action in your favor before you go to bed tonight."

"When are you coming back?" Courtney asked, with tears streaming down her face. "I need you."

"Two weeks. I'll meet you in L.A. in two weeks. I love you Baby Cakes."

Courtney sniffled, "I love you too."

Lillian put her arm around her tearful granddaughter as she ended the call with, "Thank you Herbie, you've always been my favorite son-in-law."

He laughed, "I was your only son-in-law that I know about."

36

Wearing pajamas, Lillian and Courtney were on the sofa in the living room watching television with Cora when the doorbell rang.

Cora looked at the large decorator clock over the fireplace. "Who shows up after nine o'clock at night?"

Lillian grinned. "At this time of night, it's usually burglars. We better let them know we're home." She headed for the door, with Courtney following for backup, and turned on the porch light.

Charla, looking glum, wearing a jogging suit, and appearing uncharacteristically disheveled was leaning against the wall. She had a large tote bag in her hand. Lillian opened the door and spoke sourly, "Did you come to rub salt in our open wounds?"

"I didn't come to fight. May I come in?" Her demeanor was loose and slightly off balance.

Lillian reluctantly let her in.

Charla stepped inside and handed Courtney the bag. "Here's your laptop, your smart phone, your credit cards and a check to deposit for tuition. I would advise you to plan on attending summer school to make up your classes."

Courtney took it from her. "Why? Are you feeling remorse for treating me like trash? A few hours ago, you virtually disowned me. You acted as if you hated the both of us and you were about to put me out on the street with no place to live."

Charla lost her balance slightly, and slurred her words. "Let's just say I had an ep...epiphany when I got home. I may have made a mish...mishcaculation and I need to...to..." She paused as if searching for a word.

"Apologize?" Lillian interrupted. *Couldn't have been a bitchin' call from Herbie, could it?*

In an attempt to stand at her full height, Charla spoke defensively, "Well, this wasn't entirely my fault." She lost her balance and grabbed for the hall table for support.

"I disagree completely," Lillian spat in disgust. "By the way, did you drive over here in your condition?" she demanded as she looked out the side window to see if Charla's car was visible. "Are you drunk? How much alcohol have you had?"

"I didn't drive. U-u-u-Uber's waiting, or is it Lyft, I don't know. I have to go."

Lillian slammed the door shut and kept her hand on the doorknob. "Not until you apologize," she insisted, placing a firm grip on Charla's arm with her other hand. "I'm taking Courtney back to California, and you are not parting on a sour note. You've been getting away with treating me like crap, but you are going to kiss and make up with your daughter. If you don't, I will go cancel your ride, and you can walk home." She glared at her, determined to make her comply.

The standoff lasted for a few heartbeats while tipsy Charla seemed to weigh her option, glancing at the closed door and back at her antagonists. Then her shoulders sagged.

"I'm sorry, Courtney," she said woodenly, "I didn't think things through." She gave the girl a brief perfunctory hug, and then backed up toward the door.

Lillian continued to grip the doorknob. "In spite of your lack of friendliness toward me, I am your mother, and I love you, although you make it hard sometimes." Lillian had to tip her head back to stare up into Charla's eyes. She added, "Would you care to settle things between us while we're all making nice?"

Charla blinked first and looked down at the floor as if she were going to acquiesce. A long pregnant pause ensued, looking as though she was silently rehearsing her words. She seemed to be at a loss for something meaningful to say. Her mouth opened several times, but nothing came out.

Lillian glared at Charla who refused to look at her. "I'm waiting."

After a long silent pause, Charla mumbled, "Not right now. I just can't. Not tonight."

Lillian opened the door. "Okay, but don't wait forever. I'm not getting any younger. I'd really like to know what your beef is before I'm put in the ground."

Charla paused, as if she were about to change her mind, but shrugged and abruptly walked out the door, tottering slightly as she made her way to the waiting car.

Courtney watched her leave. "I'm sorry Grandma. I guess she's not ready to talk about whatever is on her conscience." She took out her phone. "I have to call Daddy." She dialed and put it on speaker.

Without preamble, Herbie answered with, "Did you get all your stuff back?"

"Yes I did and thank you Daddy. How did you do it?"

"I called her and reminded her of the terms of our divorce settlement."

"What terms are you talking about?"

"I'll give you the nutshell version. She doesn't have to liquidate any property and pay me my share of joint assets for as long as you are in college. It's her responsibility to pay for your education and all your living expenses while you are a student. If you leave college for any reason and cease to be a student, my attorney will start the division of property process and she will have to begin selling off assets, starting with the family home of which she's so proud. Lastly, she will have to start paying me alimony because she always made more money than I did during the marriage. If she gives you anymore flack, you call me."

Courtney's eyes grew wide. "Daddy, you're so awesome. How did you ever get terms like that?"

"I'm not going to dredge up the whys and wherefores. Suffice it to say, I had an ace lawyer."

"But, Dad…"

"She's your mother and she loves you. So cut her some slack. Sometimes she's too impulsive."

"This sounds so unfair to you."

"Don't even think about my needs. I have a good job. It's your duty to get the best education your mother's money can buy for you. Whatever else you want to do after college, I will support wholeheartedly. For now, you need to go back to school."

"I guess you're right," Courtney sighed. "Grandma is driving me home this weekend. I love you Daddy."

"I love you too. Tell your grandma she's still the best mother-in-law anybody could have. Now I have to go. I'll see you in a couple of weeks."

"Bye, Dad, I can't wait to see you."

Lillian heaved a sigh. "I think I need some popcorn and a beer to celebrate our victory. Do you want some soda?"

"First I have to call Lennie with the good news." She punched his number and wandered into Lillian's bedroom.

37

The hour was late when Lillian and Cora returned home on Sunday night. They had driven Courtney back to the condominium where she lived near school and helped her tidy the place up, clean out the science projects in the fridge and stock up on groceries.

Lennie Becket stopped by, giving them a chance to meet the young man that Courtney cared so much for.

"It was nice to meet her boyfriend," Lillian commented as she carried her overnight bag into the house. "He seemed so soft spoken and polite; not at all what I would expect from an aspiring rock musician."

"I hope the past two weeks has given her a little more incentive to stay in school. She can play drums on the weekends." Cora added, "Education should be the number one priority at her age. Do you think we managed to impress that young man with the importance of it?"

"Let's have a cup of hot chocolate before we go to bed." Lillian headed for the kitchen. "As for Lennie, I think we may have gotten the message across."

When the women awoke the next morning, Celia had just come home from her shift and was setting up the coffee urn. "Welcome back girls. I picked up donuts on my way home. Coffee's brewing. It's been too quiet around here over the weekend."

She set out cereal, bowls and milk. "Now that the crisis is over, can we get back to the subject of finding some summer activities for us to do when bowling ends?"

Lillian filled her coffee cup and sat down. She brought Celia up to date on the events of the past few days. "There's still the matter of my relationship with Charla. None of this did anything to repair that, in fact, I hope she won't pull further away from me. Should I go to her and grovel?"

"No!" Celia and Cora snapped in unison.

Celia cleared her throat. "My advice is to leave her alone for a while. She needs to lick her wounds. After all, she's eating crow right now and you know that will not sit well with her."

"You're probably right. I'm sure she is a little miffed that I called Herbie and sic'd him on her case."

Celia snickered. "Yeah, those big rental dogs had nothing on Herbie. He went after her like a pit bull."

"So," Cora spoke between bites of cereal, "shall we sign up for a summer league, join the Y and do water aerobics, take a trip in your snazzy new car, or what? We need to put all this behind us and move on."

"You guys are just trying to take my mind off my broken relationship with Charla."

"Guilty," Celia said with a grin. "For your own good and your blood pressure, you need to just forget about her for now and enjoy the summer coming up. We can take some two or three day excursions; maybe go to Laughlin or Sedona. I've never been to Lake Havasu. I'd like to see that London Bridge."

Lillian eyed her. "Don't you have to work?"

"I have a lot of accrued vacation days so I can make arrangements for time off."

"What do you think, Cora?"

Cora grinned. "I think it's time to put some real miles on that car. So let's make up a list of things to do, because we aren't getting any younger."

"Yeah," Lillian agreed, "like a Do or Die List."

"Don't say die!" Celia said hastily.

38

When Wednesday rolled around, there had still been no word from Charla. She hadn't even called to see if Courtney got back to school. Lillian thought about giving her a call, but what would it accomplish. Charla was never one to apologize for anything and expecting it now was a waste of time and energy.

After bowling, the three friends headed off to the Senior Center for lunch. A few weeks had passed during the time they were distracted with Courtney and her plans to turn Charla's world topsy-turvy. When they walked into the center with food on their minds, dating was the last thing anyone wanted to think of. That man with the monstrous dogs had still not called Lillian for a date. The girls concluded he suffered from cold feet.

Lillian and Cora cued up in line at the food counter to fill their plates while Celia held three chairs at the table they chose. After paying, Lillian headed for her seat when a man she had never seen before stepped into her path.

She was about to complain, when he spoke in the most endearing Irish brogue she had ever heard. "Excuse me, Colleen," he said with a sweep of his hat and a low bow. "Squeamish McPhee—may I be getting you something to drink?"

Lillian, stunned by his boldness, was slow to respond. "My name isn't Colleen. It's Lillian."

"Lillian. Aye that is a nice name. May I help you with that?" Squeamish motioned to her plate.

"No, I can manage," Lillian replied as she studied the man. His green eyes twinkled below thick graying eyebrows while the top of his head evidenced a sparse mixture of pale red and silver hair. "You must be new here. Are you waiting tables?"

"No ma'am, I'm new to the city. I've moved over from Ireland to be near me daughter. She suggested I should be getting to know people of me own age while she works. So here I am. Let me walk you to your table."

Lillian walked in a fog as if struck dumb with Squeamish following along. "Would you like to sit with us? This is my roommate, Cora. The other one, Celia, is over there in line. We can save you this seat if you like." She gestured towards an empty place.

"Aye, that'd be fine, but only if you allow me to fetch your beverage. What would you like?" said the Irishman in his thick brogue. His green eyes seemed to bore into Lillian as she looked up at the new visitor who stood only a few inches taller than she did. Her mind flashed to thoughts of four leaf clovers, Blarney stones and fields of lavender. She shook off the silly images.

"I'll have coffee. Thank you." She shot a glance at Cora who was settling into her seat.

She smiled and winked at Lillian, whispering in her ear, "Those mojos of yours must be sending messages today."

Lillian glanced quickly down at her boobs and whispered back, "Don't be silly." Nevertheless, as she seated herself, she pulled her blouse tighter together in front, in a vain attempt to hide her ample assets. She mumbled to herself, "I really need to look into breast reduction. Those old codgers and their roving eyes are starting to annoy me. They would get a big letdown if they saw me take off my bolder holders—warning—falling rocks."

Cora laughed loudly, prompting Celia to ask as she settled into her seat, "What's so funny?"

Lillian whispered, "I'm just considering breast reduction surgery. It seems I can't go anywhere without some lonely old fart ogling my knockers."

"What are you talking about? That guy with the dogs never called you, so what's to complain about now?"

"Him," Lillian whispered as Squeamish set her cup of coffee on the table.

"I'll be right back after I load a plate. Is there anything else I can be getting you ladies?"

Cora gazed in awe at the attractive new man. "Well, he's too short for me, but maybe you would be interested." She winked at Celia.

Celia watched as the new man retreated to the food line. "Well, aren't you a breath of fresh Irish air," she whispered under her breath. "None of these other oafs in this room have ever offered to wait on us. Who is he and what Irish heaven did he descend from?"

Lillian took a bite and chewed it. "He said his name is Squeamish McPhee and he's fresh off the plane from Ireland."

When Squeamish returned with his plate, his eyes twinkled when he spotted Celia with her brilliant red hair. He extended his hand, "Squeamish McPhee."

Celia briefly shook his hand. "I'm Celia, and I don't think I've ever heard of anyone with that name."

"It's a name bestowed upon me by me late wife. She was a very bad cook and many a times, I had upset stomachs after eating her not-so-Irish fair. She took to calling me Squeamish early in our union and it stuck. Sometimes I can't remember me given name."

Celia grinned. "It's nice to meet you…Squeamish. I hope the food here is agreeable to you. We've been eating it almost every week for lunch and haven't had any incidents requiring medical care, so I think you're safe." She eyed him and smiled.

Celia whispered into Lillian's ear. "If I know anything about the Irish, I have to guess he's full of blarney."

When Squeamish rose to go pick out a desert, Cora gazed around the room as she took a bite. "Maybe this Irishman will be a little more interesting than these tired old farts that have been coming here for a long time. This place could use some new blood. Have you seen old Jim Boyd around lately?"

Celia checked around the room. "I haven't seen him since his visit after that makeover. I guess we did such a good job of it that he doesn't have time for us anymore." She shrugged. "Ask me if I care."

Cora clucked her tongue in her cheek. "Celia, if you don't watch it, you might end up growing old alone and lonely. You should give one of these freckled old farts a chance. You might find someone worthwhile around your age."

"I don't think so." Celia finished chewing a bite and added. "Men our ages are like over-ripe bananas—covered in brown spots and too soft too enjoy—if you get my drift."

Cora had to laugh aloud. "Celia, don't you know that when you peel a ripe banana, the meat is at its sweetest? They may be old, but they are squeezable. You should try one sometime. You might change your mind."

Celia smirked. "Cora, I think you're the one who needs to find an old man to…to…*squeeze*."

"You're very funny, Ann Landers. I'm over the hill, but you are still young enough to find yourself some male companionship."

When Squeamish returned to the table with a slice of pie, he took the seat next to Celia, which had freed up. He cleared his throat and timidly spoke. "Miss Celia, I was thinking maybe you would be in a mind to show me around the city sometime."

Celia looked at him as if he had three eyes.

Squeamish flushed red and started eating his pie. "Forgive me brash behavior. Forget it." Drops of sweat broke out in his hairline.

Celia sighed. "Sure. Tell you what. I'm riding with friends today and I have to work tonight, but give me a call and we'll arrange something." She wrote her number on a napkin and tucked it in his shirt pocket.

He patted the napkin. "You work at night?"

"Yes, I'm an emergency room nurse. If you wander out at night and get run down by a taxi cab, you'll probably end up in my care."

"I'll remember that," Squeamish replied with a grin. "Maybe I can think up an excuse to require an examination," he intimated in a sexual tone.

Those words made Celia rise and indicate to her friends that it was time to leave. "Are you ready girls? I've got some things to do this afternoon."

"Sure. Excuse us Mr. McPhee," Cora said politely, "we have to go. It was nice meeting you."

Squeamish rose as the women prepared to depart. His eyes dropped below Lillian's chin. "Perhaps we will meet again next week?"

Lillian smiled. "Yes, perhaps they—we will." She turned and walked briskly away mumbling, "In your dreams, Jackass."

Back in the car, Lillian chuckled. "I saw you slip your phone number to the new man. What's with that, Celia, the man hater?"

Celia smirked, "I felt sorry for him. He's nice enough and his Irish eyes were smiling. It might be interesting to hear him talk about where he came from and all that blarney."

"It's got to be your red hair. He found that more attractive than my big mojos, thank God." She heaved a sigh of relief.

Cora piped up. "You did such a great job on Jim Boyd, we never see him anymore. Is Squeamish going to be your next project? Are you going to make him disappear as well?"

Celia grinned. "It's a possibility."

39

Saturday morning, Lillian awoke late to a quiet house. She put on a robe and headed for the kitchen.

A note on the counter left by Cora stated, "The coffee is ready. Just punch the button. I've gone to an early bird sale, will return shortly. I'll pick up some pastries."

Lillian punched the button and returned to her bedroom to make the bed and take a quick shower. When she headed back to the kitchen, she noted that Celia's door was ajar and her bed made. *I wonder where she went. She didn't say anything last night about having plans today.*

Lillian had become so accustomed to having her roommates at the table with her for breakfast, that she felt lost. She poured a cup of java and sat down. The newspaper was lying open to an ad, so she browsed through the pages. The house was so quiet; she could hear the tick of the kitchen clock. She silently thanked the good Lord for bringing Celia and Cora into her life. If not for them, this might be every morning in her life. Charla still had not contacted her.

She picked up her cell phone and punched her number. *Maybe she's over her anger by now and ready to talk.*

Charla answered in a sleepy voice as if she had been out late the night before. "Mom—you woke me up."

"It's eleven in the morning," Lillian informed her.

"Eleven o'clock already? Oh my God, I need to get moving. I'm holding an open house at one."

"Wait," Lillian yelled, "don't hang up. I was hoping we could spend some time together today."

"Not today. I have a juicy listing and I promised the sellers, I would have an offer by the end of today."

Lillian mused silently; *I guess I'm not the only one on the receiving end of empty promises.* "Can I buy some lunch and come over and chat with you. We haven't talked since Courtney went back to school. Please. I'd love to see one of the classy homes you list. We need to get past whatever roadblock it is that's hurting our relationship."

"Do we have to do it today? I'll be busy trying to sell a house."

"I've been to open houses myself and I'm sure you won't be that busy. There is always down time between browsers. Most of them will be the neighbors coming around to snoop. Honestly, I've done that myself in the past."

An audible sigh came from Charla's end. "Okay. Do you have a pad and paper? Here's the address. The hours are one to four. Wait until around one-thirty."

"What would you like for lunch?"

"You decide as long as it's not something messy to eat." The line went silent.

Lillian checked through the kitchen cupboards and pulled out her cookbook. She decided to make a nice quiche for lunch. They could reheat it in the microwave.

40

Lillian was packing up her lunch for Charla and preparing to go to the open house when the front door slammed and Celia came stomping into the kitchen. She plopped down on a kitchen chair and huffed loudly. "Remind me to smack the next asshole that approaches me and wants to be friends."

She looked at Celia with wide-eyed curiosity. "Where have you been? You didn't leave any notes. I figured you must have done a double shift at work."

"Shamus called early this morning and wanted a tour guide. I wasn't sleeping anyway, so I dressed and went to pick him up."

"Who is Shamus and why are you so mad?" Lillian could hardly choke back a chuckle.

"Shamus is the real name of that Irish wacko we met on Wednesday. He seemed nice at the start, and I drove him out to Lake Mead for a tour of the dam and the bridge. Then we did a car tour through Boulder City which he liked very much."

"So what's the problem?"

"He suggested we stop at an Irish pub for brunch. I took him to O'Leary's Ale House.

"That's a nice place. I like their lamb stew."

"Forget the stew. Everything was fine through the meal, until he ordered a second and third beer. He got up and started spouting Irish ballads to some imaginary music. He was getting rowdy and started jigging around tables. It was embarrassing."

"That's the Irish. They like their suds." Lillian stifled a laugh. "So what happened next?"

"I slunk off to the ladies room and then made a fast exit out the back door and drove home."

"You left him behind? That was rude." Lillian failed to stifle a snicker.

"Not as rude as I could have been if I had to load that drunk into my car and take him back to his house." She pawed through the kitchen cupboards. "Where's the aspirin. He gave me a headache."

Lillian reached into another cabinet and produced the needed bottle, setting it on the counter. "I'm sorry your date went badly," Lillian said with a grin.

"It wasn't a *date* and don't look so smug," Celia retorted. "He was interested in you first."

"Yeah, but I don't have red hair." Lillian chuckled. "He must have thought you were his new *Colleen*."

"Yeah, well my name isn't Colleen and my hair isn't really red." She eyed the lunch Lillian was packing. "Where are you going today?"

"I'm taking a sack lunch to Charla. She's having an open house in a ritzy neighborhood, and I'm buttering her up. I want to get to the bottom of why she has such a problem getting along with me."

"At an open house—won't she be busy?"

"Have you ever been to an open house? I have and there aren't that many browsers. I hope to pry a conversation out of that stuck up daughter of mine. I need to find out what's eating her."

"Good luck with that." Celia rose and headed for her bathroom. "I need a shower to wash away the blarney I've been fed today."

Lillian arrived at the appointed one-thirty time. She parked on the street and headed to the front door of a single level home. The wide driveway led to a four-car garage. She admired the front yard landscaping with desert plants and succulents surrounding a trio of palm trees. An etched glass set of double front doors beckoned. The outside foyer leading to it was lush with flowering plants, and a little bistro set. A security guard occupied one of the chairs. She spoke to him. "I'm Charla's mother. Do you mind if I go in? I brought her lunch."

He nodded, but didn't move to open the door for her. His broad fanny seemed glued to the chair as if he were a garden gnome. His hands remained folded across his ample belly, just below the badge on his dark uniform. *It must be hard to find a rent-a-cop willing to work weekends.*

Lillian moved on quickly and entered the home. She warily called out, "Charla."

"In here," came the reply. "Take a left and then a right. I'm in the kitchen."

The arched entry opened out into a large great room furnished with comfortable sectional facing a high-definition television mounted over the massive gas fireplace. A breakfast bar and kitchen took up the rest of the room which would probably hold half of the house where Lillian lived. Beyond that, a wall of windows and glass sliders opened onto a spacious patio, infinity swimming pool, spa, and waterfall. The outdoor furnishings of pricey patio sets and an outdoor kitchen dripped of money at a level of society Lillian had never seen up close. "Good grief," she gasped. "Who lives like this? These people obviously don't shop at discount stores."

"This is nothing compared to some of my listings." Charla handed Lillian a printed glossy card with particulars about the home. "Do you want to see the rest of it?" Her cool detached demeanor made Lillian feel like a stranger around her own daughter. She tried to shrug off the feeling, reminding herself, *she's my daughter and I love her.*

After the grand tour where she saw up close the gold-plated bathroom fixtures, a shower as big as a walk-in closet, with multiple showerheads, and the enormous bedrooms, each with a private bath, any one of which would dwarf the house she occupies, they returned to the kitchen area.

"I made you some quiche to warm in the microwave. Can we eat on the patio?"

"Sure. Business is slow today. I think I may have been too optimistic about getting an offer on this place." Charla cast a frustrated glance about the room and frowned.

"Is there something wrong with it? Is the list price too high?" Lillian asked.

"I don't think so. However, it's been on the market for a long time. We've reduced the price several times. The owners live in Florida."

"Don't tell me this is their winter home." Lillian gasped. "It must be nice to be that rich."

While they ate, Lillian broached the subject she came to discuss. "Herbie mentioned your divorce decree. Why is your divorce still up in the air? I thought it was all over and done with."

"It is, but ours was a special case," Charla answered without making eye contact.

"Why would you agree to such terms? It sounds like you got a bad deal. Do you really have to pay for Courtney's education? Wouldn't that be partly his responsibility too?" Her brow furrowed to make her point. "I mean, what was your lawyer thinking?"

Charla gazed out at the pool and didn't answer right away. "I'm not going to discuss it with you or rehash past history. I agreed to it for reasons that I prefer to keep confidential—for Courtney's sake."

"You can't even tell your own mother? I'm trying to figure out why you avoid me like the plague. It hurts my feelings and you don't seem to care. What the hell is going on with you?" Lillian felt like she was talking to a stone. "Look at me, Charla?" she demanded. "What happened to our relationship?"

A voice rang out through the open patio doors. "Hello, is anyone here?"

Charla whispered, "You ask too many questions and frankly, it's none of *your* business." The shriveling glare she cast on Lillian made goosebumps rise on her arms.

Before she could verbalize a comeback, Charla jumped up, put a smile on her face, and turned her attention to the visitors. They disappeared into the many rooms in the other wing of the house.

Charla was still busy with the prospective buyers when another couple walked through the house and out onto the patio. "Are you the agent in charge?" the woman asked softly.

Still licking her wounds after the daggers Charla shot at her, Lillian jumped up and responded, "No, I'm…" she paused, choosing her words, "here to assist." She smiled sweetly. "The agent is with another couple now. I can show you around in the meantime. This, as you can see, is a lovely pool area." She made a sweeping motion with her hand and frowned. "It's so sad about what happened here."

The visitors raised their eyebrows and the man asked in a thick Hungarian accent, "What do you mean by that?"

Clamping her lips shut and acting embarrassed as if she misspoke, Lillian cast a gaze at the pool. "I shouldn't have said that. Just forget it."

The man demanded, "If you don't tell us what you meant, we won't be interested in looking at the rest of the house."

"May I ask," Lillian began, "are you from around here?"

"No," the man responded with a firm take-no-prisoners attitude. "We sold a house in San Francisco and we're looking to relocate here. We have cash and can close in one week. Now tell us what you know about this house. Is there some kind of stigma attached to it? Is the title clouded?"

Lillian didn't exactly know what a clouded title meant, so she smiled innocently. "No, I don't think so." Her gaze fell on the pool again. "The price is a real steal in view of…"

"What!" the man demanded. "Level with us!" His hardened expression on chiseled features told Lillian he wore the pants in the family. The wife remained meekly silent at his side.

Lillian assumed a sad expression. "It's terrible and I shouldn't tell you. Don't tell Miss Charla I let anything slip, please," she whispered, "I could lose my job."

"We won't say a word," the man leaned close to hear Lillian whispering.

"The price is low in order to get a quick sale. It seems the owner is in prison. He beat his wife to a pulp and drowned her in that pool." She sighed and made the sign of the cross.

The couple looked at each other and their eyes scanned the pool.

"It was such a bloody mess that the pool had to be drained, cleaned and refilled." She cast her eyes down on the pool deck. "They did a super job of cleaning up the blood. It's as if it never happened. Its lovely now, isn't it. I can show you the rest of the house if you like."

"No thanks," the couple blurted in unison as they made a hasty retreat. Feeling smug, Lillian followed at a distance as they strode swiftly to the front door.

At that very moment, Charla was coming back through the foyer with the other couple. "If you'll wait a minute, I'll be right with you," she said to the retreating people.

They looked at her as if she had two heads and sneered. The man spoke in a rude manner as they made their quick getaway, "No, thank you. We've seen all we want to see."

Lillian quickly returned to the patio and gathered up the lunch leftovers, bagged them, and headed for the front door. "I'll see you later, Charla."

There was no response from Charla, as she was busy talking up the desirable points of the property with her prospective buyers.

As Lillian exited, she looked back at the vast entryway; the elegant living room sparsely furnished with neutral décor and beyond that the large picture windows with an unobstructed view across the valley to the strip. She silently congratulated herself on having screwed up at least one sure sale. Maybe she would ask Charla where the next open house was going to be. She sighed and closed the door. *I wish I had some chalk. I could have drawn an outline of a dead body on that marble floor in the foyer.*

Let Charla explain that to her clients. She shook off the idea. *How am I going to get that girl's attention—in a healthy way?*

41

"So how was your lunch with Charla?" Cora greeted Lillian as she came through the door. "Celia told me you made her lunch and went to her open house."

"The lunch was brief, the house was gorgeous, dripping of money, and the heart-to-heart talk a bust. She just won't open up to me and then some browsers interrupted us, so I left." She frowned and emptied the bag of discarded lunch, putting the utensils and containers in the dishwasher. "There is something eating that girl and she absolutely refuses to discuss it with me."

"Would you like some coffee?" Cora asked. "I'm just about to make some."

"Sure." Lillian sank into a chair and moped. "What did you rush out so early this morning to buy, Miss Early Bird shopper?"

"I got some new clothes and a real steal on a new bed ensemble. I'm tired of the old one. Maybe I should have got you out of bed to go with me. It sounds like you would have had more fun."

"Oh, I had some fun." Her mouth curled in an evil grin.

"Celia would have had more fun too. Did she tell you about her effort to be a tour guide?" Recalling Celia's account of how she ditched Shamus, made them both erupt in loud laughter.

"At least he showed his true colors right away before any of us got involved in befriending him. Drunks I don't need." Cora filled two mugs and sat down, adding a plate of cookies.

Celia came in and joined them.

"So, how was the open house?" Celia asked.

Lillian reiterated her brief visit with Charla. Then she added, "But I got even with her. She needs to learn not to talk to me like that."

Cora frowned, "Okay, what did you do this time? Are you in trouble again? Are we all going to have to leave town?"

After Lillian told them what she had said to the prospective cash buyers, there was a burst of laughter.

Celia spoke first. "You are in for it now. You had better hope she doesn't find out what you said to those people. She's never going to invite you to another open house."

"Oh, I doubt those people will come around again. They looked shocked. They will probably steer clear of Charla's listings from now on."

Cora munched on a cookie. "We really need to find something else for you to do. Idle hands can get into a lot of trouble. Why don't we plan a vacation as soon as bowling is over? I'd like to go to Hawaii."

"Set a date and I'll put in for vacation days," said Celia.

"That sounds like a plan," Lillian agreed. "I'll get on line and see what kind of accommodations I can get. While I'm at it, I think I'll see if there are any more open houses scheduled for Charla's agency."

Cora looked over the top of her reading glasses. "Lillian, you need to find a hobby. You need to take up basket weaving or crocheting."

"I do have a hobby. It's picking on Charla. Eventually, I'm going to find out the secret she's keeping. I'm her mother but she treats me like some casual acquaintance she doesn't want to get too chummy with."

Celia cautioned her, "The harder you push, the more she is going to avoid you. If there is something she's regretting or is embarrassed about, it isn't likely she will tell you or anyone else."

Cora suggested, "Maybe you need to drive down south and drop in on Ella. Maybe she'll blab the family secrets."

Lillian's eyes went wide. "I never thought of that. I could get her drunk. She likes those flavored Vodkas and she can get real gossipy when she's tipsy, if I remember right."

Celia motioned with her hand. "So go. Pack a bag and hit the road in the morning. You can be back by Tuesday night."

"I think I'll go right now. It's still early."

"You won't make it all the way before dark and you don't like to drive at night," Cora cautioned.

Lillian glanced at the clock on the wall. "I can make it if I drive straight through. It's freeway all the way. Does anyone want to come with me?"

42

Lillian cruised down the I-15, second-guessing herself as to whether she should be making the trip alone. Cora couldn't accompany her because she was committed to substitute teaching Monday and Tuesday and the notice was too short for Celia to arrange for some days off.

By the time she reached Primm, her resolve to speak to Ella in person was crumbling. She pulled off into a casino parking lot and considered heading back home. She hadn't even bothered to call ahead and see if Ella would be home. She thought *this is nuts. Look how late it is. I can't make it before dark. I have to go back home.*

She was about to restart the car when she thought she should visit a restroom first and have a bite to eat. *I need to think. Do I really want to visit that old biddy? Do I really want to drive all the way down there?*

After lingering over a steak dinner in the casino café, Lillian wandered about the floor playing various slots and vacillating between heading south and heading home. Should she call Ella or just pop in on her? Not being able to decide, she kept playing. When she finally cashed out to leave, darkness had descended over Primm. A check of her wristwatch nearly shocked her out of her shoes. It was midnight. She had visited the ATM numerous times, feeling guilty every time for wasting more of her hard-earned bingo winnings. Each time she shrugged off the moment. *It's my money and I don't really have to leave any of it to anyone. Still, it was a waste.*

Looking out at the darkness, she felt ridiculous. She was supposed to be in San Diego by now and here she was, at the state line. She looked back at the casino floor and the hotel check-in desk beyond. She wasn't tired, having drunk three cups of coffee with dinner. She was still licking her wounds after the encounter with Charla and at the same time, gloating over running off some customers. She finally made a decision and walked to the car.

43

Sunday morning, Cora was in the kitchen eating when her phone buzzed. She picked it up absently without looking at the caller I.D. "Hello," she answered with a mouthful of pancakes.

"It's Charla. Did I wake you up?"

Cora swallowed and came to attention. Charla never called her unless something was wrong. "No, I'm eating breakfast. What's up?"

"I'm trying to track down my mother. She's not answering her phone. I got a call from Courtney. She has been calling her grandmother repeatedly with no answer. Is she still asleep? Did she let the battery in her phone run down again? Did she die in her sleep?"

Cora paused a moment to contemplate how she should answer and not rat on her friend. Evil thoughts crossed her mind. *You hope she died in her sleep so you don't have to be bothered with her anymore you...you...*

"Cora, are you there?"

"I'm here, and no, no and no to your questions. You just saw her yesterday. What makes you think she died in her sleep? She's fine."

"Then why doesn't she answer her phone?" Charla demanded.

"She went on a road trip. Maybe she can't answer because she's driving."

"Where did she go? She has to stop sometime and return her missed calls?" Charla's voice sounded snotty as it usually is when dealing with her mother.

Cora didn't miss the tone of voice. "Maybe if you took more of an interest in your mother, she would tell you her plans, even invite you along."

"I saw her yesterday, but I'm trying to sell a house. I can't ignore my customers."

"Yeah, so I hear. Maybe if you had made a promise to spend today with her, you would know where she is right now." *I wish I didn't feel so spiteful. Charla's attitude is catching.*

"She left before I could do that."

"And you don't have a cell phone?" Cora's impatience was showing in her voice. She thought about Charla's lack of concern for her mother every other day of the year—why all the anxious concern now? Did she have a guilty conscience?

"Would you please go see if her car is in the driveway?" Charla pleaded.

"Sure. But I told you, she went on a road trip." Cora made no move to go to the front window.

"Just do as I asked. It will only take a second."

Cora put down her fork, eyeing the breakfast that would be cold by the time she returned to the table. She went to the front window. "Lillian's car is not here. I told you…"

"Yeah, yeah, yeah—she went on a road trip. Where did she go and did anyone go with her?"

"She went alone. She was going to…to…"

"Where was she going?" Charla demanded.

Cora heaved an audible sigh. "She decided to go visit Ella."

"Why would she do that? She can't stand my great-aunt. They get along like oil and water."

"We all have a duty to put up with relatives we don't like. It's common courtesy." *Like the way I'm putting up with you now.*

"When did she leave? She was at my open house until about two."

"She didn't leave until around four. I thought she should stay until this morning and get an earlier start, but she seemed anxious."

"That was stupid. As slow as she drives, she wouldn't get down to Ella's place until lights out. My God, what was she thinking?" Charla huffed. "I really don't need this."

Cora's fears were beginning to surface. Maybe Lil misjudged how far her new car would go on that battery and little tank of gas. Maybe she fell asleep at the wheel and crashed. Maybe a carjacker stole her new automobile and she is wandering along the freeway. The possibilities are endless—all of them frightening.

"Cora, answer me," Charla shouted.

"Answer what?"

"I said, did she go off and forget her telephone?"

Cora took off walking towards Lillian's bedroom. "I don't know. I'll look for it." She quickly checked all the places where someone might set a phone down and forget it. She found Lillian's sitting on the bureau. "Her phone is here. At least I think it is." She picked it up, but when she activated it, the screen indicated a dead battery. "The battery is run down."

"How about that one she bought for Courtney." Charla's voice sounded snotty as if she still resented Lillian's interference.

"I don't see any other cell in here. Maybe when she was packing, she accidentally picked up the wrong one. Try that number and see if she answers."

"I don't have that number. Do you?"

Cora sighed. "No, but give me a while to find a charger and then maybe I can find it in Lillian's phone. In the meantime, relax. Your mother is a big girl."

"Ha," Charla spat. "Lately she's been acting like a child. I don't know what to do."

Cora sneered at her phone. *I could tell you what to do, but you wouldn't like my suggestion and it might involve having to visit a proctologist afterward.* Instead, she kept her cool. "I'll call you if I find a number." She ended the call.

If I was brave enough, I could tell that uptight ballsy bitch where to go and what to do, but it's not my battle.

Cora found the charger, took the dead phone into the kitchen to plug it in. The screen lit up and she scrolled through the call list until she found the number for Courtney's phone. She picked up her own and dialed the number, certain that Lillian would answer. It immediately went to voice mail.

"Lillian, where are you?" she said with increased apprehension. "Call me back. You picked up the wrong phone when you left. Charla is looking for you. Call me or call Charla."

44

A sliver of sunlight peeked through the gap in the drapes and fell across Lillian's face, waking her. She glanced at the clock. It was early. Instead of rolling over to go back to sleep, she rose and showered.

After sitting in her car in the dark for a few minutes the night before, watching the taillights of passing cars on the freeway, Lillian had opted for prudence and safety. She got out, grabbed her small suitcase from the back seat, locked up, and headed for hotel check-in.

After breakfast at the hotel café and a brief stop at the gas station to top off her tank, she hit the road, heading south.

She still had not called to see if Ella was home. Kicking herself for that, she decided to pull off the freeway at the next opportunity and do it. She had to scrub that plan when the next rest stop south of the state line had barricades up barring entry. Signs announced renovations in progress. "Damn." She kept driving.

When the off ramp to Zzyzx came up, on a whim, she slowed down and took it. She had traveled this freeway countless times over the years, and always wanted to see where that road would lead, but had never taken the time to do it. She forgot all about calling Ella.

The pavement ended and the road seemed to be leading into the desert. She began to feel that maybe she had made a mistake or perhaps she was avoiding a visit with Ella. *Maybe I should give up and go back home.*

Slowing to a crawl, Lillian began looking for somewhere to turn around when a few buildings came into view and a sign directed her to the Desert Studies Center. There weren't many people around this time of morning.

Having come this far, she decided to relax and do the tourist thing. She remembered seeing a brief documentary on television about this little oasis and the quack snake oil vendor that founded it. She pulled up in front and parked.

After an hour of browsing the Center and walking about the decaying structures of the former health spa, she was back on the road. She drove slowly, turning over in her mind the option of heading home, or turning south. The overpass was swiftly coming up and she needed to make a decision. She really didn't like Ella, and to be honest, this detour was another excuse to avoid the visit. *That old bat won't tell me anything anyway.*

She swung to the right and took the ramp heading north. By the time she reached the state line, she needed a coffee break, so she pulled off and drove to Buffalo Bill's parking lot. She recalled passing this way many times over the years, and she had never stopped to see this casino with the old roller coaster that never seemed to be operating. Curiosity got the better of her and she indulged it.

After locking the car, she walked away as a distant noise chimed. It wasn't her phone because that wasn't her ring tone. Looking around briefly, thinking someone had left their cell in a car, she shrugged and continued toward the entrance. The temperature on this spring Sunday was rising and she wanted to retreat to an air-conditioned place for a while.

During the drive, she had been hearing an annoying noise intermittently. She thought it was the radio and she pounded on that button to stifle it. Then she concluded it was something going haywire in her car engine. It must be some of the bells and whistles built into these new ones to tell you if you need to have an engine check. She resolved to take it back to the dealership when she got home, and complain.

Entering the front doors was like stepping back in time. The building had the feel of a cavernous mining operation. Her eyes swept over the interior and up to the high ceiling. An elevated track resembled a mining rail and fake workers on dollies wound around the room. A water tower replica stood in the middle of the vast casino floor.

She barely noticed the slots as she wandered around in search of somewhere to buy something to eat. She found the food court and ordered a sandwich and drink at The Dog House burger joint. As she waited for her order to come, she let her eyes roam over the surrounding décor and hoped the food was better than the name the place suggested. *Who names a restaurant The Dog House?*

After finishing the meal, she took her coffee and wandered about the casino floor, eventually settling for one machine and indulging in some relaxing play while finishing her drink. Between the loud piped in music and the ringing bells and mechanical sounds of the slots, even if her cell rang, it would go unheard. She actually enjoyed the long respite from phone calls.

Her chosen slot machine seemed to be on a hot streak, giving back more than she put in, so she played on. She continued to turn over in her mind the idea of going to see Ella, but now it was too late to do it this week. She could plan a trip next week and maybe Cora would come along. She hit the bet button again, upping the ante.

A scruffy man with several days' growth of beard and noxious body odor slid into the seat beside her.

Lillian glanced sideways with disdain, and instinctively clutched her handbag closer to her body as she continued operating the slot. Her encounter with that purse-snatcher weeks earlier flashed through her brain and her senses sharpened. Ordinarily she would have cashed out and moved away to another area when someone offensive got too close. In this case, her machine was hitting hot and heavy, racking up winnings and she was reluctant to move.

She wrinkled her nose and made an effort to ignore the man. He looked like some of the homeless people prowling the streets of Las Vegas, pushing their shopping carts, and begging for change.

His clothing reeked of sweat, soil, and stale cigarette smoke. His long hair stunk from lack of any recent shampooing. The filthy rats nest was in such disarray that no self-respecting head lice would choose to live in it.

She edged slightly away from him and scanned the casino floor, looking for a security guard. *Where were they when you needed them?* The fight-or-flight argument was turning over in her mind, and she had decided on the latter when the man opened his jacket slightly, and without looking directly at her, said, "Do not scream."

45

Cora ended her efforts to reach Lillian and dialed Charla.

"Did you find a number?" Charla asked without saying *hello.*

Cora read off the number. "I tried calling, but it went straight to voice. She's not answering that one either."

"I'll keep trying. I have to call Courtney back."

"Don't be raising an alarm just yet. Maybe she turned the phone off and checked into a room for the night somewhere. Maybe she just forgot to turn it back on or put it on a charger. Give her some time before you scare Courtney. Lillian will be fine."

When there was no response from Charla's end, Cora looked at the screen. The bitch had hung up on her without even saying *thanks.* She picked up her breakfast plate and dumped the cold soggy contents down the garbage disposal. "Thanks for spoiling my Sunday morning," she said aloud as she started over again grilling new pancakes.

"Who spoiled your Sunday morning?" Celia came shuffling into the kitchen and poured a cup of coffee.

After reheating the grill and setting out clean plates, she filled Celia in on the morning activities.

"It's not like Charla to worry about her mother's whereabouts," Celia commented between sips of hot coffee. "Do you suppose she found out about Lillian's little revenge at the open house? Maybe it's just as well our girl left town for a while." She chuckled.

"Courtney's trying to call her grandmother, but she left her phone at home and apparently picked up the one Courtney gave back when Charla returned her original one. Lil's not answering that one either. If I know her, she probably misplaced it too."

"It sounds like Charla thinks we need to keep her mother on a short leash. Who appointed us her custodians?"

"Who do you think?" Cora smirked.

Celia accepted some pancakes and poured syrup on them. "We should give it until the end of the day before we get too concerned about Lillian's whereabouts. She'll be back."

"I should have talked her out of the trip. A simple phone call to Ella would have been enough."

"It's early yet. If she stayed overnight somewhere, she won't get to San Diego for another four or five hours. You should call Ella around three and see if she has company yet."

Cora glanced at the charging phone. "You're right. Her number is in that phone."

Celia finished off her stack of pancakes. "All of this could be avoided if Charla would grow a heart and some feelings for her mother."

"It's going to take something really traumatic for that to happen."

Cora reluctantly dialed Ella's number.

A breathless voice answered. "This is Ella."

She started to ask if Lillian was there, when she realized Ella's voice kept talking. It was a recording. "Leave a message."

Cora vacillated between leaving a message and hanging up. She opted for the former. "This is Cora, Lillian's roommate. I'm just checking to see if Lil made it down there okay. She forgot her cell when she left here in a hurry. Call me back." She looked at Celia as if silently asking what to do next.

"Call dragon lady and tell her Ella doesn't answer. She'll have to figure out what to do next. Maybe she can call the place where Ella lives and get a message to her that way."

46

Lillian's hand froze over the play button as she glanced sideways at the scruffy bum. Her eyes fell upon the handgun in his waistband. She desperately scanned the casino floor as far as she could see without looking too obvious.

She whispered, "What do you want?"

"Give me your cash," he said as he pretended to push the play button on the machine in front of him.

"I don't have much left," she lied. She had a few hundred dollars after hitting a jackpot the night before and recouping most of her earlier losses, but she wasn't going to tell this shithead about it. "I'll have to cash this ticket out." She hit the button and it emerged a couple seconds later. She offered it to the thief. "Go cash this."

"Don't mess with me bitch. You'll yell for security the minute I try to do that. Give me your money." His hand tightened around the handle of the gun in his belt.

Lillian knew the thief couldn't get too brazen with all the cameras watching the casino floor, so she stuffed the ticket into her purse and casually sipped on her cold coffee.

The gunman became fidgety and the noxious odor of nervous sweat wafted from his filthy clothes.

"Look," she said, "if you want a meal, I'll buy you one. If you need a room for the night so you can clean up, I'll pay for one. If you need some clean clothes or anything else, I'll get it for you."

"Sure, and then you'll call the cops. You must think I'm an idiot."

"Let me tell you about the last thief that tried to rip me off," Lillian blurted, "he's…"

"I don't care! Give me your car keys," the man demanded in a forceful whisper. "I want your cell phone too, and your cash. Do it now, or I'll shoot you right here."

His face, what she could see of it, was hardened and his gray eyes glassy, as if he were on drugs.

"Are you homeless?"

"Stop asking questions, bitch, and give me your keys." He removed the gun from his waistband and pointed it at her from inside his jacket, while his eyes darted back and forth, as if watching for any security personnel.

With an audible sigh, Lillian reached into her purse and retrieved the keys and three twenty-dollar bills. She placed them in the space between the two machines. "Do you talk to your grandmother like that?"

"Shut the hell up! I said give me your telephone, too." He waved the gun while keeping it hidden out of sight of prying cameras. He picked up the keys and money with his other hand and stuffing them into his pocket. He snapped his fingers, "The phone too."

Lillian dug deeper into her bag. Her phone was missing. Panic grew and her hands began to shake. "The keys won't do you any good if you don't know where I left my car."

"I know, because I followed you in here. That's a nice ride."

Her mouth gaped at that revelation.

"Don't look at me!" He ordered. "Now give me your phone!" The left side of his jacket moved slightly as he waved the gun to emphasize his point.

"It's in the car," she blurted. "I don't bring my phone into casinos because I can't hear it ring anyway. You'll find it in the car." Truth was she couldn't remember where she left it.

"You are lying."

"So go ahead and shoot me," Lillian dared him as her heart pounded so hard she felt as if a heart attack was imminent. "You won't reach the door before they get you. Leave now while you can."

She looked around in time to see two security guards ambling in her direction. She wanted to scream to alert them.

"Put that ticket back in your machine," the thief ordered. "Wait ten minutes, then I don't care what you do, but if you give me away, remember, I know where you live."

Lillian complied with a hand trembling so violently, she had difficulty fitting the ticket into the slot. "How would you know that?"

"I'll have your car and your registration has your address. You sic the cops on me, and I'll give your address to some very bad friends of mine."

She looked away desperately in the direction of the security personnel walking the floor. When she looked back, the thief was gone. She heaved a sigh and checked her watch. Ten minutes clicked by. She cashed out and took a frantic step in the direction of the security desk when she tripped and pitched forward.

47

Cora's phone chimed and she answered.

"It's Charla. I called the place where Ella lives. She's gone on a bus tour to Sedona. She's not even home and they said my mother never showed up inquiring about her."

Cora sighed. "So she never made it to San Diego and we know she didn't go to see Courtney. Now what do we do?"

"I'm going to file a missing person's report. Maybe Highway Patrol can find her. Maybe her car broke down or she ran out of gas."

"Maybe the battery went dead. I'm never sure about those new hybrid cars. It's a long way between charging stations if she let the gas tank go dry." Cora's voice trailed off. *I can't think about that possibility.*

Celia stood by, listening to the conversation. "I'm going to call in sick and head out. Maybe she made a pit stop somewhere, like Primm, and got distracted. If she's there, I'll find her."

"A twenty-four hour pit stop is a long stop." Cora responded wide-eyed.

"You know our girl, the queen of the slot machines, it could happen." Celia grinned. "I'm going." She went to her room to change clothes and make the call.

"Cora, are you still there?"

"Sorry, I was listening to Celia. She's going to Primm to search the casinos to see if your mother stopped there and just lost track of time." *If this turns out to be another one of Lillian's big ideas for garnering Charla's attention, she's succeeding.*

"It seems like a waste of time. She could be anywhere. I think I should report her missing."

Sure, don't bother to go looking for her yourself, let somebody else do it, Cora thought.

Celia came back into the kitchen and motioned to Cora to get her attention. "Do you want to come along?"

Cora sighed, nodding affirmative. "Look, Charla, do what you think you should. I'm going to Primm with Celia. If Lillian is down there, we'll find her." She ended the call.

When the girls reached Primm in Celia's car, they initially started searching by cruising all the parking lots and structures in search of Lillian's car. That proved to be futile, as there seemed to be too many cars exactly like Lillian's model and they didn't know her license plate number.

"Okay," Celia said, "We start Plan B. Have you got a picture of our wayward roomy on your smart phone?"

Cora searched through her cell and found a selfie they took some time ago at the atrium. She showed it to Celia. "This will have to do."

Celia pulled into a spot at Whiskey Pete's and they headed for the check-in desk. She held up the phone to the clerk and asked, "Have you seen this woman? She's our friend and she's missing. Do you know if she stayed here last night?"

The clerk studied the photo. "What's her name? I'll check."

After looking at the records, he nodded. "She checked in around midnight last night and checked out this morning around ten. If she's not out on our casino floor now, you should try the other establishments across the freeway. A lot of gamblers make the rounds when they come here."

Cora and Celia separated and searched every square inch of the casino floor, restrooms, and restaurants. Cora had to pause for a moment at the display where Bonnie and Clyde's car of death was on display—testament to the fact that a life of crime does *not* pay. *Lillian was missing. Was she a victim of crime?*

The girls met up at the front door and shrugged. "Not here."

Celia started the car. "Let's do that one next." She pointed to the casino connected to the outlet mall. "Maybe she went shopping."

Two hours later and feeling exhaustion setting in, Cora was about to give up. "There's one more to search. Let's go to Buffalo Bills. I need some food and I like the hamburgers over there."

Celia looked at her watch. "It's well past lunch time and I'm starved. Let's eat."

When Celia parked and they were walking towards the door, they noted a Highway Patrol car and an ambulance idling near the door. She frowned. "Not a good sign."

Cora joked, "Somebody must have hit a jackpot and it gave them a heart attack."

48

The car cruised slowly along the street while the driver craned his neck in search of his destination. The street dead-ended in a cul-de-sac forcing him to backtrack until the correct house number appeared. Pulling to the curb, he hesitated while eyeing the immediate vicinity. The street appeared deserted at this hour on a late Sunday afternoon. He had not headed directly to this neighborhood, but had taken the long way, staying off the freeway, and avoiding areas heavily traveled by law enforcement.

Sure the coast was clear, the driver boldly pulled into the driveway beside an old sedan, got out acting as if he belonged, and walked up to the door. When nobody answered the bell, he peeked in a window beside the door. The house appeared to be deserted. He walked around the garage and reached over the top of the gate, slipping the latch and proceeding to the back yard.

The covered patio was vacant except for a cat lazing in a chair. The startled feline jumped down and ran, leapt onto the high block wall and disappeared into the next yard. The man stepped up to the sliding patio door and grasped the handle, expecting resistance, only to find it unlocked. It opened easily. He called out softly, "Mom, are you home?" A ploy often used in case any neighbors were listening.

He went to the refrigerator, took out a carton of milk, chugged a big gulp, and then returned it to its place. Somewhere in his mind, he heard the screech of his mother's voice chiding him, *"Howie, I told you not to do that!"* He jerked as if slapped and looked about, expecting to see her evil face pop up somewhere. "Go-o-o-o away, Bitch!" His automatic reaction every time *she* screamed in his memory. The package of Oreos on the counter diverted his attention and he popped one into his mouth.

Searching for more snacks, he opened what looked like a pantry, and found a washer and dryer. He stripped off all of his clothing, including his sneakers, and deposited them in the machine, tossed in a half cup of soap and pushed the start button. For a second, he was unsure what to do with the gun while his jeans were in the wash. His only option was to carry it around as he snooped.

Exploring the residence, he padded down the hall bare-assed, peeking into each room. He needed the bathroom, which he found down the hall between two of the bedrooms. He relieved himself, leaving the seat up, and then stepped into the glass-enclosed tub and took a shower, shampooing his hair and enjoying the feel of water cascading over him. Homelessness in the Nevada desert left him feeling like a tortoise. His last shower in a prison cell was a distant memory. He stood there for twenty minutes as if it could wash his past away.

After drying off and dropping the plush towel on the floor, he searched the medicine cabinet for deodorant. He found a woman's razor and some shaving cream, which he used to remove several months growth of beard, leaving the shavings where they fell in the sink. With a pair of scissors from a vanity drawer, he carefully cut off the excessively long black hair cropping it to just below his earlobes. The hanks dropped to the floor where he ignored them. The crude cut changed his appearance considerably. Anyone looking for him would be watching for someone with long scruffy hair and a beard. With that task done, his naked exploration around the house continued.

The sound of the spin cycle drew his attention back to the kitchen where he tossed his clothes and shoes into the dryer. Thirty minutes left to kill and chill.

He wandered into a bedroom where a laptop and printer occupied a small computer desk. The printer was of little interest, but the laptop looked to be top of the line. He unplugged it taking the charger as well. He tossed the bed and checked under the mattress for hidden valuables before snatching a pillowcase and inserting the computer.

Next, he riffled through a jewelry box, but didn't find anything but junk trinkets. *My grandmother wouldn't even want that crap.* A search of the closet came up empty as far as anything he could pawn. The private bath only produced a stethoscope lying on the counter. He picked it up, inserted the earpieces and checked his heartbeat. *My mother was wrong when she said I didn't have a heart.*

He carried the pillowcase into another bedroom and repeated his motions. The only thing valuable in that room was another laptop. The collection of books on a shelf was worthless. Reading had always been a struggle for him. A diagnosis of dyslexia and fetal alcohol syndrome rendered him hopeless in school. He still got PTSD recalling his mother's lip lashings and severe beatings for failing and dropping out. He shook off the memory and moved on.

The bedside table produced a vibrator and a romance novel. *Naughty old woman, I should come back and pay a visit tonight. You wouldn't need the vibrator after I'm done with you.* The fantasy brought on involuntary stirrings and he quickly diverted his attention to the medicine cabinet in the adjacent bath where there was nothing of interest. *These witches are boring.*

Entering the third bedroom produced a little better result. Another laptop, an iPod, and the medicine cabinet offered an assortment of prescription drugs. He stuffed everything into the booty bag. While pawing through the bureau drawers a wad of cash appeared. He palmed the bills. The rest of the drawers produced nothing but granny panties and super-sized bras that could have carried two bowling balls. He held one up and whistled. "Whoa, that's a bitchin knocker locker, whore." He dropped it on the floor.

The buzzer went off on the dryer, so he returned to the kitchen. After dressing in the warm, dry clothes, he stuffed the money into his hip pocket and inserted the gun back in its position for easy access.

He noticed the iPhone charging on the counter. After unplugging it, and stuffing that into his pocket, he deposited the charger in the bag. He grabbed the package of Oreos off the counter, a couple sodas from the fridge and two bottles of beer, depositing them into the sack.

After looking around the kitchen one last time, he lugged the heavy bag of loot through the house to make sure he had everything of value. The newer flat screen television was too cumbersome to conceal on his way out, so he left it. He noticed a dish on the table beside the front door with a set of car keys and some loose change in it. Pausing to contemplate his next move, he scooped up the change and grabbed the keys before departing through the same door he had entered, leaving it slightly ajar.

Cringing as the side gate squeaked slightly, he glanced up and down the street before emerging into the open. He headed for the sedan, bypassing the car he had acquired a few hours ago. He unlocked it with the key instead of tipping neighbors off with the chirp of the fob. A final sweep of his eyes around the area assured him no witnesses were present.

After setting the bag on the passenger seat, he started the car, cocking his ear. This engine he could easily hear. That other set of wheels reminded him of an over-sized golf cart. He backed out of the driveway and cruised away. The gas gauge registered full. It would be three hundred miles before he would have to stop for a refill. *That was a piece of cake. When will those suckers learn to lock their doors?*

49

Cora and Celia entered Buffalo Bills and stopped for a minute to take in the surroundings.

"This is the last one, if she's not here, I don't know what we will do. I didn't see her car in the parking lot."

Celia pointed across the room at a raised platform where a sign posted read "Security." A man in a dark uniform with a bored expression yawned and gazed out on the casino floor. She grabbed Cora's arm. "Over there. Cue up her picture and come on."

They approached him and Cora held her phone up toward his face. "Have you seen this woman? She's our friend, and she's missing. She should have been back home hours ago."

He eyed the women but didn't look at the phone. "That's the way it is when people play the games. They lose track of time."

Perturbed, Celia raised her voice. "Look at the picture, please. She's not answering her phone and we can't find her car."

He complied and recognition dawned. "Oh, yeah, she's been taken to a room back there." He pointed to a door.

"Why!" The girls chorused. "Is she in trouble?"

"Some guy…" he broke off. "I'll show you back there. She can tell you herself."

He stepped down and led them through the closed door to a room where there was a bustle of activity.

Emergency personnel were putting a bandage on Lillian's forehead and taking her blood pressure. She had a temporary brace on her right arm.

"Are you sure you don't want to go to a hospital?" one of them was asking.

When Cora and Celia walked into the room, Lillian perked up and tried to stand. The EMT put a hand on her shoulder and kept her from getting up.

"What happened," Cora asked. "We've been searching for you."

Lillian said angrily, "I was robbed!"

Celia looked closely at Lillian. "Were you mugged *again*?"

The EMT raised his eyebrows and asked, "Has this happened before?"

"It's a long story," answered Cora. At that point, she became aware of the Highway Patrol Officer standing in the corner taking notes on a pad of paper. He was relaying information on his radio to other NHP's elsewhere.

Cora heard him giving the description and plate number of Lillian's car.

"Don't tell me your car was stolen."

Lillian nodded. "The scum bag took my car and forty dollars which is all I said I had. And I can't find my phone."

"Where did this happen," Celia asked. "How did he get away with it? Did he do this to you?" She motioned to Lillian's injuries.

"I was playing the slots. The stinking bastard and I mean that literally, sat down, showed me a gun inside his jacket and demanded I give him my car keys, money and phone."

Celia chuckled slightly. "You left your phone at home."

"Oh," responded Lillian. "That's why I couldn't find it. I told him it was in the car."

Cora fingered the brace on her arm. "Is it broken?"

"No. He didn't lay a finger on me. As soon as he left, I jumped up to run to Security. I tripped over the next stool and went down, slamming my head and arm on the wood floor. I think I sprained my wrist." She touched the knot on her head. "Good thing I have a hard noggin."

Celia sighed. "You just keep testing your durability. One of these days, it will backfire."

"What made you come looking for me here?" She gave her friends a faint smile.

"Charla called. Courtney has been calling you with no answer, and Charla became concerned."

"Really—I have to be missing for her to care."

Cora gave Lillian a knowing nod. "Anyway, I found your phone. The battery was dead. I called Ella and there wasn't any answer. It turns out she isn't even home. She's on a senior bus tour."

Lillian sighed. "I guess I should have called her before I left home on this wild goose chase. I stayed the night over at that hotel on the other side of the freeway, the one with the shot up old car. Then I went to ZZYZX. By then I changed my mind about going all the way down there to visit that old bat. I stopped here to eat lunch and veg out for a while. I really intended to be home late this afternoon."

Celia chuckled. "We shouldn't let you out of the house alone anymore. Sometimes I think you need a keeper."

Lillian squared her shoulders and spoke indignantly, "I can take care of myself."

Cora raised her eyebrows and gazed at Lillian's injuries. "And you do it so well."

Celia addressed the EMT. "Can we take her home now?"

"I think she's good to go. She just needs to sign this form for the insurance."

Cora approached the NHP officer. "Is there any word on her car? Has anyone spotted it?"

He nodded negatively. "I have her address and phone number, so she'll be notified if the robber is apprehended or her car is found. You can take her home now."

A casino employee came into the room pushing a wheel chair. "I'll give you a ride to the door if you don't mind." She placed a clipboard and pen in Lillian's reach. "I need you to sign this incident report. We'll be saving the security footage in case it is needed in a legal action later." She waited for Lillian to sign the document. "The full report will be mailed to you."

"I'll go get the car and pull up to the door." Celia exited and disappeared down the hallway leading back to the casino, followed closely by a security guard.

50

Over Lillian's strenuous objections, the paramedics insisted she ride in a wheelchair to the front door. She clutched her handbag and looked down at the floor, trying to avoid all of the curious stares from other patrons. "This is humiliating," she grumbled.

Celia's PT waited at the curb. Cora folded her own lanky figure into the rear seat. Lillian moved into the front passenger seat and secured the belt.

"You take care now," the casino employee pushing the chair said. "We look forward to having you back when you are better." She smiled and waved.

The door slammed and Lillian grunted, "When pigs fly."

It wasn't until the car was gaining speed at the on ramp to the I-15 that Cora spoke from the back seat. "Want to tell us how you got into this pickle?"

"I feel like such a fool," Lillian chided herself. "I went off half-cocked. It was too late in the day to make that trip to California. I stopped for a break and before I realized, it was midnight, so I got a room."

"We know that much," Celia interjected. "The desk clerk over there confirmed it."

"What happened next?" Cora asked softly. "What did you do between leaving there and ending up at Buffalo Bills?"

"I'm so stupid," Lillian spat.

Cora reached forward and patted Lillian on the shoulder. "Now don't say that. Everyone does impulsive things sometimes."

"I started to head south again, but I got sidetracked. On a whim, I took the road to ZZYZX." She chuckled. "I guess I was still trying to avoid seeing Ella."

"You wouldn't have seen her anyway," said Celia. "Charla told Cora that Ella isn't home right now."

"Oh, well anyway after the tour of that poor excuse for a tourist attraction, I headed back towards Primm. I needed a pit stop, so I thought I'd have lunch at Buffalo Bills since I've never been there before and will probably never go there again."

"You could have called us to let us know where you were," Celia said, trying not to be too stern.

"I couldn't find my phone."

"You had Courtney's phone."

"What? I don't remember taking her phone with me. Where would it be? It's not in my purse." She craned her neck and looked at Celia. "I thought she left it at our house when her mother gave back her own phone. I'd already bought it, so I was going to keep it for a backup phone if mine got broke."

"It must be somewhere in your car. Maybe it's in the glove compartment. Maybe Courtney put it there when you took her back to school."

The light dawned. Lillian slapped her forehead and then groaned in pain. "That's what that stupid noise was that I kept hearing. I thought there was some kind of warning alarm going off because of something wrong with the engine. I was all set to take that damn car back to the dealer and complain when I got home. I'm such an idiot!"

"The battery in your phone was dead, so Cora put it on the charger. You can call Courtney when you get home. She's been worried about you."

"Has Charla been worried too?" Lillian felt smug. *Maybe she'd finally gotten some attention from that girl.*

"She seemed concerned when she called. I'll phone her now to let her know we found you." Cora dug around in her purse to find her cell.

"No," spoke Lillian a little too loudly. "Let her stew for another hour until we get home. I want her to worry."

"Why?" Celia asked.

"Let's see if she's really concerned about me. Let's see how long it takes her to call and see if I'm home yet."

Cora moaned. "That's cruel. You're just making things worse."

"I probably am, but all my efforts to make things better have failed miserably. She has a guilty conscience about something and until she comes clean with me, our relationship is always going to have a deep chasm between us. Let her strew a while."

Cora put her phone away and shrugged. "Okay, if that's what you want."

51

The conversation waned as Celia turned onto their street. When the house came into view, she slammed on the brakes. "What the..."

Lillian had been dozing and the abrupt stop awakened her. She looked around and shrieked. "That's my car in the driveway. How in hell did it get here?"

Celia slowly progressed forward but didn't pull into the driveway. She stopped at the curb across the street.

Cora's mouth dropped open when she realized something was missing. "My car is gone!"

"Did you put it in the garage?" Lillian asked.

"No. When we left, it was right there." She pointed at the driveway.

Celia grabbed her cell. "I'm calling 911. The thief that stole your car obviously found our address in it and he may be inside. We can't go in until the coast is clear."

"I bet he's loading up on our stuff now." Lillian speculated. "Pull up in back of my car so he can't move it."

Cora disagreed. "He's probably already gone and he must have taken my wheels. He knew NHP would be looking for yours. Damn! Next time I see Brown Betty, she'll smell like a garbage dump."

"*If* you see her again," Lillian corrected. "You better call the police and report it stolen. They can start looking now while we wait."

It took twenty minutes for a police cruiser to pull up to the curb. Celia jumped out and talked to the officer, explaining the situation.

He turned and eyed her purple PT and then walked over and opened the passenger door of Lillian's car. "The key is still in the ignition."

He walked up and tried the front door. "It's still locked. There's no sign of forced entry."

Celia suggested, "Go around to the back. He may have gotten in through the patio door. We left in a big hurry and may have forgotten to lock it."

She escorted the officer through the gate to the back. He motioned for her to hang back while he progressed to the patio. The door was partially open and he put his hand up, indicating she should stay put by the side of the house. He drew his gun.

After what seemed like hours but was only minutes, he came back out and waved her in. "Somebody has definitely been here but they're gone now. He escorted her to the bathroom where the hairy intruder had cleaned himself up.

Celia took one look at the mess of hair on the sink and floor and groaned, "Ugh."

A noise at the back door got their attention. Cora and Lillian walked in. "We got tired of waiting in the hot car. Was he here?" Lillian asked.

Celia pointed at the dirty bathroom. "See for yourself."

She peeked in and took a deep breath. "He shaved and gave himself a haircut. That took a lot of gall. He left wet towels on the floor. That's a man for you."

The officer stood back. "You ladies should look around and see if anything is missing. He's been here and gone and probably didn't leave empty-handed." He began speaking into his radio, passing on necessary information for the dispatcher to rebroadcast.

Cora reminded him. "Don't forget to tell them he stole my car." She gave him the make, model and description along with the license plate number. "It's old, but it's still mine—or it was until this afternoon."

Celia shrieked from her bedroom. "My laptop is gone!"

Lillian yelled out, "Mine is gone too, and he took some prescription drugs and money." When she noticed her discarded bra on the floor, she huffed, "Pervert!"

Cora inspected her room and came back with a frown. "He took my computer too." Then she returned to the kitchen and blurted, "Damn it. He took Lillian's phone that I left it on the counter—charger and all. He also took my Oreo cookies. I hope he chokes on them."

The officer relayed the information, took notes, and informed the women, "Because this involves felony auto theft with use of a firearm, I'll have a tech come out and fingerprint your car and the bathroom. Don't touch anything until they've been here and gone. They'll take some pictures and DNA samples because it started with an armed robbery at Buffalo Bills. If he's apprehended he'll go to trial on that evidence."

"What about our stuff?" Celia asked.

"He's probably pawned it by now. Notify your insurance companies and file a claim. Notify your phone company and cancel your cell service for the phone so he can't use it. Were there any house keys with the car keys he took?"

Cora nodded. "Yes, he got those too."

"Then I would suggest you call a locksmith and have your locks changed immediately. That's about all we can do now."

Lillian blurted, "Can't you use my cell phone to track him—you know, like which towers it's pinging off of?"

The officer stifled a chuckle. "You watch too much CSI on television. Cancel the service. He'll probably sell the phone"

"That's it?" the girls chorused.

"Pretty much—we don't know if he left town and if he did, which direction he went. He has a head start on us. It's in the system now so all personnel will be on the lookout for your car and him." He looked at Lillian's bandaged forehead and splinted arm. "Did he do that to you?"

She blushed slightly, "No. When I jumped up to run for the security desk and report the robbery, I tripped and fell."

The officer took one more look around and headed for the back door. "I'll be out front until someone from the department shows up to take evidence. If you think of anything else, let me know."

Cora saw him out and then asked, "Does anyone want some coffee?"

"It's a little late for that much caffeine," Lillian sighed. "We could have some tea instead? I could use a sandwich."

Celia ducked out the back door. "I'm going to move my car and take the keys out of yours. I'll check and see if Courtney's phone is in the glove compartment."

Cora yelled to stop her. "Put on some surgical gloves first! We don't need you obliterating the robber's prints."

"I have some in my car and I'll use the passenger door. Good thing you reminded me."

Cora and Lillian made eye contact. "She carries surgical gloves in her car?" Lillian exclaimed.

"She's a nurse. What if she comes upon a traffic accident—she would need them to help somebody."

"Or an armed robbery," Lillian mumbled.

The roommates where enjoying their tea and sandwiches when Cora's phone chimed.

"It's Charla," she said as she picked it up. "What do you want me to tell her?"

Lillian reached across the table and took the phone, putting it to her ear.

"Were you looking for your mother?" She grinned as she spoke.

"Where the hell have you been? Courtney is frantic."

"Well it's nice to know Courtney cares. Have you been worried?"

There was no response at first. "You are using Cora's phone so I assume you're back home. Is everything back to normal?"

"It is in a manner of speaking. An armed robber stole my car, I may have broken my wrist and I have a lump on my forehead. Other than that..."

"Well I'm glad you're back with your friends," Charla interrupted. "It doesn't sound too serious. Now I have to go. I'll call Courtney."

"But don't you want to know the rest of my story?" Lillian said hurriedly.

"Not right now. I'm putting out some fires."

"What fires? Is your house in flames?"

"Not that kind of fires. Remember my open house?"

"Yes. It was very lovely. Did you get an offer on it?" Lillian grinned as she recalled her mischievous antic with those buyers from San Francisco.

"No! Somebody has been lying and spreading rumors. They are saying there was a murder committed in the house. There was no murder! It's all false information and if I find out who started that rumor, I'm going to sue them."

Lillian scowled at the thought that her own child would sue her. She forced some sweetness into her reply. "I'm sorry you're having such a hard time. I can't imagine why anyone would want to sabotage your business." A wicked grin lit up her face.

"It was probably that bitch, Margo Halstead. She was after that listing for months when I stole it out from under her nose. Now I have to go and do damage control. Call your granddaughter when you have a chance." The call ended.

Lillian held the phone for a few beats and looked from Cora to Celia. "That woman is like a chocolate covered ice cube. She looks delicious on the outside, but the inside is cold and numbing."

Celia chuckled. "Maybe they got the babies mixed up in the hospital and she really belongs to Leona Helmsley."

Cora picked up the phone and searched through the addresses. "We better call Courtney before we forget." When it began to ring, she handed it back to Lillian. "Let her know you're safe."

52

A trip to the doctor on Monday morning confirmed the wrist was only sprained, not broken and the bump on her forehead turned out to be superficial. Lillian left the doctor's office in a huff.

Celia asked, "What are you pissed about now. That was good news."

"Yes, it was, until he reminded me that I'm not young anymore, my bones are brittle, and I need to be more cautious about my activities and who I hang out with…as if I've invited those hoodlums to rob me! He suggested I work out at a gym and acquire some muscle."

"That's good advice for all of us. We need to get back to the exercise classes. What did you tell him?"

"I told him it's not my activities that are the problem. It's the criminal element out there preying on people they think are too old to defend themselves."

"He's only looking out for your best interest."

"You may be right, but he still didn't need to remind me how old I am."

When the two arrived back home, Lillian dialed Charla's number hoping to get some of her time to discuss serious matters.

"Hi, Mom, did you go to the doctor?" The sound of a motor created a noisy background and Charla's voice sounded like it was coming from a tunnel.

"Are you driving and talking on your cell phone?" Lillian frowned. "How many times do I have to warn you about the dangers of that?"

"I have Bluetooth in my car. It's hands free."

"Oh, are you going out to show a property?"

"No. I'm headed to Phoenix to meet up with Ella."

"Why would you be going down there? Ella is on a bus tour to Sedona, isn't she?" Once again, that little stab of jealously surfaced and Lillian's heart ached. She had just been through a traumatic experience, but Charla was going in Ella's direction instead of coming over to give Lillian some tea and sympathy. She felt cheated.

"I'm her designated contact in case of a medical emergency."

"What medical emergency? You said she was on vacation."

"She was, but she suffered a stroke and is being air lifted to a hospital in Phoenix."

"Why didn't you fly?" Lillian's mind was jumping ahead already as she tried to stay in the present. Was that old reprobate that had stolen so much time from Lillian's life with her own daughter finally going to skip the light fantastic up the path to the pearly gates? Maybe she would finally stop competing for Charla's attention.

"Mom, are you still there?" Charla's irritated voice brought Lillian back to the present.

"I'm sorry dear; I was just thinking I could have gone with you."

"There wasn't time to plan and I couldn't get a plane ticket on such short notice. I'm already half-way there. Courtney is on the way and meeting me at the hospital. I'll call you with an update."

"That would be nice." The ensuing silence indicated that Charla had already ended the call.

Lillian put the phone down and sighed. "Ella stroked on the bus and she's on her way to the hospital. Charla's halfway there already. It seems that woman always comes first with her."

Celia patted Lillian's hand. "That shouldn't come as a surprise to you at this late date. It's sad to say, but Charla has built a close relationship with Ella and you can't change it. Just bide your time. Nature will take care of the situation eventually. I speak from a medical standpoint. People her age rarely recover from massive strokes. Things will work out for you."

Lillian sat silently for a while. "What's wrong with me?"

"There's nothing wrong with you. Why do you ask?" Cora commented.

"Ella is my aunt. I should have some feelings for her. I should be concerned about her health. She's the last of my mother's generation. Everyone else is dead. Why do I feel so evil and have bad thoughts about her? There's something missing in my DNA."

Celia took her hand. "People drift apart for many reasons. It's natural. Her interference in your relationship with Charla has a lot to do with it. If you don't have any great love or concern for the woman, don't feel guilty. I have a lot of shirt-tail relatives I don't like and when they die, I'll probably not shed a tear."

Cora spoke up. "If you want to, I'll drive you down there."

"In what," Celia reminded her, "your car was stolen."

"I can drive Lillian's for her. If this is Ella's final days, we should be there to support Charla. She'll be crushed."

"Don't remind me." Lillian frowned and rose from the table, clearing her dishes. In the meantime, I think I have to stop obsessing over it. I'm sure Charla will call me if Ella becomes critical. Maybe it isn't even serious. Maybe she just drank too much Vodka and passed out. I need a diversion. Does anyone want to go play Bingo?"

Celia chuckled and suggested, "We should take my car. Yours needs a major cleaning and detailing after that grungy thief used it. You can never tell what kind of cooties he left behind."

Cora added, "And what about all the fingerprint dust the cops left? The car is a mess."

"Well," Lillian responded, "I think I'll just go spray the inside with some Raid and close it up. Tomorrow I'll tackle the cleaning. Have we got any Lysol wipes?"

53

The eternal sun shone brightly on the Las Vegas valley on Tuesday morning. Lillian and Cora were preparing breakfast while Celia read headlines aloud from the morning newspaper. The chime of Lillian's phone interrupted the morning. She picked it up and commented, "Its Charla." After a deep breath she answered, "Hello."

The response was a sobbing noise and stuttering voice. Lillian took a deep breath. "Don't tell me, let me guess. Ella didn't make it."

"She's gone," sobbed Charla, barely able to speak the words.

"I'm sorry. I know she meant a lot to you." She rolled her eyes and thought; *I bet she won't cry like that when I die.* "Do you want me to come down there?"

"You don't need to." Charla seemed to regain her composure. "Courtney is here. There's nothing to do. We've arranged for burial in San Diego and now we have to drive over there and close out her apartment."

"What about a funeral? Isn't there going to be a service for her?"

"She didn't want one. She pre-arranged long ago for direct interment beside Uncle and her boys. She didn't want anyone crying over her."

"That doesn't sound like Ella. She always liked attention."

"It's what she wanted. She always told me that if people didn't come to see her when she was alive, she didn't want them hanging around after she's dead. Courtney and I will see to it her wishes are carried out. I may not be back for a few days."

"Okay then, I would just be in the way. You don't want me around."

"Now don't take it that way."

"That is the only way I can take it. For years, you and Ella have had a little admiration society of your own, and you never included me."

"Mom, this is not the time to bring up grudges. I'm hurting. I loved my aunt."

"Correction, dear; she was my aunt and your great-aunt." *Although you treated her as if she were your mother,* thought Lillian, but decided not to add to the rancor by verbalizing it.

"Whatever," Charla responded with effort to speak without sobbing. The sound of blowing her nose honked loudly over the phone. "Now she's gone and I didn't even get to say goodbye."

"You're right, there's no place for me down there. I'll see you when you get home." Lillian ended the call and looked at Cora. "My competition bit the big one. I don't suppose it will change anything between me and Charla."

"Just give it time," Cora said sympathetically. "Charla had a relationship with Ella and it will take her time to grieve. When she's done, she'll come around. You'll see."

"I should at least send flowers. Shouldn't I?"

Cora filled their coffee cups and sat down "If you're not invited to the party, you're not obligated to send a gift. I wouldn't bother. Why don't you wait until Charla gets home and then order flowers sent to her office with a condolence card? Remind her that you are still here. She'll be forced to call and thank you for them."

"I could send her a cactus...," said Lillian with an evil grin, "you know—one with lots of barbs on it."

Cora chuckled and responded with an emphatic, "No! Send a nice arrangement that says, 'I love you in your time of need.'"

"I suppose you're right. I think I'll put on some old clothes and start cleaning my car and disinfecting it. Do we have any cootie spray?"

"Let's finish eating," Celia suggested, "and then we'll all pitch in to detail your car. I suppose we'll have to take Cora shopping for a new set of wheels next."

"Don't write off Brown Betty yet," Cora cautioned. "She might turn up."

"She could, but in what condition? You might want a new car after you see what that thief does to her," Lillian reminded her.

It took two hours of scrubbing and disinfecting, but the girls finally sighed and stepped back to view Lillian's completely restored car. "She looks just like she did when we drove her home from the dealership, thanks to my roommates." Lillian smiled and wiped her brow.

"I have to admit," Celia grinned, "this wasn't as gross as cleaning up that mess the perp left in the hall bathroom. I felt like I needed to shower with Lysol after that."

Cora snickered. "Was he some kind of Yeti?"

"They don't live in the desert and carry guns." Lillian chuckled. "But now that you mention it, he did have a face only a mother ape could love."

After the girls showered and were relaxing on the back patio with some iced tea, Lillian suddenly jumped up and started for the house.

"Where are you going in such a hurry?" Cora asked. "Do you have to pee?"

"I'm going to buy a gun!"

"What?" Cora and Celia responded in unison. "What do you want with one of those?"

"I'm tired of being robbed. This was the second time. I feel like I have a target on my ass. The next loser that comes at me is going to get a big surprise."

Cora followed Lillian into the house. "Now don't go postal. Stop and think about it. You're acting in the heat of the moment."

Celia caught up and added, "You'll just end up shooting some innocent bystander. You don't know anything about guns."

"Can't we talk you out of this? Wouldn't some pepper spray be better? You can't go to jail for shooting someone with that." Cora said. "I'll even buy it for you."

"I've made up my mind." Lillian said emphatically. She picked up her purse, searched for her keys, and squared her shoulders. "Do you want to come along?"

Cora and Celia exchanged glances and shrugged. Cora said, "Come on Celia. We better go along and make sure she buys one that won't do too much damage when she shoots herself in the foot."

Celia shrugged. "The two of us can at least keep her away from the assault rifles. An angry grandmother can do a lot of damage with an AK-47."

"Don't be ridiculous," Lillian snorted. "My purse isn't big enough for anything that size. I just want something I can fit in here." She held up her handbag. "The next time I'm ordered to reach into my purse and give something to a perp, he's going to be on the receiving end of a bullet. Now are you coming?" She headed for the front door.

A couple of hours later, the three women emerged from the American Gun Shop. "Why can't I take that gun with me today?" Lillian complained. I paid for it." She had picked out a nice small used 22-caliber pistol that fit nicely into her bag. She filled out an application for a concealed weapon permit, all the time complaining about the red tape and how easily criminals obtained guns without all this *stupid* paperwork.

"Don't you pay attention to the news? There's a waiting period and you have to pass the background check. They'll call you when you can pick it up."

"I'm just an old grandma with gray hair. Can't they make an exception? Can't they tell I'm harmless? What if we get robbed in the meantime and I don't have my gun to shoot the bastard."

Cora snickered. "That's not going to happen, and besides, if you were harmless, you wouldn't be buying a gun in the first place and that purse snatcher you nailed wouldn't be wondering if he'll ever be able to father a child. If you had a gun then, he'd probably be dead—or singing soprano."

Celia piped up, "This is like closing the barn door after the horses got out. We won't get robbed again." Then a thought struck her. "Did we lock the patio door before we left?"

They all gaped at each other. Lillian headed for the car. "We better get back home, pronto!"

54

Everything was quiet on the Charla front for the next few days. Lillian tried several times to call, but there was no answer. Attempts to reach Courtney failed too. She abruptly slammed her phone down on the kitchen table. "They're treating me like I'm dead," she complained loudly Friday morning.

"Who is treating you that way?" asked Cora as she filled the coffee maker.

"Charla never called back with updates. She's ignoring me."

"You must know what it's like to clean up the remainders after someone died. It's a big job. I'm sure she wants to concentrate on that and get back to work next week. She hasn't abandoned you. She's just busy."

"I know you think you're saying all the nice words to make me feel better, but you don't need to give me lip service," Lillian grouched.

Cora sighed and tried to ignore her friend's surly tone of voice. "It's not lip service, Lillian."

"I'm sorry. I guess you're right. I remember the mess Charlie's parents left behind. After forty years in the same house, it took six weekends of garage sales to get rid of everything. His mother never threw away anything, not even used plastic bread bags and twist ties. There was old food in the freezer out in their garage that I swear contained dinosaur meat. And there were packages of frozen vegetables that went out of date when Nixon was still claiming '*I'm not a criminal*.'"

Cora chuckled. "That sounds all too familiar. People, who grew up in the great depression era as our parents did, were savers and recyclers. My parents were the same. My mother even used coffee grounds twice before discarding them."

Lillian made a gagging sound. "That's enough to make you want to give up drinking coffee."

"Maybe we girls need to think about some spring-cleaning and yard sales. We can hardly fit a car into that garage out there."

"Not this week," Lillian replied.

Celia came dragging in the front door and interrupted the conversation. "I need a bowl of cereal and a valium. I think I need to sleep for a year."

"What happened? Did you have a bad night in the ER?" Lillian asked.

"I can't talk about it because of HIPPA laws. Let's just say some tourists are complete idiots." She grabbed a bowl and poured out cereal. "This young generation coming to Vegas for the first time will put anything in their mouth, no questions asked."

Cora chuckled. "It's like they go through their infancy all over again. Whatever someone hands them, it goes in their pie hole."

Celia swiftly wolfed down a bowl of Cheerios. "Now I need a pill."

Lillian piped up. "We're fresh out of those, remember. They were stolen along with Cora's car."

Celia frowned. "Oh yeah, I forgot. I guess I'll just have to settle for a couple of aspirin. Try not to make any noise. I need sleep." She shuffled off to her room and quietly closed the door.

Cora directed her attention back to Lillian. "Maybe you should take a page out of Celia's book."

"What does that mean?" Lillian wrinkled her brow."

"I mean, Celia wastes no time stressing over why her kids and grand-kids never call her."

Courtney's former cell rang, interrupting the conversation. Lillian picked it up and looked at the caller I.D. "Speak of the Devil, its Charla."

"I'm on my way back home," she said without preamble. "Courtney went back to school."

"So you got everything taken care of. That was fast and I'm fine. Thank you for asking." Lillian responded with an acid tongue.

"Oh, well this week has been so hectic I hardly had time to do my hair. I cleaned Ella's place out of all the personal items like photos and things and then I donated her furnishings to charity. I'll drop by tomorrow. There are a few things you might want to keep."

"That would be nice," said Lillian with a smirk. "I should have been there for her burial."

"We'll talk when I get back." The call ended.

Cora spoke up. "Why bother to show up for the burial. You didn't like her."

"I just want to make sure the witch is really dead."

"Are you still going to order flowers sent to Charla's office?"

"What kind of flower says 'Remember me? I'm your mother.'"

"There is always Forget-Me-Nots—can we still get those?" Cora snickered. "On second thought, maybe just a soppy sentimental card would do."

"I'll have to think about it. In the meantime, I have to go shopping for a new laptop or some other kind of computer. Why don't they invent PC's with a way to bolt them down to the desktop? That would throw the thieves off. They'd have to go looking for a screwdriver and that would take too much time. Do you want to come along?"

Cora had been wiping down the counters and range while they talked. She threw the rag in the sink. "Sure, why not? We'll never see our other ones again. There must be a thousand messages on Facebook that we've missed by now. My emails must be stacked up too."

"Okay, then. Thirty minutes and we're out of here."

55

Charla arrived as promised on Saturday morning. She carried a package about the size of a large breadbox into the house and plunked it down on the kitchen table.

Lillian eyed it. "What's that?"

"This is a bunch of photos of your family. There are old pictures of Ella and her siblings, some of your mother, and some of you as a kid with Ella. I donated all of her household goods to a place that helps abused and neglected women and children start new lives. Her clothes went to Goodwill and I inherited her jewelry and cash."

"So she didn't leave anything to me?" Lillian smirked and pursed her lips.

"No," Charla replied flatly as if the concept was ridiculous.

Lillian leafed through the messy contents apparently flung carelessly into the box. She gathered a handful of bent, scratched and dog-eared photos and flipped through them with little interest, pitching them back into the container. "I have enough old crap like that. I don't need hers."

She picked up a framed photo and stared at the images. It was a formal pose of Ella, Charla, and Courtney taken by a photographer. The latter appeared to be about ten years old. "When was this taken?" She turned it so Charla could see the picture.

"Oh, that. Courtney and I thought it would be nice to have a three-generation picture taken with Ella. It's nice isn't it?"

Lillian clamped her lips together and inhaled deeply with indignation. She felt throbbing start in her head as her blood pressure soared like a hot air balloon. "That is not a three-generation picture. Ella is—*was* not your mother. To be three generations, she would have to give birth to you. How many times must I remind you, she was my aunt—not your *mother*," she said emphatically. "I wish you would remember that and make the distinction. It's very hurtful to me."

Charla shrugged. "I know who you are. I don't understand why you are so sensitive where Ella is concerned."

Lillian turned toward the counter where coffee was brewing to hide the disgusted expression on her face. *Sometimes the peroxide on that girl's head soaks in all the way to her heart.* "Do you want some coffee?" She proceeded to pour two mugs full without waiting for an answer.

Cora wandered in. "You're back. How was the trip?"

Charla sank into the nearest chair as tears welled up in her eyes. She buried her face in her hands. "I'm really going to miss her."

Lillian and Cora looked at each other over Charla's head and rolled their eyes. Lillian made a stilted effort to console her weeping daughter, but could only muster a brief shoulder pat. Trying her best to sound sympathetic, she said, "Would you like to talk about it?" *Why did I say that? I don't really care.*

Charla proceeded to describe every detail of Ella's last hours. "Courtney and I held her hands and talked to her. She was in a coma but they said the hearing is the last to go, so we talked to her, begging her to wake up." She stopped to wipe her tears, smearing her eye makeup, and then dabbed at her nose.

"I should have been there." Lillian said in a failed attempt to sound broken up. *Just to make sure the witch is dead.*

Charla continued to sniffle, ignoring Lillian's comment. "She never woke and finally just slipped away."

Lillian smiled with secret satisfaction. It went unnoticed by her weeping daughter.

"We saw to it she was laid to rest with Uncle and my cousins."

"*My* uncle and cousins," Lillian corrected.

"But I was the closest to her. She really was a good woman even though you didn't care for her."

"For good reason," Lillian frowned. "She was mean to me when I was a kid and I had to endure her less than satisfactory skills as a babysitter."

"Mother," Charla interrupted, "that was decades ago. You were just a kid. Get over it."

"You don't get it. She horned in on my relationship with you and interfered with my efforts to discipline you. She gloated over her success in stealing time from me—time we could have spent cultivating a close relationship as mother and daughter."

"She was good to me. I thought you appreciated that."

"You thought wrong. When we moved here to be near you, I thought I would finally have you all to myself. Wrong. They suddenly decided to re-locate also, and to where? Here! I was glad when her old man finally retired and moved them to San Diego. I thought it would give you and me more time together."

"That sounds so…cold." Charla sniffed and blew her nose.

"Well, that's how I feel. Have your pity party this coming week, and then turn the page and move on. It's not like she was your mother."

"Aren't you grieving even a little? She was the last of your generation."

"I hate to have to keep correcting you, but she was the last of my mother's generation. I am the last of my generation."

"I know. I just can't think right now." Charla blew her dripping nose again.

"I'm sorry if I don't feel the same about her passing as you do, but now maybe we can discuss our relationship and how we can grow closer together."

"I really don't know what you mean. I try to be here for you," Charla whined as she picked up her phone and began thumbing the apps.

Lillian took a big breath and exhaled. "In your own way, I guess, but I would like to have more. We never have any fun together. You are always busy. I tried to talk to you at that open house and you blew me off. Remember when you were a young mother, we used to take Courtney and go to the mall and shop until we dropped. We haven't done that since Courtney started school. You can't even find time to have lunch with me once a week. Yet, there are postings all over Facebook of you and numerous friends you've spent time with."

Charla appeared not to be listening. She was engrossed in something on the screen of her phone. She began texting someone and seemed to forget she was sitting across the table from her mother.

Cora had been silently watching the exchange between her best friend and Charla. She made occasional eye contact with Lillian, as they seemed to be exchanging unspoken words and the same thoughts. A few times, she opened her mouth to speak, but thought better of it. She finally picked up her coffee cup and walked away. "I think you guys need to talk. I'll just take this into the other room and watch television. It's nice to see you again, Charla." She made a silent hand motion for Lillian to keep trying to communicate with the woman.

Lillian reached out and covered Charla's phone with her hand. "Please, can that wait? We need to discuss this problem. I tried at the open house, but…"

Charla interrupted, "My open house was busy. It wasn't the place to have any lectures from my mother."

"Then, how about here—this is a good place to talk, isn't it?" Lillian looked around the room as if making sure they were alone. She lowered her voice and leaned in closer. "I want to know what you are keeping from me. What would cause you to avoid spending time with me? You need to let your mother back into your life. It's very hurtful always being on the outside looking in. I should be your best friend but you treat me like a stranger."

Charla paused for a few beats, glanced back down at her phone and up at Lillian. She opened her mouth as if she was about to say something meaningful, when her cell chimed. She checked the caller I.D. and stood up. "I have to take this." She slid the patio door open and stepped outside, closing it behind her.

Lillian took a swig of coffee and mumbled, "Lousy timing."

When Charla came back shortly, she picked up her handbag and headed for the front door. "I have to go. Do what you want with those photos and things. I kept the ones I wanted and Courtney took a few. The rest are yours."

Lillian called after her, "But what about our talk? Don't you want to know what happened in Primm?"

"Later. I have to go."

The front door closed and Lillian mumbled, "She could care less about my problems. It's like she lives on another planet."

Cora came back with her empty coffee cup and put it in the sink. "I heard that. Give her time. She has to get over Ella."

"Do you suppose, if I were dying, I would get any attention from her?" *Is there a way to pretend to be dead or in a coma?*

"Don't say dying," cautioned Cora. "Be careful what you wish for."

Lillian picked up the box and headed for the door to the garage.

"Aren't you going to show me what's in there?" Cora called after her.

"No. It's full of resentment and memories I'd just as soon forget." She proceeded to the garage and deposited the entire package in the trash bin.

56

The doorbell sounded several times followed by loud banging on the security door.

Cora jumped at the sudden racket. She crept to the entry and peeked out of the window by the door. Charla stood there with an angry facial expression. "Oh, no," she groaned. "The jig is up."

The racket started up again and Charla shouted, "Celia, answer the door. I know you are in there."

Cora quickly opened up. "Shush! Keep the noise down, damn it. Celia is taking a nap before she has to go to work."

"Your car is gone. I didn't expect to find *you* at home." She looked back at the driveway as if expecting to see something she missed before.

"My car was…"

Charla didn't wait for an explanation. "Where's my mother?"

Cora opened the security door and motioned for Charla to come in. "Keep your voice down."

She flounced into the living room and set her bag on the couch. "So where is the little blabbermouth? She owes me an explanation as to why she sabotaged my open house."

Cora bit her tongue to suppress a cutting reply. "She's gone to the shooting range."

"Why would that old woman need a shooting range? Has she gone off her rocker?" She proceeded to the kitchen and pulled a bottle of water from the fridge. "You don't mind, do you?"

Cora forced a smile. "It wouldn't matter if I did."

"So what is she doing at a shooting range? She doesn't know anything about guns." She took one long swig from the bottle and set it on the counter.

"She bought a pistol and she's learning to use it."

"Oh for God's sake, what is she thinking? Why would she need to do that at her age?"

Cora's brow furrowed and she spoke in a forcibly controlled voice. "In case you have forgotten, she has been robbed twice and our house was burglarized. She feels she needs to arm herself in case it happens again."

"That purse snatcher didn't get anything—when was she robbed—what do you mean your house was burgled? Nobody told me about that. What are you talking about?"

Cora motioned for Charla to sit down at the kitchen table. "Maybe you need to focus for a few minutes and let me tell you what has been going on with your mother. She tried to tell you the other day, but you were in no mood to listen and you left abruptly, cutting her off. Don't you want to know what happened during those hours that she was missing and we were frantically trying to find her?" She stared at Charla. Her makeup was impeccable and there was not a hair out of place. Her dress and shoes shouted designer labels. She offered Charla a chair. "Can I get you some coffee?"

Charla grabbed the bottle of water and sat down. "No this is fine."

The muffled sound of a cell phone chimed and Charla started to rise to go answer it.

Cora placed her hand on Charla's shoulder and pushed her back down. "Let it ring. It's time to talk."

"But…" She twisted in her chair looking longingly in the direction of the living room. "What if it's important?"

"Not as important as what I am about to tell you."

57

While awaiting approval to become a heat-packing mama, Lillian had been sneaking off to the gun range for instructions on how to shoot the *thing.*

The instructor was very patient with her when she fumbled the practice piece; shot wildly, missed the targets completely, and at one point, nearly shot the instructor in the foot. His quick reflexes avoided disaster. After that, he replaced the live ammo with rubber bullets. They could maim but not kill.

"Are you sure a container of pepper spray won't do?" He asked politely when it appeared Lillian was in over her head. "I have some for sale."

"You don't bring pepper spray to a gun fight, Sonny!" Lillian insisted. "I've been attacked twice. The next time, the advantage is going to be on my side of the muzzle. Now let's get on with this." She pointed at the target and fired several shots. The first five hit the back wall and bounced to the floor. One hit near the bullseye. "See, I'm getting the hang of it."

The instructor moved around behind her and replied with enthusiasm, "I see that. Maybe you'll get as good as *my* grandmother."

"Was your grandmother a crack shot, too?" Lillian asked as she closed one eye, sighted down the barrel, and pulled the trigger.

"She tried, but she only succeeded in taking out my grandfather's kneecap. He never walked the same after that." He laughed softly.

The instructor reminded Lillian, "Hold the gun with both hands and place your feet slightly apart so you can keep your balance." He demonstrated for her. "Squeeze the trigger with just your finger, not your whole hand."

"Are you kidding me—both hands? I have to learn to shoot one handed because I have to pull it out of my purse. I won't have time to do it your way."

"Okay, let's try it that way." He stepped behind her once again to avoid wild shots.

Lillian held the gun in one hand. The weight of it made her wrist tremble when she squeezed the trigger. Nothing happened. "What's the matter with this stupid thing?"

"You're out of bullets and out of time."

"Oh, dear, I guess we better schedule another practice session." She looked at her watch. "I have to get home now Sonny, but can we do this again tomorrow?"

"Sure, how much ammo can you afford?" He grinned.

Lillian looked at the targets and mentally tallied how much she had already expended and what it cost her to replace the things stolen from their house. She shrugged. "Money is no object."

"Okay, then," *Sonny* replied. "I'll see you tomorrow about the same time. This has been fun." He stepped sideways and put his hand on Lillian's practice piece, gently taking it from her. "Tomorrow, we'll practice with your own gun. Okay?"

A few minutes later, Lillian gleefully left the gun store with her new purchase. She had permission to own and carry a weapon of granny destruction.

Lillian noticed Charla's car parked at the curb when she drove up. *I wonder how she will react when I show her my smoking hot pistol,* she thought, *but, first, I have to go pee.*

244

She slipped as quiet as possible into the house with the intention of making a bathroom stop before facing Charla.

"Is that you, Lillian?" Cora was calling from the kitchen. "Look who came to see you." She turned her back to Charla and made a real scary face, drawing her finger across her throat in a slashing motion. With clenched teeth and bulging eyes, she mouthed *open house.*

Lillian paused a moment and took a tentative step towards the kitchen. "I have to pee first." She ducked into the hall bathroom. While taking care of the immediate need, she hurriedly tried to think of a response in the event Charla started in on her about her vengeful actions. How was she going to defend herself against that?

A couple minutes later, she emerged and walked nonchalantly into the kitchen, took a bottle of water from the fridge and plunked down in a seat across from Charla. She let her bag drop to the floor beside her chair. "Is there any coffee?" she asked, trying to sound cheerful. Anxiety, however, brought on nervous sweat in her armpits. She swigged on the water as if she had come in from a hike in the desert.

Cora sniffed the air. "You smell like gun powder. Have you been shooting those bullets or eating them?"

Lillian opened her bag and withdrew her new purchase. She set it down gently in front of Charla. "Ain't she pretty?"

Charla backed up slightly and eyed the piece as if Lillian had just placed a cockroach in front of her. She reached out and with her fingertips, gently rotated the pistol so the barrel didn't point in her direction. "You aren't honestly going to carry that thing around in your handbag, are you?"

"Sure I am," answered Lillian defiantly. "What good is a gun for self-defense if you keep it locked up in a safe? I've named her Betsy."

"Please put *Betsy* away for now," said Charla, eyeing the offending item on the table.

Lillian was having devilish fun watching Charla squirm with discomfort, so she ignored the request while she went to the counter and poured herself some coffee. She sat back down, pulled the gun closer to her side of the table and eyed Charla. "Now, to what do we owe the pleasure of this visit?"

Cora jumped in, "I was filling her in on your escapade to Primm, our cars getting stolen and our house being burglarized. I thought she should know."

Lillian sighed. "Charla, this could all have been avoided if you would just open up to me and tell me your deepest darkest secrets so we can wipe the slate clean and start a new relationship."

"We're back to that again." Charla frowned and looked away as if studying something crawling up the far wall.

"I was going to visit Ella and see if she would spill the beans. But now, that's not possible."

"She wouldn't betray my confidence anyway and that's not what I came here to talk about." She brushed an imaginary piece of lint from her dress. Cora set a bag of lemon cookies on the table and took a chair. "So why were you in such a snit when you started pounding on our front door? You were mad as hell about something to do with an open house."

Lillian caught the implication, smiled slyly as she took a box of bullets out of her bag and dumped a few on that table. She picked up the gun and playfully began dropping a little brass bullet into each chamber of the snub-nosed six-shooter. "I'm going to practice with this tomorrow at the range. She took aim at a potted plant by the back door."

Cora's long reach shot across the small table and forced Lillian's hand down towards the floor. "Didn't your mother ever tell you not to play with guns in the house?"

Lillian set the piece on the table. "So what were you so angry about that you had to storm over here unannounced?" She smiled at her daughter.

Sweat beaded on Charla's forehead and her face seemed frozen. Finally, she swiped a hand across her brow and exclaimed, "Whew. It's hot in here. I…I…I don't remember. It must not have been important. I have to go back to the office now." She stood up abruptly, nearly knocking the chair over backwards, righted it, and headed for the front door. "I'll call you next week. We should do lunch."

Lillian mumbled, "I won't hold my breath."

The front door closed.

Lillian burst out laughing. "That was fun. So she did a little sleuthing and found out that I scared off some people at her open house."

"She was really mad when she came in. She acted like she was ready to kill you."

Cora eyed the loaded gun. "Please take the bullets out of that thing and put it away."

Lillian complied and dumped the bullets onto the table. "It's funny how she backed off at the sight of a little gun. Of course, I was just having fun intimidating her. I certainly wouldn't harm my own daughter."

"Not on purpose anyway, but a granny with a loaded gun is enough to make anyone forget why they got mad in the first place."

58

Cora was busily engaged in putting away groceries when Lillian came into the kitchen. She wore a pair of white slacks and a red tank top, over which she had on a loose floral patterned blouse. Her feet sported jeweled gold slippers to match her gold earrings.

"Where are you going all dressed up like that? Did that guy with the big dogs finally call you?"

"No. The guy with the big horn called me," she said with a big grin on her face.

Cora furrowed her brows. "Who are you talking about?"

Lillian laughed. "Herbie's back in town for a couple of days and asked me to meet him for dinner."

"Where is he staying?"

"I don't know where he stays. He didn't say. He asked me to meet him at the Orleans." She picked up her purse and pawed through it.

"Make sure you have your keys and cell phone. If you keep getting lost when you leave the house, I'm going to have a tracking device installed on your ankle."

Lillian smirked. "I'm only going to the Orleans. How lost can I get?" She reached into her bag and pulled out the gun. "And besides, I have a new homing device here for any homies that might need a bullet or two when they try to make a non-deposit withdrawal from my wallet."

"Put that thing away!" Cora chided. "You're not even sure how to use it yet. You really shouldn't be brandishing it about."

"I know how it works. I want to show it to Herbie. Now I have to go."

Cora eyed the package of steaks on the countertop. "I guess these can wait. I was going to grill tonight, but they will keep. You have fun. Tell Herb not to be a stranger. I'd like to see him too."

"I'll invite him for dinner tomorrow night. How would that be?"

"Sounds like a plan. Behave yourself."

"What does that mean?"

"You have that look on your face. You're planning to do an end run round Charla and get into her business; I know you are."

"Herbie's been out of the country. Why would he have any idea what's eating that girl. It's just a dinner. I want to hear about his trip."

Lillian arrived a little early; valet parked, and made her way through the casino to the spot where Herbie said he would meet her. After picking up a Pina Colada at the bar, she took a seat at a nickel poker machine and played while waiting. She rarely came to this establishment, preferring neighborhood casinos, closer to home. A glance at her wristwatch indicated Herbie was late.

With her back to the bar, and engrossed in playing, she failed to notice the man quietly approaching her. He tapped her on the shoulder and startling her so that she nearly dumped her drink down the front of her blouse. Instinct made her want to reach for the gun in her purse, but her hand was holding the glass.

The man laughed and kissed her on the top of the head. "My heavens, Lillian," he chuckled. "You're so jumpy." He sat down beside her and put a friendly arm around her shoulders. "It's good to see you."

Lillian smiled, set her drink down and kissed Herb on the cheek. "How's my favorite ex-son-in-law. I've missed you. And in case you haven't heard, I have a good reason to be jumpy."

His gazed roamed around the casino floor. "I've missed you too." He stood. "Shall we go? I have reservations at the Prime Rib Loft. I hope you're hungry."

"I've been saving my appetite all day. I love their food." She left the drink and followed him. He had not changed much. He still looked delicious in his suit and tie with his hair meticulously combed. It was thinning and graying on the sides, but didn't detract from his overall good looks. His complexion appeared a bit pale after a few months in France's wet climate, but he'd tan up if he stayed here long enough. She marveled at his tall muscular build, evident in the shoulders and the upper arms where his jacket pulled a little too tightly. "Have you kept up your routine of working out?" She grabbed his arm and squeezed playfully.

"You bet. I have to stay in shape. Tell me what you've been up to lately and why you're so jumpy. I feel out of the loop since Charla and I…uh—split."

"I'm still sad about that and I think Charla is mad at me for siding with you. I don't understand that girl anymore. I thought the two of you made such a nice couple. Your divorce was the last thing I would have expected. I'm still in shock. What happened?"

"We put on a good face for Courtney, but trouble began a long time before the split."

The conversation stopped while the host showed them to their table and handed them menus.

After placing their orders, Lillian asked. "Have you seen Courtney?"

Herb smiled warmly. "Yes she was my first stop upon landing in L.A. She looks so different. I'm trying to absorb the blue hair and nose piercing. She filled me in on The Band and her desire to be a drummer."

"What do you think about that? Did she tell you what we think they should name their band?"

"Yes and I like it. Thank you for not discouraging her from chasing her dreams. She has my support too, but I made it clear she has to finish school. Playing small venues on the weekends will give her a chance to cut her teeth on the industry, but education is the priority."

Lillian scowled, "Did she tell you that I bought her a set of drums and Charla destroyed them? I guess that tells you what she thinks of her daughter's aspirations to be a musician."

"She told me. I promised to get her another set. Don't tell Charla." He motioned for the waiter and ordered a scotch.

"Did you meet Lennie? She seems to be totally infatuated with him."

"I did and yes he is a nice kid. I made him a deal."

"What kind of deal?"

"I promised him that if those two kids stayed in school and graduated as expected, I would help them break into the business. I know many people and I can get them started. I even paid to print up some ads for them. How did you think of the name, *Pulsation*?"

"It wasn't easy. We must have looked up a hundred names on the internet. Do you know how hard it is to find one that's not already in use by some band somewhere in the world? That was the most fun I've had with her. She found out I'm not all boobs and no brains."

Herbies eyes automatically dropped to Lillian's assets but politely did not linger. "I've always known that. I have a great deal of respect for you and for Charlie as well when he was alive. Now, what has Lillian been up to besides tattling on my ex-wife?"

"I'm afraid I've been a very bad old lady. Do you really want to hear about it?" She smiled coyly.

When the meal was finished, Lillian had recounted all her tales of muggings and the destruction of her old car, emphasizing Charla's total lack of interest in her escapades and problems.

When she was finished, Herbie whistled. It sounds like you and Charla have a lot of work to do on your relationship. I wish I could help, but I don't think I should get between the two of you. Charla seems to have moved on so well that she has no time for anyone but herself. I'm sorry about that."

"Don't be sorry. It's not your fault. Do you have any clue as to why she has distanced herself from me? We never do anything together. I don't buy her excuse that she is busy with her business all the time. There has to be something else. Moreover, I think she has a boyfriend. She doesn't know that I saw them together once."

Herb seemed to fall asleep with his eyes open for a second. He stared off into space.

"Herbie, are you with me?" Lillian tapped a spoon on her glass to get his attention. "Where did you go?"

He turned his attention back to her and sighed. "I have a good idea what she's keeping bottled up, but it's not up to me to spill the beans. She has to tell you when she's ready. Now, I suggest we go get an ice cream sundae at the food court for desert."

Lillian patted her full tummy. "Are you kidding? I have no room, but I'll watch you eat one. Come on."

While watching Herbie consume the concoction, Lillian tried again. "You know what Charla is hiding, don't you. She's my daughter and nothing she has done would make me turn against her. You were married to her for over twenty years. Please tell me so I can put this to rest." She waited while Herb seemed to be turning things over in his mind.

He avoided eye contact as he shoved the empty dish aside; a vague sadness seemed to cloud his eyes. "If Charla wants you to know, she'll tell you. I'm sure she's staying tight-lipped for Courtney's sake. It would be best if you just let it go and work at establishing some sort of amicable middle ground with her. Dredging up history serves no useful purpose. That's all I can say." He checked his watch. "Now I must bid you goodbye. I have a two-day gig at the South Point. We start at ten. It's so nice to see you again. Take care of yourself." He kissed her on the cheek and turned to go.

Lillian called after him, "Call me once in a while and let me know how you're doing." The words were lost amongst the musical chirps and noises emitted by the carousels of slots and a loud outburst from somebody that must have hit something on a machine. She grumbled to herself, "Damn it, what the hell is the big secret? Somehow, it has to do with Courtney."

She watched his back until he disappeared around the corner. She mumbled, "Damn, I forgot to invite him to dinner and I didn't get a chance to show him my new gun."

59

When the bright morning sun streamed into Lillian's bedroom window, gradually rousing her, she sat up and threw the covers aside. She experienced a feeling of failure and frustration.

The dinner with Herbie was nice, but garnered zero clues into the reason for Charla's behavior. She thought about it. He had a strange look on his face when she mentioned seeing Charla with that man at Bellagio. Was he hurt that she had moved on? Was the divorce his fault? Had he cheated on her? Had she cheated on him? Was that why they split? She had so many questions and still no answers. Maybe she should take everyone's advice and give it a rest. A new project might help take her mind off it.

She put on some old jeans and a tee, made a quick cup of coffee, and carried it to the garage. The house was silent as a tomb. Cora had borrowed Celia's car to go sub in a classroom while Celia slept.

This was a good time to start digging into the boxes in the garage. It has been three years since the three women set up housekeeping together in Cora's home. She would probably never use any of the household goods again, and it was time to get rid of the crap so they could get at least two of their three cars into the garage. It would help cut down on the auto theft problem if they could park their cars inside.

The first box she opened sparked memories. It contained several years' accumulation of photos and family memorabilia she had always planned to organize in a scrapbook but never got around to. She carried it into the dining room and began spreading the contents out on the table. Forget about cleaning the garage, this was her new project. She picked up the loose photos and thumbed through them. There were envelopes full of pictures taken back when cameras still used film. The box contained years of memories that silently called out for attention, where does one start?

She grabbed her handbag and headed to the store for supplies and a book or magazine to tell her how to organize the mess.

An hour and a half at Michaels and two hundred dollars later, Lillian dragged half a dozen bags into the house. She dropped them on the table and headed to the kitchen for a cold iced tea. Scrapbooking already proved to be expensive and exhausting, but she was eager to get started. Settled with her cold drink, she started thumbing through the how-to book, and mentally planning the project.

As she commenced digging into the box and sorting the contents, a peaceful calm descended on her.

60

Celia shuffled out of her bedroom later that day, past the closed double doors to the dining room, and into the kitchen, where Cora was baking cookies. "Where's Lillian?"

Cora scooped chocolate chip cookies off the hot sheet onto racks to cool. "She's in the dining room reliving the past."

Biting into a warm cookie, Celia complimented the baker, "Umm, these are good. I'll be having milk and cookies for my dinner." She headed to the fridge to retrieve the milk jug.

Cora motioned with her head to the room where she found Lillian when she came back home from teaching. "It looks like she's been in there all day. I poked my head in and spoke to her, but she barely looked up. She has photos and stuff spread out on the table. She's muttering to herself, all engrossed in what she's doing. She hasn't even come out to get a cookie. I know she can smell the aroma. I noticed bags from Michaels sitting on the floor."

"I thought she threw out that box of stuff Charla dropped off. Did she have a change of heart all of a sudden?"

"No, this is a box that's been in the garage ever since she moved in. I think she's scrapbooking." She shoved another cookie sheet into the oven and set the timer.

"Maybe it'll get her mind off of her problems with Charla. I hope she's finally found a hobby. Did she say anything about her dinner with Herbie?"

Cora picked up a cookie and ate it. "She was supposed to invite him to dinner tonight, but she forgot. Apparently, her attempt to pry information out of him about Charla went nowhere. He wouldn't tell her anything either." She started to take another warm morsel and then put it back. "I'm going to spoil my appetite for dinner if I keep this up. We're grilling steaks."

Celia finished her snack, put three cookies on a plate, and headed for the dining room. "I guess I'll say hi and see how she's doing."

Lillian looked up when Celia entered. "Don't mind my mess. I started to clean the garage but decided it was too hot out there. I've needed to do something with this crap for a long time. I thought it would be fun to learn to scrapbook." She indicated the page she was working on with stickers, ribbon, and scissors. "Look how cute this is when you cut the photo down to just the subject and put a frame around it. It's so precious."

"Yes it is. Is that Courtney?" Celia asked pointing at a baby picture.

"No, it's Charla." She handed Celia a book she had already finished. "This is Charlie and me, our wedding and honeymoon and the years until Charla came along. It's kind of skinny because we were too poor to spend money on photography."

Celia thumbed through it. "I didn't know you took a honeymoon. I thought you said you couldn't afford one."

"Well, we called it a honeymoon. It was one night in a hotel on the Lake Michigan shore. That's all we could manage." She continued to snip and paste. "This is the next album. It starts with Charla's birth and all her childhood events up through the time she left for college."

"Wow. How can you remember all the dates and sequences of these events? After all these years, I would have forgotten when anything happened. Most of the time, I don't even remember my own boys' birthdays."

Celia picked up a stack and sifted through them. She noted that Lillian had meticulously written on the back of each photo the name of the subject and the date taken. "I'm afraid I have never been this thorough about preserving memories." She put the stack back where she got it. "It looks like you have a lot of work ahead of you. Don't forget to come and eat dinner. Cora is grilling steaks. Have some cookies in the meantime." She retreated and closed the door.

Returning to the kitchen she exclaimed, "Holy crap on a cracker. Did you see the mess in there? We won't see her for days unless we go remind her to eat, drink and go to bed at night. She's obsessed."

"Better that than her obsession with Charla and whatever deep dark secret she thinks Charla is keeping from her. Personally, I think the woman is simply stuck up and ungrateful to her mother for all she has done for her over the years. Notoriety in the Las Vegas social circles has put that woman on a self-made ivory pedestal and she thinks she's too good to come slumming around her mom. It's shameful."

Celia went to the fridge and started pulling fresh vegetables out. "My radar tells me there is something deeper going on. Something she has buried and doesn't want to see the light of day. You know Charla; she's all about public image." She set up the cutting board and started making dinner salads. "Remember when we saw her at the Bellagio on the arm of that good looking guy? Maybe she's carrying on with a married man and he was in town for a booty call."

Cora chuckled and started to season the steaks. "Yeah, I remember. He could call on my booty anytime he wanted, married or not. He was hot."

Celia paused and eyed her roomy. "Cora, take a tranquilizer. You're too horny for a woman your age. Do you want me to call up Jim Boyd and invite him to dinner? I could find somewhere for me and Lillian to go for a few hours while you call his booty."

"I said I could do somebody hot. He doesn't qualify, and besides, last I heard he's engaged to that woman he met at the mall. You can take credit for that, Celia, since you thought it would be a good idea to give the man a makeover. Apparently his lady likes peeling back the layers with all the brown splotches on that old banana to see what's inside."

Celia laughed. "You have a dirty mind. I'll never look at another banana again without thinking about what you said. You've ruined them for me."

Cora grinned. "Then you'll have to settle for grapes. I haven't thought of an analogy involving them yet."

"Lucky for the grape growing industry," said Celia with a grin.

"However, I can come up with plenty of jokes about nuts," Cora added.

Celia put up her hand to stop Cora from elaborating. "How do you keep your mind on teaching with all those fruits and nuts in your brain?"

The oven timer went off and interrupted their banter.

A scream emitted from the dining room, nearly causing Cora to drop the pan of cookies. She quickly set it on the tile counter and they both ran to the source of the outburst.

Lillian came rushing out of the room. "Where's the insect spray?" Her eyes were big as saucers and she headed for the cabinet under the sink.

Cora and Celia cautiously peaked into the room. "What the hell set her off?" Celia asked.

"I don't know. I wonder if it's safe to enter," replied Cora.

Lillian rushed back and began spraying the carpet, the box, the baseboards, the windowsills and the assorted mess on the tabletop. "Quick! Get out and shut the doors!"

"Calm down, Lillian. What in the hell scared you so much?" They were standing outside the closed double doors.

Lillian was checking the floor to make sure no noxious intruders were trying to escape through the gap between the doors and the floor. For good measure, she sprayed along the gap. "I was engrossed with my project when a cockroach crawled out of the box and ran across my hand. God, I hate those things!"

Celia and Cora laughed.

Cora said, "All of this for a little roach?"

"I want to make sure his relatives die if they come looking for him." She headed back to the kitchen to put the spray away. "I guess my job is done in there for tonight." She shivered. "I hate bugs."

Celia chuckled. "I'm surprised you didn't pull out your gun and shoot the thing."

"You're brave enough to kick the bejesus out of a thief, but you go postal with a can of Raid when you see a little bug," said Cora waving her hands in the air.

"It wasn't little. It was gigantic," Lillian asserted indignantly.

Celia laughed. "Should I call the coroner to retrieve the *gigantic* body in there?"

Lillian straightened up after putting the can away. "Now you guys are just mocking me."

"It's our duty," said Celia. "We're you best friends."

While enjoying their steak dinner, Lillian spoke up. "I've been thinking..."

"Oh, God," Cora interjected, "here we go."

"Let me finish my thought. I'm just saying that while I'm working on organizing all those photos and memorabilia, it might be nice if I start writing my memoirs to leave for Courtney. Somehow, she was under the impression I was born old and never did anything in my life besides babysit with her. I gave her a thumbnail version of where I came from and how Charlie and I got together."

Cora mockingly looked surprised and responded, "You mean there's more?"

Celia looked at her with a crooked grin. "Kids don't care where we came from as long as our bank accounts are there if they need them."

"Well that's a little cynical, don't you think?" Indignation was evident in Lillian's voice.

"It's the way I feel. I haven't heard from my kids in months. It's obvious they no longer care. I've learned to deal with it and I no longer care either."

Cora ignored Celia's remark and asked, "Do you even know how to write anything?"

"I went to college, but I have no idea where to start putting down on paper anything about my life. You're an English teacher, where do I start?"

Cora thought about the question while she finished the last bite of steak on her plate. "My first and foremost suggestion would be—leave out the trip down the birth canal. That vision will lose your reader on the first page."

Lillian chuckled. "That just spoiled my appetite. Then where do I start."

"Finish your scrapbooking. Get it all organized, and then just write a commentary following along page by page, photo by photo until you get up to the present. As you go along, little snippets of experiences will come to mind and you can include them like points of interest on a scenic tour. It's only for Courtney anyway. Give her the necessary vital statistics, places, names, and funny happenings. Don't dwell on sad stuff. Keep it light and amusing. She might want to share it with her children in the future."

"She says she isn't going to have any, as she puts it, 'brats'."

Celia started clearing the table. "I still think that's a lot of effort for very little reward."

"Maybe you should consider doing something like Lillian is doing. Your boys may not appreciate it now, but if you left them something to read after you're gone, they might gain a new appreciation for you and decide not to make the same mistake with their children. We all need to know where our roots are. I regret not making an effort to find out where mine came from," said Cora.

Celia chuckled. "My roots are assumed to be in the cabbage patch where my mother always claimed she found me."

"I'll go you one better. The reason I grew so tall and skinny and developed this beak I have for a nose is because my mother contended she found me hanging around in the middle of Dad's Iowa cornfield scaring the crows away."

"That's mean," Lillian commented. "My mother was nicer. She said she found me in a litter of cute little bunny rabbits out in Daddy's barn."

Cora eyed Lillian's huge knockers and laughed. "Somehow bunny rabbits don't come to mind when claiming you were found in a dairy farmer's barn."

Lillian stuck her tongue out and crossed her eyes. She snarled kiddingly, "You're just *udderly* jealous of my assets." Then she turned on her heel chuckling, and strode back toward the dining room.

Celia hollered after her retreating friend, "You better air out that room before you start playing with your memories again. I don't want to have to call the coroner to pick up *your* dead body!"

61

A week went by and the roommates only saw Lillian when she came out of the dining room to eat or retire for the night. There were dark circles forming around her eyes from lack of sleep.

Finally, at dinner, Celia asked, "Are you about finished traipsing through the past? We miss you and I'm worried that you aren't eating or drinking enough. Is all this really worth it?"

"You wanted me to find a hobby, didn't you?" Lillian replied.

"Yes, we did," agreed Cora. "I can't wait to see all those albums you have made in there. Can we look at them yet?"

Lillian finished chewing a bite of pork and grinned. "I'm finished. Would you like to see them after dinner?"

"We would love to," said Celia enthusiastically. "Let's do that first and then bring out the desert as a celebration. We're going to get our roommate back."

Lillian opened the doors to the dining room. All the albums were sitting in order on the table. She motioned towards her masterpieces. "You guys go ahead and browse while I clean up all these clippings and trash." She commenced gathering the trash bags and headed for the garage.

Celia grabbed the second volume. "I want to start with this one where Charla first comes on the scene. I want to see if there are any clues as to what makes that chick tick." She sat down and began thumbing through the pages. In the first picture of Charla as a newborn, she could clearly see that she was taking after Charlie. She leafed quickly through the album up to the last page where Charla was graduating high school. She had her arm around a young classmate. She drew in a breath and whispered to get Cora's attention.

"What?" Cora frowned with concern.

"Look at this picture. Do you see anything familiar?" She held the book closer to Cora and pointed at the photo.

"That's a snapshot at Charla's high school graduation. So?"

"No, look at the young man with her. Who does he look like?"

Cora studied the picture for several beats and drew in a breath. "Oh my word, how could Lillian miss that?"

"Should I point it out to her?" Celia asked in a whisper.

Cora shook her head. "Not yet. What's in the next album?"

Celia closed that one and picked up the next, skimming through it. "These appear to be Charla in college years, dance performances, rally squad, etc. etc. Oops, here's that same classmate again. They must have gone to the same university. They look real cozy." She turned a few more pages. "Here's Charla's college graduation. There's that fellow again. He's looking more and more like…"

"The guy we saw at the Bellagio, right?" Cora whispered.

Lillian walked back in just then and the girls curtailed their discussion. "This is really lovely, Lillian," Cora said with a sly grin. "You've done a nice job." She pointed out the fellow graduate with Charla and asked his name.

"Oh, him," Lillian huffed. "He and Charla went all through high school and college together. I had hopes that they would marry someday, but they were never anything but friends. Charla came to Las Vegas to make a career in show business and met Herbie. That boy went to Yale law school, met a girl, married and fathered about six kids. I can't remember his name, exactly. I wrote his first name on the back, Marshall; but for the life of me, I can't remember his last name. It had something to do with a term used in law, which is why he said he had to become a lawyer."

"Where does he live?" Celia asked.

"He has a practice in Michigan somewhere. I'll have to ask Charla if she remembers his name."

Celia and Cora exchanged amused glances.

"What?" Lillian frowned.

"Oh, nothing," Cora said. "We were just curious because he's in a lot of these pictures. "Did he break Charla's heart?"

"I don't know. She never said anything to me. Of course, she was here, and we were still back east. She moved on and married Herbie and they always seemed happy, until recently. The divorce came as a real shock to me. I was blindsided."

Celia closed the album and headed for the door. "This is fun, but I have to work tonight, so I'm going to take a nap."

Celia retreated to her room, closed the door, and turned on her new computer. She had a specific search in mind. She knew she would not sleep until she got her question answered.

62

Charla was on the phone, when Lillian suddenly appeared and slammed the office door behind her.

On this late afternoon, she had come to Charla's office and stormed in uninvited. She hadn't heard from her daughter in all the weeks she had been putting together the albums.

She discovered that life does not flash before your eyes. It takes weeks of sorting, pasting, cutting and fussing to take that walk down memory lane. She had gone through all the range of emotions one can experience when looking back. She missed Charlie more than ever now and had to stop at one point to cry and have a private pity party behind closed doors. She felt cheated these last few years by Charla and her hoity-toity attitude towards her own mother. She had kept the hurt to herself most of the time, but now there was going to be a showdown. She had had enough.

The set of albums remained on the dining room table where the girls left them after a thorough inspection.

Celia and Cora first noticed the clues in the photos and ran with them through the internet, solving the mystery of Charla. The next day, the roommates called Lillian back to the dining room, armed with their detective work and pointed out the evidence. Charla had been harboring the truth for years and had erected walls around her personal life that she didn't want torn away to expose her deceit.

Now Lillian was here for a confession.

Charla hung up the phone and eyed Lillian's handbag. "Tell me you don't have a gun in that purse."

"Relax, it's in my car." She plunked down in a chair across from her daughter.

Charla looked especially beautiful today. She'd let her hair down and it fell in soft waves around her shoulders. Expertly applied makeup and the soft blue of her dress brought out the color of her eyes.

She eyed her mother for a few beats and then asked, "So why are you here?

"When were you going to tell me about Courtney's biological father?"

Charla abruptly rose from her desk. She closed the blinds that separated her office from the lobby and opened the door slightly to inform her secretary, "Hold all my calls."

"How did you find out?" Charla blurted the words as her face first turned white and then gradually beet red. "Nobody is supposed to know."

Lillian waited a beat then spoke. "Does Courtney know?"

Charla looked away, fiddled with some papers on her desk, as if contemplating another lie. When she looked up, she displayed only the tiniest hint of resignation. "I'm not going to discuss this matter here." She looked at her watch. "It's almost quitting time. Why don't I go pick up some Chinese food, and meet you at my house in say, an hour?"

"Don't try to put me off," Lillian said vehemently. "We're going to get everything out in the open."

"We will, but not here. Meet me at my house." She rose from her desk, opened the door to urge Lillian to leave, saying, "I'll see you shortly."

Lillian pursed her lips, but didn't argue in front of the office staff. "One hour. Don't be late."

As Lillian made her way back to the car, she could feel Charla's eyes burning holes in the back of her head. She mumbled, "I bet she doesn't show up."

Distracted, Lillian nearly clipped a car as she backed up to leave the parking space. A loud honk jolted her out of a daze, prompting her to slam on the brakes. Chiding herself, she grumbled, "Get it together, Lillian. You've got a rip snorting showdown ahead of you."

63

Lillian knew that Charla would never think to bring dessert, so she stopped at a bakery and picked up cupcakes.

She was waiting outside the house when the hour expired, and Charla hadn't shown up. She started to steam. "I knew she'd dodge the issued." After fifteen more minutes went by, she started her engine and prepared to leave. "I wonder what her excuse will be this time."

Her cell phone rang. She stopped the engine and answered. "You're late."

Charla ignored her. "I was delayed. I'll be there in ten minutes."

"Sure." Lillian hung up.

Twenty minutes later, Charla drove into her garage. Lillian hurriedly exited her car and joined her. "You can get arrested for leaving an old lady to die in a hot car."

"I didn't leave you in a car. You have air conditioning. You can roll down the windows." She punched the button to close the garage door.

The house was silent except for the sound of an air conditioner running. Temperatures outside were creeping up to triple digits early.

Sight of the swimming pool in the back yard, made Lillian wish she had brought a swimsuit. However, she wasn't here for a social visit. This was truth or consequences.

After plates were set out at the table and containers of Chinese food opened, Lillian broached the subject again, as they dug into the chow mien and sweet and sour pork.

"Are you finally going to tell me the truth about Courtney's father? Does she know?"

Charla took a few seconds to answer. Resignation was apparent on her face. "She only knows I have a boyfriend. She's never met him. I've kept them separated, because she might become suspicious if she saw him."

"How could you keep such a secret and be so deceitful with your husband for so many years?" Lillian was livid. "He is a wonderful man and deserves better." She recalled the hurt in Herbie's eyes when she was plying him with questions at dinner.

Lillian saw for the first time ever, tears well up in Charla's eyes. She turned away and went to the counter to get a tissue from the box. After dabbing them away, in a voice barely audible, she whispered, "He knew."

"What! How did this happen? The cat is out of the bag. You may as well come clean with me. This is what has been coming between us all these years. You were afraid I might catch on and blab to the wrong people. I know you have a reputation to uphold and you are worried I'll destroy it. You have so little faith in me. I'm your mother, but you, and not this issue is what's torn us apart. You need to tell me the truth!"

Charla took a deep breath and paused as if to compose her thoughts. "This can't go any further than this room."

"What do you take me for—the town gossip? Have more faith in your mother."

"I have to ask, though, how did you figure this out."

"I didn't. Cora and Celia did when I showed them the photo albums I've been working on for weeks. I took up scrapbooking. When they saw your high school graduation photos, they thought something looked suspicious. They tackled some detective work on the internet. It didn't take long. Courtney looks enough like a young Marshall to have been his twin."

Charla looked stricken. "So they know too?"

"Don't worry. They won't tell anyone. They really don't give a shit about your love life."

Charla took a deep breath and let it out. "When Marshall Court went to Yale, I moved here in an effort to divert my attention away from the feelings of abandonment. He was—still is, the love of my life. I thought we would take up where we left off when he was finished with law school. I thought he would come here, start a law practice, and marry me."

"But he didn't." The pained look on Charla's face made Lillian's heart bleed for her daughter.

"Instead, he broke up with me. I was devastated. I even contemplated suicide."

"Why didn't you say anything to your father or me?"

"I considered myself an adult and you guys still lived so far away. I had to handle it myself. I met Herb on the rebound and he seemed like he'd be a good husband. He was. He was never jealous or possessive of me and supported my career. He was away a lot on gigs and I supported his career."

"I know that. Now why did you cheat on him?"

Charla dabbed at the tears that wouldn't stop. "I didn't mean to and it wasn't anything I ever expected to do. Herb was out of town when my dance troupe was performing for a law convention. I was in the front line of dancers doing the high kick when I looked down at the audience and nearly fell off my high heels. Marshall was in the front row. Our eyes met and locked and that was the beginning of our affair. I don't remember the rest of the show that night. I was in a trance, operating like a robot. All the old animal magnetism we had in high school and college came roaring back like a tornado."

Lillian drew a breath and raised her eyebrows. "You were sleeping with him all those years ago in high school and when you went off to college together at the University of Michigan?"

Charla diverted her eyes. "Yes. I couldn't help myself. I worshipped him."

"I'm surprised you didn't get knocked up."

"We took precautions. He had his law career mapped out ahead of him and I wanted him to succeed because it would mean a wonderful life for us."

"I had no idea." Charla's pained expression brought tears to Lillian's eyes. She swiped at them.

"When the show was over that night, he hung around and waited by the stage door. I followed him like a lamb to slaughter, as he led me to his room. We didn't even exchange many words until after we made love. It was a night I shall never forget. It was as if all the years of separation evaporated and we were back in college hitting it like two horny students in a dorm room. I couldn't help myself. I still can't and that's the night I became pregnant."

Lillian noticed the pupils in Charla's eyes dilate as she talked about Marshall. "Jesus. You get horny just thinking about him. Don't you have any shame? He's married and has six kids he's still raising. He's going to run for Governor. Haven't you considered what this could do to his career if the news got out that he has an illegitimate daughter? If it hits the headlines that a man of his stature has a two-decade affair going on with a mistress—it could mean political suicide."

"I know. That's why it has to remain secret. And, I never told him about Courtney."

"You're joking. You named her after him. Being pregnant is somewhat hard to hide. Didn't he ask questions?"

"I didn't see him for a couple of years after that momentous night. He was busy with the law firm that he and his wife started. I couldn't contact him for fear his wife would find out. So I never told him." Even after all these years, guilt of her deception showed on her flawless features, revealing worry lines between her eyebrows.

"A father has a right to know about the children he creates."

"I thought our lust filled night was going to be only that one time. I never dreamed he would contact me again. So, when I found out I was pregnant, I told Herb he was going to become a father."

Lillian noted that Charla was fighting back tears.

"He's been a good one too, but didn't he wonder why his child didn't resemble either side of our families?"

Charla frowned and looked down at her hands. "He knew why."

Lillian's mouth gaped open. "He knew! Why did he not leave you right then?"

Charla breathed deeply and fidgeted with her brightly painted fingernails. "Herb has been sterile since he had mumps in his teens. He had no hope of fathering children. When I turned up pregnant, he had to admit that he had purposely kept it a secret. He said he loved me and was afraid I wouldn't marry him if I knew I could never have children with him. I nearly fainted when he confessed that omission to me. I assumed he would file for divorce immediately."

"But he didn't."

"No." Charla said wistfully. "His own father had abandoned the family years before, and he wasn't going to do the same to an unborn child."

Lillian spoke lovingly about her former son-in-law, recalling how he calls Courtney his *Baby Cakes*. "He became Courtney's father and doted on her as if she were his own. It takes a big man to raise another man's child when his wife has cheated on him."

"I loved Herbie with all my heart for that, but I always knew our time would come to an end. He made that clear. He did his duty to provide Courtney with the father figure she deserved. We stayed together for her, but we were never intimate again. When Courtney went off to college, he filed for dissolution of our marriage."

"Maybe it's none of my concern, but weren't you scared to death you would become pregnant again with your *lover*? I mean, I know how one can be careless in matters of the heart." *What am I saying? I've never been careless in my life with sex. I was married to Charlie. He was my first, last, and only. I haven't seen another man naked since Charlie passed away. Face it Lillian, you never had the chance to be wanton and careless.*

Charla hesitated to answer.

"You did something, didn't you, Charla." Anger began to rise in Lillian. "What did you do?" She demanded.

Charla looked away. "It's past history, Mother. It doesn't really matter now."

"Answer me, damn it!" Lillian didn't mean to yell, but her voice rose involuntarily. She was losing patience with Charla's reticence.

Charla dropped her gaze to her hands resting on the table, and in a barely audible voice, replied, "I had a tubal ligation immediately after giving birth."

Lillian slapped the table angrily. "Well that explains everything. Your daddy always wondered why you never gave us another grandchild to enjoy along with Courtney."

"I never wanted to make that mistake again in the event Marshall came to visit. We didn't make plans to meet again since he was here for that convention, but eventually, he did return again and again."

"So all those years you were married to Herb pretending things were fine, you were sneaking around behind his back carrying on with your backstreet romance. When did you find the time?"

"It wasn't easy, but we managed. Marshall expanded his law practice, opening a satellite office in Las Vegas, so he would have an excuse to be in this area. I called in sick on the nights he made it to town on the pretext of consulting with his up-start young lawyers running the local office. You thought I was working late shows while you babysat, but I wasn't." Her eyes darted to Lillian and then quickly away.

"What about Marshall? Is he going to divorce his wife and marry you? I know you're still carrying on with him after all these years. I saw you with him once." Lillian immediately regretted that confession.

"When did you ever see me with Marshall? We…never mind, I don't want to know."

"So, is he?"

"Is he what?"

"Is he going to finally marry you?"

Charla frowned. "Not anytime soon. He loves me and when he visits, we get together. The fire still burns hot between us, but he can't leave his wife. There is a lot at stake. He still has kids to put through college and his wife is a formidable attorney. She's never lost a case. She would take him to the cleaners if she ever found out about us. She has aspirations of becoming First Lady someday."

"So, all this is why Herb got such a good deal in your divorce. If this scandal became public, it could ruin both you and Marshall."

"That's about it. I love Herb because of the man he is. Who else would have taken on the job of raising my daughter? I would have gladly stayed married to him, but it was his choice to end the farce. I couldn't give up Marshall. He's like a heroin addiction to me and I'm his."

"Twenty years is a long time to sneak around and have an affair with a married man."

"I know, but we can't help it. Herb has moved on. Courtney has gone to college. I'm not getting any younger. Marshall still sees me as the girl he fell in love with in high school. He's all I have now. Someday, maybe circumstances will change for him and he'll be free to bring me into his public life. I can wait."

Lillian shook her head. "You are such a fool! Affairs rarely turn out the way you want them to."

"I have a lot of years invested in this one and I won't give up hope now."

Lillian shrugged. "Suit yourself. Now, my friends and I have enough sense to know this is your business and we won't tell anyone, least of all Courtney. This issue, as far as we are concerned will end here. I just want you to know I love you and would like to spend some time simply being your mother and friend. Now that you know that I know, can't we start a new chapter and maybe have lunch once a week or go shopping together? I'm getting older. I won't live forever. I'd like to leave this world knowing we've said all we have to say to each other and there are no issues left on the table."

Charla contemplated that idea for a while. The cell phone in her purse on the counter rang and she started to rise, but stopped. "Please don't tell Courtney that Herb is not her father."

"That's something you need to settle with your daughter. You said she knows you have a man in your life. It could explain some of her rebellious attitude toward you. Keeping her on the fringe is not good. Get it all out on the table. What if there was ever a medical issue.

"Courtney is plenty healthy. I don't think I have to worry about that."

"Don't wait until there is a life or death situation that forces you to tell her the truth," cautioned Lillian. "She won't hear it from me. I've seen her with Herb. She loves him and he dotes on her. I won't have anything to do with destroying that relationship."

"I know I have to tell her sometime, but not right now. This has to stay confidential. If I tell her the truth, she might pursue looking for Marshall and it could upset the balance we have now in *our* arrangement. It could be disastrous."

"Did Ella know about you and Marshall? Did she know that Courtney was the result of your dalliance?"

"She knew, but she didn't hold it against me. She wasn't judgmental and would never have betrayed me to anyone, least of all you."

"What does that mean?" Lillian blurted indignantly. "Oh, I know, it was just one more thing she could use to draw you to her and away from me."

"Now don't take it that way. She respected my confidences and she loved me like a…"

"Don't say it," Lillian interrupted. "It only makes me angry." Lillian rose to put her plate in the sink. "It's time for these delicious cupcakes." She brought the box to the table.

"I don't eat carbs," Charla objected as she sneered at the frosted little devils as if they had horns.

Lillian urged, "Go ahead and live a little. You can work it off on the treadmill tonight…or some other way. Is Marshall due back in town anytime soon?"

Charla didn't get the joke.

"I'm kidding," Lillian chuckled.

"They look delicious, but please share them with your roommates."

Lillian reluctantly closed the box. "I'm glad we had this little talk. I'm sympathetic with your hesitance to come clean with Courtney. I don't want her hurt either. Now that we have this all out in the open and I understand why you've avoided me for so long, can we put it all behind us? I promise I won't speak of this again and I'm wiping your slate clean. Maybe we can hit the mall on Sunday and shop until we drop. You're not working are you? It'll help get our minds off all this drama."

Charla didn't answer right away as she dumped the remainder of their dinner in the kitchen trash and put the plates in the sink.

The hesitation didn't escape Lillian's eye. "Well? I'm not getting any younger."

Charla turned from the sink and smiled. "I can't think of anything I'd rather do. Have you been to the Summerlin Town Center?"

"It's too hot out for that. Can we go to the newly remodeled Boulevard Mall?"

"Sure. I'll pick you up Sunday morning and take you to breakfast first." Charla walked Lillian to the front door and held it open for her.

"I'm looking forward to it. I love you." Lillian reached up and put her hand on Charla's shoulder to pull her down so she could plant a smooch on her daughter's cheek. She squeezed her hand and hesitated a moment before leaving.

As she walked away, she felt a twinge of disappointment that Charla had not responded with those four little words she ached to hear. *I love you, Mom.*

Lillian was feeling euphoric when she started the car. She had finally reached Charla on a close and personal level, something she had not been able to do in years.

Charla had not returned her sentiment, but that would come in time. She felt sure of it.

She exited the gated community and pulled into traffic. Her mind was going back over their conversation and she drove robotically. She was almost home before she realized how far she had come. She stopped at a red light, her mind completely preoccupied. When it changed to green, she hit the gas, and a tremendous explosion erupted as colliding cars jerked her to attention. Unable to avoid the impact, the trio of bent metal spun around and came to rest in the middle of the intersection. The air bags inflated and something solid smacked Lillian's temple. Everything went black.

64

Cora mopped the kitchen floor and started putting things away when Celia joined her. "Where's Lillian?"

"She left late this afternoon armed with the information we found for her. She said she was going to confront Charla and try to settle things between them. That was very clever of you to go directly to the internet and search high school yearbooks for Charla's senior class. I never would have thought of it."

Celia took a yogurt from the fridge and commenced eating it. "Sometimes I get bored, I browse, looking up old classmates. Honestly, who cares about twenty-year-old history? Courtney is oblivious and Herb is a great father. Apparently, Charla is the only one who can't put it behind her. She has let her shame destroy her marriage and her relationship with Lil. They need to turn the page and get on with living."

Cora's phone chimed, interrupting the conversation. She eyed the caller identification. Only the number appeared. She answered.

Celia watched her expression change to wide-eyed shock and then panic. She hung up after listening for a few minutes, ending the call with one last statement. "Send pictures to my email address so I can forward them to my insurance company. They can decide if they want to have it towed."

"They found your car." Celia grinned. "I take it Brown Betty has bit the dust."

"Brown Betty is Burnt Betty. That little bastard was trying to avoid main roads, so he wound up in some little mining town north of Tonopah. Did you know there is a place called Manhattan, Nevada?"

"No."

"The town's people are a rough take-no-prisoners bunch of old miners. When the little twit went into one of the local bars and tried to sell them the stolen computers and phone, they got suspicious. A couple of them tried to take him down and hold him for the County Sheriff. He ran, crashed my car, and it caught fire. His ass is cooling in jail and everything he stole burned up."

"Will he be brought back here?"

"In a day or so and Lillian will have to identify him." Cora's eyes brimmed with tears when she thought about her dependable old brown sedan. "I'll never see my car again."

"Don't cry. It's only a car. They've arrested the little twerp. The hair and fingerprints he left behind is enough to convict him. It's not like he was a smart thief."

Cora swiped away the tears. "I guess I better change clothes. Can you drive me to a dealer? I may as well see if I can find a good used car. This really sucks." She frowned and walked away.

"Wait." Celia called after her. "It's too late. They're all closed now."

Cora stopped in mid-stride. "Oh, I didn't realize it was so late. I didn't even eat dinner. I need a shower."

Celia was just finishing her yogurt and considering making a cup of tea, when her phone chimed. She answered and when she hung up, she ran to Cora's room.

"Get dressed! We have to go," yelled Celia.

"Relax. I'm not in that much of a hurry," Cora replied as she peeled her clothes off to take a shower. "You said the car lots are all closed now. I'll have to wait until tomorrow."

"No, we have to go now. Lillian has been in an auto accident. The hospital called me. They know she's my roommate."

With Cora in tow, Celia used her key card to enter through the same door the ambulances use. She checked the board for the cubicle number in the busy ER where they would find Lillian.

Emergency room personnel were busy taking vitals and going about the usual diagnostics. A portable x-ray machine arrived. Cora and Celia stood aside and waited until the room cleared out. A bandage covered the side of Lillian's head and the skin was turning color around that eye. The white of her right eye had turned red.

Cora approached the bed, took her hand and squeezed it.

There was no response. "Lillian, can you hear me?"

Celia walked over and spoke with the EMT's that had brought her friend in and were doing their paperwork. "You brought my roommate in after the accident—Lillian Crocker. What can you tell me?"

The handsome young man looked at her with a blank expression. "I can't tell you anything."

"Yes you can. I'm on record as one of the people who can make medical decisions for her and I work right here. I can look it up myself once it's in the computer. So tell me now, what happened."

The young man looked to the nurse sitting at the desk as if to get permission to violate HIPPA law.

"Give him the okay, Susan," Celia said to her co-worker.

Susan nodded. "You can tell Celia anything. She practically runs this place."

The EMT looked at his notes. "There was a three-car collision. Patient sustained blow to the temple and possible fractured ankle. She was unconscious when extricated from the car. If you want to know who caused the crash, you'll have to ask the police. That's all I can tell you." He handed Lillian's identification and insurance card to Celia, picked up his clipboard and joined his co-worker who was changing the sheet on the gurney.

Celia rejoined Cora at Lillian's bedside. "Has she said anything yet?"

"No. She must have a concussion."

Celia read the machines that were monitoring her friend. "Her vitals seem to be okay. The x-rays should be ready soon. I'm going to chase down the doctor on duty and see if he knows anything."

Time seemed to drag on. Cora kept talking to Lillian. "I know you're in there somewhere. You need to wake up. You're scaring me. Wake up, Lillian." She patted her hand and shook it gently.

Lillian grinned and moaned softly. "You can stop now. I hear you. Did you call Charla?"

Cora sighed with relief. "Jeepers creepers, I thought you were going to die on us. How's your head?"

"It hurts. I've had worse migraines than this." She looked at Cora as if she were a stranger. "Are you the nurse? Where's Charlie?"

"You mean Charla."

"No, Charla lives in Las Vegas. I mean Charlie. Why isn't he here?"

Cora let go of Lillian's hand and looked out into the hall to see if she could spot Celia. "I'll be right back." She retreated hurriedly to go in search of help.

She caught up with Celia around the corner. "Come quick. Something is wrong. Lillian thinks Charlie is still alive. I think she's got amnesia."

Celia made for the cubicle with the doctor in tow.

He checked Lillian's pupils and vitals. "I'll see if I can speed up the test results." He left.

Cora and Celia both studied Lillian with concern. "Do you know who we are?" Celia asked.

Lillian chuckled. "Yes, I know who you are. I'm just yanking your chain. My ankle is killing me. Did I break it?"

"Lillian," Celia chided, "knock off the jokes. You about gave us both heart attacks. What's with the dramatic performance? And yes, it looks like you have a broken ankle and you took a huge conk on the noggin."

"I've reminded you time and again to fasten your seat belt. You forgot and when you pitched forward, your head must have taken out the rear view mirror." Celia gave an audible sigh. "I hope you've learned your lesson this time."

Lillian touched the side of her head and winced. "I guess I wasn't thinking so clearly when I left Charla's house."

"Can I have some aspirin? I've got a pounding headache."

"The best I can do is Tylenol." Celia disappeared and returned a minute later with water and two tablets.

"Now what the heck are you trying to pull, you little imp," Cora asked.

"I want you to call Charla and tell her I'm here. Then clear out and let me be. We had our confession session just before the accident. We kissed and made up—that is I kissed and made up. She didn't return the gesture. I want her to think I'm dying. I need to hear from her own lips that she still loves me."

"That will come as you repair your relationship," Celia assured her.

"This accident has given me pause. My life can end in a heartbeat and I want her to realize that. I need her to say the words out loud."

"I could put a bug in her ear," Cora suggested. "Maybe she just naturally assumes you know it."

"No. Let me hear it from her without any of you prompting her."

Celia agreed, "Okay, we'll do it your way. You will be here a few hours and then they will transfer you to a room for observation overnight while they keep a lookout for complications from the head injury. I'll call Charla."

"And I'm going to play dead for a while." She closed her eyes.

65

Charla was just getting out of the shower when her phone chimed. She picked it up, saw Celia's number and contemplated ignoring it. She didn't like Celia very much. She was always nagging her to *be nicer to your mother. Spend more time with your mother.* It was really none of her business. She set the phone back down and continued to towel off.

She had slipped into some casual slacks and a sleeveless silk blouse when the phone chimed again. She eyed the number. "That woman is persistent," she complained aloud.

Grudgingly she answered, "What is it now, Celia? Did my mother trip over her own feet again?" She put the phone on speaker and set it on the bathroom counter while she applied makeup.

"Stop being such a bitch, Charla."

"To what do I owe the pleasure of this call?" Charla primped at her hair as she spoke. She brushed a tiny speck of mascara from the corner of her eye, picked up the tube and began applying it to her eyelashes as she talked.

"I thought you should know that your mother had a car wreck on her way home. She's at my ER, unconscious. You should come as soon as you can. Do you remember where I work?"

"Yes, Celia, I remember. Is it serious?"

"We don't know yet. You need to come."

"I'll be there as soon as I can." She hung up, ran a comb through her hair and applied lipstick. "It's probably another one of her bids for attention," Charla mumbled as she headed for her car.

Charla moved towards the cubicle, where Lillian lay with her eyes closed.

She approached tentatively.

Monitoring machines beeped softly and an IV dripped slowly.

Charla noted the black eye and bandage. This looked like a repeat of that other morning a few months ago when the roommates called because Mom tripped and hit her head.

A nurse popped in to check the readouts on the monitors. "The doctor will be in shortly." She left.

"Mom," Charla spoke softly, "you can wake up now."

Cora appeared in the room. "I know what you're thinking. You remember when she fell in her bedroom. This is more serious. She totaled her new car. We're lucky she's not DOA."

"What happened? I noticed some cops around. Was everyone from the accident brought here?"

"Yes," Cora answered. "I spoke to one of the officers. He said your mother's car was an unfortunate victim when two other speeding cars ran a stop light. I think she has a serious concussion."

"When will she wake up?" Charla eyed her mother. "*Will* she wake up?"

"You'll have to ask the doctor. It could be days before she responds to anything." Cora waited a beat and then asked, "I'm sure she told you that your secret is out."

Charla's head jerked up and she opened her mouth to respond.

Cora raised her hand to indicate she didn't need to say anything. "Don't worry. Celia and I aren't going to tell anyone. It's your family business and you can handle it any way you want. However, just in case this injury is more serious than we think, I have to ask you one thing."

"Not that it concerns you," Charla said indignantly, squaring her shoulders as if ready for a fight, "but what?"

"Did you two get everything hashed out and all of your differences settled? It's important to do that when there is a chance your mother won't be coming back from this."

Charla drew herself up to her full height and glared at Cora. "It's really none of your business what goes on between my mother and me, but yes we had a long talk and made plans to get back on track."

Cora pressed on, seemingly undaunted by Charla's snotty attitude. "Good. You have a lot to make up for where your mother is concerned. I hope you find it in your heart to say all the right words and do the right thing. She isn't getting any younger. Now I will leave you. If there is anything that remains unsaid, it's time to take care of it. Even if she's in a coma, she may be able to hear you. So be nice." She turned on her heel and left.

Charla glared at Cora as she retreated, then turned her attention back to the still figure in the bed. Lillian had not moved a muscle. The only indication of life was the gentle rise and fall of her diaphragm as she breathed and the steady beep of the heart monitor. Bruises were forming on her face as Charla watched.

Charla thought back to the last few minutes of their dinner that evening. Lillian took the news in stride, although she took her shots, chiding Charla for her indiscretions. She promised not to tell Courtney. When she left, her brief kiss and the words "I love you" gave Charla pause, after all the deception and neglect of her mother over the years. She was too slow to respond and Lillian left without any reciprocation for the gesture.

Taking Lillian's hand in hers, she sighed and a tear dripped from the corner of her eye. "I'm sorry, Mother for everything. I should have had more confidence in you. I'm sorry I've been such a bitch. I honestly don't know how I got to that point, except that I was being so selfish and immersed in my obsession with Marshall. I let it color my attitude towards those closest to me—you, Courtney and Herb. I should have been putting all of you first."

By now, the tears were coming in torrents and Charla was having difficulty getting the words out. "I'm so, so sorry for everything. I love you and I want you in my life for a long time. Please come back to me. Please wake up." She sat down in the chair beside the gurney, squeezed Lillian's hand and put it to her wet cheek. "I'm begging you to please come back. I want you to move in and live with me after you get out of the hospital. Come back."

Celia interrupted the heartfelt speech when she peeked into the cubicle. "Excuse me," she whispered, "I need to do something." She lifted Lillian's eyelids briefly to check her pupils and then turned abruptly and left.

Within a minute or two, orderlies came in and started unplugging things.

"What's happening?" asked Charla as she scooted the chair back and stepped aside in a panic.

"We're taking her to radiology for a brain scan. You can wait here or go to the waiting room. This will take a while. You might want to take a coffee break." They wheeled Lillian out.

Charla sat back down in the chair, looked around the cubicle where Lillian's bed was a minute ago, and felt at a loss as to what to do next. *What if this is it? What will I do if I never get the chance to make it up to her?* She took a tissue from her bag and wiped her eyes.

It was time to call Courtney. She should be here too.

66

The roommates had been hovering nearby and met Charla as she came out of the cubicle. They had stood close enough to overhear most of Charla's sentimental plea. Those words were what Lillian had wanted from her daughter. They exchanged satisfied nods when hearing them. Nevertheless, they were duty bound to carry on the charade for as long as Lillian wanted. They were feeling smug, until Celia peeked in and saw signs of trouble.

After the orderlies took Lillian to x-ray, Celia felt a brief moment of pity for the woman standing before her, but it passed swiftly. "Would you like to go to the cafeteria for a cup of coffee?"

She felt like gloating a bit, but hid it well as she noted that Charla had cried enough tears to wipe her face of all traces of makeup. She was still beautiful without all of that Estee Lauder crap. She didn't have any skin flaws that needed to be covered.

Ample freckles were Celia's cross to bear and she had long ago given up trying to obscure them with foundation. She was satisfied to see the air let out of Charla's inflated ego for once and see her humility at Lillian's bedside. Now maybe her closest friend will finally have what she wants most…her daughter back.

"Did your mother say anything while you were with her?" Cora asked as if they had not been eavesdropping. "Did she wake up at all?"

Charla nodded to the negative. "I don't know if she heard anything."

"Not even a flicker of recognition?" Celia asked. "Did she squeeze your hand or respond in any way?"

"No."

"Excuse me." Celia checked her wristwatch. "I'm going to my locker and change into scrubs. My shift starts soon, but first I'm going up to Radiology to see what's happening with Lil. You two should take a seat in the waiting room. I'll catch up to you."

A few minutes later, Celia settled into a seat beside Charla. "The news is not good. Lillian has bleeding on the brain. They are taking her to surgery. It could be hours before she wakes up."

"So you're saying that she didn't hear anything I said to her back there," said Charla, as she nodded towards the ER. "Did I just make a fool of myself for nothing?"

Celia paused for a moment to control the urge to slap the woman. Keeping her voice down to avoid making a scene, she replied, "This isn't about you. Your mother could quite possibly die. It's all on your conscience if you wasted twenty years shoving her away because of your deception. So consider your performance at her bedside a rehearsal for when she really wakes up. Stop thinking about yourself and start thinking about her. You'd better pray she comes back to us. You have a lot to atone for."

After a pause to absorb the slap down, Charla stood. "I have to pick Courtney up at the airport."

Cora and Celia watched as Charla squared her shoulders and headed for the door with her chin held high.

67

Celia returned to the ER to start her shift and Cora waited at the front entrance for Charla and Courtney to return. It was midnight.

She dozed off involuntarily around one a.m. for a few minutes when someone tapped her on the shoulder. She looked up to see Courtney. She smiled a drowsy smile and yawned. "Hello sweetheart. How was your flight? I'm so glad you could make it." She glanced at her watch. Two hours had passed since she fell asleep. She felt so tired, she could hardly move.

"Flying is boring. Where's Grandma?"

Cora rose, stretched her neck and shoulders briefly, and headed towards the elevator bank. "Follow me. She's in recovery. It's so late, we may not get in to see her, but it won't hurt to inquire about her."

Courtney was dressed in mismatched clothing with rubber thongs on her feet as if she had jumped out of bed, thrown on the nearest clothes from her bedroom floor and dashed out the door. Her hair was in disarray and there was no sign of having applied any makeup.

Charla on the other hand, had apparently found time to apply makeup and comb her hair. *Image is everything to that girl, even at three in the morning.*

"Excuse my clothes, Cora. Mother called to say she had a seat on a late flight for me and I had to race to the airport to make it. I didn't even pack a bag. I sure got some disagreeable looks when I went

288

to the ticket counter with a one-way reservation and no baggage. I practically got strip searched at Security. Like where would I hide a bomb in these skin-tight jeans and tank top? I don't know how many times I had to explain the situation."

"It doesn't matter how you're dressed, dear. You are here now and your grandma will be very happy to see you when she wakes up."

"If she wakes up," Charla interjected glumly.

As they rode in the elevator, Cora remembered Lillian's last words to her. "Now leave me alone and let me play dead." She had intended to feign a coma hoping Charla would apologize and say the magic words she so wanted to hear. However, somewhere between those words and the arrival of Charla in ER, Lillian had actually slipped into unconsciousness. All of Charla's heart-felt words and tears were for naught. Lillian had not heard any of it.

Only Celia noticed the change and became alarmed. She had sought out the doctor and that's when hospital personnel sprang into action.

Cora had been in the surgical waiting room when the doctor came out to report make his report. She commenced relaying what she knew to Charla and Courtney. "According to the surgeon, they successfully stopped the bleeding in her brain. Prognosis is guarded."

The nurses allowed a five-minute visit as she ushered the three into the room. ICU at this time of night was silent as a funeral parlor and all the staff talked in hushed tones. Hooked up to a respirator and monitors, Lillian looked about as dead as you can look and still breathe. Her ankle had been set in a cast. IV fluids kept her hydrated while a bag caught the urine. A thick bandage covered the side of her head where she had taken a blow to it. Her face had swollen and the skin around her eyes had turned a deep purple. She was ashen and still.

Courtney burst into tears. She took Lillian's hand and rubbed the back of it. "Grandma, I love you. Please come back to us."

There was no response. Lillian didn't have to pretend to play dead. She actually looked the part.

Cora moved forward to put an arm around Courtney's shoulders. "Please don't cry. It will take a while for her to come out of sedation. She'll be okay." *I wish I could be sure of that.*

Charla moved around and took Lillian's other hand. "They won't let us stay long. We have to go now, but we will be back first thing in the morning. We love you."

I wish she would have said that when Lillian was awake. Cora swallowed hard. "I have a favor to ask."

"Anything," Charla replied as they left the room.

"I don't have a car. Can you drop me off at home?"

Courtney piped up on their way out the hospital door. "Where's your car? How did you get here?"

"I rode here with Celia, but she's working now. As for my car, that puke that held your Grandmother up also stole mine right out of our driveway. I guess nobody has filled you in about that. Have you Charla?"

Charla shrugged. "I guess I haven't had time. I'm exhausted. Let's get you home. I'm sure Courtney is tired too. Will you need a ride tomorrow?"

"I don't know. Maybe I can borrow Celia's PT."

Cora rode silently in the back seat of Charla's Cadillac. *After my long talk with her about Lillian's robbery and the burglary of our house, Charla didn't have enough interest in the whole thing to relay it to Courtney. I wonder if when...if ever, she would have gotten around to it. If there is one thing, I know for sure...that family has a serious lack of communication.*

When Cora exited the car, she was stunned when Charla said, "Call me when you get up if you need a ride." The woman she could barely tolerate was being nice now. She hardly knew how to react.

She shrugged and replied, "Thanks for the offer, but I think I'll call for a rental car. My insurance will cover it and I won't be a burden to anyone. Lillian may be out of it for a while and I'll be back and forth to the hospital."

Charla smiled. "Okay, but if you change your mind, let me know."

Courtney blew Cora a kiss. "Thanks for everything, Cora. I don't know where Grandma would be without you and Celia." She rolled her eyes in her mother's direction to make her point. "We'll probably see you tomorrow...I mean later today."

Cora waved and started thinking about how good her bed was going to feel. It had been a long day.

68

The hours dragged into days, the days into weeks. The school year ended, meaning Cora's job substituting was over for the summer.

Celia was juggling her night shifts with long visits to Lillian's bedside and trying to catch up on sleep during the day.

With Lillian out of the house, Cora felt like she was in suspended animation. Instead of the companionship and laugher of their coffee times and breakfasts, there was only silence. She even wished she had a little dog to keep her company. She filled the hours with belated spring-cleaning. She repainted her bedroom and redecorated the hall bath with new paint, wallpaper border and new linens in an effort to erase the vision of that hairy intruder giving himself a makeover in the room.

Every afternoon, she went to visit Lillian's bedside. Her friend didn't appear to have recovered consciousness, but she was showing signs of movement in her arms and legs. Whether it was voluntary or not remained questionable. However, it did give Cora hope.

The task of finding a new car to replace Brown Betty took some of her time. The more she looked, the more confused she got. She finally settled on a slightly used Prius. All the while, Cora worried over Lillian's status. Her friend was always occupying the back of her mind.

The long-term recovery facility across from the hospital had taken over Lillian's care and she occupied a room with two beds. A scrawny anorexic old woman with sparse hair and no teeth occupied the second bed. She barely acknowledged Cora's friendly greeting each day.

Cora was impressed at how caring Charla had become over the trying weeks. She was there almost every time Cora or Celia visited. Cora's attitude toward Charla had begun to soften. Maybe she wasn't the bitch the roommates had tagged her to be. Maybe it had really been her tug of war between her clandestine personal life, her guilty conscience, and her desire to keep the truth from Lillian. The woman was attentive to her mother in her time of need. Perhaps they could learn to tolerate each other after this.

Courtney had flown in a few times over the weekends, but returned to school, keeping in close touch by phone.

Celia explained, "These things take time. The brain operates at its own pace. She'll come out of it." Her glum facial expression didn't match those optimistic words.

All the same, Cora observed that each day, her dear friend grew gaunter as she lost weight. The head wound from surgery healed and her hair grew back in that spot, but still she didn't respond to stimuli. If she wanted to play the role of dying drama queen for Charla's benefit, she was performing an Oscar winning act.

Cora had just about given up hope. She parked her Prius in the lot and sighed. Today she would have a talk with the doctor. Maybe it was time for Charla to let Lillian go into hospice care and proceed toward that place where she will rest in peace. It was clear she was in severe decline. She would talk to the doctor and then to Charla.

The summer temperatures had risen to triple digits and a blast of warm wind ruffled her short dyed brown curls as she made the walk to the front door of the care center. She felt as if she had been through this before, all those years ago when her husband was failing at the end of his life. He had passed while still in a hospital room. Cora never expected to have to go through somewhat the same thing again. Lillian was always so full of life, eager to be on the go, daring in her escapades. The vision of Lillian in her sombrero heading off to visit Charla's office in her *Spanish Cadillac* made her laugh softly. She mumbled, "I can't save you from this caper, my girl. It's time."

She inquired at the nurse's station as to when the doctor would be making his rounds.

"He's in Miss Lillian's room as we speak. You can catch him with her if you hurry."

Cora swiftly made her way through the maze of hallways leading to Lillian's room. Her heart beat faster as she approached. She anticipated a serious talk with the doctor about running brain function tests to see if they needed to let Lillian go. She rounded the corner, pushed the partially open door aside, and approached the tall burley doctor standing at the bedside blocking her view of the patient.

When she came around to the foot of the bed, she nearly swooned and had to grab a nearby chair.

Lillian's eyes were open.

"Lillian," Cora gasped. "You're awake!"

The doctor turned to address Cora. "Yes, our patient woke up this morning. I consider it somewhat of a miracle, and the good care we provide here." He smiled in satisfaction. "It looks like she will make a full recovery given some time."

Cora moved up to where she could take Lillian's hand and squeezed it. "Oh, my God, do you know how badly you have scared all of us? I thought we were going to be burying you."

Lillian looked over at Cora with vacant eyes. "Who are you?" Her speech was slightly impaired due to the feeding tube in her throat that had kept her alive. The doctor had already removed the oxygen mask, leaving deep marks in Lillian's wrinkled cheeks.

Taken aback, Cora gasped and didn't reply right away. She looked up at the tall physician. "What's wrong? Why doesn't she know me? We've been friends and roommates for years."

Lillian burst out with a weak chuckle. "I'm just kidding. You're my daughter, aren't you?"

"What?" Cora felt her heart sinking. "Have you got amnesia?"

Lillian laughed weakly again. "I know it's you, Cora. I'm just practicing my act for when Charla comes in. Has she been to see me?"

"She has devoted every single evening to you. I've never seen her so attentive. I think you put the fear of God in that woman."

"Good, then, my plan is working. If she thinks I'm dying, I'll get her attention."

"Lillian, this is no time to be goofing off. You need to get well so we can take you home. So knock off the silliness."

She directed her attention to the doctor. "What's going to happen now? She's been resting long enough. Can we get her up and walking soon? Her muscles must have atrophied by now. What's next?"

"I'm ordering intensive physical therapy. We'll keep her until she can walk with a walker."

Cora smiled. "That's what I wanted to hear." She glanced down at his left hand—*no wedding ring*. She glimpsed his smile, his straight teeth, his ice blue eyes, and his rosy complexion. It wasn't often she met somebody taller than her own six-foot stature. She suddenly found herself wondering what he would be like in the sack. She had never dated a doctor. She shook her head and pulled herself away from the imaginary affair. "I have to call Charla."

Lillian blurted, "No, don't call her yet. She still hasn't said the words I want to hear, and if she thinks I'm going to croak, maybe today will be the day."

Cora was about to inform her that Charla had said those words a hundred times in the course of the last few weeks while Lillian was in her deep sleep. Of course, they went unheard. She opened her mouth to say so, but thought better of it. "Okay, what do you want me to do?"

The doctor interrupted them. "I have to continue my rounds. You two women have some catching up to do. Lillian, tomorrow you will start therapy. We'll remove that tube immediately and send in some soft foods for you. Now I must go."

"Thank you, Doc, for all you've done," Cora said as he left the room. "Now, Lillian, you've caught up on your rest and I see you have not lost your sense of humor. How do you want to handle this?"

"Tell the people here not to let on to Charla that I'm awake. If she comes by when she closes her office today, I want to surprise her. Can you be here when she arrives, and looking very grim? She needs to think I'm done for and they are going to pull the plug."

"Lillian, your daughter has been through the mill, dealing with this. As I told you, she has been here faithfully every night after work and every weekend. She has said repeatedly how much she cares for you. I've seen her cry a bucket of tears. She has apologized endlessly for her behavior over the last two decades. Why do you want to drag this out? Just ask her to say the words."

"You know how she is and how controlled she can be. If she thinks this is the end, maybe she'll feel something for me. Really feel something. Please."

"Lillian, she has proven that she loves you, and you are only going to make her angry. I know that she is sorry. If you…" Cora shrugged. "Okay. I'll call her and say we have to have a serious discussion about your prognosis and I'll meet her here when she gets off work. I'll head her off at the door. You be ready."

When Charla appeared a little later, Cora noticed dark circles around her eyes and worry lines in her forehead that all the makeup in Macy's couldn't hide. It was obvious the strain of having to keep her business running and be at Lillian's bedside for these past weeks was finally taking its toll. For an instant, she thought about blurting out the fact that Lillian was awake and going to make a full recovery. Keeping Charla on the hook like this was not fair.

Ultimately, she remained loyal to her friend and kept quiet. *I hope that Lillian will come to her senses and stop playing dead in an effort to keep Charla close.*

69

The grim look on Cora's face as she came in the front door, made Charla's heart skip a beat. "Is she alright?" She searched Cora's face for a positive change in expression.

The reply wasn't encouraging. "You need to try and talk her back to us. Keep telling her what you have been for the last few weeks. Make her come back to us." Tears formed in the corner of Cora's eyes, to add to the drama. "I'll hang out for a few minutes in case you need me." She turned and stepped into the nearby restroom.

Charla braced herself. By Cora's demeanor, she gathered that there had been little improvement in her mother's condition since her last visit. She headed for the room. She had to tell her something and this was such an awkward time to do it, but she couldn't avoid it.

The room was dim, being on the shady side of the complex in late afternoon. Lillian lay very still as if still in a coma. Every evening that Charla came by after work, it was the same. Maybe it was time to let her mother go, disconnect the feeding tube and IV, and let nature take its course. It was a decision no daughter ever wanted to make, but maybe it was time. She was so concentrated on watching Lillian that she didn't hear Cora hovering outside the door.

"Mother, I'm here." She took Lillian's hand and squeezed it. "Even if you don't know it, I've been here every evening since your accident. I've prayed for you. I've begged you to come back to us." Tears began to flow down her cheeks.

She sobbed, "I love you so much and I am so sorry I wasted all those years avoiding you. I want you to know that. I am grateful to you and Dad for helping me raise Courtney. I'm proud that you are my mother. I'm going to miss you so much. I wish you would come back, even if only for a little while. I need you. Courtney needs you and sends her love. I want you to be around for her college graduation. I want you to be here to see her walk down the aisle and get married."

After a pause to take a tissue out of her bag and dab at her dripping nose, she continued, "I just want things to be better than they were before your accident. I'd do anything for you— anything. Words can't express how much I love you." She squeezed Lillian's hand and wished for a response.

Cora entered the room and positioned a chair so Charla could sit down. "Take the load off," she whispered.

Charla complied and looked up at Cora. "I don't know what more to do."

Cora grinned. "I'm sure she heard you." She reached out and yanked Lillian's big toe. "Wake up you old hag. You aren't leaving us yet," she demanded.

Charla's mouth dropped open and she exclaimed, "Cora!"

Lillian's eyes popped open.

"See, you just have to use language she understands." She giggled.

"Mother, have you been awake all the time? Were you faking?"

"What do you think? I just wanted to hear you say you love me. I woke up this morning. What day is this? How long have I been asleep?"

"Five weeks, you lazy old slacker," said Cora. "You've been sleeping long enough. It's time to get back to living."

"Five weeks! I missed five weeks of bowling! " Lillian huffed. "What in hell—the last thing I remember is leaving Charla's house."

"We had lunch together. You never made it home." Charla held Lillian's hand as if she could never let it go.

"Where did I go? How did I wind up here? Where is here?"

Cora spoke first. "Didn't you ask your doctor when you saw him?"

"No. He didn't explain anything."

"We told you once already, before your brain surgery, but you probably don't remember. Your car was involved in an accident at an intersection close to our house. Apparently, Angel was the tuna salad in a sandwich made by two red light runners. You got a serious concussion and you are lucky to be alive. The airbags saved you, but you forgot to wear your seat belt. Your noggin took out the rearview mirror."

"However, you are fine now—or you will be with some physical therapy," Charla added.

"What happened to my car?"

"Don't even think about that. You can get another one. You won't be driving for a while anyway."

"Maybe never," she frowned. "That's two cars in a matter of weeks. I won't be able to afford insurance now."

Charla laughed. "Really, mother! You nearly died and the only thing you are concerned about now is the cost of car insurance?"

Cora chuckled. "We'll figure out something. I have a car now so we'll get by just fine. You'll be coming home soon."

"I'll hire a nurse and physical therapist to work with you, Mom. We'll get you back to normal real soon. This time, I really will buy you a car, whatever one you want, no limits. I mean it this time."

"Can I have a Cadillac?" Lillian grinned and studied her daughter for a few beats. "You've changed. You're more like the daughter I remember before all the—before the troubles."

"We ironed all that out the day of your accident. We had agreed to put it in the past and go forward with a new relationship. Do you remember that?"

Lillian paused as if searching her memory. "Have you done anything about it?" She looked Charla in the eye.

"My main concern has been you. We need to get you back to one hundred percent. That's all I'm concerned about now."

Cora patted Lillian's free hand. "I'm going to leave the two of you now. Maybe you still have things to talk about. I'll be back tomorrow.

By the way, see if you can find out if your doctor is single and available. He kind of tweaked my fancy." She winked meaningfully.

Lillian sighed. "I've been on the verge of meeting Saint Peter at the Pearly Gates and all you can think about is finding an eligible man to *tweak your fancy?*"

Charla burst out laughing. "Is that how you old broads refer to your aging sexual urges now—fancies?"

Cora responded with a shrug. "You could say that. It sounds better than the more graphic term—*I'm horny.*"

Lillian rasped, "I remember you saying you didn't want another man that had to reach for his knee to scratch his balls."

"I did and I meant it. But your doctor looks as if he's young enough he doesn't need a jock strap to hold everything up to keep from tripping over it."

Charla laughed. "Is this how you always talk about old men? It sounds so…"

"I know," Cora interrupted, "we're a couple of bawdy broads sometimes. After all, if you can't have *it* you can at least enjoy talking about it."

All the animosity between Cora and Charla seemed to have gone away for the moment. Charla reached out and put her arm around Cora. "I'm glad you're Mom's friend. I can't tell you how much I appreciate what you do for her. I'm sorry I've been such a bitch."

Cora hugged the woman back. "I think we can forgive and forget and learn from all this. Now I will leave you. I'm sure you've got a lot to talk about." She waved and quickly left the room.

Charla turned her attention back to Lillian and commenced bringing her up to date on significant events from the past few weeks. She carefully omitted any reference to Marshall. She needed to tell Lillian about the latest disheartening news, but decided to delay that until she had more information and until Lillian was stronger.

"I'm starving," Lillian said. "This damn tube irritates my throat when I try to talk."

Charla jumped up. "I'll go find a nurse and see if they can bring you some gelatin or pudding. They need to take that out. I'll be right back." She left in a hurry, leaving her handbag on the bedside table.

Deep inside the bag, a cell phone began to chime. Lillian's instinct was to reach for it and answer, but she found her arms to be extremely weak. She lay impatiently while the phone rang and then finally quit.

Charla returned. "The nurse is going to bring you something to eat. The doctor left orders for them to remove your feeding tube and give you soft bland meals for a few days."

"Your phone rang while you were gone," Lillian rasped, motioning towards Charla's purse with a weak wave of her hand.

Charla reached in and checked. "Courtney called, I'll dial her. I think she would like to hear your voice." She held the phone to Lillian's ear.

When Courtney answered, Lillian smiled and said, "When are you coming to visit your old granny?"

A loud hoot erupted from the phone and Courtney yelled, "Grandma's awake. I'm so excited. When did this happen?"

"A little while ago; I guess I'm going to live now. Can you come and visit? Bring your Lennie with you."

"I have exams all week, but I'll get a break after that. I'll be there as soon as I can. I love you and can't wait to see you, Grandma."

"I love you too. Talk to your mom before you hang up."

At that moment, the nurse came in, put on vinyl gloves and prepared to remove the feeding tube. Charla stepped out of the room, not wanting to be witness to that procedure. "I can't talk long, Honey, I have to help your grandma eat something. What's up?"

"It's so great to have her on the mend. I miss her so much. What I really called about is to ask if you got the test results back yet. Do you know yet?"

Charla took a deep breath and let it out. She did not want to break this kind of news to Courtney over the phone, so she lied. "Not yet. Come home as soon as you can get here and we'll talk. I should know everything by then. When is your last final exam?"

"I'll be done and on the road by Friday afternoon. I'm worried about you."

"Don't worry. This is fixable. Your Grandmother is anxious to see you. I love you. See you Friday night." She punched the end call button.

Sleeping had been out of the question since Marshall called a week ago on his burner phone. He called to report that his wife has cervical cancer and the prognosis isn't good.

Charla's first reaction had been a brief glimmer of hope for a future with Marshall after all. However, after Googling that kind of cancer and reading all the papers, reality set in.

The research explained the causes of cervical cancer—HPV. Charla's heart sank. For the past twenty years, the only man she had relations with was Marshall and she knew that this news meant she was at risk as well. She made an emergency appointment with her OB-GYN. The results came back yesterday. She called Marshall back and begged him to go to his doctor and take the test to see if he carries the virus. It was logical to assume that if he's having unprotected sex with two women and both of them have the same disease, he has to be involved.

His reaction was not what she expected from the man she had loved all her life. He went ballistic over the phone, accusing both his wife and his mistress of cheating on him.

Charla was deep in thought with her phone still in hand when the nurse came out of Lillian's room and retrieved a food tray from the cart. Pushing the thoughts out of her head, she followed the nurse back into the room and seated herself beside Lillian. "Let me help you with that."

The nurse paused for a minute. "It might be difficult to swallow for a while. Those tubes irritate the throat. Just take it slow." She cranked the bed up so Lillian's head was more elevated and then left them alone.

Charla dipped a spoon into the gelatin and said, "Let's give this a try. If you can't do it, I'll go get you some Ensure and a straw."

"No you won't," Lillian objected. "I'm not that far gone. Give me that spoon." She grabbed it, promptly spilling the contents on her bedsheet. She pulled the sheet up and sucked the glob off.

Charla grinned. "That's my spunky mom. Welcome back."

70

The medical facility was abuzz with morning activity when Courtney entered and made her way down the hallway. Orderlies were busy changing vacant beds and others were carrying food trays into various rooms. She breezed by a cafeteria where patients in wheel chairs were eating at round tables.

Confused by the maze of hallways, she stopped at a nurse's station to ask directions, and then took off again. When she found the room she wanted, she cautiously entered. An African-American woman occupied the bed nearest the door. Courtney smiled and waved. The woman barely acknowledged the gesture. She moved on to the other bed.

Lillian was napping. Her partially consumed breakfast sat on the tray table. Courtney gagged at the sight of congealed oatmeal and runny rice pudding.

Courtney took a seat and quietly waited. She noted that grandmother had lost a lot of weight, noticeably in her sunken cheeks and the increased wrinkling on her arms. She thought back to just a few months ago when Lillian referred to herself as fluffy—not fat or pudgy. The fluff was gone, replaced by sagging skin and dark bags under her eyes. It made tears well up in Courtney's eyes. This was not the fun-loving spunky grandma who rescued her from the storm Courtney had created over the dog situation.

As she studied Lillian, she briefly considered visiting UNLV to see if she could enroll there next term because she felt like Grandma needed her here. Then Lennie popped into her mind and she discarded that idea. *I could take her to California with me. She could stay in the condominium while she regains her health. She—that wouldn't work; she probably wouldn't appreciate Lennie staying overnight all the time. In Grandma's eyes, I'm still a virgin. Ha!*

Lillian stirred, opened her eyes, and looked around, her gaze coming to rest on Courtney. She smiled with delight. "Courtney, how long have you been sitting there? Why didn't you wake me?"

"I didn't want to disturb you. I just came in. I drove up last night after exams. How are you doing?"

"I'm just peachy keen, as you can see. I caught the red light runner epidemic. I was just minding my own business when boom! Nevertheless, I'll be fine now. Where is Charla?"

Courtney glanced out the window at the hospital across the way. "Mom had something else she had to do this morning."

Courtney had checked Charla in for surgery at five this morning. She had waited in the surgical area waiting room until the doctor came out to say her mother would be in recovery for several hours. Then Courtney breathed a sigh of relief, grabbed a fast breakfast in the hospital cafeteria, and walked over to see Lillian.

"Is she having an open house today?"

Lillian's hoarse voice interrupted Courtney's thoughts and she turned her attention back to her grandmother.

She lied. "She's across the way...visiting a friend." Her smile wasn't selling it.

"Courtney, I know that look. What's going on?"

She couldn't keep it in any longer. She burst into tears and dropped her head onto Lillian's shoulder.

"Courtney, baby, what's the matter? Why are you crying? Now you're scaring me. Did your mother have a face-lift that went wrong? Tell me."

Courtney reached for a tissue, wiped away the tears and blew her nose. She paused, trying to find the right words.

"Mother went into surgery this morning. They had to take out all her female organs and a portion of her colon and small intestine because the cancer had spread. She's in recovery."

Lillian's eyes widened. "What? What do you mean *cancer*? She seemed fine yesterday when she was here. What has she been keeping from me? There she goes, doing it again, keeping things from me. Damn!"

"I'm not supposed to tell you, but I can't keep you in the dark. That man she's been dating—the bozo that comes into town, boinks her and then blows out again—he apparently gave her the HPV virus. She had full-blown cancer...stage four."

Lillian's hands flew up to her face as tears welled up. "I knew something was wrong. She looked really tired and haggard the last few days. She should have told me. How does she know this guy passed the virus to her?"

"His wife has it too. She had surgery a few weeks ago and is undergoing chemotherapy as we speak. He's an asshole."

"Oh, dear, did Charla notify him of these circumstances?"

"She didn't want to tell me, but I nagged her for the truth. She told him and he accused both his wife and my mother of cheating on him. He won't even go to a doctor and see if he is a carrier. He will just keep going on about his philandering ways and infect all the women he screws. How could she get involved with a jackass like that?"

"Did your mother tell you who this turd is?"

"I don't know his name. If I did, I would find a way for him to pay for what he's done."

"I know his name." Lillian closed her eyes a minute. "Don't tell your mother this came from me, but if he has put her life in jeopardy, I think the world needs to know so that other women are protected."

Courtney perked up, dabbed at the tears still escaping her eyes and gaped at Lillian. "How could you know his name? She was always so cagey about it. She wouldn't tell me whom she was seeing. She never brought him around to the house when I was home. It's as if she's been leading a double life for years. Who is he...somebody famous?"

Lillian pursed her lips as if trying to hold back the words she had vowed to keep secret.

"I'm begging you to tell me, Grandma. I'm not leaving until I find out."

"Don't ever tell your mother this came from me, because I promised her I'd never tell you."

"I promise." Courtney took Lillian's hand and squeezed it. "Now who is he?"

"The day I had my accident, your mom had finally confessed to me about the other man in her life besides your daddy, Herb. I think you should know the truth, but it didn't come from me."

"Their love affair began way back in high school." After Lillian relayed what she knew about Marshall Court and Charla's more than twenty-year affair with him, Courtney sat in a daze in the chair she had dropped into at the name, *Marshall Court*.

Her brain was connecting the dots. She could barely say the words aloud. "He's my biological father? She even named me after him! How could she do that to me? What was she thinking?"

"I suppose, like all mistresses, she thought he would leave his wife at some point and marry her. When they were in high school together, I thought they were just friends that hung out a lot. It started back then. They kept a big secret. He broke your mother's heart when he married that other woman. Herbie has been an excellent father for you, and don't ever forget it. He loves you with all his heart. He is an innocent victim in this. Don't let it change the way you feel about him."

"He will always be my daddy. This other guy, the sperm donor, he's going to regret everything he's done."

"What are you going to do?"

Courtney took her iPhone out of her back pocket. "I am the social media generation. If Marshall Court thinks that he is blameless and getting off scot free, he has another think coming. By the time they discharge my mother from the hospital, that turd's political ambitions and marriage will be history. I'll bring you copies of the gossip rags from the supermarket. Now I need to get back to the hospital."

"Not without me." Lillian made an effort to throw her covers aside and rise up.

"You can't go yet. Besides, she's still out of it." Courtney tucked the covers back around Lillian.

"When they put her in a regular room, I'll come and check you out for a visit. I think you could probably take a ride in a wheel chair across the parking lot. The weather is beautiful out there."

Lillian's head sank back into her pillow. "Okay. I'll make sure they let me take a shower. Could you go to my house and get me some clothes?"

"Aren't you rushing things?" Courtney had to grin at her grandmother's spunk. She was coming back from near death and now she wanted some street clothes already. "I'll call Cora and have her bring you some things. How is that?"

"I didn't think of that. I'll expect regular updates today."

Courtney rose and started to leave. "I love you Grandma." After blowing her one final kiss, she left. She had a wicked task ahead of her. The laptop was in the car. The words she intended to speak on the video she was going to post were forming in her brain. Vengeance was in her soul. However, it would have to wait.

It was evening before Charla was ready for visitors. Courtney pushed Lillian's wheelchair into the room and over to the bedside.

Lillian took Charla's hand. There were IV tubes and wires attached all over. Lillian noted the pale skin. Without makeup, Charla could be any other plain Jane on the street. This version was the girl she raised and wanted back. When the makeup and designer clothes went on, the personality changed to someone Lillian didn't know and often didn't like.

"Why didn't you tell me about this, Charla?" Lillian scowled at her daughter. "I thought we were going to be up-front and open with each other from now on."

Charla hesitated as if searching for words.

"Well?" Lillian prompted, "I'm not getting any younger."

"I'm sorry. You had just begun to come back from your accident. You needed rest and time to rehab. I didn't want to burden you with my problems."

Lillian squeezed Charla's hand. "Okay, then. Let's get one thing straight. We are in this recovery thing together. I'm going to help you and you're going to help me. When does your chemo start?"

"I don't know. Why do you ask?"

"Because I have to make sure I'm out of this chair and walking by then so I can go with you and hold your hand while you puke."

"Oh, please, Mother, can we not talk about that now? Courtney is staying here a few weeks to help me. You need to concentrate on walking so you can go home. I'll be there for you as soon as I can get well enough to drive. We'll both be there to help you. Now I need to sleep." She closed her eyes as if to dismiss both of them.

Courtney took Lillian back to her room and tucked her in for the night. "I'll be back tomorrow, Grandma. Don't go anywhere." She kissed Lillian's cheek. "I love you."

"I love you too. See you tomorrow."

That evening, Courtney plugged in the laptop, logged on to social media and made a video. "Hi. My name is Courtney Marsha Romaine and I am the bastard child of…."

Thus began the systematic destruction of Marshall Court's aspirations for higher office. It went viral in hours.

71

"It was a nice service," Cora said as she walked across the lawn at the cemetery and weaved through the parking lot to locate her car. "There were more people here than I would have expected."

Cora glanced back to where the casket sat poised over the open grave. Workers stood silently by at a respectable distance, waiting to finish the interment. She couldn't hold back the tears. "They had so little time together after they ironed everything out. I'm so sad for her. Charla visited Lillian every day after she could get around after her surgery. She walked her mother up and down the hallways and really seemed to have done a complete turnaround in her attitude. Even as she was preparing herself mentally for all the bad side effects of chemo, she faithfully showed up to help Lillian through rehab and I think that encouraged both of them to get better faster. They even talked about living together after they both got well."

Celia wiped away a tear. Her eyes were red from crying as well. "Charla mention that she planned to sell that big two-story house and have a new one built all on one level so that Lillian could live with her. She was really making a sincere effort to atone for past sins. This just isn't fair. Life is not fair sometimes. Courtney appears absolutely crushed and even Herbie looks completely devastated. It was so nice of him to come back when they needed him most."

"I think he still loves Charla. After all, they were married for over twenty years. He came back when Courtney told him about Charla's cancer, and he was there every minute to wait on her when she got out of the hospital, so that Courtney could help Lillian. He didn't leave until Charla could drive herself to work again. It's a shame that woman didn't realize what she had with him. She threw it all away."

Cora sighed. "Lillian had high hopes that they would reconcile. Courtney would have liked that."

"I'm witness to disappointments every day I work in ER. Some things are not meant to be."

Cora started the car. "Courtney told me that after she plastered the internet with scandal about Marshall Court, the news rags latched onto it like dogs with a big piece of prime rib. They literally destroyed any chance he ever had to run for high office, and his wife is divorcing him. Other women have come forward accusing him of infecting them. Charla wasn't his only dalliance."

Celia snorted, "Good for them! He deserves it. He turned his back as soon as Charla told him he was carrying an STD."

"There's a post funeral reception at Charla's house, so I guess we better get going."

"Who's handling it?" Celia asked. "It looks like everyone she knew was here."

"Herb hired a caterer."

As Cora drove, Celia dabbed at escaping tears. "Lillian is going to need us more than ever now. And we need to make sure we are here for Courtney too."

"She's going to need lots of moral support. Marshall is demanding a DNA test to prove her claims that he fathered her."

"I've heard it all before. That's what philanderers do. They poke every available woman, and then deny accountability. You see it all the time. However, I don't think he has a leg to stand on. Courtney is the spitting image of him when he was her age. It's hard to deny that. It didn't take us long to figure that out as soon as we started looking at the photo albums Lillian put together."

"He's even threatening to sue her for slander. Can you beat that?"

"I hope she counter sues. At any rate, his aspirations for high office are shot all to hell."

Cora parked at the curb in front of Charla's house. They waited for Courtney and Herb to pull into the driveway and help Lillian out of the car and into a wheelchair. She had been walking with a walker up until Charla became critical all of a sudden. The shock seemed to drain all the strength from Lillian and she reverted to a wheel chair most of the day. She wasn't quite back to her old self yet and still needed more physical therapy. She had suffered a severe setback by the unexpected death of Charla.

Everyone thought things were going to turn out for the good. The doctors had removed the cancer and scheduled her for chemotherapy. She had even managed to put in a few hours in her office. It was a real shock to everyone when Charla went into cardiac arrest sitting at her desk. A blood clot had hit her lung. She was gone in an instant and medical staff could not revive her.

Marshall had severed all communications with her. The sorrow was present on Charla's face and in her eyes when Cora ran into her during visits with Lillian in the rehab hospital. At that point, Lillian was walking with a walker and looking forward to discharge. This tragedy had put her back in a wheelchair, too bereft of energy to walk.

Herbie very gently pushed the chair up the walkway to the front door and into the great room by the kitchen. He positioned the chair by a side table and brought her a cup of coffee.

Cora and Celia followed and took seats by their friend. People streamed in the open front door, and quietly greeted others whom they knew. Some expressed their condolences to Lillian, while others hovered around Courtney.

"Can I get you a plate of food," Cora asked Lillian.

Lillian absently responded, "Sure," while never taking her gaze off Courtney. "Did you know that Herb is going to move back in here while he settles Charla's estate?"

"That's nice. He loves Courtney. He's not about to abandon her now," Celia commented while holding Lillian's hand. "Cora and I are going to take care of you. Aren't we?"

Cora nodded. "No doubt about it. Now, what should I bring you, Lil?"

"Anything, as long as it doesn't have onions in it. I don't need to have a case of the runs tomorrow. I have to get back on my feet so I can check out of that place where the doctors parked me. I'm sick of it."

Cora suggested, "Why don't we just take you home with us today? Between the two of us, we can get you up and walking again. You've been there too long now. Come home with us. Celia has already lined up a therapist to come to our house every day to work with you. How would you like that?"

"Do you mean it? Won't I be a burden? Don't you have school to teach?"

"That doesn't start till September. We're going to get you back in shape so you can bowl in the fall. That hospital is too slow. What are they trying to do, max out your insurance? We can do a better job and do it faster."

"Then you can start by getting me something to eat. I'm starved." Lillian brightened and even managed to chuckle softly. "I guess I have to start a new chapter in my life. I wonder if that old fart with the big dogs would still be interested in an old woman with a gimpy leg and brain damage. I guess I could learn to like horses—I mean dogs. Did I mention he looks like that actor, what is his name...Sam Elliot?"

Cora grinned. "A few months ago you thought I might like him."

Lillian looked down at her chest and laughed. "On second thought, maybe he wouldn't be interested in me anymore. The assets he seemed to be so enamored with when I met him seemed to have had the air let out of them. Look at these." She punched her flattened form jokingly. "I've lost so much weight that they've taken to hanging around my knees when I stand up"

Celia laughed. "She's back."

If you appreciated this story, please post a review on the site where you purchased it. Thank you for your interest and be kind to your mother.

Made in the USA
Las Vegas, NV
31 October 2021